*Beacon of Hope: Episode I*

# Paths into Darkness and Light

Jeffrey A Hallett

ISBN:  979-8-9921902-2-9   (paperback, 2nd edition)
       979-8-9921902-3-6   (eBook, 2nd edition)

Library of Congress Control Number: 2025905835

Illustrations by Jessica Nagel (@colorful.and.wild)
Cover design by Holly Dunn (@hollydunndesign)
Developmental editing by Amelia Beamer

Dragon's Trove Press, Livermore, CA, USA

# Chapter List

# Illustration List

# Acknowledgments

Works of passion and creativity require a village, or at least this one did. I could not have done it without the help of many special people supporting, encouraging, and otherwise helping me bring this to life. I'm deeply grateful to every one of them:

My mentor and coach, Bernie, someone I consider a true Renaissance man, for his wisdom and encouragement,

My daughter, Elyse, for providing unwavering support and optimism while suffering through multiple snippets, excerpts, and drafts from start to finish,

My editor, Amelia, for her insights that helped me see this story and characters in ways that inspired me to go beyond ordinary,

My illustrator, Jess, for her creativity and inspiration in bringing these characters to life,

My beta readers, Sabrina and Trista for their investment of time, patience, and invaluable honesty.

And last but not least, to many other friends and family for their encouragement and support.

Thank you all. I could not have done it without you.

# Forward

Thank you for taking a chance on this book. I do appreciate it. Just to be honest up front, I wrote this book solely as a project of passion. I just felt it was something that would challenge me, but that it was something I could do and would learn something valuable by doing it.

Writing a book has been on my bucket list for a long time, mostly because it took a long time to actually come up with an idea that I could feel passionate enough about to put in the work and, frankly, one that I thought others could find worth reading. I wondered more than once if I'd ever come up with one, but then, like most good things in our lives, it came unexpectedly out of nowhere. Apparently, being patient and letting something happen naturally was one of the first writing lessons I needed to learn.

In writing this story, I've become quite invested in Tricia, her friends, and her foes. I deliberately tried to make Tricia a bit atypical for these types of stories. There are parts of me, and of many people I'm close to, blended together in her and the other characters. It wouldn't surprise me if you saw some of those same qualities in yourself or others that you know too, and if you do, then I'll feel some measure of success and satisfaction. As I stretched myself by writing this book, I wanted Tricia's journey to stretch her.

In the end, my sincerest hope is that you do find some enjoyment in reading it and that Tricia's story will help inspire us to push our boundaries, be the best version of ourselves, and enable others to be the best versions of themselves as well, no matter what the world throws in our path or how it pressures us to be otherwise.

You are here to make a difference, to either improve
the world or worsen it. And whether or not you
consciously choose to, you will accomplish one or
the other.

– Richelle E. Goodrich


Our challenges don't define us. Our actions do.

– Michael J. Fox


I believe there's a hero in all of us, that keeps us
honest, gives us strength, makes us noble.

– Aunt May, *Spiderman*

# Tricia

*I should have swiped the other way,* she thought disgustedly as she walked down the street toward home. It was a warm, pleasant evening with a light breeze. She could even smell the ocean as it gently whirled around her. Normally, that smell would have made her feel happy inside, but tonight, she barely noticed. Doctor Tricia Carling had her shawl wrapped snugly around her, not so much for warmth but more to just shield herself from the other people out on the street. The city of Crystal Bay really came alive at night, especially in this area around the university near where she worked in one of the research laboratories, but after the social train wreck she just experienced, being in a throng was really the last place she wanted to be. She walked briskly, grateful she'd worn comfortable shoes. The restaurant wasn't far from home, but she didn't wear dress shoes very often, and the last thing she needed was a blister on top of everything else.

*Why do I let Marni talk me into these things?* she lamented. On her own, Tricia would never get involved with dating apps like this, but Marni pushed her to just give it a try. "It'll help you get out more and meet people," Marni insisted. She was meeting Marni the next morning for brunch, and without a doubt, Marni would want every single detail. Just as Tricia rolled her eyes, a troublesome wisp of blonde tumbled down into her face. No matter how she tried to fix her hair, that bit always seemed to have a mind of its own. She tried to blow it out of her face unsuccessfully, but it just playfully and annoyingly batted at her cheek as she walked. *I swear, if I shaved myself bald, that lock of hair would STILL find a way to pester me.* She reached into her bag, pulled out an elastic hair tie, and pulled her hair back into a makeshift bun. Satisfied she had it tamed for now, she glanced down at her commpad in her purse and saw the message she was expecting from Marni, "I want to hear EVERYTHING tomorrow 😊 😉!" Tricia sighed, and as if on cue, that same lock of hair dropped down in her face to taunt her. She gave it a twist and tucked it back behind her ear...as if it would stay anyway.

The evening had started well enough. She arrived just a few minutes early to find Martin already there—points for being punctual. He was dressed casual but nicely, a good match for the blue floral sundress she'd chosen. He smiled and waved to her, and she returned the smile and the wave. *At least he looks like his profile*—add a few points for appearance and honesty.

"I called earlier to confirm the reservation," Martin told her—more points for some attention to detail, not bad so far. "They said it would just be a few minutes. I guess they aren't used to people being here on time," he said with a wink. She smiled. *Promising, promising...*

They were quickly seated and given menus and water straight away. After a quick glance at the menu, Martin said he would like to order a bottle of wine and asked her if she preferred red or white. Tricia said she preferred red. Martin flagged down the waiter and ordered a bottle. A few minutes later, the bottle came. The waiter uncorked it and poured a small amount for Martin to sample. After making a bit of a performance of swirling the glass and swishing a sip in his mouth, he declared the wine suitable. The waiter poured for them both, set the bottle in the middle of the table, and both of them ordered an appetizer. The waiter thanked them both and left.

Tricia picked up her glass, gave it a quick swirl, inhaled deeply through her nose, and then took a sip. Martin watched her closely, smiling. "So, what do you think?"

It really wasn't her favorite. Frankly, she was a bit surprised he didn't ask more about her wine preference before taking it upon himself to order, but nothing to make a big deal about. "It's fine," she said, taking another sip.

"Just 'fine'?" he pressed. "Really, what do you think of it?"

"Well, ok then," she said. "I like the bouquet and the strong fruit flavors up front, but it goes a bit flat after that and finishes more on the astringent side than I typically care for." He did ask.

"So," he chuckled, "Are you some kind of wine snob?" He tried to make it sound humorous, but it came off a bit strained.

"No, I'm not a snob," Tricia replied, a bit ruffled. "I just know what I like. I did say it was fine, and I meant it."

"So yeah, you're a wine snob then," he jabbed with a grin.

Getting a bit annoyed now, Tricia started, "Look, if I were actually a snob, I probably would have said something more along the lines of..."

"Hey, folks! Who gets the calamari?" The waiter broke in, looking back and forth between the two of them and holding a plate of calamari ceviche in one hand and one of bruschetta in the other.

Tricia raised her hand, silently thanking him for the save.

The waiter nodded and set the plates down in front of them. He asked if they needed anything else, and they both shook their heads.

The tension momentarily broken, Tricia tried to put things back on a more positive note, "Your bruschetta looks quite nice." Martin nodded but seemed overly preoccupied with placing his napkin into his lap just so.

Tricia started to sample her calamari. "How is it?" Martin asked. "It's very good," Tricia replied carefully, lightly covering her mouth as she still chewed a piece. "Better than 'fine'?" Martin teased with a mischievous smirk on his face. "Yes," Tricia smirked back, "much better than 'fine'."

"You know," he continued, "I never could figure out how someone could eat that." gesturing toward her plate.

"Well, it's really quite straightforward," Tricia retorted, looking down at her plate. "The invention of utensils has made it even easier," she quipped, looking up with a smile just in time to see Martin taking a bite from a piece of bruschetta he held between his thumb and forefinger. He paused mid-bite, and his eyes widened a bit. *Ugh...bad timing, Trish,* she thought and winced a bit. He carefully set the piece back down on his plate, wiped his mouth with his napkin, and took a rather large sip of wine.

"Um, so, why don't you tell me a bit more about what you do, Martin?" hoping to pull off another quick recovery. After a short pause, he began a very long and detailed description of his company, what they did, what he did, and how well he did it. His appetizer went forgotten in favor of sips of wine periodically to keep his vocal cords lubricated. Tricia worked on her appetizer, routinely nodding and giving the occasional 'mmm-hmm'. Martin happily fed on those bits of encouragement and continued on...and on...and on...

Finally, Tricia finished her appetizer - most of Martin's bruschetta was still untouched - set her fork down and took a long sip of her wine. After breathing for a while, she decided that the wine really was a little better than just fine. *Seems the wine has been breathing more than Martin has.* She suppressed a small giggle.

Martin, however, caught the twitch in her facial expression. Frowning a bit, he asked, "Did I say something amusing? Or am I just boring you?"

"No, no," Tricia said quickly to reassure him, "It's not that at all."

"Well," Martin continued, now getting slightly irritated, "what is it then? I feel like maybe you're trying to sabotage this date."

"What do you mean?" Tricia replied, somewhat more defensively than she'd intended. "What do you mean 'sabotage' it?"

"Well, other than insulting me a couple of times, you haven't hardly said two words since we've been here," he said accusingly.

"I'm sorry if it feels that way to you. I really don't mean anything by it. It's just that I'm the kind of person who is very comfortable listening and someone who feels like saying something when I believe I have something truly worthwhile to say."

His eyes narrowed a bit. "As opposed tooooo....?"

Tricia drew her shawl a bit tighter around her shoulders at the thought of what came next. Her reply, she reflected with just a touch of regret, made it clear to them both that wine and appetizers were where that date would end. They split the check, and now here she was, walking home quite a bit earlier than planned.

Part of her wanted to be irritated at Marni for talking her into this, but Tricia knew deep down it was on her. Marni was just trying to help in her own way, and in the end, Tricia had gone along with it. She'd always assumed meeting someone, settling down, and having a family was all in her future, but it would happen in its own time. Tricia wasn't in any rush, and she knew one thing for sure, when it happened, it wouldn't be because she met some stranger by exchanging some messages through an application on her commpad. That might work for Marni, but it wasn't for her.

Gratefully, her townhouse was located just off the university campus where she worked, so she arrived home in short order and pressed her thumb against the lock to open the door. Adding to her frustration, the lock decided to pick that night to be stubborn, forcing her to retry it three times before finally giving in to her. She tossed her bag down on the small table by the door, went into the bedroom, flung the shawl across the top of the bed, and let herself drop face-first into the duvet. She took a deep breath and let it out slowly, letting her lips flutter.

As she let herself sink into the fluffy comforter, she was distracted by a small thump on the bed next to her head and looked up just in time to see Rascal, the small black kitten she'd taken in last year, padding across the bed towards her. Rascal rubbed her face on her cheek, purring very loudly in her ear. She couldn't help but smile and rolled over to scratch her head. "You still love me, though, don't you, fuzzball?" Rascal mewed softly and purred even louder, eating up the attention.

Tricia picked up Rascal, still rubbing her ears, kicked off her shoes, and went back out to the front room to retrieve her commpad from her purse. She set Rascal down, and as Rascal proceeded to rub vigorously up against her calf, Tricia read the message from Marni again.

She quickly typed a reply, "Yup, will tell you all about it at brunch tomorrow morning. 10? Usual place?"

A <thumbs up> image came back a few seconds later. Tricia put the commpad on the charger and squatted down to rub Rascal's back.

"That's right, Rascal," she chuckled, "she'll will hear all about it, but she isn't going to like it."

"Oh, Tricia," Marni lamented, "Tell me you did not say that."

Tricia had her head down, focusing intently on the small swirls she was making in her hollandaise sauce with her fork.

"Did you really use the words 'droning incessantly'?"

Tricia sighed a bit and looked up at Marni. "Yeah, I did," she admitted.

"Whatever possessed you to go with that? Of all the things you could have said?" Marni chastised.

Tricia knew Marni was right. It was a showstopper, and she knew it when she said it. *WAS I trying to sabotage the date?* she thought to herself. *Probably.*

"I don't know, Marni," Tricia admitted, not just a little bit exasperated with herself. "He just got so irritated all at once and started accusing me. He just couldn't seem to get that I was perfectly content to listen and take it all in, and then it escalated and started getting ugly, and I guess I was just done with it at that point." Tricia put down her fork and wiped her mouth with her napkin.

Marni sat back and folded her arms across her chest, putting on that look Tricia had seen so often, the look a schoolteacher gives her star pupil when she pulls a D on a quiz.

Doctor Marni Haskell had been Tricia's best friend since they roomed together in college as freshmen. It hadn't started off well. They had been about as opposite as you could get. Marni was a few inches shorter than Tricia with curly red hair, sparkling green eyes, lots of curves, and a big, bubbly personality that made her the center of attention whenever she walked into a room. She was the embodiment of the best things coming in small packages. After a couple of tense weeks at the start of the semester, though, something just gelled. Tricia felt Marni really understood her, what being an introvert really meant: not that she hated people or being around people, just that at times she found them exhausting and really needed her own space.

Marni seemed to make it her mission to make sure Tricia didn't let herself get too isolated, dragging her out to mixers and other events from time to time. Somehow, though, she always knew when to let Tricia have her space too. Tricia generally felt when they went out together that the two of them made anyone who thought blondes had more fun think twice, but they did have fun together, and she appreciated Marni's authenticity and genuinely compassionate nature - even if it was underneath a razor-sharp wit and a smart comeback occasionally.

Tricia, on the other hand, provided Marni a sense of moderation, sensibility, and realism that Marni needed every now and then. Whether it was to buckle down for midterms, her latest romance, or just the latest shiny object, Tricia felt she provided some centering that Marni needed from time to time. They became inseparable throughout their undergrad.

They shared breaks together, visiting each other's families. They fought at times, but every time, they made up with crying and hugs. Marni was there for her when her dad was killed before their senior year; if it weren't for Marni, Tricia wasn't sure she would have finished college. It was a painful time for her, and she likely would have ended up in a very dark place, but thanks to Marni, it didn't come to that. Tricia was Marni's maid of honor right after graduation and then was there for her after the divorce two years later. They were thrilled when they both were accepted to doctoral programs at Crystal Bay University, and after being awarded their doctorates, Marni with her MD and Tricia with her PhD in optical physics, luck kept them together still, with Marni accepting a post in the Novel Gene Therapy department in the university hospital downtown, and Tricia being offered a lead research position in one of the advanced research laboratories on campus.

Marni took a deep breath, exhaled, reached across the table, and patted Tricia's hand. "Well, there's always next time," she said.

"Oh no," Tricia replied quickly, "there isn't going to be a next time."

"You can't give up after just one date, Trish."

"Oh, yes, I can," Tricia said, with an air of finality, making an I'm-so-done-with-this gesture with both hands. Before Marni could get out another word, Tricia put the nail in the coffin, "Nope, I'm done with it. I've already closed down the profile and deleted the app. I'm not doing that again, Marni."

Marni gave her that wide-eyed puppy dog look. No, it wasn't going to work.

"Oh, look, Marni. This just isn't for me. This isn't how I want to meet people. I need to meet people, more like me, not just half at random, based on a concocted profile and a few messages."

"Do other people like you actually come outside where you can find them?"

"Sometimes," Tricia chided back, "you just have to know where to look."

"When you can be bothered to look, I suppose."

Tricia shrugged and took the last bite of her Eggs Benedict—Marni had polished off her breakfast sandwich already—and signaled the waiter for a refill on coffee.

Taking advantage of the opportunity, Tricia decided to change the subject. "Hey, if you're not doing anything next weekend, why don't you come up to The Ridge with me?"

Marni's face cast significant doubt on the credulity of Tricia's suggestion.

"Seriously, come up. The weather is getting nice, and I have a lot of work to do on the place. I've let it sit idle for far too long."

Marni scoffed. "You know I don't know one end of a hammer from another, Tricia."

"That doesn't matter, Marni," Tricia pressed. "It would be great to have a second set of hands or even just some company."

The Ridge was a family cabin about 2 hours outside of the city, not quite in the mountains, but a bit further up than the foothills. The property had been in Tricia's family for generations. It had been part of a deed grant program from the government. After sufficiently improving the properly and living on it for a specified period of time, the land was turned over to the family free and clear. It was surrounded by lush trees and was well isolated from anyone else for miles.

Her great-grandfather had made a very smart move by letting the forestry service set up a small depot on the edge of their land, so the cabin was much better equipped than most of the other properties in the area. The forestry service maintained the road and made sure there was water and electricity. Tricia had to pay for what she used but didn't have to worry about the lines or plumbing. The service's maintenance depot was on the very edge, so they never came around the house, and they were hardly ever there anyway, so it was a great arrangement. There weren't even any land taxes.

The only catch was that the family couldn't sell the property. The deed granted them ownership in perpetuity, provided the land passed directly from parent to child. Should they no longer want the property, or if there were no children to inherit it, it passed back to the government; the family would get a modest payment, but nowhere near what it was really worth these days.

Sadly, Tricia had ignored the place for several years now. Her dad had been killed during one of their trips up to The Ridge, so the thought of going there was very painful for a long time, and until recently, she just hadn't been willing to deal with the memories.

"Speaking of the place," Marni asked, "have you heard from your mother at all?"

Tricia shook her head. "No, not a word since the court case."

"That's a good thing then, maybeeee?" Marni said hesitantly, trying to paint a silver lining on a touchy subject.

Tricia shrugged. "Probably. Honestly, I don't ever really expect to hear from her unless, of course, there's something she wants."

Her mother, Marys, had left them and divorced her father when Tricia was in high school. Shortly after her father's death, she had brazenly tried to challenge the will and take custody of the place away from Tricia, but given the terms of the deed, the judge dismissed the claim essentially out of hand. It never even made it to court, but the thought of losing the place did put the spark back into Tricia, reminding her that it was a very special place and that it really meant something to her.

Now that she had a good solid income and time on her hands, Tricia had decided to get the place back into shape so she, and someday her family, could enjoy it and build their own memories there. She had the roof replaced in the spring, but it needed a lot of cleaning, furniture replaced, and other general maintenance. It would be a project, but one she knew would be worth the time and money.

Tricia pushed the memory aside and, not yet willing to let Marni off the hook, circled back on her invitation. "Come on, Marni, it'll be fun. Even if you don't want to help, we can still bring a couple of bottles of wine, have a fire outside, watch the stars...it'll be great."

"Hmmm, now you're selling it, Trish." Marni chuckled. "Truth is, I've got plans next weekend, and if I'm lucky, I'll get nibbled on by something other than mosquitoes."

They both laughed. "Well, if you change your mind or plans fall through, you're more than welcome. I'll be going up more regularly now that the season is changing. There's plenty to keep me busy up there, and it is a great place to get away from things from time to time."

"Sounds lovely, Trish, I'll definitely take you up on that invitation—" Marni paused, feigning thoughtfulness "—but maybe *after* you've fixed the place up enough that I don't have to go out behind a bush to do my business," Marni smirked and took her napkin out of her lap, tossing it onto her empty place. "I hate to eat and run, but I have a shift this afternoon at the hospital, so I need to get going. Do you have anything else going on this weekend?"

"Nope, nothing much." Tricia was quite happy about that but didn't want to give Marni anymore to tease her about. "I have a few errands, and I want to get to the gym sometime today, too."

Just then, the waiter dropped off the check. Tricia grabbed it just as Marni's hand slapped the table. Marni wrinkled her nose at Tricia in mock irritation.

"I got this one, Marni. You can get going so you're not late."

They stood up, hugged, and Marni walked out the door, hailing a taxi that had just pulled up. Tricia took the check over to the counter, scanned the payment code from the register, and acknowledged the payment request with a tap on the commpod unit in her ear. She turned just in time to see Marni get into the taxi and pull away.

*She's one in a million,* Tricia thought gratefully and walked out onto the busy street.

# Visions

Tricia sat at her workspace, staring at her monitor and stirring her coffee absentmindedly, while she waited for the simulation to complete. The team was building up to a major milestone, an experiment that would be a huge achievement in their work if it succeeded. *If this simulation would ever complete,* she thought with a huff, drumming her fingers on the table.

Behind her, she could hear Alex rattling around at the storage racks in the back of the lab. She could also faintly hear the morning news stream from Jamal's workstation. It was common knowledge around the lab that Jamal had a big crush on Tamara Rawlins, the program host, so the morning broadcast of CrystalClear was a staple part of their morning routine. Tricia didn't mind. The program had some interesting guests and did a good job of presenting the local news and city events; being in touch with what was happening was generally good for the team. Besides, Jamal was an absolute machine, so if the news stream helped him feel more productive, so be it.

The workstation finally chimed, and the simulation refreshed to show the results. Tricia pushed her glasses up on her nose and tucked her hair behind her ear. She leaned in to inspect the results and scowled a bit. They weren't favorable. The resonance harmonics were still too high. *Well, there is no good data or bad data. There is only data,* she reminded herself, saved the results, and sent the team a link to review after she briefed them on the outcome. She took a sip of her coffee and scrunched up her face. It was stone cold, so she tossed her glasses down on the workspace, pushed back her chair, and made her way to the front of the lab, where the team maintained a small break area. Alex always made sure there was a fresh pot brewed and ready to go.

"Anything good on the stream this morning, Jamal?" Tricia called out as she poured herself a fresh cup.

"Now you know he doesn't actually *listen* to the show, don't you, Doctor C?" Alex jumped in, grinning broadly.

"I do...mostly." Jamal retorted in mock defense, and they all laughed. Alex dumped what she'd salvaged from the storage racks on one of the lab tables, tugged on Jamal's lab coat sleeve, and they joined Tricia in the break area.

Armed with fresh cups of coffee, Tricia had just started updating them on the results of the simulation when they were interrupted by someone opening the lab door. The lab administrator stuck his head in and looked around.

"Hey, Jack!" Tricia called out and waved. "We're over here. Come on in."

Jack came in trailed by two young people; students, most likely Tricia guessed. The first was a thin woman about Tricia's height with short medium brown hair and bright green eyes. The other, a man, was easily six feet tall with dark eyes and hair. Both of them wore nervous smiles as they followed Jack to the break area.

The team stood up as Jack and the two newcomers arrived at the table. "I've got your new interns, Trish," Jack said, sweeping his hand toward the two students. "Doctor Tricia Carling, this is Nikki Robbins and Steve DiCicero."

Tricia smiled and shook their hands in turns. "Pleased to meet you both. Welcome to the Advanced Imaging and Optics Lab." She turned her attention back to Jack. "I have to admit you caught us a bit off guard. I thought they weren't supposed to arrive until next week, Jack. We haven't prepped for them yet." The reaction on Jack's face told her she probably came off more irritated than she'd intended.

"Well," Jack shuffled a bit, "it turns out they were available early, so rather than wait, we decided to bring them by this week instead. I dropped you a message this morning. It was a rather short-notice change in schedule. Sorry about the surprise."

*This morning? Seriously?* Part of her wanted to rip Jack a new one, but she forced herself to stay calm. It wouldn't bode well to terrify the interns on their first day.

"This morning? Sorry, I didn't see it. I've been focused on running a new simulation this morning and haven't checked messages since I first got in." Tricia took a quick breath to dispel her irritation. "Hey, it's certainly not a problem though. We can shuffle things around and make it work." She looked back to the new interns. "We are more than happy to have you."

Jack looked at the interns and then back to Tricia. "Ok, then. I'll leave you to it then. Let me know if there's anything I can do to help."

*A little more advanced notice would be nice,* she thought, forcing a smile. She shook Jack's hand, and as he left, she turned back to the new interns.

"It's really an honor to meet you, Doctor Carling," Nikki said apprehensively. "I read your paper from the optical physics conference last year. It was amazing, really revolutionary."

"What did you think about the quantum wavelet coupling concept?" Tricia asked, deliberately testing her a bit.

"Um, well, to be honest, a chunk of that went over my head, but from what I did understand, the coupling would solve quite a few problems aligning mixed energy constructs," Nikki answered tentatively, blushing a bit.

*Smart*, Tricia nodded approvingly. "Well," she chuckled, "that observation probably puts you ahead of most of the conference attendees."

They all snickered at that. "Here, let me introduce the rest of the team." Tricia gestured toward Jamal first. Jamal was a stout, stocky man just a few inches taller than Tricia. No one was surprised to hear that Jamal had played rugby as an undergraduate. His round face wore a big, broad smile that was capped with long flowing dreadlocks. "This is Jamal Okunwe." Jamal shook both of their hands and welcomed them. "Jamal is a PhD candidate and is doing his thesis work on what we are doing here. We are hoping he will stay on with us after he completes his degree." Tricia gave him a side smirk, and Alex playfully nudged him with her elbow.

Tricia then pointed to Alex. Alex was a few inches shorter than Tricia, very petite, with striking black hair and piercing black eyes. "This is Alexandra Garcia. She's our full-time lab technician. She can literally build anything out of scraps and handles most of our computer and electronics components."

"Everybody calls me Alex. Welcome aboard!" Alex added on, giving them one of her signature big smiles.

"So," Tricia said, clapping her hands together, "we probably should start with a tour." The Advanced Imaging and Optics Lab was her pride and joy, and any irritation she might have still felt from the interns' surprise arrival was completely purged by her excitement to show it off. "This—" she spread her hands wide "—is our break area. Coffee here. Small fridge for cold drinks and lunches there. Hot and cold water dispenser over there. Everyone is responsible for washing cups and dishes. We don't use single-serve cups or utensils here, so you may want to bring in your own. You can leave them in that cupboard over there. Just so you know, anyone caught leaving dirty dishes gets to wash everyone's for a week. K?"

The two interns nodded.

"Cool." Tricia acknowledged. "Before we see the rest, feel free to drop your stuff here and grab a lab coat out of that cabinet. Pick anyone you like. It'll be yours while you are here. I'll get Jack going on making name tags for them. We have a laundering service for the coats and smocks that is provided by the university, but we'll go over all of that a little later."

Nikki and Steve set their bags down on the break table and proceeded to select their coats from the cabinet. Once properly outfitted, they returned to the group, and they all started the tour.

Tricia showed them that the lab was essentially laid out in a series of concentric circles. Around the outer edge were the break area, a couple of small conference cubicles, some storage cabinets and racks, and extra worktables. On the inner ring of the layout were the various workspaces for the staff and tables where they assembled and performed bench tests on the projectors, sensors, and analysis equipment used in the experiments and to carry out any other pre-experimental work or equipment development.

"And at the center," Tricia proudly announced, "we have the centerpiece of our lab, our main stage if you will." She walked the group up to an octagonal chamber in the center of the lab.

The chamber was roughly twenty feet across and looked to be made entirely of glass except for a black frame around each of the eight transparent walls and circling the octagonal top and bottom. One of the chamber's walls was actually a sliding door consisting of two panels that separated left and right. When the door panels slid closed, they sank back into the frame and latched, becoming nearly indistinguishable from the other seven walls.

"This is our full-spectrum high-energy projection and measurement isolation chamber. In here, we can generate high-intensity projections of the visible and near-visible spectrum with nearly nanometer precision and measure emissions down to nearly an Ångström unit. The walls contain dynamic polarizing filters that allow us to control how much, if any, ambient energy flows in and out of the chamber. Plus, the glass is nearly unbreakable; you could drive a truck into this structure, and you likely wouldn't put a scratch on it. This is where we conduct our major experiments."

"We call it 'The Hot Spot,'" Jamal chimed in with a wide grin.

Tricia smiled, "Yes, we do." She turned to Nikki and Steve. "Alex and Jamal will bring you up to speed on all the capabilities of our Hot Spot here and the other equipment in the lab. There are also a lot of safety protocols we'll need to make sure you're up to speed on before you can jump in, but we'll get you going right away."

They paused for a several seconds letting it all soak in before Nikki finally broke the silence, "It's all incredibly impressive Doctor Carling, but what exactly are you all trying to do here?"

"How much time do you have?" Alex joked. Tricia gave Alex a playfully dismissive wave of her hand, and with a mischievous grin, she beckoned them to follow her back toward the front of the lab. When they'd all collected in the break area, she motioned for them to have a seat at the table and got everyone a beverage from the refrigerator.

"We are working on a new technology we call Immersive CoSimulation. Put simply, we are trying to create remote physicality or virtual instrumentation. Our work will take concepts like Augmented or Virtual Reality to a new level by allowing people to physically interact with a remote environment using holographic technology."

Steve took a deep swallow of his drink. "Doctor Carling, it sounds like you're trying to make that room from that old science fiction show where a computer could generate some fictional scene, and people would go in and interact with it like it was the real world."

"Something like that, Steve," Tricia agreed, "but not quite so grandiose. We aren't trying to recreate entire environments, but we are building more on concepts of remote work that came about during the pandemic in the early 20's. Back then, remote workers could only interact with information they could share over the network. Any work that required hands-on actual materials or equipment still required people to go into the workplace."

Tricia got up and quickly fetched what looked to be a wrap-around headset from one of the lab tables. "Imagine a telepresence where one worker is physically in an office conference room, and another is working remotely, perhaps wearing an immersive VR headset like this one. The person in the conference room can pick up, say, a whiteboard marker and write on the whiteboard, but with conventional VR, the remote worker can only watch. With what we are trying to do, now imagine that the remote worker has an avatar projected into the room, and that avatar also has physicality, allowing it to also pick up the same marker on behalf of the person who is remote and write on the same whiteboard as the worker in the room."

"That's incredible!" Nikki exclaimed. Jamal and Alex just sat back in their chairs with their arms crossed, smiling.

"Now, let's take it one step further," Tricia pressed onward, "Imagine there is no physical whiteboard or marker. Imagine now, when the present worker and remote worker want to collaborate, they ask the system to project a whiteboard and marker. The projected whiteboard feels solid. Both the avatar *and* the person in the room can pick up the projected virtual marker and 'write' on the projected whiteboard. Both of them see the writing and drawing appear just as if the marker and whiteboard were physically there. At a command, the virtual marker can be told to change colors so they can write in red or blue or green. At another command, the marker transforms into an eraser. Virtual dynamic instrumentation accessible to both remotely and physically present coworkers."

They were both dumbfounded. Tricia glanced at Jamal and Alex, sitting there smugly. Jamal made the 'mind-blown' gesture with his hands. Tricia snickered.

Nikki finally spoke up, "It's game-changing, Doctor Carling. Our whole definition of 'the workplace' and 'collaboration' will shift dramatically. Specialists can be brought into any situation at any time to solve problems. People can operate in hazardous situations remotely in complete safety. In an emergency, a surgical specialist could operate on a critical patient who might've died previously because the specialist was too far away. It's absolutely astounding."

"But Doctor Carling, it seems the real key here is the physicality part." Steve countered. "If I remember, this kind of thing was tried years ago using force fields, but they could never figure out how to make the force fields small or precise enough." Tricia nodded, encouraging him to go on. "Force fields were like the rail gun. The smallest one they could make required a nuclear reactor and was roughly the size of an aircraft carrier. It could never be made practically applicable, and the technology was abandoned."

"Yes, Steve, that's absolutely correct." Tricia agreed. "Yes, we learned that light energy and Maxwell's Equations could only get us so far, but the breakthrough happened a few years ago when we finally discovered how to detect and tap dark matter and dark energy. Can either of you tell me what you know about dark energy?"

Nikki sat forward and folded her hands on the table. "For over a hundred years, scientists have been exploring the concepts around our expanding universe but could not explain, using conventional theories, that is, how the universe was continuing to expand or why it seemed the expansion was accelerated at vast distances." Tricia nodded enthusiastically and waved her hand for Nikki to continue.

"Scientists eventually theorized that there must be some kind of invisible dark matter and dark energy making up the missing mass they observed in the universe and providing the forces necessary to continue to drive the universal expansion. This was all highly theoretical and could not be proven until about a decade ago when we created the first detectors and collectors for dark matter and dark energy. The scientist who figured it out won the Nobel Prize if I remember correctly."

"You do remember correctly, Nikki," Tricia jumped in excitedly, "and you described it perfectly. Yes, *that* was the breakthrough that's making what we are doing possible." Tricia looked at Steve. "We are using dark energy to do what force fields could not, to create the physicality we need for our projected instrumentation."

"And that's where the wavelet coupling comes in?" Nikki asked.

Tricia smiled and nodded. "Exactly."

Steve scoffed a bit and countered again, "But Doctor Carling, it's still very theoretical, isn't it? I mean, yeah, we've figured out how to collect and study dark energy, but it sounds like the application you are proposing is well beyond where we are, isn't it?"

Tricia's eyes lit up. "Not as far as you might think, Steve, and definitely no longer just theoretical. We've done it."

"What do you mean, you've done it?" Nikki asked.

Tricia pointed to the Hot Spot in the center of the lab. "The Hot Spot has been fitted with dark energy collectors and emitters. We've already been able to use projections of dark energy to affect physical objects, albeit on a very limited scale. There, inside the chamber, is our prototype for what we call a 'multiphasic integrator'. That's our big next milestone, our next big experiment. Our design for the integrator will allow us to weave fields of the regular electromagnetic spectrum with controlled fields of dark energy, to mix dark energy with projected holograms, giving them the perception of being tangible objects."

"How close are you? How far away is this?" Steve stammered.

Alex stepped in, giving Tricia a short break to take a drink, "Weeks. We're assembling the arrays we need and are nearly done with the software that will control the projections and collect the data. Doctor C has been building the simulations that will hopefully provide the parameters we need for our first test of the multiphasic integrator."

"And," Tricia picked up without skipping a beat, "that is where we were when you came in this morning. I'd just finished running a simulation and was in the middle of sharing the results with the team. Long story short, we still have a lot of work to do. The simulation results indicate we have some potential problems with the resonant harmonics between the two energy fields. Those resonant effects could be extremely catastrophic if we don't sort it out."

Nikki perked up immediately, "My previous project was using some algorithms to dynamically adapt and dampen harmonics in resonant systems. The application was the laser pulse systems in cold fusion reactors, but holograms are essentially based on laser technology. Maybe some of that could be helpful?"

Tricia nodded while taking another sip. "Perhaps it could. We're open to any ideas, and I'm already feeling good about how you both are going to fit in around here." She took a quick look at her watch and felt her stomach give a small rumble. "Hey, it's almost time for lunch. Why don't we take lunch, and when everyone is back, say one-ish, we can finish going over the simulation results? Then I'll hand you two over to Jamal and Alex to get a deeper look into what's happening here and how we are doing it."

Everyone smiled, nodded in agreement, and broke for lunch.

"Like you mean it, Carling." said the deep voice behind her. Tricia jumped. Marni giggled. Tricia turned to look, and sure enough, Sensei Tim was standing right behind her. She put her hand to her chest to slow her racing heart. *How can such a massive guy move so silently?* she wondered.

They attended martial arts class every other week, and tonight, they were doing striking and blocking drills. A couple of years ago Marni had suggested that Tricia do this with her. Marni felt she wanted to be better prepared to walk around the hospital parking garage, especially when she was on the late shifts, and had recruited Tricia for moral support. Tricia hadn't been too sure at first; the class was rather crowded, and this kind of thing was seriously outside her comfort zone, but it had become a regular routine for them, and, if the truth were told, Tricia did come to enjoy it after a while.

The class was taught by Sensei Tim. He was an intimidating man, towering over Tricia and most of the rest of the class, wide-shouldered and powerful. He had been special ops in the military at one time, but they didn't know much more as he avoided talking about it much. They did know he was highly ranked in multiple forms of martial arts and had been a combat training instructor in the military as well. He'd left the military after several tours of duty overseas. Now, he works event security with the campus police and teaches this class on the side. The class was available to students for elective credit and open to university faculty and staff, so it included a broad mix of people.

Despite originally joining just to keep Marni company, Tricia found that she especially enjoyed the exercise portions of the class. They were a good change of pace to just going to the gym. She also really enjoyed the precision and discipline of the kata, the short sequences of techniques and transitions they learned to build mastery over the forms, build balance, and make the flow of movement smooth and natural. She felt that practicing those forms, along with the meditation exercises they did, really helped her connect with herself in a deeper way and be in better tune with her own body. As for the rest of it, like these drills they were doing now, she wasn't so sure, but she was getting a lot out of the class, and it did give them something to do together.

"Check your stance, Carling," Sensei Tim corrected, stepping in front of her. "Bend those knees a bit more and shift your weight up on your toes." She adjusted her stance. "Yeah, good, just like that. Now, throw the punch...slow motion."

She simulated throwing the punch with her right hand and held the pose at the end. Sensei stepped back and looked at her form. "When you throw that punch, rotate those hips." He tapped her right hip with the back of his hand. "Rotate and put your weight into the strike. Let your weight come forward on that front foot."

Tricia obliged, rotating her hip and shifting forward.

"Better," he said, "now flatten that wrist. Remember, you want everything that's Tricia Carling to be focused into that one-inch square right here on the front of your fist." He tapped her first two knuckles, then slapped his palm into her outstretched fist.

Her fist literally disappeared inside his huge hand, but she held her stance strong. "Yes, Sensei!" she replied with emphasis.

"Good...now, strike!" Tricia reset and punched his open palm, emphasizing the hip rotation and weight shift.

"Good...again!" She punched faster this time, hearing the satisfying smack as she made contact.

"And again!" She struck a third time, faster and harder yet.

"Good! That actually smarts." Sensei Tim grinned. "Carry on."

After class was over, Marni hurried out to use the restroom before their usual after-class late supper. Tricia was packing up when she saw Sensei Tim approach her out of the corner of her eye.

"You got a minute, Carling?" he asked.

"Sure, Sensei." She stood up, lifting her head to make eye contact. *I wish I had a step ladder for these chats.*

He was standing there with his hands on his hips, and his face said there was something important on his mind. He was typically rather stoic and somewhat reserved, but she'd learned when he had something to say, it was usually worth hearing.

"Why are you here, Carling?" he finally said softly and thoughtfully.

Blindsided, Tricia just stared at him, lost for words. Her mind raced to come up with a good answer, but before she could muster one that didn't sound trite and unsatisfying, he sighed softly and interjected, "Yeah, I thought so. You should probably give that some serious thought."

Still confused that he would pose such a question, a puzzled expression crossed her face. "Why do you ask, Sensei?"

"Simple, Carling," he said, his deep voice softening a bit. "When I look at you, I see a good student, and frankly, that disappoints me." Tricia started to speak, but he held up his hand to stop her. "It disappoints me because I think I could be looking at a great student."

Her puzzled expression shifted to surprise. This might've been the last thing she expected to hear in this conversation.

"You could be, but you need to find your gut, find what motivates you, down deep." He tapped his temple. "You have it up here," then tapping over his heart, "but you need to have it in here. Having it just in your head won't be enough for you to reach your full potential. Do you get what I'm saying?"

Tricia nodded slowly. "Yes, Sensei. I think I do."

"Good. Have a think about it and we'll talk again when I see you in a couple of weeks then." He turned and walked back to the front of the room to collect his gear.

Tricia stared after him for a few seconds, then turned to see Marni waiting just outside the door. She waved, picked up her bag, and joined her in the hall.

"What was *that* all about?" Marni asked.

"Oh, nothing serious. Just a pep talk. At least, I think it was." Tricia replied, still digesting what Tim had told her, and they left for dinner and drinks.

*It is a beautiful sunset,* she thought. The one they called Purity—all the Liberators of Gaia took code names—looked out the window of the train. She loved the changing colors, especially when it started to get dim, and the warm peach on the horizon faded to the soft sea green and then into the dark blue of the oncoming night. As beautiful, relaxing, and riveting as that view was though, her eyes could not avoid drifting down to where the true legacy of mankind was moving past her: the piles of trash by the tracks, the dilapidated buildings covered in graffiti, lots filled with wrecked cars or other rubbish barely contained by rusted, broken chain-link fences. She turned her eyes away in disgust, but the crowded interior of the train was no better to her. Under the seat in front of her, a fast-food wrapper sat next to an empty cup that rolled back and forth with the jostling of the train. Overlapping faded smells created a sense of staleness and overuse. People were packed together, trying to pretend they were alone on the train, making themselves as small as they could whenever the lurch of the train made them bump against each other. A couple argued a few seats down, but no one seemed to care. A disheveled man pushed through the door between cars and rambled down the aisle, nudging people out of his way as he mumbled loudly to himself, but no one even seemed to notice him. In fact, they went out of their way *not* to notice him. At best, she observed, they have complete apathy for each other. At worst, they likely resented each other's very presence.

*Well, that's something we have in common, I suppose*, she thought to herself, closing her eyes and letting her head rest back on the top of the seat. Since joining the Liberators, she'd helped them get what they wanted: publicity, notoriety, and greater awareness of their cause to stop destroying the planet and live in harmony with it. Their hearts were in the right place, but they needed guidance and focus. She'd helped them write their manifesto and get it published. She'd helped them plan and organize their protests and their recent more flamboyant demonstrations. She was very committed to the Liberators' cause, but while they were useful, they didn't need to know her entire vision. They were moving to the next phase of the campaign tomorrow. She sighed. After months of preparation, finally, tomorrow, her real plan would begin. She silently reaffirmed her dedication to it. She didn't choose the name Purity because she was pure of heart or spirit or motivation—she felt quite the opposite, really—but rather because she was pure in her intent and focus, pure in the simplicity of her vision and directness of her solution.

Yes, she was completely committed to their vision of seeing humanity live in harmony with the planet, but in her mind, the best way for humans to live in perfect harmony with the planet was for there not to be any.

# Catastrophe

**W**ith each stroke, Tricia flowed smoothly through the water. She focused on making each stroke efficient and clean so she could get the most out of each lap she made.

*Stroke...breath...stroke...*

*Strong clean kicks...stroke...breath...*

She saw the wall approaching, and with one more stroke, she tucked, rolled, planted her feet against her wall, and pushed off into the next lap. Only four more to go.

Instead of her usual gym routine, Tricia had decided to swim this morning before heading into the lab. The team had been putting in a long set of nights getting ready for today, and she felt a good swim would be relaxing and put her in the proper mindset for the big event. Today is the day they run their big experiment, the first fusion of holograms with dark energy, the milestone they've been working toward for over a year.

Tricia especially loved this place to swim as it was a saltwater pool. She found it to be very soothing, and it brought back her special times at the beach. Her father had regularly taken her to the beach when she was a little girl, and the feeling of being in the saltwater reminded her of the happy memories she had of those times. There was still a little bittersweet, though. She felt the sadness that he was gone, but those memories, and others like them, were special to her. Plus, from where she lived now, the beach was an hour away, and the public transportation to get there was painful on a good day, so the pool would be the next best thing. *Maybe if the experiment today was successful,* she thought, *the team should do a day at the beach sometime to celebrate.*

Tricia finished her last lap, hoisted herself out of the water, and sat on the edge of the pool, dangling her feet in the water. She checked her time; it was pretty good, considering she hadn't done any laps in a while. While she checked her pulse, she looked up at the school mascot emblazoned on the wall next to the pool. The stylized, cartoonish alligator grinned down at her, ready to take on all comers, and reminded Tricia that she had the highly successful university athletics program to thank for her having access to facilities like this.

The Crystal Bay University Caymans were highly respected in collegiate athletics. They had forgone their football program about a decade ago, which many felt would be a huge mistake, but the men's and women's soccer, rugby, and lacrosse teams were consistently nationally ranked, having won numerous national titles. Additionally, the swim, diving, and basketball teams were always at the top of their conferences and occasionally made the national tournaments as well. Tricia was always bothered by the fact they used the wrong spelling for 'caiman', but she accepted it was probably just easier for Americans, and especially American donors, to remember.

Tricia remembered arriving as a freshman shortly after the school had decided to end its football program. There was still a lot of controversy on campus about the decision as quite a few students no longer had sports scholarships for football, and many influential alums were irate to see their school no longer represented by their favorite sport. It didn't matter that the program had not historically done well on the national scene. It was a matter of tradition and nostalgia. With donors and alumni deliberately withholding large donations in protest, the school was experiencing some serious financial problems, forcing some cutbacks in many programs, including scholarships, housing allowance, and many non-academic programs. Tricia recalled feeling the pinch herself when she first started.

The school, though, persevered and invested in other team sports that were actually much less expensive to fund. They started having success in those other programs, and alumni, seeing some sense in what the university was doing, started to donate again. The entire athletic program got a massive boost when the USA shocked the world by taking the bronze medal in men's rugby at the most recent Olympic Games. The team coach and four of the starting fifteen were all from the Caymans' national championship team. The donations really started pouring in after that bit of publicity. While Tricia had always been a bit skeptical of student athletics, particularly at these elite levels, they did contribute a lot of funding to the university, and she had to admit she enjoyed taking in a rugby or lacrosse match on occasion. *Go, Caymans!* she thought as she wrapped her towel around herself and headed into the locker room.

Fortunately for her and others, the university believed the entire campus should benefit from the money the athletic programs brought in. Most of the facilities were available to the entire student body, faculty, and staff, and the university also subsidized many programs available to them, such as the martial arts class Tricia and Marni took with Sensei Tim. Further, as a research faculty member, Tricia was entitled to 24/7 access to all the athletic facilities on campus and to a reserved locker in this facility. After she had finished showering, she dried off, dressed, and then put her towel and suit into her tagged mesh laundry bag. This was perhaps her favorite perk of all; she only had to drop the bag in the bin by the door, and the next day, her things would be clean, dry, and back in her locker, ready for her to use. There was no need to take a wet towel and suit into the lab and have them ferment in her bag all day while she worked. All told, the facilities were a fantastic benefit, and Tricia made use of them liberally.

Normally, on a day like today, Tricia would stop by the bakery on the way to the lab and get something special, but today, Nikki and Steve would be covering it. Yesterday, she'd caught Jamal and Alex trying to convince them that it was tradition for interns to bring in treats on the day of their first big test or experiment in the labs. She let the joke go on for a little bit, but when it looked like they were starting to buy it, Tricia stepped in. In the end, Nikki and Steve volunteered to bring something in any way. When they turned to go back to their work, Tricia wagged a finger at Jamal and Alex as a light admonition against hazing the interns. Alex giggled, and Jamal shrugged with a clownish grin on his face.

When she arrived at the lab, Tricia was pleasantly surprised to see that Nikki and Steve had not only kept their word but scored bonus points doing it. There were freshly baked croissants on the break room table, and they were still warm. Tricia helped herself to one, poured a cup of coffee, courtesy of Alex, no doubt, and wandered over to where Alex and Nikki were in deep discussion.

After reviewing some of the work Nikki had previously done on controlling harmonics and resonance, the team felt there was a solid opportunity to use some of those ideas in their configuration. Nikki had worked closely with Alex on building a resonance feedback controller and integrating it with the system they were planning on using today. Tricia had helped Nikki build a model of the controller in the simulator, and based on everything they'd seen so far, it looked very promising in managing the harmonics that Tricia had been worrying over in previous simulations. In fact, that's exactly what Nikki and Alex were discussing; they had just run a new simulation and were tweaking the final parameters for the controller they would use later in the day.

Still munching on her croissant, Tricia eavesdropped for a bit. Satisfied with the discussion, she started to turn away but, Nikki and Alex, having caught her listening in, both turned to look at her. With her mouth still full, Tricia waved her hand, signaling them that she had no comment, and then, looking at Nikki, she raised the half-eaten croissant and gave her a thumbs up. Nikki smiled, nodded, and then resumed her conversation with Alex.

A few hours later, the entire team sat in the break area doing their final debrief for the big test. The croissants were gone. All that remained was a sad pile of crumbs in the box. In principle, the design of the experiment was fairly simple. They would be creating a simple polyhedron suspended in space inside the Hot Spot using the holographic emitters. Once that was established and stable, they would attempt to fuse the holographic surfaces with dark energy. If the experiment worked, they would end up with a stable polyhedron that would repel a one-inch ball bearing that would be dropped from a magnetic clutch in the top of the Hot Spot directly above the top of the polyhedron. True to his sense of humor, Jamal had rigged the release for the bearing with a fancy red ribbon that hung down next to the main control station.

Tricia was stirring her coffee as each member of the team gave a short report of where they were. Jamal was currently discussing where he felt they were with the final integration between the dark energy conduits and the holographic emitters, "...and finally, just to be sure, I replace some of the primary leads with higher bandwidth cabling. I was a bit concerned the lower grade ones might not be able to handle what we'd be sending through them today and didn't want any problems from that."

Alex started to chime in, but Jamal held up his hands and nodded, "Yeah, I know it was a long shot but better safe than sorry."

It was Steve's turn next, "Not much new to report today. I ran a full diagnostic and systems check after Jamal swapped out the cables just to be sure, and it looked fine. The emitter and sensor arrays all look good. Spectrum sweeps on the holographic and dark energy systems are well within tolerance for the run today."

Tricia nodded and turned to Nikki. "How about the feedback controller, Nikki?"

Nikki glanced at Alex, who returned her glance and then responded, "It checks out. Alex and I did a little tweaking of the parameters, and we think this new set will help manage some of the fringe effects we were still seeing in the simulation. I updated the settings in the controller, and it's looking good." Alex nodded to confirm.

Tricia rubbed her chin. "Any reason to re-run the simulation just to make sure?"

Alex took this question, "Don't think so, Doctor C. The tweaks were minor, and honestly, it's unlikely those fringe effects would have been a concern today. However, since today's theme is 'better safe than sorry', we went with the new set. It's purring like a kitten."

Under other circumstances, Tricia might have questioned this decision, but seeing the team looking so confident and enthusiastic, Tricia just smiled and nodded instead as Alex continued, "As for me, the rest of the electronics racks look good. Recording systems are calibrated and ready to go. I've made sure we have extra capacity for the collectors and servers in the lab. The data will be coming in too fast to sync with the network servers in real time, so we will be buffering it in the lab first, and then we'll upload it all to the network storage later. I've also double-checked the power feeds and made sure Facilities has the extra power conduits online in case we overdraw on the primaries. I'm more concerned about any spikes we might get than the baseline load we'll put on them. Better safe than sorry, right?" Alex smirked and shrugged.

They all chuckled.

Tricia could feel the excitement building in the room. They were close and the team knew it. Still, she had to do her duty. She looked directly at the team and asked point blank, "Ok folks, what are we missing? How is this going to go sideways?"

She waited patiently for them to answer. The gears were turning in each person's head, trying to look for any detail, no matter how small, that might get cause them to fail today. Finally, the team looked at each other, and then back to her. Nikki shook her head. Jamal shrugged. The rest stayed silent.

"Ok, then," Tricia proclaimed, putting down her pad, "On the count of three, thumbs up or down to go. One....two....three!"

Each member of the team put a thumb up, with Alex putting up both of hers. Looking into each person's eyes in turn, Tricia finally added her thumbs up to the rest. The team breathed a sigh of relief and anticipation. "Let's light it up!" she said, and they all broke to their respective stations.

Tricia looked over the master console one more time. Everything was sitting solidly green. The equipment was warm and ready to go. She looked again at the team. They were clearly excited. *If this works…WHEN this works*, she corrected herself, *this is going to be huge.* "Load it up, Jamal. Put up the box." Tricia instructed.

"Aye, Captain!" Jamal said, adopting a very bad Scottish accent. The 'box' was, in reality, a three-dimensional regular dodecahedron, with each of its twelve sides being a regular pentagon. Jamal scrolled through the assortment of geometric shapes in the system library, mumbling to himself, "Dodecahedron…dodeca…ah, there it is: regular Platonic solid."   Jamal selected the configuration to load the specifications into the emitter controllers, and the shape sprang into life in the middle of the Hot Spot, glowing steadily, casting a slightly yellow hue on their faces and the rest of the lab behind them. They had done this part countless times, but it was an important first step.

"Alex, how does it look?"

Alex checked the sensor stream and responded, "It's looking good, Doctor C. Energy variations on the order of one part per billion…very stable. Power flows are steady. No spiking."

Tricia nodded. The butterflies were starting to flutter in her stomach, too. The next step was the part they'd never tried before. They'd done each of these sequences before, multiple times, but never together. This was it.

"Ok, Jamal." Tricia tapped Jamal on the shoulder. "Let the dark energy flow."

"You got it, Doctor C," Jamal replied. Even he was very serious now, anticipating this key step. He tapped in the dark energy control program. They couldn't see the dark energy directly, but they could all see a moiré pattern start to form on the surface of the glowing dodecahedron. The colors on the surface of the hologram started to shift and swirl as the pattern slowly covered the entire surface.

"Wow, it's beautiful!" Nikki commented. The entire team grunted and hummed in agreement.

"Alex, what are you seeing?"

"Energy levels still stable, Doctor C. Still looking good."

"How are the harmonics, Nikki?"

Nikki checked her panel. "Harmonics are consistent with what we saw in the simulator, Doctor C. All good so far."

Tricia looked at the glowing, swirling object in the Hot Spot. *This is amazing!* she remarked to herself, momentarily mesmerized by the swirling patterns of color and shadow. So many years work, and, if they succeeded—and it certainly looked like they were about to succeed—if they actually heard the steel ball bearing plink as it bounced off the surface they'd created from comingled energies, it wouldn't be just ground-breaking; it would be *magical.*

"Are we ready to drop?" She asked the team.

"Wait, Doctor C," Alex said. She checked her panels and then went to the main panel on the wall. "Power levels are climbing. It's drawing more power."

"Same on the dark energy," Steve added. "The dark energy conduit load is increasing, too."

The polyhedron started to pulse slightly, the pattern on its surface was breaking down and becoming more chaotic. It was beginning to look much less beautiful and much more angry.

"Hey, team," Jamal said urgently, "I think we have a problem."

"What's going on, Jamal?" Tricia asked.

"The harmonics are building…really fast!" he responded, the worry and fear in his voice coming through clearly.

"Ok, I'm calling it." Tricia called out, "Steve, shut down the emitters. Pull the plug on them. The dark energy, too."

"Got it, Doctor C!" Steve responded and urgently tapped the control screen in front of him.

As they watched, the polyhedron in the Hot Spot started to glow more brightly. Even more alarming, it began to expand inside the chamber. The pattern on the surface started to fluctuate between chaotic and regular patterns, looking at first like a regular mosaic and then disintegrating into pure chaos, then reforming again. They could all hear a low humming sound starting to build in the room.

Tricia yelled out, "Talk to me, team! What's happening?"

Jamal checked a couple of the instrument panels quickly. "The harmonics are still cascading. I think we are in trouble. It looks like there is enough energy already in the system that the harmonics are continuing to just feed on themselves. I think we've hit some kind of hysteresis effect, some kind of threshold. I'm pretty sure it's going to overload, Doctor C. I don't know if the Hot Spot can take it."

"What about the feedback controller?" Tricia asked, looking for any option she could find at this point. The brightness and the humming sound both continued to grow. The polyhedron was swelling and starting to pulse, expanding and contracting over and over, faster and faster.

Alex yelled from across the lab, fighting to be heard over the growing hum filling the lab, "I'm not sure it's working, Doctor

C. Uh, wait...check that. Honestly, looking at these readings, I think it might be making things worse. The resonances are multiplying."

Tricia thought for a second, then called out. "Alex, hit the polarizers in the glass. Darken the walls as much as you can. Let's see if we can contain it. Nikki, see if you can shut down the resonant feedback controller. Maybe taking it out of the picture will cause it all to dissipate."

They both moved instantly. Alex frantically worked the Hot Spot controls. The glass started to darken, but after a few seconds, it started to flicker, darkness rippling across the surface of the glass walls, and finally, they flashed back to transparent again. "The polarizers are no good. The energy must be too much for them. They are fried!"

Nikki responded right after her. "I can't access the controller either, Doctor C! I can't shut it down!"

By now, the polyhedron in the chamber nearly filled it and was glowing like a small sun. It was swirling with light and color and patterns of dark. It was beautiful and terrifying. The humming sound was deafening, almost to the point where the team couldn't talk over it anymore.

Tricia made a snap decision. "Team, get out of here! Run! Evacuate anyone with you that you can find. Pull the alarm on the way out and call the emergency responders!"

"What are you going to do?!" Jamal yelled after her.

"I'm going to try to pull the connector on the feedback controller. Maybe that'll shut it down, and we can salvage this." She frantically waved them on. "Don't worry. I'll make it out either way. Just GO!"

The team looked at her, all with frightened and worried looks on their faces, but obeyed her and ran out of the lab door.

Tricia could no longer look directly at the chamber. Shielding her eyes with her hand, she ran to the feedback controller. The cable connector was near the bottom of the equipment rack. Wasting no time, she pushed the rack over to expose it and reached down to disconnect the cable. She grabbed the coupler to twist it free, but her hand snapped back immediately. The connector was wickedly hot. She looked at her hand, and blisters were already forming where she'd touched it. *There's nothing I can do with this. I'm out of time,* she concluded and turned toward the door to make her escape.

She had just taken a step, though, when the system finally overloaded, and the blazing dodecahedron dissolved in a burst of light. For an instant, she saw the waves of energy leap from the chamber, a mosaic of light and dark, twisting and churning. The waves hit her, lifting her off the ground. Every muscle in her body locked tight, her back arched, and her fingers splayed outward. She convulsed and spasmed, suspended in mid-air, as the energies surged through her. Every nerve in her body was on fire. Tricia wanted to scream, tried to scream, but the only scream she could manage was in her mind. Any kind of response or attempt to save herself was utterly impossible for her. In that moment, death would have been a mercy.

After a few eternal seconds, the energies dissipated, and Tricia fell to the ground in a heap. She lay motionless, fighting to breathe, while tears streamed down her cheeks. As the blackness took her, she could only hear the pops and crackles of overloaded circuits in the emptiness. The humming sound had stopped. The chamber had gone dark, and then, so did she.

# Aftermath

Her eyes didn't want to open. They weighed a ton as if she had been asleep for a century, but something inside her said it was time. Digging deeply, Tricia forced them open anyway, only to immediately shut them again. The room was dim, but even that small amount of light needed getting used to. She opened them again, squinting and blinking while her eyes adjusted. Finally, she could open them fully. *Where am I?* she wondered. Turning her head slightly toward the sound of soft beeping, she saw a bank of medical equipment. Some of the machines showed her heart rate, blood pressure, and breathing. Some others were likely controlling the IVs she saw hanging next to her bedside. *Hospital?*

She felt something on her face, covering her nose and mouth. *Oxygen probably*, she assumed, but when she tried to reach up toward her face, her hand wouldn't move. Tricia tried to sit up, but the strap across her chest only gave her a couple of inches of movement. Even so, that was just enough to make her head swoon. She groaned a bit and sank back into the bed.

When she opened her eyes again, there was a woman's face peering down into hers. "Welcome back, Doctor Carling." the woman said to her softly and gently. "It's so good to have you back with us."

Tricia again tried to sit up, but the nurse gently pressed downward on her shoulders. "No, just stay still. Let me get the doctor for you." and she disappeared through the door. Looking down again, Tricia could see the edge of the oxygen mask. Past that, she could see the restraints holding her down on the bed: straps at her chest and knees and then soft manacles securing her wrists and ankles. She was puzzled, but for now, she wasn't up to doing anything about it and trusted the doctor would have answers for her.

She looked again at the equipment, beeping and chiming softly. Tricia noticed an odd swirling of light faintly around the equipment. She then looked toward the window and saw the same patterns there around the gaps in the closed blinds. *Something else to ask the doctor about it seems.*

Before she could ponder that any further, the door opened, and in walked a portly but distinguished-looking man, roughly ten years older than Tricia, wearing a tie and a medical coat. He approached the side of her bed, bent over, and looked into her eyes. Satisfied by what he saw, he stood back up and, in a very proper British accent, introduced himself. "Hello. I'm Doctor Gerald Smythe, with a 'y'. Do you know who you are?"

Tricia nodded. The doctor just continued to stare at her.

Taking the cue, Tricia mumbled through the oxygen mask, "Tricia Carling."

"Excellent." the doctor replied, making a note on the large tablet he was carrying. The nurse returned to the room, carrying a large white cup with a long, flexible straw. "And I see you've already met Nurse Chen," he added. Doctor Smythe nodded to the nurse. She came over to Tricia's bedside, set the cup down on the small table next to her, and reached down toward her. The nurse gave a sharp tug, and Tricia felt the mask come loose. The nurse carefully lifted it away from Tricia's face and then held the end of the straw down to her lips. The cool water felt wonderful as she eagerly sucked it in.

"Easy, Doctor Carling, easy...go slow," the nurse advised her. Tricia obediently drank slower, savoring each swallow.

"Shall we open these up then?" the doctor asked her, walking over to the blinds on the window.

Tricia nodded, still sipping.

The doctor pressed a small button to the side of the window and the blinds rotated, admitting more of the bright daylight outside. Tricia stopped sipping, and squinted and blinked, again having to adjust to the brighter light. The swirls she saw before intensified around the now fully exposed window. The effect made her feel slightly nauseated, but having the room brighter definitely made her feel better. Some of the haze in her head started to clear, and she felt a bit of energy return to her body.

She tugged again against her restraints. "Are these still necessary, Doctor Smythe?"

"Oh, yes, of course," he replied. "While you were unconscious, you were having occasional episodes of convulsions and spasms, and we didn't want to take the chance that you'd injure yourself on the IVs and equipment leads if you were to have one while you were unattended. However, it's been a couple of days since you've had one, and since you are conscious, I think we can dispense with these now." He nodded toward the nurse.

Nurse Chen came to the bed and quickly unbuckled the various straps, letting them fall down the bedside to the floor. Tricia started to try to sit up, and the nurse quickly came to her side, putting one hand on the back of her neck and another on her shoulder, supporting her. "Easy does it," the nurse cautioned, "you still have some IVs and leads attached, so let's be careful moving around, shall we?" She helped Tricia slowly sit up, rearranging tubes and wires as she did. Tricia could see that she had an IV in her right arm, a clamp on her right middle finger, and several leads coming out of the front of her hospital gown near her neck. Reaching up with her left hand, she felt the leads attached to her temple and just below her ear at the base of her skull. Whatever happened, it wasn't a small matter, given how closely they were monitoring her.

Sitting up on her own, Tricia took a deep breath and gently stretched her shoulders back. She was rewarded with several pops and cracks in her back. She was scared to ask the next question, but there was no sense in putting it off. Tricia looked up at the doctor and asked, "So, you said I hadn't had an episode for a couple of days. How long have I been in here?"

The doctor pulled over a tall chair from next to the equipment rack, positioning it next to Tricia's bed. He sat down and took off his glasses, tucking them into the upper pocket of his coat. "So, Doctor Carling," he started.

"You can call me Tricia, Doctor," she interrupted.

"Very well, Tricia. I want you to try to stay calm. Can you do that for me?" he asked gently.

Tricia nodded.

"You've been with us just slightly over a week."

Tricia sighed in relief. "A week. Well, that's better than the months or years I thought you were going to say."

Doctor Smythe smiled. "Well, yes, I suppose it did sound a bit dramatic, didn't it? Apologies for that."

Tricia chuckled, "Just a bit. So, what happened?"

"Honestly, we were hoping you could tell us, Tricia," Doctor Smythe admitted. "The emergency responders rushed you in here right after the accident at your lab. Do you remember the accident?"

Tricia hesitated, thought, and finally shook her head. "I mean, I remember the experiment, and it started to overload. I tried to shut it down, but I don't remember a thing after that."

Doctor Smythe nodded and made some more notes on his pad. "Unfortunately, your team..."

"They are all right, aren't they?" Tricia asked urgently.

"Yes, yes, they are fine, but, as I was saying, unfortunately, they don't really know any more than that either. It seems much of the recorded data was destroyed by whatever happened, leaving very little record, but they are still sorting through what they have and have agreed to pass along anything they might find."

He paused for a moment, and Tricia used the break to ask the nurse for more of the water. The nurse handed her the cup and Tricia sipped some more, slowly, while the doctor continued.

"Being fully honest with you, Tricia, we didn't have much hope for you when you came in. You had suffered severe neurological shock, and it appeared as though most of your major organs were on the verge of completely shutting down. It was touch and go there for a while, but cutting the long story short, your recuperative abilities surprised us. Within a couple of days, you'd stabilized—still in critical condition—but we believed you were going to at least survive at that point, even if we didn't know what condition you'd be in long term. Needless to say, when you woke up on your own today, and to see you sitting there, knowing who you are, having a lucid conversation with me is as astounding as it is a relief."

He patted her hand and smiled broadly at her. Tricia put the cup down and smiled back. "Well, believe me, Doctor, no one is happier to be a complete surprise to you than I am."

The doctor and nurse both laughed. He stood up and pushed the chair back. "Of course, we'll have quite a battery of tests we'll want to run, but while I'm here now, let's check a few basic things quickly, shall we?"

Tricia consented, and Nurse Chen helped her lie back down on the bed. The doctor started with some basic questions: her name, her address, her occupation, the names of her team, and her birthdate. From there, he pulled back her eyelid and flashed a light back and forth across her eyes. The swirling and pulsing she was seeing twisted and turned as the light moved across her field of vision. He then asked her to touch each of her fingers, in sequence, to her thumb, first on her right hand, then her left. Finally, he ran the tip of his stylus across the bottom of her foot. She flinched; she'd always been extremely ticklish on her feet.

Doctor Smythe made several notes and then looked up at her. "That's all quite excellent, Tricia. Naturally, we'll still do a full suite of tests on your motor functions and coordination, as well as cognitive function, but your basic responses are spot on."

He tucked his pad under his arm and asked, "Are you feeling any pain or discomfort anywhere, Tricia?"

Tricia gingerly moved her arms and legs, hands, and feet, then flexed her neck a bit side to side. "No, just some general aching and stiffness. Guessing that's probably normal for being in bed for over a week. The only thing I am noticing is that I see some odd patterns in the light, there at the window, and here at the monitors." She pointed at each in turn.

"Hmmm, is it obstructing or interfering with your vision?"

"No, I don't think so."

Doctor Smythe held up his tablet toward her. "Can you read this without any difficulty?"

"Yes. No problem reading that at all. I just see some faint swirls and flashes kind of moving around on top of it all."

"Very well, Tricia," the doctor replied, making a few more notes on his pad, "I will make sure we get you down to an ophthalmologist as well to have your eyes checked out. He or she will be able to see if there's anything going on there with which we need to be concerned. It might just be some residual effect of the neural trauma you experienced, but we will want to be sure."

Tricia nodded and thanked him.

"Unless you have any further questions, Tricia, I will leave you once again in the capable hands of Nurse Chen. She's been by your side almost nonstop since you've been here." He turned to leave and then stopped and turned back to her. "Ah, I almost forgot. I will also let Doctor Haskell know that she can come see you tomorrow. We practically had to call security to keep her out of here after you were admitted."

Tricia chuckled, "Yeah, that sounds like Marni."

The doctor nodded and left. Nurse Chen looked down at Tricia. "Is there anything you need? Anything I can get you?"

"I'd really love some more water if that's ok, and if it's not too much trouble, I'd really like some help getting in there," she said a bit sheepishly, pointing toward the water closet.

"I think we can arrange that, Tricia" Nurse Chen smiled.

"Thanks, Nurse Chen; I'd really appreciate it."

"Of course. And call me Lori. Doctor Smythe is a bit old-school and insists on maintaining the formality and being proper and all, but I think we can drop a bit of that for the rest of the time you're here."

"That's great, Lori, and thanks again for everything you've done, taking care of me and all."

"Of course, Tricia," Lori replied and started to unclip the leads so Tricia could get out of bed. "The doctor really did speak for all of us when he said we were thrilled today when you finally woke up. I had a feeling you'd surprise us all, and I'm ecstatic you proved me right!"

The next morning, just as Tricia was finishing breakfast, the door to her room burst open, and Marni flew into the room. She made a beeline to Tricia and gave her a huge hug, almost causing Tricia to choke on the bite she was still chewing. After she released Tricia, Marni flopped down on the side of the bed next to her and, in a very melodramatic manner, said, "Gerald, oh, pardon me, Doctor Smythe, told me I could finally see you, so I made sure you were the first person I saw today. Aren't you lucky?" Marni beamed at her.

"Nobody's luckier," Tricia agreed, smiling back.

"So, how are you feeling, Tricia?" Marni asked, "Technically, I'm not part of your care team, so they aren't allowed to really tell me anything, but I do have my sources, of course." Marni winked at her.

"Oh, of course you do," Tricia teased her back. "I'm doing fine, Marn. I was a little fuzzy when I first woke up, but I'm doing a lot better now. A bit achy here and there, but otherwise, pretty good, under the circumstances." Although the swirls were still there in the window directly behind where Marni was sitting, she saw no need to mention the thing with her eyes just yet. The whorls of light gave Marni the appearance of having a halo, but Tricia knew her friend was certainly no angel. Tricia chuckled softly.

With a jolt, Tricia suddenly remembered...*Rascal!* "Oh, my goodness," she exclaimed, "Marni, can you get over the apartment right away? I've been here a week...poor Rascal is probably starving!"

Marni patted her shoulder, "Fret not, Tricia. When I found out what happened, I went there first thing and used the emergency code you'd given me. She's fine. Little Snot still won't have anything to do with me, but the food has been disappearing when I stop by, so I assume she's eating okay. I also changed the litter yesterday. Yeeech! I don't know how you stand that."

Tricia giggled. "Well, when you love something, you kinda have to put up with all its faults, don't you?" and she poked Marni in the shoulder.

Marni stuck out her tongue. "Oh, and I told Sensei what happened, too. Not everything, but I mentioned you had an accident at work and were in the hospital. He waived his no-show rule for you. Said to tell you he hopes you're back on your feet soon and to take as much time as you need."

Marni then gestured toward the closet with her thumb. "Also, you may not have seen it yet, but I put together a bag for you from your apartment. The nurse said she put it in there and would let you have it when the doctor cleared you to have personal items. Some clothes, your commpad, a few other basics...nothing fancy."

"Thanks, Marn. I really appreciate that."

Marni turned fully toward her, and her face became very serious. "Tricia, what happened? Really?"

Tricia sighed. "Honestly, Marni, I don't remember a whole lot of it. We were doing the experiment, and it got out of control. I made the team leave, told them to get help, and I tried to shut it down. I don't remember anything after that. I guess I wasn't successful, was I?"

"Not *successful*?! You idiot!" Marni said, her joyful façade abruptly stripped away. She slapped Tricia across the shoulder lightly, but she meant it. "What were you thinking? Trying to stop it?"

Marni was visibly shaking now, and her voice cracked. "When they brought you in here, you were barely alive, Tricia. I was here when they brought you in. I saw you lying on that gurney while they rushed you to the ICU. They honestly didn't expect you to live through the night. For crying out loud, you actually coded at least once, maybe twice…I can't get a straight story. You nearly died, Tricia!" Tears started to flow down Marni's cheeks.

Tricia was speechless, and it was all she could do to not start crying herself.

Marni looked up to the ceiling and took a breath to compose herself. She reached up, brushed away one of the tears with a finger, and swore under her breath. "Now look what you made me do. I'm going to have to redo my eye makeup now."

They both laughed. Marni reached down and took Tricia's hand. "Look, I know you were just being you. That's the kind of thing you do. You put yourself second to save something else, and I know that will never change, but can you at least promise me you'll just be smarter next time? Think, will you? If anything happened to you, they might as well dig two graves."

Tricia smiled and nodded, squeezing Marni's hand.

Marni squeezed back and then let go. She took a tissue and blotted her eyes and cheeks. "Hey, I've got to get back to work…after I clean myself up, of course…but I'll stop by again later, ok?"

"Sure, that'd be great. I'm clearly not going anywhere, so I'll be easy to find."

Marni put her hands on her hips. "True, but that doesn't mean you still won't find some way to get into trouble."

Tricia made an X over her heart with her forefinger and held up her hand. "I'll be good, Marn. I promise."

Marni gave her one more smile, waved, and she was gone.

A few days later, Tricia was sitting cross-legged on her bed reading an article on her commpad. Marni had come by first thing in the morning for a quick visit, and then Tricia had been put through a battery of motor control and function tests. She was still sitting in the scrubs they'd given her to wear during the testing. The tests were quite extensive, and while they hadn't yet given her any indication of how well she'd done, overall, she felt really good. Her vision still had that odd aftereffect, but the stiffness in her muscles was nearly gone, as were the other small bruises and abrasions. They told her if all her tests came back positive, she would be discharged in a couple of days, and she was more than ready to get going.

She heard a light knock on the door and looked up to see Nurse Chen poke her head in. "Are you decent?"

Tricia nodded.

The nurse stepped in part way through the door. "Your team from the lab is here to see you, if you're up for it, of course. If not, just give the word and I can ask them to come back another time."

"No, I'm good, Lori. Please send them in."

The nurse turned and waved her hand. As she stepped back, Jamal, Alex, Steve, and Nikki filed into the room. Alex walked straight to Tricia's bedside, bent down, and gave

Tricia a big hug. When she pulled back, her eyes were wet. "It's so good to see you, Doctor C," she said, smiling and wiping her eyes.

The team grouped up behind Alex, and each of them offered their own greeting, gratitude, and happiness to see her looking so well.

"We've really missed you down at the lab, Doctor C. How are you feeling?" Jamal asked her.

"Well, I'm doing pretty well, all things considered," Tricia responded, keeping it light. "The doctors haven't given me the results of all the tests yet, but if they go well, I'll be out of here in a few days, they say. You know me. I'm getting pretty stir-crazy in here, so fingers crossed."

They all chuckled. Tricia followed up, "So I'm almost afraid to ask, but how's the lab?"

Jamal answered first, "Overall, it's not as bad as it could be. The sensor arrays are a mess, and we had a lot of burnouts in some of the desktop equipment outside the Hot Spot, but most of the emitter systems and other control circuitry came through it relatively unscathed. We figure a few weeks for some replacements to come in, and then some assembly and tuning, but we figure we can have it all back together in six, maybe eight weeks at the most."

Steve picked up from there, "Yeah on the whole, it's looking doable. The bad news is that most of the data is corrupted beyond recovery. Even Sorceress Alex couldn't scrape it together, so we don't have any real record of what happened. Your doctor asked us to try to provide any information we could, but we're sorry Doctor C. We just couldn't retrieve anything."

"Well, if Sorceress Alex couldn't find anything," Tricia teased, and Alex grinned broadly, "then yeah, we'll have to figure it out another way. Um, I have to admit, my memory of what happened is a little fuzzy." She ran her fingers back through her hair, tucking her rogue lock back behind her ear. "Can you give me the short recap?"

"Sure," Jamal answered, "Essentially, we were successful, at least initially, but the harmonics cascaded, and there was a huge buildup and spontaneous release of resonant energy. The system destabilized, and the Hot Spot couldn't contain it. You made us leave and then tried to disconnect the resonant feedback controller, but you couldn't, and you got caught in the overload."

*That's right*, Tricia remembered. *I burned my hand on the cable coupling.* She looked down at the palm of her right hand, but there was no trace of any burn at all on her hand. *Odd...there's nothing there now...nothing at all.*

Nikki pushed herself to the front of the group. Tears started to run down her face as she picked up where Jamal had left off, "We did as you asked...got people out and pulled the alarms. We heard the overload from outside the building and could see the light burst." She wiped her eyes and continued, "The responders came right away and asked us to show them where to find the lab. We walked in with them, and when we saw you lying there, we thought...we thought you...that you were..." and she broke down into sobs.

Nikki knelt next to the bed, crying. "It's all my fault, Doctor C. It's my fault this happened to you."

Tricia put her palm on Nikki's hand. "I doubt that very much, Nikki."

Nikki wiped her eyes and again. "I messed up the feedback controller. I reversed two of the control parameters by accident. Instead of dampening the harmonics, we think it caused them to amplify and cascade instead. We ran it through the simulator, and it confirmed that once the resonance reached a certain point, it would just keep feeding off itself. By the time we caught it, it was already past the point of no return. If I'd gotten it right, it never would have happened, and you wouldn't have gotten hurt."

Tricia pulled Nikki up by her shoulders and gave her a hug. Patting Nikki's back, Tricia reassured her, "No, don't do this to yourself, Nikki. Mistakes happen. We're scientists. Stuff goes sideways. We all share the blame, including me; our safety protocols shouldn't have holes in them that let simple mistakes turn into scenarios like this."

Tricia pushed Nikki back gently and tipped up her chin to look her in the eye. "We'll all do better next time, yeah?"

Nikki smiled weakly and nodded. Tricia smiled back and pointed her toward the box of tissues sitting on the stand next to her.

With the air cleared, the team sat and chatted. They shared some of the news—of course, Jamal had all the headlines to share from CrystalClear and took a lot of teasing for it—and they discussed a bit of how to get started putting the lab back into shape. Tricia was very happy that they'd come and even more relieved to hear that the lab was salvageable.

After about an hour, Nurse Chen came in carrying a tray and informed them that her patient needed to get some more rest and eat her lunch. They said their goodbyes, and Tricia promised to let them know when she'd be released. The nurse hustled them out of the room and then reminded Tricia to eat all of it so she could recoup her strength and get herself out of there. Tricia gave her a salute and, realizing she actually was pretty hungry, dove into her lunch.

# Discovery

*T*hump
*Thump*
*Thump*

Tricia focused on the sound of her footfalls striking the treadmill, synchronizing them with the beat of the music coming through her earbuds, pacing herself with the music. The console of the treadmill showed she only had a few minutes left in the program she'd chosen. She frowned a bit and glanced at her watch. It was showing the exercise monitor. She felt like she was barely breaking a sweat, and according to her watch, she was right. Her heart rate was barely elevated, not even close to her normal cardio range.

It had been almost two weeks since she was discharged from the hospital. When she was released, the university and her medical team had put her on a two-week short-term leave from work to ensure she fully rested and to monitor her start of a gradual return to normal life. Originally, the doctors had wanted six weeks, but both she *and* the university had strenuously questioned that recommendation, especially since the doctors couldn't point to anything specifically wrong with her to justify such a long furlough. All her cognitive, motor, and physiological tests were perfectly normal, and other than a reduced appetite and the persistent swirling in her vision, there was nothing to indicate the ordeal she'd been through. The reduced appetite they wrote off as being consistent with such a prolonged period of rest, and they would continue to monitor her vision. They still couldn't find anything physically wrong with her eyes and continued to believe it was an aftereffect of the shock to her system and would fade eventually.

The first few days of her sentence, as she called it, were pretty good. When she got home, Rascal was beside herself with excitement that Tricia was finally home. She mewed, rolled on the carpet, and followed Tricia everywhere, headbutting her for attention at every opportunity. Tricia had left the apartment in a bit of a shambles the morning of the accident, so laundry, dishes, and other cleaning chores occupied her for a bit. Eventually, though, there were only so many odds and ends to do, so many books to read, so many shows to watch, and only so many walks she could take before she started to go stir crazy. Her energy levels were off the hook, and she needed something to do, or she would lose her mind.

And there were the dreams, very intense, vivid dreams she was having every night now. Last night, she was flying over the city. She could feel the wind on her face and flowing through her hair. Beneath her, there was a low thrum she felt from the city, like it had a pulse, and she could sense it, feel it pulse through her. She felt powerful and alive. Above her, the sun shone brightly, and she turned up toward it. She flew directly toward it as it called to her. She closed her eyes and felt the light and warmth on her skin growing stronger, more vibrant...and then she woke up. It had been like that every night since she was discharged, but again, it was most likely the result of doing too little and being cooped up for too long.

Tricia had asked if she could go up to The Ridge to get some change in scenery, but they'd asked she stay in the city. If something should happen, she needed to be close to medical assistance. They were being understandably cautious and conservative; they still really didn't know what had happened to her. No data related to the accident had been recovered by the team, so they were flying blind in terms of what happened to her and what might happen next. They had reluctantly agreed she could resume moderate exercise and other normal personal activities provided she took it easy and notified them of any adverse effects she might experience.

The treadmill chimed to indicate that the program had completed and that it was time to enter the cool-down interval. Tricia slowed to a walk as the treadmill whirred, lowering itself to a more level position. She checked her watch again. To her surprise, the watch showed her heart rate dropping rapidly, almost back to a normal resting rate. *This was too easy,* she thought to herself. Her weight training circuits had been the same. She had expected some kind of atrophy from the accident and the time spent in the hospital, some decline from what she was used to doing, but she had experienced almost the opposite. She had ended up doing her sets at two levels above her regular settings on each weight station. Even then, it still wasn't challenging; she felt like she could do the whole stack if she tried. Of course, that was silly, but it was just one more indication that more rest was not what she felt she needed right now.

She wiped her forehead with her towel. In a few days, she would have her two-week evaluation. Her team of doctors—yes, she had a *team* of doctors, the very thought of which made her roll her eyes—would put her through an exhaustive battery of tests and decide if it was safe for her to go back to work and resume her normal life. Given how she felt right now, she couldn't imagine not passing the evaluation, but they were erring on the side of caution. Further, the university had made it clear they were deferring to the doctors to decide when it was safe for her to return. They were taking no chances either, so she desperately wanted the tests to go well. She *needed* them to go well. It was time to get on with life.

Since they'd given her permission to return to normal personal activities, Tricia took that to include the martial arts class she took with Marni, so she let Marni know she'd be coming, and they met up for it as usual. Marni was very happy she was back. Even Sensei Tim made a point to welcome her back, including a stern caution to take it easy and to let her know if she needed to take a break at some point she should feel free to excuse herself. Tricia appreciated his support. It felt good to be back.

To her chagrin, though, tonight included those blocking drills she didn't like, the same ones they were doing in the last class she took right before her accident. Tricia was making the most of it, though. She remembered the tips and pointers Sensei had given her the last time and was focusing on her form, shifting her weight, and the other points he had told her.

Marni, of course, was being Marni. Happy to have Tricia back meant a little extra trash talk and taunting during the drills. Despite not being highly athletic, Marni was quick, and Tricia was having trouble getting through her blocks. Marni would grin at her and make some taunting comment like, "Ooooh, you can't touch dis" under her breath, not so loud that Sensei could hear it, but enough that Tricia could. Any other day, Tricia would just smirk back and not let it get to her, but today, that smirk was creating some real irritation.

*Yes, I can touch dis, smart aleck*, she thought to herself. Her focus and determination sharpened. Marni barely blocked the next couple of punches, and she gave Tricia a slightly mocking "oooh" face, teasing her a bit more. *Enough!* something deep inside Tricia said, and as if she were suddenly a spectator in her own body, she watched what happened next in slow motion.

She felt the punch that she threw sail past Marni's block like it wasn't even there and make full contact with Marni, squarely connecting in the center of her chest. Marni yelped and winced, her arms coming forward as she fell backward. Marni's feet came up, and she landed flat on her back on the gym floor, eyes closed, grimacing in pain.

The world snapped back to normal speed. Marni cursed and pushed herself up on one elbow, the other hand going to her chest where she'd been struck. Tricia's hands flew up to her mouth in shock. She heard Sensei behind her call a halt to the class.

"Jeeeeez, Tricia! What are you doing?!?" Marni yelled at her, rubbing her chest.

Tricia flew down to her side, laying a hand on her shoulder. "Oh, Marni, I'm so sorry. I don't know what happened."

"You PUNCHED me, Tricia!" Marni blurted out. "Hard! Really hard!"

By then, Sensei Tim had gotten over to them and knelt down beside Marni on the opposite side from Tricia. He supported Marni's shoulder with his hand. "You ok, Haskell?"

Marni sat up. "Yes. I think so, Sensei." She was still wincing, taking shallow breaths to avoid the pain.

"Can you show me, Haskell?" Sensei asked.

Marni looked up and nodded to him. She opened the front of her gi and pulled down the neckline on the tank top she was wearing under it. There was a bruise starting to form just to the left of her sternum. It was already turning purple.

"Hmmm, you need to get that looked at, Haskell. Unlikely anything is broken, but get it checked anyway." Sensei told her. He looked at Tricia and looked back at Marni. "Take a seat, Haskell. Class is pretty much over anyway. Sit the rest out."

Marni got to her feet with a little help from Sensei and Tricia and gingerly walked to the back of the room. She settled down with her back to the wall next to her bag, the jacket of her gi still open, gently rubbing her chest.

Tricia started to follow her, but Sensei tapped her arm and gestured for her to return to her spot on the floor. Tricia nodded, picking up on his cue that a few minutes for things to settle down might be a good idea, and took her spot as the rest of the class formed up for cool down and closing exercises.

When class was over, Tricia immediately turned to go see Marni, but Sensei Tim caught her. "A word, if you please, Carling," he said sternly.

Tricia winced, knowing she was going to get chewed out and probably deserved it. She looked over to Marni. Marni gave her an ok sign and then waved her on to answer Sensei's summons. Tricia turned and, head hanging, walked over to where Sensei was solemnly waiting for her. He turned his back to the rest of the class as they gathered their things to leave so the two of them would have a small amount of privacy for their discussion.

"First off, you know I need to read you the required riot act about 'control', don't you, Carling?" he started. "What happened?"

"I…I, uh…I don't know, Sensei." Tricia stammered. "We were doing the drill, and honestly, I was tired of getting blocked. The next thing I knew, she was on the ground."

"You lost control, Carling."

"Yes, Sensei, I did." Tricia sighed and hung her head again.

"You just got a real-world lesson on why control is so essential. You tagged your friend pretty good. She's going to feel that for quite a while, you know."

"Yes, Sensei. I know." Tricia's voice waivered a bit.

"Control is more than just physical," Sensei went on to explain. "It's mostly mental and emotional, about focus, awareness, and attitude. Without those, physical control is pretty much impossible. Do you see what I mean?"

Tricia nodded, her face awash with regret and guilt.

"All right, Carling." He put a hand on her shoulder. "I know you already feel terrible, so there's no point rubbing it in further. You got the point, am I right?"

"Yes, Sensei, I got it."

"Ok, good." Sensei's demeanor softened a little. "Second, how is that hand? Any pain or discomfort?"

Tricia looked down at her hand, turning it over and back. She wiggled her fingers and clenched and unclenched her fist a few times. "No, Sensei. It seems fine."

"Good. Keep an eye on it, though. I have to admit your form must've been perfect, or a punch like that would likely have broken a finger or your wrist. Another reason why control is so important," he added, drilling in the lesson a bit more.

"Yes, Sensei. I will." Tricia agreed.

Sensei stepped a bit closer and lowered his voice. "Now, the last thing. I don't want to send mixed messages because I don't like seeing what happened today happen in my classes, but remember when you were here last, and I asked you why you were here? We talked about purpose?"

"Yes, Sensei."

"What you did, even though it was careless, was an example of what happens when what we teach here is backed up with purpose and intent and why that is so important to what I'm trying to teach you all. I saw that punch, Carling. Honestly, I'm not sure I could have blocked it."

Tricia looked up at him. He was right about the intent part of it, for sure. Obviously, she didn't want to hurt Marni, but in that moment, she had decided she was not going to be blocked anymore. Something inside her had responded to that.

"Have you thought any more about what we talked about last time, Carling?" he asked.

"Somewhat." She lied a little, but she needed to think. "But maybe we could talk about it next time, Sensei? I think I've honestly had enough for one day, and I'd like to see how Marni is doing."

Sensei nodded. "Oh, and between you and me, Carling, I'm betting Haskell learned a lesson about shooting her mouth off too." He smiled and winked.

Tricia smiled back. "I don't know, Sensei. It is Marni, after all."

He chuckled and gave her a short bow, dismissing her from class. She returned the bow and headed back to where Marni was still sitting against the wall, her head leaning back and her eyes closed.

Tricia knelt down beside Marni and put her hand on Marni's shoulder. "I'm so sorry, Marni," she said, her voice waving a bit.

Marni looked over at her and gave her a weak smile. "Oh, I know you are. I know you didn't mean it." She reached over and gave Tricia a big hug, or at least the biggest hug she could, with the swelling blossoming on her chest.

Tricia returned the hug gratefully. After they separated, Marni stood up slowly. Tricia picked up Marni's bag for her and put the strap over her own shoulder.

"So, are you up for a drink?" Marni asked.

"No, I don't think so," Tricia replied. "Not tonight. I think I'd rather go home."

Marni smiled and nodded. "Well, if you're going to carry my bag, the least I can do is give you a ride."

Tricia smiled back. "Sure. That would be great. Thanks!"

Even though all seemed to be forgiven with Marni, Tricia was quiet most of the way home. Marni tried to make some small talk, but Tricia's mind was still spinning over what had happened, so she didn't contribute much to the conversation beyond the occasional head nod or grunt.

Tricia did her best to cover up the anxiety building in her from what had happened, but by the time Marni dropped her off, she was shaking so hard she could barely unlock the door. She pushed the door closed behind her, dropped her bag by the couch, stripped off the top of her gi, and rushed into the bathroom. She threw cold water on her face and stared at herself in the mirror.

*What's happening to you?* she thought to her reflection.

It wasn't just too much rest or pent-up energy. Something was going on with her. Something she didn't understand. Something out of her control.

She grabbed the glass on the vanity, filled it with cold water from the tap, and sucked it down. She carefully set the glass down next to the sink and, tipping her head back, she wiped her face with the towel. Tricia looked at herself in the mirror again. A realization came over her. "The accident..." she said to her reflection, a reflection she wasn't sure she recognized right then. She squinted and leaned in to look more closely at herself in the mirror. *What ARE you now?*

Tossing the towel down, she felt the back of her hand hit the glass and topple it over the side of the vanity. She saw it fall, but then, suddenly, the glass was in her hand just a few inches off the floor. She slowly stood back up, staring blankly at the glass in her hand. *What is going on with me?!?*

Aware she was shaking again, she tried to set the glass down on the vanity, but the bottom of the glass struck the vanity counter awkwardly. Instinctively, she squeezed to keep from dropping it again, and the glass shattered in her hand. Shards scattered across the vanity into the sink as she pulled her hand back. Blood gushed from a deep cut on her palm. She grabbed the towel again and wrapped it tightly around the wound, applying pressure and elevating it to stop the flow of blood.

Tricia looked one more time at her reflection. Her heart was racing, and her ears pounded like a bass drum with every beat. The room began to churn. The swirling in her vision was a wheeling torrent of shimmers and pulses on top of her reflection. Fear welled up inside her. She thought she was going to faint. She dropped to one knee and put her head down, the elbow of her cut hand still propped up on the edge of the vanity. *No, Trish.* she told herself, *keep it together. This is no time to panic.*

She pushed herself to her feet and made her way into the main room. It was dark except for the glow of the city and its streetlights shining in the window. She sat down on the floor in the middle of the room. *Gotta pull myself together,* she thought, and took a few deep breaths. *Better....better....* She crossed her legs and put her hands on her knees. *Just like the meditation we do as part of cool-down in class...breathe....relax....*

Tricia focused on each breath. In deep...hold...out slow. She felt the fear start to abate. Her heartrate started to slow. She turned her thoughts inward, turning her attention to each part of her body, encouraging herself to relax, to focus on getting herself back under control.

She turned her feelings deeper and felt...something. *Stay focused,* she reminded herself, but she felt something around her. Not just around her but pulsing through her as well. It was like sitting in the ocean, the waves ebbing and flowing around and through her. It was completely unknown, something she'd never experienced before, but deep down, she knew it wasn't something to fear. It was connected to her somehow, part of her. She focused on the rhythm she felt in the way it moved and pulsed and found it relaxing, even comforting.

Tricia reached toward it with her feelings and touched it. It responded to her, flowing into her even more. She could feel now she was drawing power from it. Holding onto the feeling, she opened her eyes. The swirling in her vision had intensified, pulsing, twisting, but for the first time, she noticed the swirls weren't random. They coalesced around the sources of light and energy around her, and the swirls connected her with them. The pulsing she saw matched the rhythm she felt in whatever was enveloping her. *It's all connected,* she realized.

She closed her eyes again, and this time, rather than opening herself up to it more, she gently pushed against it with her feelings. The tides and currents around her responded, receding, drawing away. She pushed a bit more, and they flowed away entirely. She sensed them, moving and pulsing at the edge of her feelings, but she no longer felt immersed in them. Tricia gradually opened her eyes, and her vision was clear. There were no swirls, no pulses, just the light coming in the window.

She concentrated on holding those tides at bay, and as she felt them churning around her, she also became aware that she felt a bit...less. Tricia felt a little weaker, somewhat sluggish. She started to feel more fatigued, and her stomach started to growl. *Is that why I've been less hungry?* she pondered. *Has my body been feeding off this, drawing power from it somehow?* She shook her head. It was a lot to fathom all at once. Tricia carefully opened herself to the flows, just a bit this time, and they rushed back in toward her. Her body eagerly drank up the currents that surrounded her, and the hunger and fatigue faded.

The realization then dawned on her that this was what she had been experiencing since she woke up in the hospital. Images flashed through her mind from the past two weeks, her time at the gym, and what had just happened in class. Enhanced strength, speed, endurance...it's all a result of her connection to this. She then remembered the burn on her palm, how it was gone when she woke up and looked down at her hand. She gently removed the towel. Where she thought she would need stitches, she saw a cut that looked like it had happened days ago; the skin had completely knitted, and where she was bleeding profusely just minutes ago, there was only a pink line. *Enhanced healing, too, it seems.*

She pushed the flows away and again felt them recede. After pausing a moment to gather herself, Tricia pushed herself up and stood. It was definitely harder to get up than it had been the past couple of weeks, but this, she reminded herself, was normal. When she let those flows in, the flows with which her accident had somehow connected her, *that* was something else, something more than normal. She'd need to figure out what that something else truly was and the extent of what it was capable, the extent of what *she* was now capable. So far, it had been both extraordinary and terrifying, but tonight, she'd taken an important step—she now knew it was there, and, more importantly, she started to have an idea about how to control it, to take it on her terms.

Her first order of business, though, was to raid her refrigerator. Without the energy flowing through her, she was increasingly ravenous, almost as if her body suddenly wanted to make up for the past couple of weeks all at once. Fortunately, the fridge had plenty of leftovers from meals that, up until now, she hadn't been hungry enough to finish. As she ate, Tricia found that she had to focus almost constantly to keep the flows away, but she hoped with practice and time, controlling them would be a skill she could master. Sated, she took a shower and went to bed, and, for the first time in weeks, she slept deeply, without dreams.

# Routines

The gray van pulled up quietly next to the building, its side entry still cast in the last shadows of the night. A faint orange light had just started to appear in the eastern sky. A stray cat, trying to get in a little more hunting time before morning, scattered behind a dumpster as the hiss of the van's air brakes broke the early morning quiet.

The rear door of the van opened, and a tall, muscular man wearing gray coveralls looked out. Satisfied there was no one around, he pushed open both of the back panel doors and gestured to the team. "Let's get going, guys," he said to them. "We are running a bit late, so we need to be snappy about it."

He gestured toward a shorter, stockier man. "We'll take care of the pickup inside." He looked at the other two, a thinner man and a woman. "You two take care of business out here, ok?" All three nodded in agreement. The two larger men unloaded two hand carts and went to the service entrance on the side of the building. The taller man typed in a code. A light flashed green, and the lock clicked free. The two men took their carts inside.

The thinner man emerged from the van carrying a metal sphere about the size of a basketball. The woman followed close behind with a basket of spray paint in one hand and a short trapezoidal box made of PVC hooked over the elbow of her other arm. They walked to the corner of the service alley next to the main street. She set the PVC frame on the ground near the corner, and he placed the metal sphere on top of it, nestling it into place.

He took a small device out of his pocket. "I've got this if you want to get started with that," he said to her.

"Sure thing," she said. She picked up her basket and walked a few feet away to a large open space on the wall. She liked this part. It was creative and artsy. Plus, she'd done it multiple times now and was pretty good at it. She picked up a can, shook it for several seconds, and started spraying the wall.

The man made an exasperated 'pfff' as he worked on the commpad in his hand. The device was emitting some very unhappy beeps and chimes, clearly not cooperating.

"Something wrong?" she asked.

"Every time we do this, these things just keep getting bigger and more complicated," he complained.

"Well, Opus wants bigger and splashier demonstrations, so Purity is just trying to accommodate that. Getting bigger is part of the plan." the woman offered, switching colors.

"Yeah, but I just wish she'd let me help with the electronics. I don't think that's her strength, and they just seem a bit, well, unreliable at times." He tapped another set of buttons. A display turned yellow, and a progress bar appeared. "Thing is, she just won't let anyone near these things when she's building them."

"As long as they end up working, I wouldn't worry about it," she advised. "Opus trusts her, and so far, she's delivered. Just make sure you get it right. Between you and me, she's all pretty and sweet on the outside, but Purity's got an edge. I wouldn't want to be on her bad side."

"Truth." the man agreed. An indicator flashed green on the pad in his hand. "Hah!" he exclaimed. "Got it!"

"Yup. Me too," the woman said. She put the can of spray paint back in the wire basket and stepped back to admire her work. A blue and green image of the Earth, wrapped in breaking chains. The symbol of the Liberators of Gaia.

The man stepped up behind her and looked over her shoulder. "Nice," he complimented, and they slapped hands in an exchange of high-fives.

The service door popped open, and the other two men emerged pushing the carts. The carts were loaded with canisters and bags, almost overflowing. The taller man looked at the wall and then looked approvingly at them. "Good job, you two. Now, please give us a hand with this so we can get out of here. Be careful, too. A couple of these containers look like they might come open, and you don't want to get poked with any of this stuff." The thinner man's face scrunched into an 'ick,' and they came over to help. Picking up this kind of waste wasn't glamorous by any means, but it did pay the bills and, more importantly, gave them cover for their other, more covert activities.

The team quickly loaded the waste into the bins in the back of the van. The woman tucked her basket of paints into the corner, and the group climbed into the van. The taller man took a second to look around one last time, and satisfied everything was in order, he pulled the door shut as the van slipped away into the waning shadows. No one was around to see them go, but people would be starting to show up soon.

And they would get quite a show to start their morning.

The morning sun was warm on Tricia's face as she left the fitness facility. She looked up and closed her eyes, letting it beam down on her. Gently, she reached out with her mind and felt the now familiar flows circling around her. She touched them lightly, and they stirred in response, eager for her to draw on them, to give her power. A gentle push and they settled back down, patiently waiting for her to call on them. After several days of practicing, she was confident she finally had a solid grasp on when she would, and, more importantly, when she would not, draw on this new source of power.

The meditation technique she learned in class and had used that first night she fully discovered her new connection to those waves of energy had served her well. There were times it was more challenging to hold them at bay; when she was excited, or she exerted herself, it seemed her body craved the strength their power gave her, making it all the harder to resist. Overall, though, Tricia felt like she was starting to get the level of control she'd need to avoid unwanted surprises, surprises like broken drinking glasses and hurt friends...or worse.

Despite how drained she felt, Tricia walked briskly across campus toward the lab. It had been a good workout, and the fatigue was very satisfying. After she had started to learn how to control the way she accessed her new abilities, it did not take long for her to realize that she received no benefit whatsoever from any exercise she did while her power flowed through her. In fact, the first workout she did exclusively without her powers was brutal and confirmed the concern she had earlier about atrophy. She had to drop at least one level of intensity on every station, including her cardio, but she pushed through it. The difficulty was compounded by how much she had to concentrate to keep her powers out of it; the harder she worked, the more her body craved the energy around her and tugged on it. Tricia pushed through, though. After a few workouts, she finally felt like she was back in her groove, and now her routine started each day with a workout first thing every morning, just for her, no enhancements. There would also be another workout later in the day, more of a training session, really, when she was sure she had the facility to herself. In many ways, that one was even more challenging.

When her lab building came into view, a wave of nervous excitement came over her. Tricia was excited to get back to work, but the memory of what had happened to her there was still strong, scary and unpredictable, and it would take her some time to get over that.

Memories or not, in her desire to return some normalcy to her life, she had gambled with her assessment the other day. Tricia bit her lip a bit, recalling what she'd done, but she was so desperate to get off her medical team's radar. The more "exceptional" she continued to appear to her doctors, the more likely she'd have to endure more tests and scrutiny. The more she was poked and prodded, the more likely she feared they would find out there was something going on with her, something different and unusual. No, continuing to be seen as "exceptional" on her tests was not really in her best interests.

She was fairly sure she could suppress her abilities for the exam, but she was concerned that going cold turkey might also draw unwanted attention. If her body had really been drawing on these energies ever since her accident, then that effect was what her doctors were used to seeing. A sudden or drastic change might end up being even more suspicious.

In the end, she split the difference. It took a lot of concentration, but Tricia did her assessment, channeling only a minute trickle of her power. Maintaining a consistent level at such a small amount she found to be exceptionally challenging, almost blowing it a couple of times. Two of the tests had to be repeated due to inconsistent results, but her gamble paid off. She passed the assessment handily, and ultimately, the doctors were pleased that her results were more in the range of what they considered normal. It led them to believe that whatever had hyperstimulated her system in the accident might finally be passing, and they found that encouraging. Fortunately, the cut on her hand from the broken glass had fully healed, so that wasn't a factor either. Their only observation was that she was slightly underweight, so they cleared her to return to work half-time with strict orders to eat more and put on some weight. She promised them she'd do her best to put on a few pounds before her next evaluation in two weeks. If that evaluation was positive, she'd be fully cleared and wouldn't have to see them again for three months. Tricia resolved that she'd eat a pack of skunks—*a surfeit of skunks, I think it is, actually*—if it would keep her out of any more testing.

Tricia peeked in through the door window before she keyed her way into the lab. The team had their heads down, already busy. She took a deep breath and closed her eyes for a second. *Game time*, she thought and opened the door.

Alex was the first to see her and squealed out her name with a huge smile. The rest of the team reacted immediately. It reminded Tricia of the meerkats she'd seen on one of the nature channels. They popped their heads up to see her, all of them except Jamal. He had his headphones on and was intently watching his monitor. His back was to the door, and he hadn't seen or heard a thing. Tricia could see he had the news stream going, and she snickered a bit seeing him so intently fixed on it. *As usual,* she thought, happy to see things looking so normal.

The headline on the screen reported that the Liberators of Gaia had been busy again this morning. From the pictures she could see, it looked like they had set off another one of their smoke bombs somewhere downtown, but she couldn't make out exactly where. Alex walked over and swatted him on the shoulder. When he looked up, she pointed in Tricia's direction. Jamal beamed when he saw her, tossed his headset down on the desk, and hopped off his stool to greet her.

The team came up to meet her and engulfed her in a huge group hug. She gladly returned each of their smiles and thanked them for welcoming her back. Alex put a hand on her shoulder and turned her toward the break area at the front of the lab. Over the table, Tricia saw a banner saying, "Welcome Back, Doctor Carling." On the table were a balloon bouquet and a cake bearing the same message. She couldn't help but be a little choked up. *It is good to be back.*

Nikki picked up a knife. "Is cake on the menu, Doctor Carling?" she asked.

Tricia gave her a sly smile. "The doctors told me specifically to eat cake, so who am I to argue? Cut me a big slice, Nikki." She was sure one of her doctors actually did tell her that when they were admonishing her for being underweight. Most likely, he was joking at the time, but Tricia was perfectly fine with taking his expert advice at face value.

Nikki smiled and started slicing the cake. Jamal took care of passing the slices around while Alex got everyone a fresh cup of coffee.

After a few helpings of cake, multiple rounds of coffee, and a lot of general catching up, the welcome-back party had started to wind down. The team had given her a small 'welcome back' present, a T-shirt that showed an exploding atom, a flask boiling over, and a broken test tube dripping something green, all encircled with letters that said "Forget lab safety. I want superpowers!" *If they only knew*, Tricia thought to herself when she opened it, but she did find it funny, if a bit too close to the mark. She took off her lab coat and put it on over her blouse. They all toasted it with a cheer and their cups of coffee.

With the festivities drawing to a close, Tricia decided it was time to switch gears. "So, what's been happening around here?" she asked them collectively.

Alex and Jamal did most of the talking. Nikki and Steve had been occupied mostly by midterms since the accident. In fact, they had to be taking off shortly for their last exam, but they contributed where they could. As each of them shared, Tricia took notes, frequently interrupting to ask a number of pointed questions about how the repairs on the lab were progressing and other points of interest. While she was genuinely concerned with getting their work back on track, getting the lab back to full working order now had a personal stake as well. She knew she would be needing it for herself as well.

Most of the work Alex and Jamal had been doing consisted of taking inventory of the damaged components, replacing components out of parts stock where they could, rewiring burned-out circuits, and filling out requisitions for equipment and parts they didn't have on hand. The university had relaxed some of the signature requirements on purchasing, but some of the bigger items would need Tricia to review and approve before they could be procured. She added that to her growing to-do list for the upcoming week.

Tricia put her pen down, pushed her glasses up on her nose, and tucked her misbehaving hair behind her ear.

Looking directly at Alex and Jamal, she cut to the heart of what she really wanted to know, "So, where are we exactly?"

Jamal answered first, "Long story short, nearly all the workstation equipment—computers, monitors, analytics, comms, that kind of thing—are replaced and ready to go. The Hot Spot itself is working at a basic level."

Tricia frowned a bit. "What does that mean?" she probed.

"Well," Alex chimed in, "the basic EM emitters are fully functioning, as are the standard collectors and sensors inside the chamber. We can generate and scan the full electromagnetic spectrum fully to spec."

"That's great," Tricia responded. She was especially glad to hear this part. Those functions were exactly what she'd need for the personal tests she was planning. "What's not working?"

Nikki answered this time, "None of the advanced holographic imaging systems are working. We need to replace most of the focusing coils for those. The dark energy conduits are scrap as well. They were totaled and have to be rebuilt."

"Quite a few of the requisitions waiting for your signature are to get us the parts we need to reconstruct those." Alex piled on.

Tricia checked her watch. It was getting close to lunch, and she would have to check out soon. If she was caught violating her work restrictions, it wouldn't go well with either her doctors or the university HR department. She took off her glasses and hung them over the collar of her T-shirt.

"Ok", she said after a brief pause, "let's dig into those requisitions and the reconstruction plans tomorrow morning. Since we are rebuilding, let's make sure we are upgrading where we can along the way. I have a feeling the university will be somewhat sympathetic to helping us, so let's shoot for more than the status quo, shall we?" She winked at the team. They chuckled in response and gave her a thumbs up.

"When can we fire up the Hot Spot so I can take a look?"

Jamal shifted uncomfortably. Alex responded, "Unfortunately, not until next week, Doctor C."

"How come?" This was not the news Tricia wanted to hear.

"The university has scheduled a full safety inspection for this weekend," Jamal explained. "They were ok with us doing some basic diagnostics while we were repairing the systems, but any actual operation is strictly taboo until they've had the wiring and structural integrity verified by a team of inspectors."

Tricia huffed. Definitely not the news she wanted, but it wasn't the end of the world. At least the Hot Spot was operational, or at least operational enough, and a week wasn't that long to wait. There was still quite a lot of testing and experimentation she could do without the Hot Spot in the interim.

She nodded. "Ok then. Let's go over those plans and requisitions tomorrow. We can run a few diagnostics and do what we can to make sure that the inspection goes without a hitch. I still have a lot of catching up to do, so one step at a time then." Tricia looked at the team. They were watching her very expectantly. "Thanks a lot for the warm welcome back, guys. It really means a lot. I'm really excited to be back. You guys have done a fantastic job while I was out, and I know we are all really looking forward to getting things back up and continuing where we left off."

The team smiled and nodded. Nikki and Steve excused themselves for exams, and the rest wished them good luck. As they left, the research department admin stuck her head in the lab.

"Doctor Carling?" she called out, looking around the lab. She finally saw them sitting in the break area. "Oh, there you are. Can you swing by the office on your way out today? We have some paperwork to review with you, and there are some things you need to sign."

Tricia waved at her and answered back, "Oh, hi, Brenda! Absolutely. In fact, I think we're about done here for today, so unless the team has something else really important to go over right now, I'll walk over there with you now."

Brenda gave her an ok sign and waited patiently by the door while Tricia gathered her things and put her lab coat in the cabinet. Jamal and Alex agreed there wasn't anything else pressing to talk about and volunteered to clean up. Tricia thanked them again for the cake and for taking such good care of things in her absence. She gave them both a short hug before following Brenda out the door.

As Tricia walked with Brenda, she couldn't help but reflect again on how great it really was to be back. The work the team had done in her absence was really stellar, and while she had complete confidence in them, she was always pleased to be proven right.

# Trials

Tricia approached the fitness facility and, as expected, saw that the front lobby was dark. This facility was the same one where Sensei Tim held class, and Tricia knew it typically closed early for general use on certain days of the week. As a member of the faculty and staff, though, she had after-hours access. She went to the side door and scanned her badge. The door clicked open.

She went to the lobby to sign in, acknowledging the caution that there was no attendant on duty and that she was responsible for her own safety. Obviously, the security system had a record of her entering the building, but that alone wasn't enough to transfer liability from the university to her for using the facility after hours. *Acknowledged*, she thought as she signed the book at the front desk.

As she left the lobby, motion sensors snapped the hall lights on for her, illuminating her way to the weightlifting rooms. The powerlifting suite was the first room she encountered. She paused briefly to look in through the window. That room was for extreme weight training to prepare for events like the

Olympics and other world-level competitions. It contained the equivalent of a couple of automobiles and was probably more of what she needed if she truly wanted to test her limits, but that wasn't her goal right now, and that room wasn't available to her, even if it was. To get access to that room, she would need to be accompanied by a member of the training staff to spot for her and make sure there were no safety problems. Having someone else along was just not an option for her, at least not now.

The next room, however, was her destination, the free weight room. Tricia went in, and the lights flickered on. While there wasn't as much weight in this room, what was here would suffice for her immediate training plan. She turned the window blinds closed and laid a one-hundred-pound dumbbell in front of the door for good measure. *No surprise interruptions*, she assured herself.

Her plan, the one she'd been working with for a couple of weeks now, was simple. Tricia had done a lot of research on weight power training. She'd had less luck on programs for training and controlling her speed—likely she'd need to improvise something, probably up at The Ridge away from any possible spectators— but there was a lot of information on powerlifting. More specifically, she was especially keen on the mechanics and techniques for lifting extremely heavy weights. World-class powerlifting wasn't just about building raw strength in order to lift more weight. It was also very much about technique and, more to her needs, about training to apply the right amount of strength and force to lift the weight at hand, efficiently and precisely, with no wasted effort.

Tricia set down her bag and stripped off her sweats, revealing only a support top and compression shorts. *Another good reason not to have any spectators*, she chuckled to herself. On the advice of pretty much every website she'd read on training safety, she had invested in a set of knee supports, a weight-lifting belt, and gloves with wrist braces. She wasn't sure she needed it all at this point—her strength and speed seemed to include some kind of natural reinforcement for her body—but safety was foremost on her mind, so she strapped them on. Tricia looked at herself in the full wall mirror and grinned. She either looked really good or really ridiculous. How she looked didn't matter, though. She needed to ensure she had control over her strength, and so far, her approach was working.

Her workout plan was simple. Tonight would consist of a circuit of chest presses, squats, and deadlifts. She would do a series of strength ladders, meaning she would start with the lowest weight that was just beyond her ability to lift without her powers and draw just enough of her powers to lift that weight consistently and smoothly for five reps. She'd then add weight and repeat until she either maxed out the weight she could do or topped out the weight she could put on the bar. Then, she'd work back down.

*Easier said than done.*

It was a good program for her. Not only did it help her truly understand and control her strength, but it forced her to exercise precision in how she drew on her powers. Her tendency was to pull too much; the first time she'd tried this routine several days ago, she had almost thrown a fifty-pound dumbbell through the mirror. Tricia quickly learned the strategy of slightly drawing below what she thought she'd need; as with most things, it was easier to add more if she found she needed it than it was to take away. She clapped her hands together twice and began loading the bar on the rack over the chest press bench.

Tricia started with just two plates and screwed down the lock nuts on the ends of the bar. She checked the door one last time to make sure she'd at least have some warning before someone pushed their way in. Two plates she could probably explain away, but once she started adding more, there would be no simple explanation. "I'm wiry" or "I'm just stronger than I look" wouldn't only go very far if she was caught with several plates on the bar.

She lay down on the bench and looked up at the bar. The bench shifted slightly under her. Tricia scowled a bit and wiggled a bit to test it. *Hmmm, seems all right, I guess. I'll leave a note for the staff to check it when I leave,* she decided and gripped the bar with both hands. Simultaneously, she sucked in a deep breath, drew on her power, and pressed the bar upward. It resisted, so she drew a smidge more and succeeded in lifting the bar free of the rack. Holding it above her, she lowered it to her chest and then pressed it back upward, exhaling.

*One*

She lowered it again, sucking in another breath.

*Two*

Her arms shook a little. *Steady...keep it smooth,* she prompted herself.

*Three*

The weight felt like it was getting heavier, so she drew in a small amount more. The weight lightened, and her arms firmed up.

*Four....Five.*

The bar rang as she slid it back into the rack and let it drop. Tricia sat up. "Good lift," she said to herself, "but I definitely undercut it a little too much." She resolved to pay closer attention to that on the next set. Pushing her lock of hair back out of her face, she stood up to unscrew the nuts and add another couple of plates.

Two hours later, Tricia was sitting on the bench by the mirrored wall. Her knee supports and weight belt were lying at her feet by her gym bag. She'd already put down three protein bars and was taking a long drag on her water bottle. As expected, there wasn't enough here to fully test her limits. She had maxed out the squats and deadlifts. She probably could have done significantly more on the presses, but she just didn't trust that wiggly bench after all. It was all good, though. Overall, she was pleased with how it went and was satisfied she was getting a good handle on how to control her strength.

Tricia tugged on the strap of her gloves. They made a loud ripping sound as the hook-and-loop fasteners pulled free. She tugged the gloves off, dropped them into her bag, and leaned forward, resting her elbows on her knees. *Do I even have limits?* she wondered as she took another long drink of water. Even in the short amount of time she'd been training, she had already noticed she could draw more than she could when she first started. *Will I just keep being able to draw more and more? Will I hit some kind of ceiling, or will the day come when my body just can't take the stress anymore and gives out?* She shook her head and sighed. *Humans spend their entire lives trying to push their boundaries, find their limits. Most never do.* She looked at herself in the mirror and shrugged. *Maybe that's part of how I stay human. Maybe at some point, I'll simply need to accept that I might never find my limits, no matter how hard I look or how far I go.*

She stuffed her equipment in her bag and zipped it up. *Won't stop me from trying, though.*

*I LOVE this!* Tricia thought to herself as she ran. *It's like flying low!* She loved the feel of the wind in her hair, snapping her ponytail behind her. The scenery flew past her while the birds overhead seemed to be soaring in slow motion. *Being strong is one thing, but this is something else entirely. It's exhilarating!* she marveled as a bug suddenly struck her goggles, creating a dark green smear across her vision. *Yeeech,* she thought, making an ick face. *Well, mostly exhilarating.*

She had come up to The Ridge early that morning loaded with ideas on how to use the isolated location to help her test and learn to control her speed. While the uneven terrain with its gravel and pothole ridden roads and trails wasn't ideal, she needed the privacy more. If anyone ever saw her running at this kind of velocity, her picture would be all over the network streams in a matter of minutes.

Tricia had run this ten-mile course four times already this morning with one simple goal: to learn how much endurance she had and how fast she could really be. It was clear already that her endurance was more than up to the task. Her heart rate and breathing were only slightly elevated after each run. The only remotely adverse reaction was how hungry she was after each circuit. She was so hungry, in fact, that she had no choice but to eat almost an entire meal in between trials.

She had realized early in the middle of the first run that the trickiest part of her enhanced speed was maintaining balance and footing. She had hit a patch of gravel and barely saved herself from going down and likely making a return visit to the hospital. *Not a conversation I want to have with the doctors,* she had thought to herself and forced herself to pull back a bit until her reflexes had caught up with the rest of her enhanced speed. With each run, though, her confidence grew, and she was able to push herself more each time.

*Ah, there's my finish marker. Almost there,* she realized, spotting the cone she'd put next to the road to warn her when she was getting close. Seconds later, Tricia came to a stop in front of the cabin and quickly tapped her watch to stop the running timer. *Heart rate good...breathing good...feeling good,* she thought and peeled off her goggles. She turned them over in her hand to look at the soiled lenses. She flicked another bug carcass off and half-wiped the smear away with her thumb. *Bleeech. Disgusting. Glad I thought to bring these, though. Otherwise, this nasty would be all over my face.* She made another gag face and then reached up to pull the hair tie out of her ponytail. As she ran her fingers through her snarled hair, she felt several other insect bits hit her fingers and fall out to the ground. *Ew, brushing that out is going to suck too.*

Tricia looked down to check her time and tapped her watch in disbelief. She knew her smartwatch didn't have mechanics that would get stuck, but it still seemed to be a natural reaction when the watch said something unbelievable. The stopwatch still stubbornly showed that only a few minutes had elapsed. *Ten miles in only a few minutes?!? That's insane!*

She quickly did the math in her head. *This seriously makes me the fastest living thing on the planet,* she thought. Her first run had felt almost leisurely, and it was still a five-minute mile pace. *That was some world-class speed,* she thought, still processing what she'd learned. *After three more runs, I'm a race car,* she mused, *and I know I still have more left in the tank.* A deep growl from her stomach interrupted her. "Ok, so maybe I need to put something into the tank after all," she muttered to herself and went inside to get something to eat.

As she started to mercilessly ravage a large bowl of pasta bolognese, Tricia pondered two important points about her elevated appetite. The first, more in the short term, was that she was probably going to have to make a supply run before the day was over. This was her fourth full meal of the day, and she wasn't close to being done with her training plans. Fortunately, there was a convenience store at the base of the foothills. If memory served, though, it likely meant she would be eating a lot of box macaroni and cheese and canned mystery meat this weekend. She shrugged. *It won't be great,* she thought, shoving in another mouthful, *but I can make do with that for this weekend. Next time I come up, I'll make sure I bring more provisions...a lot more.*

*What's more important, though,* Tricia continued thinking, grabbing a piece of bread to mop up the rest of the sauce in her bowl, *is how my powers are related to these increases in my appetite. There's no question they are. I just need to figure out how and why. Somehow, my metabolism is now directly linked to how my body is channeling and processing these energy flows to give me these powers, and it burns a lot of calories doing it.*

She took a long drink of water and grabbed a chocolate chip cookie to round out her meal. *Perhaps it's related in some way to how consistently I can draw on these powers, too,* she pondered, taking a big bite of her cookie. Tricia had noticed early on that the intensity of the energy sources around her did not seem to be a factor in how much she could draw. Indoors or outdoors, afternoon or evening, bright sun or deep shade, she could draw a relatively consistent amount of power. *The less intense the sources seem to be, maybe the harder my body needs to work to deliver, and the hungrier I get to make up for it. Maybe my body is acting as some kind of regulator or converter...or...something, I don't know. Again, the more I figure out, the more questions I have.* Frustrated, Tricia shook her head, brushed cookie crumbs off her shirt, put the empty bowl in the sink, and headed outside to start setting up for the afternoon. *But I am sure of one thing. At the rate I'm burning calories, I'm probably going to have a very disappointing conversation with the doctors about why I'm not putting on weight.*

"Pilot holes? We don't need no steenking pilot holes!" Tricia said a couple of hours later as she tightened down the last screw. It was a paraphrase of a line from an old comedy, one of her dad's favorites and one they had frequently shared for a laugh. Tapping a bit of her strength, screwing the two-by-four to the oak fence post was no problem at all. *Just have to be careful not to strip the screw head, or worse, twist the head off,* she cautioned herself. A couple of ruined screws lay on the ground by her feet, testifying to her concern.

Tricia dropped the screwdriver into the toolbox and stepped back to admire her handiwork. *Simple, but clever,* she thought. The two-by-four had a smaller section of wood attached with a hinge just above her head and had a small latch that would hold it up at a right angle when set. She reached up and held the hinged piece horizontally while she clicked the latch into place. *Just like the seat for a tiny dunk tank,* she mused. She flicked the latch with her finger, and the hinged piece swung down. *Excellent.*

"Since I don't have a tiny person to sit on it, I'll just have to go with the next best thing," she joked to herself and pulled a lacrosse ball out of the box at her feet. As much fun as a doll might have been to use—the thought still amused her—Tricia concluded that something relatively heavy, solid, and regularly shaped would be better suited for her next test, so she picked up a box of lacrosse balls before she had come up. She reset the small platform and carefully set the ball on top of it. Again, she flicked the latch, releasing the platform, and the ball dropped neatly into her hand. *This is going to work great.*

Tricia picked up the tape measure and measured the distance from the ground to the set platform. "Five feet, nine inches," she muttered, "that's...1.75 meters." She did the math in her head. "A two-second drop. I'll have two seconds to make the catch once I pull the release."

She started unwinding the ball of twine tied to the latch and paced off five yards. Like she was doing with her strength, using her ability in short bursts like this would not only show her what speeds she was capable of but also help her develop control and precision using it; to make the catch, she not only had to be fast enough, but her timing and coordination needed split-second accuracy.

*Ok, let's do this*, Tricia thought, pumping herself up. She planted her to take off and took up the slack in the twine. *Three...two...one...* She inhaled sharply and gave the string a tug. She saw the platform release and took two steps before she watched the ball thump on the ground.

"Well, that was anticlimactic," she said disgustedly to herself. She walked over and picked up the ball. *Nothing...what happened?* Tricia wondered as she tossed the ball up and down in her hand. Then, she thought back on her runs earlier in the day. *Of course*, she realized, *when I ran earlier, I didn't trigger my speed. As I pushed myself, it kicked in on its own.*

She reflected on how each of her other abilities had a different "feel" to her that helped her to sense them uniquely. Endurance and healing came without any effort on her part at all; when she drew on the flows, they essentially came for free. Strength came easily as well, but she knew what that felt like when she used it. *I'm going to have to find that 'feel' that triggers my speed before I can do this,* she concluded. She dropped the ball of twine and ran.

Tricia pushed herself, and, within a few seconds, her ability kicked in, accelerating her forward. *There it is!* she exclaimed to herself and skidded to a stop. She immediately took off again, paying close attention looking for that precise moment when she felt her speed activate and fixed that feeling in her mind.

"Ok. Ok, I think I've got this," Tricia muttered, and before the feeling slipped away from her, she started to run back toward the cabin, gripping the sensation tightly in her mind. She clearly felt her speed trigger from the first step. She stopped by the ball of twine she had dropped, celebrated with a quick fist pump, and closed her eyes. Tricia took a minute to focus on that feeling, triggering and releasing her speed over and over without moving, trying to build the memory she'd need to activate her speed on demand.

*Now!* Tricia grabbed the twine, triggered her speed, and tugged. In slow motion, she saw the ball start to drop. She felt herself accelerate toward it. *I've got this!* She stretched her hand out for the ball and then winced in pain as the ball bounced off her collarbone instead. She slid into the fence, grabbing her shoulder, and watched the ball carom off into the underbrush. *That's why I never wanted to be a goalie. Sheesh, those things smart.* She rubbed her shoulder until her healing finished its work, and the pain subsided.

Tricia rotated her shoulder a few times and reset the apparatus, taking a new ball from the box. She walked back to her five-yard mark and set up for her next try. Again, she triggered her speed, tugged the string, and took off. She watched the ball drop in slow motion and reached out to grab it, only to watch it ricochet off her palm, bounce off a tree trunk, and vanish into the woods.

She put her hands on her hips and blew her hair out of her face in frustration. "Physics is not my friend right now," she grumbled. Tricia fetched another ball from the box. "Duh, Tricia," she said to herself. "Force and momentum are still just a function of mass, acceleration, and velocity, right? Marni will be the first one to remind me that even without my strength, at these speeds I still impart a lot of force. I've just got to be more exact, more precise." She placed the ball on the platform and walked back to her marker. *Soft hands, Trish,* she reminded herself and yanked the string.

A couple of hours and several more lacrosse balls later, Tricia decided to call it a day. Late afternoon was giving way to early evening, and streams of sunlight were shining low through the gaps in the trees. She'd honestly lost count of how many attempts she'd made, but, in the end, she'd been able to make the catch consistently, progressively starting from increasingly longer distances. Her last one had been a spectacular fingertip snag just barely off the ground that had made her smile to herself. Running the numbers told her that not only was she very fast over these short distances but assured her that she was finally starting to build the control she craved.

*Now, just one more thing before I make that food run,* she thought and trudged off into the brush to hunt for lacrosse balls. Finding at least some of them would mean she wouldn't have to buy another box, and that would make it a *very* good day.

A little later, after a hot shower and a meal of box macaroni and cheese, Tricia relaxed on the couch in front of a fire in the fireplace. Her legs were crossed in front of her. The fire took the chill out of the air that was so common in the mountains this time of year. A paper plate stained yellowish orange and a paper cup of wine sat in front of her on a makeshift table hastily constructed from a piece of iron grate and a couple of cinder blocks from the shed. The box of lacrosse balls, now nearly full again, sat by the door.

The meal left her feeling very content and happy. Despite how bad she knew that box mac'n'cheese was for her, every kid had happy memories of eating it, and she was no different. The wine in the paper cup had made her laugh, too. *As long as I'm having wine with boxed macaroni and cheese, I might as well go all in and have it in a paper cup,* she'd thought, snickering to herself. Funny as it was, she hadn't really had much choice in the matter. All the other dishes were dirty from the earlier meals in the day, and she just didn't feel like doing them, so paper it was, funny or not.

Tricia had her eyes closed and was winding down from the busy day by meditating in the soothing warmth of the fire. She focused on her breathing, slow and steady, simultaneously tapping and releasing the flows, feeling them sweep in and recede. Tricia opened her eyes briefly. The flows swirled and pulsed around the fire, refracting the firelight into twisting rainbows that shimmered brightly through the room. *It's really quite beautiful,* she thought to herself and closed her eyes again.

Holding the flows, she began to practice activating her strength and her speed in turn, like putting a car into gear without stepping on the gas. Even sitting perfectly still, she could sense each ability engage, waiting for her to draw on it. Tricia released her strength and speed and focused on the flows themselves coursing through her body. She could feel them ebbing and churning. She relaxed, letting her breathing synchronize with the rhythm:

Swell...breathe in...recede...breathe out,

Crest...fall,

Flow in...and as she drew her breath, there was a new feeling – slight, but undeniable, almost an urge. She pursed her lips and exhaled slowly,

*Flow out.*

Heeding the sensation, she gently pushed on the flows, not away from her but directing them outward. She felt them respond and instinctively reached out with her hand along with them, eyes still closed. The flows changed direction, weaving toward her outstretched hand. Tricia felt them collect there, building. *Incredible*, she thought to herself, and tipping her head slightly to one side, she pushed slightly. The pooled energy released suddenly, giving her the sensation of popping a bubble with bubble gum. She saw a flash of light through her closed eyelids.

"What the heck?" she muttered aloud, and her eyes snapped open. She looked around the room carefully, but there was nothing there. *That looked suspiciously like a camera flash*, she thought, and feeling a bit paranoid, she got up and looked out the front door. Seeing no one there, she returned to the couch. *Was that me?* she wondered, looking down at her own hands.

Eyes open, she tried to repeat what she'd done. It was harder trying to concentrate on both watching and moving the flows, but as the flows moved toward her hands and started to pool there, her hands began to glow with a bright white light. Her eyes widened. Astounded, she fought to keep her concentration, to keep the flows building. The glow intensified. She felt nothing physically from it, but it was becoming too intense to look at directly. Tricia then made the same push she had before and felt the popping sensation. The entire room was instantly doused in a flash of light brighter than daylight. She gasped in surprise and slammed her eyes shut against the brightness. When she opened them, the room was covered in afterimages and bright spots. She blinked several times as her eyes readjusted. Tricia looked down, and her hands were no longer glowing. The flows had returned to their normal pattern.

She held her hands up in front of her, first looking at the backs and then turning them to look at her palms. "Well, that's new," she muttered to herself, still trying to absorb this latest discovery.

For the next several minutes, she repeated the light pulse, trying to change the amount of flow, how long she let it build, and any other variation she could think of. She found she could even let the flows build, making her hands glow, and then pull them back without releasing the pulse. "This'll come in handy when the power goes out." she joked out loud, but deep down, her humor was masking a complex mix of excitement, wonder, and apprehension.

She closed her eyes and again concentrated intently on how these flows felt and what she thought they were doing. She slowly directed the flows to her hands again and felt the build start. *What if I don't pop the bubble? Can I just let it flow?* she wondered, and instead of the sudden push to release the pulse, she kept nudging the flows past her hands. They responded to this new direction, and she felt them ripple out of her hands. To her, the sensation was like warm water running down her arms and off her fingertips. It was soothing and relaxing and...

...there was a new smell in the room, a new smoky smell adding to the smoke from the fire. Hotter. Closer. She released the currents of energy, opened her eyes, and gasped. Her paper plate was in flames on the grate tabletop in front of her. Next to it, the top of the paper cup was singed, and the wine inside it was steaming. She cursed and grabbed the blanket next to her, throwing it over the burning paper plate.

The hot wine and paper cup went flying across the room. She vigorously patted the blanket to put out the burning plate. Through the blanket, she could feel that the metal grate tabletop was hot, hot enough that without the blanket insulating her hand, she likely would have a serious burn to show for it.

Having extinguished the plate, she flipped over the blanket. It shook in her hands as the adrenaline surged through her. Sure enough, the blanket bore a charred mesh pattern where it had been scorched by the grate surface.

She tossed the blanket onto the floor in a heap and collapsed back on the tattered couch, letting her head sink back into the cushion and took a few deep, slow breaths to calm down. When her heartbeat had stopped pounding in her ears, she sat back up. "That's enough for one day, I think," she said under her breath. What she had learned today was incredible, awesome, and scary. Gaining more control over her strength and speed was a huge step forward, and she was thrilled with the progress she'd made there, but this, this was something new, something that was legitimately dangerous if she lost control. That frightened her far more than breaking a few glasses by accident.

*I need to get to the lab, use the equipment there to study this, get some actual data. I need some real answers,* she decided and started to clean up the mess she'd made. Sleep that night came slowly for her, but it did give her time to think very carefully about what she would do next and, unfortunately, to worry about what else she might discover.

# Foundations

Tricia paced nervously outside the classroom, waiting for Sensei to arrive. She had told Marni earlier that she wouldn't be able to meet before class as they had planned. Marni didn't mind, suggesting instead that they do something after class, and Tricia agreed that a drink after class would be great.

*I'm sure I'm going to need it*, she thought as she waited for him to arrive. As it turned out, she didn't have to wait long.

"Hey, Carling."

She jumped at the deep voice right behind her. *How does such a large man move so quietly?!?*

"Hi, Sensei," she replied.

"You're here early," he said, swiping his badge across the door reader. "Where's Haskell?"

"She's coming separately."

Sensei Tim held the door open for her. She gave him a nod in thanks and slipped past him into the dark room. The lights flickered into life. He came in behind her and pulled the door closed.

"You're looking a little lean, Carling," he observed. "Is your recovery still going all right?"

"Yeah, I'm doing fine," she replied. "The doctors are on me to put on some weight. It's hard because I'm trying to get my fitness back, too, and I'm burning through a lot of calories."

"I know some good supplements you could try." he offered. "Dense in high-quality proteins. Throw 'em in a blender with some berries, kale, and milk a couple of times a day, and you'll see a difference pretty quickly. I can send you some links after class if you want."

"Thanks, Sensei. I'd appreciate that."

He nodded, rummaging through his gear bag. "I assume you didn't come here for nutritional advice, though, am I right?"

"No. I'm glad I got some, but no," she admitted, smiling nervously. "I wanted to talk before class about what you said to me a few classes ago when you asked me why I was here."

"Ok." He stood up and turned toward her with his hands on his hips. "I'm all ears."

Tricia took a shallow sigh and paused to get her thoughts straight. "When I first started, it was really to keep Marni company. She really wanted to do this and convinced me to do it with her. I guess we figured we'd keep each other motivated."

"Not an uncommon way to get started, actually." Sensei agreed.

She nodded and continued, "As I got into it, though, I started to really appreciate the exercises we did. The workouts felt really good, and I felt like I was learning something, something useful."

"And now?"

"Now I realize it's more than that. I've learned that the things you teach us here help me with my personal focus, help me be more disciplined, to understand my body, and how to be in better control of it and myself in general. Does that make sense?" She paused, a bit nervous about how he'd respond.

Sensei Tim stared her squarely in the eye as if he were reading her on the inside. Tricia shifted her feet a bit. He dropped his hands off his hips and stepped toward her.

"If there is a right answer to the question of why you are here, that's about the closest I could ask for," he told her directly. She sighed in relief.

"There really is no right answer," he explained to her. "People are here for lots of reasons, and why they are here only really matters in terms of what they can get out of what we do here and what I have to offer as a teacher. Your answer, though, is the one I needed to hear for what I had in mind when I asked it."

"And what might that be?" she asked, relief shifting into curiosity.

"I also run an advanced class," he told her. "It's not in the catalog. It's by invitation only. It's for people I think have high potential, who want to really get something out of what we do at a deeper personal and physical level, who I think could benefit from making the commitment it would take and following through on it."

Tricia looked at him dumbstruck. *Not the way I saw this conversation going,* she admitted to herself. "Um, I'm really honored you'd offer, but am I really ready for something like that?" she finally asked.

"I'm not going to blow smoke up your butt, Carling," he said seriously. "You'd be coming in quite a bit behind the other students. You are honestly behind where you should be, but I think if you work at it, you'll catch up fairly quickly. It would be hard. We do much more intense physical workouts and a lot of sparring. I'm not easy on anybody in there, and you wouldn't get any special treatment. In fact, I'd likely be harder on you than anyone else at first because you have the most ground to make up, but I think you can do it."

Tricia nodded, but before she could speak, he held his hand up to stop her.

"You don't have to answer now. The advanced class normally meets at the same time on the off weeks from this class, but we are on a break right now. We won't be picking back up for a few weeks, so you have time to think about it. It's a big commitment, so best you really think it over before making a decision."

Tricia smiled and nodded. "Thanks, Sensei. Either way, I'm very grateful for the offer."

He nodded and looked up at the door. Some of the other students had arrived and were looking in through the windows in the door. He waved at them to come in. The door swung open, and a small group of people streamed into the room. Marni was at the back and waved to Tricia when she came in. Tricia waved back and made her way to the back of the room to meet her.

Tonight's class proved to be a fun one. Instead of some of the drills she found less interesting, tonight Sensei worked them through various *kata*. Tricia found these short, choreographed sequences of techniques to be challenging and fun. Not only did they help develop a level of precision and mastery of the individual techniques, but they also made her think, and she really liked the way the techniques flowed from one to another and put them into a context that felt more practical and useful. Each one was like a little dance that blended grace and purpose.

After completing a review of the *kata* they'd done before, Sensei was now in the middle of teaching them a new one. He stood at the front of the room, calling out the next technique as he demonstrated each in sequence.

"Left down block!" he called out.

In synchrony with the rest of the class, Tricia swung her left arm down. She made a few small adjustments to her stance and arm position, waiting for Sensei to call out the next technique. *I wish he'd hurry up,* she lamented. *Holding these stances like this is brutal...probably why he does it.* She huffed a bit.

"Right front kick!"

*Ah, that's better*, she thought in relief as the class kicked in unison.

"Pivot back to horse stance, fists on hips." The class shifted back to the starting position. Sensei surveyed the room, checking everyone's position. "And....shake it out."

The entire class sighed in relief. Tricia hugged each knee up to her chest, shaking out the burn. She bent over and put her hands flat on the floor, stretching her hamstrings.

And an idea came to her.

*It would be cheating, wouldn't it?* she asked herself.

*No, not cheating,* she debated. *It would be learning, killing two birds with one stone.*

"Ok everyone," Sensei called out, "let's go through it a couple more times slow, then we'll pick up the pace. Back to the starting position, horse stance facing front. Fists at your hips."

As the class shuffled into position, Tricia finalized her decision. She sank down into the horse stance and drew in a tiny flow of her power. It was hard to only draw a small amount. *Easy*, she told herself, *we only want a little...just enough to feel it.*

Sensei called out the first technique, "Right punch!"

*Strength*, she thought, and Tricia punched. She felt the ever-so-slight increase in power. Any burning in her quads evaporated immediately.

"Left punch!" Sensei commanded.

Tricia punched left, holding her level of power small but as steady as she could.

"Pivot right, front stance!"

She turned, keeping the flows at ready but releasing her strength. Her thighs started to complain a bit, but she pushed it aside to keep from breaking her concentration.

"Right center block!"

*Speed this time.* Tricia delivered the block. To anyone else, the block looked snappy, but she felt the touch of her enhanced speed in the maneuver.

"Right downward block!"

She swept her right arm down. *No kick would touch me*, she thought with satisfaction.

"Left front kick!"

Tricia shifted from speed to strength and delivered a kick she figured would probably break in a door with ease. The extra power threw her slightly off-balance, and she landed awkwardly, but even so, she couldn't help but smile slightly as she checked her form and made a few tweaks to her stance and posture.

"Left punch!"

She punched again, twisting her hips, feeling the power flowing into the strike.

Tricia continued to couple one of her powers with each technique as Sensei walked them through the routine step by step. *This is perfect*, she thought excitedly, shifting her abilities to coincide with each transition from one technique to another. *Not only is this great practice, but it's also giving my abilities some actual application, putting them into some useful context.*

Sensei took them through the new kata a few more times, working them up to full speed by the end of class. As he increased the tempo, Tricia found it increasingly difficult to keep up, but she knew that would come with practice, practice she now could do anytime she wanted, anywhere she wanted.

After the cool down and Sensei dismissed the class, Tricia met Marni in the back of the room. Marni looked at her and grinned. "Wow, you look really happy. I take it you enjoyed class tonight?"

Tricia hadn't realized she was smiling so broadly. "Yeah," she admitted, "Yeah, I really did. I really think I got a lot out of class tonight." *In more ways than one,* she thought. "How about you?"

"Well, I didn't walk away with any bruises, so I'd call that a good day." Marni teased and gave Tricia a soft elbow to the ribs.

"Well, you weren't shooting your mouth off tonight either." Tricia shot back and gave her a wink. Marni rolled her eyes mockingly. "Come on then," Tricia said. "Drinks are on me tonight."

"Now you're talking." Marni laughed, and they left.

Instead of going up to The Ridge on the weekend to train, Tricia had decided it was a good time to use the lab and do some tests on her powers instead. She'd gotten up early, did some yoga to stretch out, and ran through a few *kata* enhanced with her abilities to warm up a bit. She even tried mixing in some of the new light pulses and heat projection, but since she hadn't practiced with them very much, working them into her new routines was going to take more time. After a big breakfast to fuel up, as she put it now, she headed off to the lab. The time to get more quantitative—more analytical—with her abilities was now seriously overdue.

Tricia stuck her head in the lab door cautiously and looked around to make sure no one was there. No one should have been, but her team was diligent, and someone may have wanted to get some extra work done. *Coast is clear*, she thought to herself and pushed the door shut.

Tricia drew the blind on the door window, grabbed her lab coat from the cabinet, and tapped the commpod in her ear. It chimed obediently. "Interface with the lab voice command control system," she instructed.

"Connecting," the device replied.

After a few seconds, a different voice took over the conversation. "Control AI for the Research Laboratory Automation engaged. Hello, Doctor Carling."

"Hello, CARLA," Tricia responded. *Alex and Jamal do love their acronyms*, she thought and chuckled.

"Please state your pass phrase to complete authentication."

Tricia cleared her throat a little and replied, "Back off, man! I'm a scientist."

"Pass phrase and voice print confirmed. How can I assist you today, Doctor Carling?" the slightly mechanical alto voice requested.

"We have a lot of work to do today, CARLA. First, engage the hazardous experiment protocol, please." She smirked. Tricia was always amused when she caught herself being polite to the AI systems, using 'please' and 'thank you' and talking to it as if it was a person. *Well, when they take over, it's best to be on their good side, I suppose.*

"Hazardous Experiment Protocol engaged," the system responded.

First and foremost, the hazardous experiment protocol required the computer to monitor her life signs. If something were to go wrong, and her vital signs showed her life was at risk, the computer would notify first responders and shut down the lab equipment. Since she was here alone, Tricia believed this was an important safety precaution.

Secondarily, but equally important to her, it also allowed her to prevent people from walking in unexpectedly by securing the doors. "Restrict entry to the lab, CARLA. Access on my authorization only."

The system chimed, and she heard the lock engage on the lab door. "Access restricted, Doctor Carling."

Tricia slipped on her lab coat and looked around the lab. She was impressed with how much the team had done since the accident. The university had really stepped up as well by expediting the requisitions for replacing the damaged equipment. Everything looked very polished and new. *Let's get it dirty, shall we?*

Tricia picked up her bag and paused for a moment to look at the Hot Spot in the center of the room. *Where it all started,* she thought, and after another pause, took a deep breath and walked into it. She thumbed the door release, and the glass panels slid closed behind her. She put her bag down in one corner of the chamber where she was fairly sure it wouldn't be in the way and went to the center.

"CARLA, experiment setup please. Disable network uplink and save all experiment parameters and data locally under 'Carling Spectrum Test.'" *We'll keep this between us, CARLA. No records on the network storage where someone might see it.*

"Acknowledged Doctor Carling."

"Polarize the chamber panels to prevent ambient light contamination, please." The walls of the Hot Spot darkened in response until they became completely opaque.

"CARLA, establish safety parameters for the duration of the experiment."

"Please specify the safety parameters."

Tricia thought for a second. She'd need to expose herself to a fairly broad range of the near-visible electromagnetic spectrum to test her abilities, but at the same time, she needed to avoid anything that might cause her harm. *Low infrared to medium ultraviolet should be enough for today,* she decided. "Set the working range of the spectrum between one millimeter and two hundred and fifty nanometers with a hard cap at plus/minus fifteen percent."

"Safety range engaged, Doctor Carling," the system replied. The system would now warn her if she asked it to generate any wavelengths that exceeded the range she specified and would reject any requests that exceeded the hard safety thresholds at either end of the experimental spectrum.

Tricia rubbed her hands together. *Let's get down to work, shall we?*

"CARLA, give me a broad spectrum across the specified working range, six thousand lumens equivalent."

The chamber flared into life, filling the interior with a bright white light. *Just like a summer day at the beach*, she thought. "Set this as the working baseline, please." CARLA chimed in response.

Tricia went to her bag and pulled out a piece of iron rebar. The shed at The Ridge had a pile of it in various diameters, and she'd found bending it to be good for experimenting with her strength. *Not so good for the hands, though*, she thought, pulling out a pair of leather work gloves. It hadn't taken long for the rough surface of the twisting metal to scrape her hands raw, but fortunately, whoever had left the gloves in the shed had small hands like hers.

Tricia pulled on the gloves and took the piece of rebar in her hands. She reached out and felt the flows around her and drew on them, but to her surprise, they were sluggish. She drew on them harder and tried to bend the iron bar, but she could barely put a dent in it.

*What the heck is going on here?!?* she thought in frustration. She pulled harder on the flows around her, but they remained just as sluggish and weak. She put everything she had into bending it, gritting her teeth, her arms shaking, but it wouldn't budge any further.

"This was so easy in the gym and up at The Ridge," she muttered, pacing the floor. "What's going on *here*?"

"I'm sorry, Doctor Carling," the computer replied, "Can you restate the question, please?"

"Ugh!" she exclaimed, "I wasn't talking to you, CARLA. Just hold on." She put the rod back down on her bag, disgustedly pulled off the gloves, and tossed them down on top of it. Tricia then peeled off her lab coat, rolled it up, and dropped it on the floor next to her bag. She grabbed the bar with both hands, opened herself to the flows, and, to her surprise, bent the bar. Not as easily as at The Ridge, but it bent.

Tricia looked at the bar, puzzled, and her mind started to race. She looked down at her lab coat on the floor, then she looked at her bare arms, then at the bent bar again. *My lab coat?* she pondered. *My clothes?* Realization swarmed over her. *Of course, when I've been working out before, I was wearing athletic gear, lightweight shorts and tops. The lab coat is thicker and denser. Somehow, it must interfere with my ability to draw on the flows of energy.*

She then looked down at her T-shirt—the "forget lab safety" T-shirt the team had gotten her had seemed appropriate for the occasion—and the jeans she was wearing. *Well, the door's locked, and the chamber walls are blacked out. Only one way to find out, I suppose,* she decided, and, with the debate now over, Tricia stripped down to her underwear. She folded her shirt and jeans and laid them on top of her lab coat. She then pulled on the leather gloves and picked up the iron rebar. Holding the iron firmly in her hands, Tricia turned, saw her reflection in the glass wall, and couldn't help but laugh out loud. *I look like I could be Miss April in a calendar on the wall of some backwater gas station.* Tricia pulled effortlessly on the flows around her and, with a quick yank, straightened the bar effortlessly. *That did the trick,* she affirmed, *so yeah, ready to go.* She glanced again at her reflection in the glass. *In my underwear. I hope this doesn't get any weirder.*

"First test, CARLA," she said. The system chimed in response. "Call this the 'energy level test', please. Start at ten thousand lumens equivalent. Step down by one thousand at each interval and pause for my confirmation. At one thousand lumens, step down by one hundred. At one hundred, by ten, and at ten, step down by one until we reach zero."

"Confirmed, Doctor Carling. Ready to begin on your signal."

"Begin, please," she commanded. The chamber brightened considerably. Tricia had to blink and shield her eyes for a moment until they adjusted, but when they did, she couldn't help but marvel for a moment at what her eyes showed her. The room had burst into a field of cascading ribbons and vivid bursting suns whirling around her. *Beautiful, like I'm seeing the moment of creation.* The double chime indicating CARLA was ready interrupted her moment of tranquility. Getting down to business, she put a right-angle kink in the iron rod just as easily as she had straightened it moments before.

"Continue," she commanded and saw the light dim ever so slightly. Another chime confirmed the second interval at nine thousand lumens. Again, she bent the rod without any effort.

Tricia continued for the rest of the test, torturing the iron rod, checking for any impact on her strength as the light around her dimmed with each step. The pulses and swirls in her vision diminished at each stage until, finally, they winked out and took her strength with them.

When she finished, she moved on to other tests, varying different wavelengths, frequencies, and intensities to determine the relationship between the energies around her and her abilities, hoping to better understand their nature. She also tested the intensity of the light pulses she could now generate, building and releasing pulses the lab computer measured for her until they were so bright she couldn't look at them anymore.

When the latest test was complete, Tricia took a deep, cleansing breath and looked down at the clock on the monitor in front of her. *Almost lunchtime*, she thought. She had just one test left, and her stomach was starting to growl a bit. She had already exhausted the protein bars she had brought, and all she had left was a jar of the protein shake Sensei had recommended. She looked longingly at it sitting in her bag and then turned away. *Nope. Saving that for last,* she promised herself.

"Last test, CARLA," she said.

"Ready, Doctor Carling."

"Label this the 'heat output test'. Give me a spectrum histogram on the display next to a total power curve. Sample the interior of the chamber in real-time, please." The monitor shifted to the displays she requested. Tricia thought for a second and then added, "Please record an energy heat map

of the chamber as well. No need to display it during the test."
*I can review that later. It'll be interesting, I'm sure.*

"Confirmed," the computer responded.

"Begin test," Tricia closed her eyes and channeled the flows out through her hands as she'd done in the cabin. She felt the air warm in front of her. She looked at the monitor and watched the spectrum shift into the infra-red and the energy curve began to swing upward.

She pulled more and flowed it forward. The room started to get warmer, and the curve on the monitor steepened.

CARLA chimed and reported, "Ambient temperature increasing, Doctor Carling. Eighty-nine degrees and rising."

Tricia glanced at the displays on the monitor and then pulled a bit more.

"Chamber temperature now ninety-seven degrees and rising."

*More*

"Chamber temperature one hundred and sixteen degrees and rising."

*More still*

"Chamber temperature one hundred and thirty-nine degrees and rising."

Tricia looked again at the monitors. Her eyes widened at what she saw. *At this power level, I could melt one of those pieces of rebar. I could melt iron, and I'm hardly trying,* she realized as a drop of sweat dripped off her nose.

"Danger! Chamber temperature one hundred and fifty-seven degrees," CARLA interrupted. "Ambient temperature exceeding safe operating tolerances." A warning indicator turned red on the display she was watching.

*That's enough,* she decided and cut off the currents flowing into her. The energy curve dropped sharply on the screen, and the spectrum histogram flattened out. Sweat ran down her cheeks, neck, and chest. The interior of the chamber was unbearably hot.

"End the test, CARLA, and store the data. Maximum ventilation in the chamber. Open the door, too, please."

The system chimed in acknowledgment. Tricia heard the ceiling fans start to whirr, and the chamber door panels slid open. Tricia felt a blast of cool air hit her, and the chamber started to return to a more normal temperature.

She walked over to her bag, rummaged past several protein bar wrappers, her leather gloves, and a few badly contorted pieces of rebar, and pulled out her towel. Her underwear was damp from the sweat running off her, and the heat had made her feel a bit light-headed. Tricia started patting the sweat off her body and sat down next to her bag, putting her back against the cool glass wall of the chamber.

After a few minutes, she reached over and took the bottle of protein shake from her bag. She unscrewed the lid and took two large gulps. She exhaled sharply, relishing the feeling. *Sensei was right about this stuff*, she thought. She turned and wiped the sweaty outline of her back off the glass. *I need to wrap this up and get out of here.*

Tricia addressed the computer, "CARLA, transcribe final observations, please."

"Ready. Proceed with your observations, Doctor Carling," the AI answered.

Tricia took another swig of the shake. "First observation. As expected, my strength was unaffected by the intensity level of the ambient spectrum until overall intensity dropped into the single lumens. As long as I can see—as long as the patterns are present in my vision—I can maintain a consistent power level. Next observation."

The computer chimed, and she continued, "Note also that while my appetite was triggered after doing the test runs, further confirming the role of my metabolism in the process, it was less than I have experienced in other practice and experimentation sessions. I believe the purity of the energy sources here made them easier to convert and process than natural ambient energy sources. Long story short, I need to be careful as my actual mileage may vary outside in the real world. Next observation."

The system chimed again, and she paused a second, considering her next entry. "Also, as expected, only energies in the visible and near-visible spectrum are available to me. Similarly, any energy I project is also limited to the visible and near-visible spectrum, manifesting as either white light or infrared. Other variations may be possible in the future, but right now, it seems those are my only options."

She paused and then decided to add a bit more. "Note also that even the moderate level of output I produced today was more than sufficient to cause blindness or other potentially lethal physical harm to another person and cause significant damage to property. I must never lose control of these abilities, even for a split second."

One last pause, just to make sure there was nothing else. "End transcription and close the experiment, CARLA. Save all data and cross-index the tests, data, and video. Oh, and terminate the hazardous experiment protocol if you please."

"Saved...index complete. Standing down from hazardous protocol."

"Thank you, CARLA," she answered. *Just one more thing to do.* Her bra was still slightly damp, but overall, she was dry enough to get dressed, and having finished the shake, she felt much more human again. Tricia pulled on her clothes, gathered her bag and lab coat, and walked out of the chamber to her desk. Using her desk computer, she logged in using the system administrator credentials. She navigated to the directory containing the system logs and found the entries related to her experiment. *I'll probably get fired for doing this if anyone finds out, but I can't afford not to do it either*, she thought and deleted the log entries from the morning's activities.

Tricia then pulled out her portable memory stick, plugged it into the port, and transferred the data package from her experiment onto it. She browsed the files quickly to make sure the data was all there. Satisfied she hadn't missed anything, she unplugged it and deleted the data from the lab server.

"CARLA, please run a full system diagnostic of the Hot Spot and all connected accessories. I'll check the result when I come back Monday morning." She couldn't do anything about the building access records, but in the unlikely event someone noticed anything and got suspicious, the diagnostic would give her something she could use to make up a rational explanation for what she was doing there.

"Initiating diagnostic. Estimated completion in roughly four hours."

"Thanks, CARLA."

Convinced she'd covered her tracks, she tucked the memory unit back into her bag, zipped it, and returned her lab coat to the cabinet at the front of the room. Tricia took one last look around as she pushed the door open. "Now," she said under her breath, letting the door close behind her, "I think there's a double cheeseburger out there with my name on it."

# Forks

It was a beautiful warm evening. The sky was already getting dark, with hints of oranges, greens, and deep blues lingering in the western sky. A fresh breeze blew through the trees. Yet, despite the warmth of the evening, Tricia had put on her sweats and had pulled up the hood of her sweatshirt, carefully tucking her hair inside, before heading home.

The day had been somewhat aggravating. Another group of auditors and inspectors had visited the lab spontaneously and spent a good part of the afternoon poking through the equipment, asking questions, and otherwise distracting the team when they had work to do. Tricia understood the university's caution and the need to fully understand what happened, but since she was still on restricted time, every minute in the lab with the team was precious, and these interruptions were frustrating at best.

As always, the best way to deal with stress was to work it off. For a chance of scenery, she'd decided to go to one of the athletic training facilities up by the field houses on the opposite side of campus from the gym she normally used. It wouldn't be in use in the evening, and most importantly, it had equipment she could use to practice with her enhanced speed and agility and even get in some exercises with the punching dummies.

It turned out to be a good call. The place was completely deserted, so she got the chance to put in some good practice time controlling her abilities and work up a good sweat without a lot of prying eyes around. Interestingly enough, she realized it was the same facility where Sensei Tim's advanced class would occasionally be meeting. *I really owe him an answer on that soon,* she reminded himself. *He's a good guy and pretty patient, but it was a special favor, and he won't be patient for much longer.*

The only downside of her choice of facility, though, was that the walk home from this part of campus took her very close to a rather shady and sketchy part of town. She probably could have taken a longer route, but she was looking forward to getting takeout from her favorite Thai restaurant on the way. *Curry waits for no woman,* she mused, but there was no need to take unnecessary chances either. She was just the type to attract unwanted attention— petite, blonde, alone— so putting on the hoodie and baggy cut-off sweatpants seemed the smart call, and if she got a little too warm on the walk, so be it.

Lehman Hall came up on her right, marking that she was almost to the edge of campus. Just past it lay a staff and faculty parking lot bordered by a well-lit street that would take her to curry heaven. As Tricia rounded the corner by the lot, she started to hear voices coming from the far side of the deserted parking lot. At first, she just heard a few guys talking and laughing, but then she heard a girl's voice, likely a student...and she was definitely not laughing. She sounded very frightened. Tricia stopped to listen more closely. *Nope, she's clearly not enjoying the party*, Tricia thought. *Well, I guess the curry's going to have to wait after all.* Tricia started walking toward the group.

"C'mon honey, we know a great place just over there. It'll be fun." They were crowded around the girl, hemming her in.

"No, no thanks guys. I really need to get back to the dorm. I have studying to do." The girl, yes, obviously a student, most likely a freshman, tried to make it sound friendly, but her voice was shaking. She clutched her backpack close and tried once again to make her way through the group, unsuccessfully. Tricia started walking a little faster. By now, she was sure these guys weren't students; this part of campus bordered a less reputable part of the city, and most of the students knew to avoid it at night. This girl must've missed the memo.

"Well, howzabout we walk you to your dorm? We ain't never seen a dorm before, 'specially the girl's dorm, right guys?" They hooted and laughed.

"Sorry, guys aren't allowed in the dorm. I really need to go." She pleaded desperately, again, trying to push her way through, and again, being denied.

"Look honey, I really think you'll have a lot more fun if you come with us. We will show you a really good time," said the tallest one, obviously the ringleader. Tricia didn't think he and the girl likely shared the same definition of "really good time."

Just as he grabbed her by the arm, Tricia called out, "That's enough, guys. She said she needs to get back to study, so best you just back off and let her go study, yeah?" If she were lucky, just getting called out might be enough to get them to back down.

They all turned, and the ringleader glared at her.

*Yeah...nope...not even close.*

The leader pushed the girl into a smaller guy. Catching her, he took her by both arms and held her in place. The other two guys flanked the leader, still looking menacingly in Tricia's direction. The ringleader jabbed his finger in Tricia's direction. "You need to take off and mind your own business! Keep sticking your nose in, and we'll show you a good time, too!" All of them jeered and laughed.

*Here we go, Trish. You'd been wondering what use these abilities could possibly be, and here's our chance. We are all in now.*

Tricia drew on the energy around her. As she expected, it was more difficult than when she had just been practicing at the field house. *It's the heavier, thicker clothes*, she realized. *Should still be enough...I hope.* As she drew on the flows around her, the energy pulses and swirls flooded her vision, circling the parking lot lights and flowing toward and around her. The effect confirmed she was tapped in, but the swirls obscured her vision in this dim light. *Ugh! This is really going to be tough*, she thought when she had a quick spark of inspiration. With some bravado she hoped would at least be a little intimidating, she reached casually into her bag, pulled out her sunglasses, and slipped them on. The swirls and pulses sharpened, bringing the lot around her, and the punks, more into focus. *Much better*, she thought.

"Well, if you boys think you have what it takes, then let's have a good time, shall we?"

The ringleader and his two wingmen started to close the distance – the fourth stayed back, holding the girl tightly to make sure she wasn't going anywhere. Tricia assumed a combat stance and took a deep breath. *Be calm. Remember what Sensei taught you.* She recalled a previous lesson, one of Sensei Tim's famous 'real world' classes, where they worked specifically on scenarios like this, situations where they would be outnumbered in a fight. "Remember two important things," Sensei had said. "First, try to isolate your opponents; don't face three if you can maneuver to only face two, or one, at a time. Second, and most important, greater numbers will eventually win, so do whatever it takes to render your opponents unwilling or unable to keep fighting as soon as you can."

The ringleader suddenly yelled and charged at Tricia. Regardless of whatever powers she had, physics was still in play, and she knew immediately that her one hundred and thirty pounds wasn't going to fare well against his charging two hundred plus.

*Momentum, though,* is an entirely different thing, Tricia thought, anticipating his punch, and planted her right foot. As he threw a clumsy right, she channeled some extra strength, grabbed his arm, and twisted, redirecting his charging bulk directly into the wingman coming up on her right side. With a heavy grunt, they tumbled onto the asphalt.

The first wingman wasn't far behind, though, and came in hot, throwing a left cross straight at her head. She drew next on her speed and watched as he shifted into slow motion, the punch now sliding slowly toward her. She easily stepped under the punch and drove her left elbow squarely into his sternum. Quickly, she pivoted, putting all her weight behind a strike directly into his kidney. With the extra speed, she knew those strikes felt like getting hit with bricks, and he buckled immediately to his knees, clutching his chest, wheezing, and swearing when he could get the breath for it.

Tricia took a second to look over at the girl and the other guy. He wasn't even hardly holding onto her anymore. Her arms had dropped to her sides, and her backpack was lying on its side on the ground next to her. They were both just rooted to the ground, staring in disbelief at what they were witnessing.

Glancing back over her shoulder, Tricia saw the other two back on their feet, grimaces of rage on their faces, coming for her. Again, drawing on some enhanced speed, she moved to the left side of the wingman and, hearing Sensei's advice ringing in her ears, drove a short thrust kick into the side of his knee. She heard the crack as he screamed and dropped to the ground, clutching his leg. *He's going to need crutches for a while*, she figured, *but now it's two-on-one.* The ringleader was already starting to turn back toward her.

Out of the corner of her eye, she saw that the first wingman had gotten enough breath back to try a half-hearted lunge for her while he thought she wasn't looking. It wasn't even really a good attempt; she easily side-stepped his grab, and a well-placed punch to the side of his head made the odds even.

"I am going to *MESS YOU UP!*" the ringleader screamed as he advanced towards her. He drew his hands up into fighting position; his fists clenched so tightly she could see his knuckles whitening. She side-stepped slowly to keep him turning, stalking her. *Smart*, she thought, *he's taking his time now.* Suddenly, and much faster than she expected, he stepped forward and drove his left fist straight for her face. Caught off guard, she attempted a block, but it was late coming, and the strength of the punch drove her arm squarely into her nose.

Her eyes welled up with tears immediately, and she staggered back a bit. She reached up with her right hand, touched her nose with the back of her hand, and was met with a trickle of blood. She cursed to herself.

The ringleader must've thought he finally had his chance. He barked out a laugh and came at her with a big right roundhouse, putting everything he had into it to finish her off. On reflex, her left hand flew up, and she discharged a pulse of blinding light right into his face. The flash lit the entire parking lot like a bolt of lightning. Instinctively, he threw his left hand upward to try to shield his eyes. Unfortunately for him, he'd already committed to throwing that punch, and now, being completely off balance, he had no way to stop it. With a burst of speed, she grabbed the flailing punch and, swapping her power for a pulse of strength, rolled in midair, slamming him hard onto the asphalt. She completed the roll, driving her entire weight into his chest, trapping his arms with her legs, and thrusting her left arm up under his chin, pinning his neck against the ground.

She paused for a second, breathing hard, watching him struggle to catch his breath through the choke hold, fighting her weight on his chest. A wave of rage suddenly burst through...

...and in that moment, she was back in her dad's car that summer before her senior year. It was just after sunset. They were headed up to The Ridge for the weekend and had stopped at that little gas station just outside of the city at the edge of civilization they jokingly called it. Dad was taking off his seatbelt. He glanced over to her and told her to wait here while he went in to pay for the gas and pick up a few odds and ends. He said he'd only be a second.

*No Dad! Don't go...please...*

He shut the car door, and she watched him push the door to the station open.

*No, not again...*

She saw the flash of light and heard the report of the gunshot.

*Nooooooooooo......*

He had no idea two men were robbing that station. He just walked in. They panicked, and in that instant, they took him. They took him from her for a few hundred dollars, a couple of six-packs of beer, and a handful of beef jerky. All she could do was stare out of the car window as they ran out, jumped in their busted-up truck, and spun wildly out of the station. They had taken her only real family, the one person who had dedicated himself to making her dreams come true. Her rock. They took him and, in turn, nearly took all her dreams and future, too.

Tears welled up in her eyes behind the sunglasses. All those years of anger and rage finally unleashed poured out into this one moment.

As for this girl over there, Tricia knew nothing about her or what her story was, but this girl could be just like her. Coming from nothing, where someone gave up everything to get her here, to give her a chance to live her dream...and these scumbags were going to ruin it for her, in the most brutal and traumatic way imaginable for her, trying to take her future just like those other scumbags almost took Tricia's.

She looked down into the ringleader's bulging eyes. Her father's killers were never caught. Those murderers never had to face justice. So many selfish, thoughtless people...all the hurting...all the pain...taking dreams and futures away from other people. Suddenly, this one punk became all of them to her, an effigy for her pent-up anger and outrage—she leaned in closer, almost nose to nose with him.

"They got away with it, but you sure as frak won't," she hissed into the ring leader's face. The rage continued to swell, to fill her, consume her. She could feel the energy inside her coursing, pushing outward. Her right hand was poised near the ring leader's head. The air around the palm of her hand started to glow softly at first, then with growing intensity. She could feel the air getting hot. Steam started to rise off the asphalt near his face. He started to squirm, first in discomfort, then in outright pain. "Stop! It burns! Stop, please!" he gurgled, pleading. *Why should I?* she thought.

Then, she heard a small gasp and looked up at the girl. The fourth punk was long gone. She had sunk to her knees next to her backpack, just kneeling there, and met Tricia's eyes. That look in her eyes…no longer amazement, but sheer terror. Not of the gang any longer, but of Tricia herself. That girl was now dumbstruck and horrified by what she thought would happen next, what she thought she was about to witness.

*This is what that dark place looks like,* Tricia realized in that moment. *This is what Marni pulled me back from after Dad was killed. I can't give in to this. I can't.*

Tricia hung her head and, with a deep breath, subdued the torrent created by her anger. The heat dissipated. The punk stopped squirming and just went limp, panting and wheezing. She released the pressure on his neck and grabbed him by the collar, hauling his face roughly up to hers. "You aren't worth it." she said, "You'll get what's coming to you, the right way," and with a quick open palm strike to the face sent him into unconsciousness.

Tricia stood up slowly, releasing the rest of the energy within, breathed deeply a few times, and stretched her back. With her forefinger, she wiped away the lingering wetness in her eyes from underneath her sunglasses, composed herself, and surveyed what was left of the gang. The ringleader was down and out. The color was already returning to his face, and other than what might pass for a mild sunburn, he showed no other ill effects from her episode. The other wingman was also still unconscious but breathing. The last one was whimpering, holding his knee. *They'll be ok,* she decided and walked over to the girl. Tricia squatted down next to her and told her to call 911. The student provided a few details to the dispatcher, hung up, and looked back at Tricia. "They are on their way. Five minutes, they said."

"Are you ok?" Tricia asked her, putting a hand gently on her shoulder.

"Yeah, I'm ok. A little shaken, but ok," the girl said. She reached into her backpack and pulled out a small, sealed packet containing one of those single-use antiseptic wet wipes, tore it open, and handed it to Tricia, gesturing toward her nose. "Mom's got a thing for germs." She shrugged with a little half-smile.

Tricia smiled back, thanked her, and cleaned off the rest of the blood. She put the used wipe into her hoodie pocket.

The girl had been staring at her intently. Finally, she worked up the courage to blurt out, "What you did...that was incredible! Who *are* you?!? *WHAT* are you?!?"

"I'm just a friend," Tricia replied softly, "A friend who wants you to promise to be more careful about where you go off campus at night, ok?" The girl nodded.

The police would be here any minute— she already thought she could hear the sirens in the distance— and Tricia was not ready to have that conversation. She gave the girl one last assuring squeeze on the shoulder, stood up, retrieved her bag, and made her way back out to the front of Lehman Hall. She stopped to pack her sunglasses and hoodie into her bag and made a beeline to the restaurant for that curry.

By the time she had gotten there, she had cooled down, and the adrenaline had worn off. Between the fight and the effort she had exerted using her powers, she was ravenous. "I'll take two orders of the yellow curry, please...medium...brown rice. For here, please," she told the waitress at the counter and then collapsed into a booth. She just needed to sit and relax for a while. Then she'd head home.

Tricia got home about two hours later. The curry had been amazing as usual, and she felt very warm and content inside., The walk home and full stomach had helped her finish winding down. The evening's activities were finally catching up with her, and she was feeling exhausted. She took a long hot shower and started streaming the local Crystal Bay News feed as she got ready for bed. The special report they were broadcasting caught her attention. There, on the screen, was the girl from earlier that night. A reporter was there with her in the parking lot behind Lehman Hall, lights from the police cars flashing in the background, reporting on an attempted sexual assault that was averted by a "mysterious stranger". Tricia tapped up the volume just in time to hear:

"So, do you know who your rescuer was? Did she tell you anything about herself?"

"No, she didn't," the girl answered, "but she was amazing. Absolutely incredible. She probably saved my life tonight."

"Well, she might be watching right now. Do you have anything you'd like to say to her in case she is listening?"

"Just thank you, and that tonight, you were my beacon of hope. You inspired me, and I know others will be inspired by you, too."

Tricia turned off the stream. *Beacon of hope...I kinda like that*, she grinned to herself, but then, in the same instant, that girl's terrified look and that punk's face slammed into her mind, replacing the smiling face she had just seen on the news stream. She sat down on the bed, wrapped her arms around her knees, and hugged them to her chest. Rascal hopped up on the bed and plopped herself down next to Tricia, purring loudly and rubbing her head on Tricia's thigh.

*Face it, Trish*, she thought, scratching Rascal's ears absentmindedly. *You got lucky tonight. If those goons had known what they were doing*—she reached up and touched her swollen nose—*this all could have gone very differently. And let's be honest about it. You came way too close to doing the unthinkable. You almost lost it. You almost let it get the better of you. You very nearly crossed a line you could not have come back from. That beacon of hope could've become a monster in just a single instant. You can't ever get that close to that line again. You have a decision to make...if you're going to do this, you're going to have to do more than just control these abilities. You're going to have to control* YOURSELF *and commit to learning how to really* USE *these powers so they don't use* YOU *instead.*

Tricia sighed, flipped her hair back, smoothed down the legs of her pajamas, and rolled over to turn out the light.

*Tomorrow, I'm giving Sensei my answer on the advanced class.*

After tonight, she knew her decision. Deep down, she knew she had known for a while. More than anyone Tricia knew, Sensei Tim embodied strength and power under absolute control. So much of what she'd learned in his basic class had been instrumental in learning to manage her abilities already, so if there was one place she could learn to make the transition from doing no harm to actually mastering her powers, safely using them in the real world to help others like she did tonight, it would be with Sensi in his advanced class.

*I sure have got a long road ahead of me,* was her final thought as sleep overtook her.

LEHMAN HALL

# Darkness

Purity forced herself to focus on the clicking of her heels on the sidewalk to distract herself from the noise around her. It was still a bit early, but the city was already waking up, eager to start the end of its week, and there were already more people out and about than she particularly cared for. *Everybody's working for the weekend,* she thought. Her habit was to get an early start so she didn't have to deal with the morning crowds, but she was getting a slightly later start today. Even so, she decided to take the chance on the coffee shop and treat herself to her favorite, a lavender latte.

Thankfully, the line was short this morning. She gave her order to the teenager behind the counter while she fished around in her bag for her wallet. When she looked up, he was just staring at her blankly. Purity leaned in with a small smile, looked at him over her glasses, and asked, "So, am I going to pay for that, sweetie, or is this on the house?" He blushed a bit and rang up her order. She tapped her card on the console and went down to the far end of the counter to wait for her order. She knew she was attractive, but she was old enough to be this kid's, um, aunt…yes, aunt, she decided. The aunt who routinely forgets birthdays and makes inappropriate jokes when she visits. She chuckled softly to herself. She didn't mind the occasional attention, but she was too focused on other matters right now to care about it, and, frankly, it was going to become irrelevant very soon anyway.

When they called her name, Purity walked up to the counter and picked up her drink. She tasted it, careful not to burn her lips. Very hot, but very delicious, as always. She admitted humanity did have its bright spots, just not enough of them, but she'd keep enjoying a lavender latte for as long as she could. She left the shop and picked up the pace; she was now well behind where she wanted to be today.

She arrived at the back door of the building and tapped the key code. This part of the building had been storage, but she and the rest of the Liberators had converted it into a makeshift base of operations and her laboratory. She set her things down on a table and went to the computer to check the results of the analysis on the data samples she'd let run overnight. With every iteration, the results steadily improved, but frowning a little, she was disappointed that the uptake rates still weren't where they needed to be, especially on the male component. Purity entered these new values into her computer simulation, and, as she suspected, these rates would not be enough to reach the critical tipping point for her plan. She huffed a bit and put her hands on her hips.

*Not to worry though,* she assured herself, *this new batch should give us a significant boost.* She went to the incubation vats and checked. They were pretty much ready, so she went ahead and added the aerosolizing solution and the signature blue and green dyes that earmarked the demonstrations by Liberators of Gaia. *We can't forget about the showmanship now, can we?* she chided silently. They thought it was all about the message, getting the attention, making a public splash with the devices she made for them, but to her it was about the science, and her vision, and the next "demonstration" was just a few days away. Satisfied that preparations were in order, she turned off the light and left to go about the rest of her day.

Tricia pulled the rental truck up to the side of the loading platform and killed the engine. She climbed down out of the cab and checked the sign next to the open loading entryway: Performance Fitness Supply. She tried the entry door next to the loading dock, but it was locked. *Loading door is wide open though. Somebody must be home,* she thought and easily leapt up onto the platform.

"Hello! Anybody here?" she yelled into the emptiness.

"Yeah. Hold on," a voice answered. Moments later, a man appeared wearing gray coveralls. He was still chewing a bite of something and wiping his hands on the front of the coveralls.

"Hi. I'm picking up an order," she told him.

He nodded and swallowed. "Sure. Go around to the front of the office. Larry'll help you out."

"K. Thanks!" She waved and let herself out the door at the bottom of the steps leading down from the loading area.

A few minutes later, Tricia had circled the end of the building and entered the front door. The small reception area had posters of fitness equipment up on the walls. As she entered the door, a younger man stood up behind the small counter facing the door.

"Welcome to Performance Fitness. I'm Larry. What can I do for you?"

Having found her quarry, Tricia approached the counter. "Hi, Larry. I'm picking up an order. It should be under Carling."

"Glad to help," Larry replied. "Do you have your order confirmation by any chance?"

Tricia fished her commpad out of her bag. She quickly located the message with the confirmation code and held it up. Larry scanned it and started scrolling on the computer screen in front of him.

"Yup. Here it is," he said, still scrolling. "Wow, quite an order. Two full sets of plates...a long bar...couple of short bars...multi-function rack...combat dummy. You buying for a gym?"

"No, just for me and some friends." She answered, prepared for this kind of questioning. "We're all going in together on a shared home gym."

"Got it. You all must be pretty serious." Larry looked through the order again. "Hey, about this combat dummy, Ms. Carling..."

"*Doctor* Carling."

"Sorry. Doctor Carling. This combat dummy is top-of-the-line. I'm not one to turn away cash, but being honest, if you don't need something this heavy-duty, the next model down is still a good one and could save you a lot of money."

Tricia thought for a moment, reflecting on her sessions with the dummies she's used at the field house during her workouts and the beating she routinely gave them. Shaking her head slightly, she looked him dead in the eye. "No, I'm pretty sure I need the heavy-duty one."

Larry looked more skeptical. "Are you sure? I can get you a good deal on one that's more suited for the average person."

"Pretty sure. Thanks, but I'll stick with what I ordered."

Larry shrugged. "Ok, if that's what you want."

*Average, huh?* Tricia decided to poke him a bit more, just for fun. "That comes with a full warranty, I assume?" she asked, completely deadpan. "Not just manufacturing, but if I break it during a workout, it'll be fully covered?"

Larry looked at her. He was clearly trying to decide if she was being serious or not. "Of course. One year replacement."

"Good," Tricia said, "just wanted to be sure."

"Tell you what," Larry said, grinning at her, "I'll go one step better. If you break it, I'll not only replace it, but I'll refund you thirty percent of the purchase price."

Tricia smirked and called his bluff. "You'll put that in writing?"

Larry turned to the computer and typed. Shortly, the printer clicked and spat out a new copy of the invoice. He put it down on the counter between them, pulled a pen out of the cup next to the monitor, and circled the guarantee he just added. He then initialed it with a flourish.

Tricia chuckled, folding the invoice, and tucked it into her bag. She took out the truck keys and put them on the counter. "Truck's out back by the loading dock. Feel free to move it however you need to load my order."

"Super," Larry said, "I'll get the guys going right away."

"Hmmm, any way someone could assemble the dummy for me?"

"Shouldn't be a problem," Larry answered. "It's a slow day today. No charge for that, but the guys might appreciate a tip for it, though."

"That can be arranged," she assured him.

"Ok, well, it'll be a while. You're welcome to hang here. There's a coffee shop and some other places you can hang out in, too, get a drink or whatever." He pulled a small pamphlet out of an acrylic holder on the counter. "There are some discounts in here you can use if you decide to do that."

"Sounds great. As long as I'm taking the day off for this, I might as well make the most of it." Tricia smiled back and slid the pamphlet into her bag.

"Is the number here good to send you a message when we're done loading?"

"Sure is," Tricia confirmed, pushing the door open to leave. "Catch you in a bit, Larry. Thanks for the help!"

A short while later, Tricia put down her book and stretched, letting the midday sun splash across her face. She checked her watch. *Shouldn't be too much longer now*, she thought and took another sip of her coffee. *I could get used to this not working on Friday thing.* She didn't normally have coffee in the afternoon, but this exotic elixir of creams and syrups hardly qualified as coffee despite the shot of espresso.

Sirens Coffee was right where Larry told her it would be. Sipping again, Tricia took a few moments to look around the business center surrounding her. At one time, this had clearly been a very industrial area dominated by warehouses, but now it was transforming and developing into something a bit more upscale. Across from her was the fitness supply, and next to that was a restaurant supply, a bulk office supplies depot, and one of those big box warehouse stores. On the corner it looked like a laser tag place was going to be opening soon. To her left was a small diner and a craft brewing taproom, and on the right, she saw a dance studio, martial arts dojo, and a discount furniture outlet. "Very up and coming," she muttered to herself. "I'll need to check it out again."

Voices on her right drew Tricia's attention. Turning to look, she saw a small girl, maybe four or five, and what was probably her mother standing in front of the dance studio. They were watching a video of a woman in mirrored tights doing some kind of interpretive dance. The little girl was completely mesmerized by her.

The girl looked up at her mom, pointing at the screen, and said, "Mommy, I want to dance like that girl."

The mother leaned down and squeezed the girl's shoulders, "I know, dear. You'd be beautiful, I'm sure."

"Can I take lessons here, Mommy?" the girl pleaded.

"I don't know sweetie. You know since Daddy left things have been difficult," she answered sadly.

"But Mommmmmeeeeee, I really want to!"

Tricia looked more closely at the two of them. The mother was wearing dark slacks and a navy blue linen shirt. In the reflection of the window glass, she could see "Inlet Shores Culinary Supply" embroidered on the pocket. *Probably works at that restaurant supply over there*, Tricia surmised. *On a break, I'm guessing. Probably can't afford day care either.* The girl was clean and well cared for, but her clothes were clearly not new either. Tricia's heart went out to them.

As she watched, a young man stealthily walked up behind the mom. He was probably in his late teens, maybe twenty. The mother was still bent over talking to her daughter about the lessons, and as Tricia watched, the man started to slowly move his hand toward the exposed open top of the mother's bag on her shoulder.

*Oh no, you're not*, Tricia resolved, her sense of moral outrage flaring. She glanced around quickly to see who might be looking and bolted out of her chair. Her speed allowed her to cover the short distance in just an instant, and she grabbed the man's wrist. She channeled her strength, and her hand became a vice grip, halting his hand abruptly in mid-motion.

His head whipped around to look at her, and as he opened his mouth to speak, Tricia pressed her finger to her lips and squeezed, not enough to injure, but enough to let him know she was not to be trifled with. He got the message and snapped his jaw shut. She checked that they had not drawn the attention of the mother and daughter. Satisfied they were still preoccupied with their conversation, Tricia looked the man in the eye, nodded her head toward her table, and gave his wrist a slight twist as she started walking him in that direction. He came along begrudgingly, occasionally sucking air through his teeth when he felt the pressure on his wrist.

When they got to the table, Tricia relaxed her grip slightly. "What's your name?"

"J...J...Jimmy," he stammered out.

"Have a seat, Jimmy. Let's chat." She said, releasing his wrist. He plopped down in the chair, rubbing his wrist. Tricia sat down across from him. Jimmy looked right, then left, and back again, like a trapped animal.

"Relax, Jimmy," She told him, "Besides, trying to make a break for it isn't a great plan. Trust me on that."

He stared at her, and, finally accepting the situation, his shoulders slumped.

"Tell me, Jimmy. I don't suppose you overheard any of that conversation between that mom and her little girl, did you?" she asked him.

"No, ma'am," he answered.

"Don't call me ma'am."

"Uh, ok," he said and swallowed hard. "No, I didn't."

"Well, Jimmy, that little girl has a dream. She wants to take dance lessons, but it's pretty clear that's a single mom barely trying to make ends meet. Look at them, Jimmy. I want you to really *see* them."

Jimmy turned to look toward the mother and little girl. They were still talking in front of the dance studio window. To Tricia, it looked like the little girl was winning that discussion, and it made her happy to believe she would.

"That mom probably barely makes it paycheck to paycheck, and yet she is doing everything she can to do the best she can by her daughter. I'm going to guess that she's going to find a way for that little girl to get her dance lessons, but I don't think someone lifting her wallet would make that any easier, do you, Jimmy?"

Jimmy, still looking at them, shook his head. Tricia could see the guilt starting to form on his face.

"Look at me, Jimmy," she instructed. He turned to look at her and withered under her gaze, struggling to make eye contact. "I don't know your story, Jimmy, but you look like the kind of guy who can do pretty well by himself if he puts his mind to it without resorting to this kind of thing. Am I right?"

"Yeah, "he answered, "probably."

"Glad to hear it, Jimmy," she said. Her commpod chimed in her ear. The voice told her she had a message from Larry at Performance Fitness Supply. Tricia stood up, "Ok, look, I've got someplace I need to be now, but I think we are done here. I'm giving you that chance to prove it to yourself, so I hope you make the most of it."

Jimmy just sat there, looking up at her. Tricia leaned down and again locked eyes with him. "*Now* is a good time to get started, Jimmy."

He took the hint, stood up, and turned to go. As he took a couple of steps, Tricia called out to him, "Oh, and Jimmy?" He turned to look back. "In case you get second thoughts, just be aware that this kind of thing is going to become much harder to get away with in this city very soon. Do you understand me?"

"Yes, m...Yes, I do," He said and walked off.

Tricia watched him disappear into the parking lot. The mother and daughter had moved on by this time. *Hope you get your dance lessons, kid*, she thought and drained the last of her coffee. Tricia listened to the message, and, as she'd expected, it was Larry telling her the truck was loaded and she could come back over when she was ready. *Excellent timing,* she thought and went back into the shop to dispose of her trash and use the ATM in the back corner.

When Tricia returned to the truck, Larry was standing on the loading dock with the keys. He tossed the keys down to her. "It's all ready to go. Drive carefully. I would be really careful going over any speedbumps if I were you."

She looked at the truck and noticed it was indeed riding quite low. "I'll be careful. Thanks, Larry!"

"You need any help unloading that?"

"No thanks, Larry," she replied, "I think I have it covered." She reached up and handed him several bills folded in half. This is for the guys."

"They'll appreciate it. If you need anything, don't hesitate to call." With that, he waved and disappeared into the back of the warehouse. Tricia walked around to the open back of the truck and mentally checked off the inventory in the truck against her order. The guys had even partially assembled some of the racks and such. *Nice! That'll make unloading and putting all this together a lot easier.*

Tricia noticed the assembled sparring dummy glaring at her from the front of the truck's cargo box. He was tightly strapped to the hooks on the wall with his spongy orange muscled torso and deep, menacing scowl facing her. 'Combat George' was painted in white letters across the black weighted base.

"Well, George, I'm going to warn you. You're in for some rough times ahead," she said to the figure.

Tricia answered on George's behalf, deepening her voice, "Bring it, Tricia! Give me your best shot."

"All right then, George," she answered again, in her normal voice, "but just remember, you asked for it," and slid the rolling door of the truck closed.

*Tick. Tick. Tick. Tick.*

Tricia, eyes closed, focused on the ticking of the mechanical timer sitting on the counter next to the stove. The rhythm was soothing, and it helped her to meditate, but it was also very distracting. It reminded her of the casseroles she had cooking in the oven, and, after the day she'd spent, she was ready to do some serious damage to one of them. The others, she hoped, would get her through her training plan for the weekend.

She had made it up to The Ridge with her cargo without any serious problems. The truck had, in fact, bottomed out a couple of times on the uneven roads but had pulled through in the end. The act of unloading and storing the equipment she'd purchased had proven to be some valuable practice and training by itself, and by the end of the afternoon, the weights and racks were stacked neatly in the small barn behind the cabin. Her plan was to convert at least part of the barn into a training area. Starting on that was part of her training plan for the weekend.

George and the wall mirrors, though, were stored inside the cabin, at least for now. She didn't trust the rats, squirrels, and raccoons not to be tempted by George's brightly colored foam covering, and the mirrors were just too breakable to leave out there unattended. Tricia disliked the idea of having to look at herself all the time, but the mirrors were included with the package she'd purchased, and she had to admit that being able to use them to check her form while training was helpful. She would hang them tomorrow, but until then, here they were in the main room, leaning against the wall next to where she was currently meditating, safely out of harm's way.

*Breath in....hold....out. In....out....*

Tricia reached with her feelings, and the flows were there, as always, gently swirling and rolling. Relaxing further, she pushed deeper with her feelings, like moving her hand back and forth in the ocean, waves pushing past and then receding. She pushed further, deeper...and paused. She sensed something different under the surface, another flow, one she'd not noticed before. *Something new*, she thought, *like the riptides or undertows...underneath...not visible until you feel them.*

Cautiously, she reached for them and tried to draw them toward her as she did with the light energies. These flows, however, resisted her pull. She tried just opening herself, seeing if they would come to her on their own, but they lingered just at the edge of her perception. *No, don't pull...coax? Invite?* she wondered, and, as best she could, she tried to coax these new flows toward her. They wavered for a moment and then accepted her invitation.

Tricia gasped a bit as the new flows rushed towards her. She felt them swirl around her body, immersing her. She held her breath for a second, waiting for some backlash, some sensation to occur, but none came. *Feels like being in a jacuzzi*, she thought, relaxing, and letting herself experience this new discovery.

As she felt the seething churn of these new flows, Tricia started to perceive a new impression from them, a sense that they wanted to expand, to extend....*to push*, she realized. She opened her herself to that feeling, just slightly. As she gave the flows more free rein, she felt a lightness, a sense of freedom, a sensation of...

*Floating?*

Holding her concentration, Tricia reached down cautiously with her hand. Where she expected to feel the floor, she felt only open air. She reached further down, feeling underneath her backside and crossed legs, but still, there was nothing but open space. She cautiously opened one eye and looked down. *I AM floating! How is this possible?* Then she turned and looked in the mirror against the wall next to her, "What the..." she exclaimed in shock and lost her concentration entirely. The flows receded, and she fell.

"Ugh!" she grunted loudly as she hit the floor. She rolled over slightly and rubbed her butt cheek where she'd landed. *Was I seeing things?* she wondered. *What WAS that?* She turned toward the mirror and folded her legs underneath her, sitting on her knees while she stared at her reflection. Cautiously, she coaxed the flows again. They responded more quickly this time, and as they entwined her once again, she watched her reflection in the mirror.

To her amazement, dark streaks formed in her hair, spreading out from her scalp down the length of her hair, and within seconds, her blonde hair was laced with broad strands of dark ebony. Her jaw dropped at the reflection she barely recognized, and she gently grazed her image in the mirror with her fingertips in disbelief.

"*That* is absolutely...freaky!" she exclaimed softly, turning her head slightly from side to side. She reached up and pulled out her hair tie, freeing her ponytail, and shook her hair fully out. All of it was a tangle of blonde and black chunks, interwoven such that if she hadn't known, she wouldn't have been able to tell which was her natural color. Tricia combed her fingers through it and rubbed some of the dark strands between her fingers. "Feels normal enough," she muttered.

Abruptly, she smiled and then laughed. She let her head drop and clapped her palm to her forehead, still laughing.

After a few moments, she looked up at the mirror. "Seriously, Tricia," she said to her reflection, "a few minutes ago, you were literally levitating off the floor, and your *hair* is what is freaking you out right now?" She chuckled a few more times. "Well," she finally concluded, "if any of this was ever going to manifest itself visually somehow, there are a lot worse ways it could show up than my hair color."

Past the shock of her unexpected transformation, she ran her fingers through her hair one more time, then clapped her hands on the top of her thighs. "Ok, let's get back to it."

Tricia, feeling the flows still around her, once again yielded to the pushing feeling and watched herself start to rise off the floor. *Amazing*, she thought to herself, *just amazing. A feeling of near-total weightlessness*. She pulled back on the feeling a bit, and she lowered smoothly back to the floor.

She stood up, brushed off her legs, and looked around the room. In the middle of the room, the combat dummy sat there scowling at her, giving Tricia an idea. "Sorry, George," she told the dummy, "I warned you there could be some rough times ahead. I apologize in advance for what might happen next." She reached out with her hand in George's direction and coaxed the flows in its direction. She felt the pushing sensation shift, and as she watched, a shadowy shimmering wave emerged from her hand and hit the dummy in the shoulder, making it wobble and spin slightly as if she'd physically struck it.

"Cool," she said, smiling. *More*, and she coaxed more of the flows, directing them at the hapless dummy. A slightly larger, denser, but still translucent flow struck George squarely in the chest, toppling him backward. Tricia glanced again in the mirror, but where she saw the flow emerge, the reflection showed nothing but empty air between her and the awkwardly tilted combat mannequin. *It seems I can see it, but likely no one else can*, she noted to herself, and again pulled back the flow, letting the dummy pop back to its upright position, wobbling as it settled.

"So," she said, reflecting to herself, "I can project energy in the form of heat, and I can concentrate it to form light. I can project this to strike or move something. I wonder..." She once again coaxed the flows towards poor George, but as they started to move outward, she deliberately held them back. The flows started to swirl in front of her, coalescing into a circular shape at the tips of her fingers. The shape stretched from her waist to her nose. She moved her arm side to side. The circular shape moved with her. Tricia checked the mirror. As before, the mirror showed nothing, but when she held up the shadowy plate, it was like looking through warped tinted glass.

"Sorry again, George," she said and strode over to where the scowling figure was waiting patiently for her. She swung her arm and struck the dummy with the front of the shimmering disc. She could see the foam depress on the dummy's surface, and it flew back away from her, crashing into the back wall of the cabin. The windows in the cabin rattled, and a picture that was hanging on the wall flew off and smashed on the floor. The paneling on the wall had a hole punched in it where the dummy had landed against it.

"Whoaaa," was all she could say, astounded, as she looked back and forth between the wobbling dummy, the hole in the wall, and the shimmering disc at the end of her hand. To the side, she caught her reflection in the mirror, and a face looked back at her that was both familiar and, suddenly, unfamiliar; a face that was hers but was now outlined in black and blonde, one that now had a new unknown to sort out and understand before it would be entirely hers again.

Tricia pulled back the flow, and the shadowy disc vanished. She ran her hand over the hole in the wall and groaned slightly. "Add that to the list of repairs I have to make," she grumbled, but as what she'd actually done sank in, any regret about the minor damage she'd caused was quickly washed away by amazement and excitement over her new discovery. "But so worth it," she added as a grin spread across her face.

Eager to continue exploring this new facet to her abilities, she closed her eyes again and focused on the new flows, feeling them surge and swirl around her. *Hmmm, I usually feel the flows surging through me. These roll and slide over me, outside of me. What if, instead of pushing them out, I pull them inside?*

Impulsively giving in to her curiosity, she directed the flows inward, eager to answer her own question. She involuntarily sucked in a sharp breath as the flows entered her. The moment they did, she instantly felt as if every atom in her body were about to explode, as if she'd fly apart, scattering every quantum of matter in her being across the cosmos. On the verge of panic, she shoved the flows away from her, and instantaneously, she was whole again.

Tricia grabbed a fistful of the front of her shirt and reached for the back of the couch to steady herself. She bent over, panting. She sank down on the arm of the couch and took several deep breaths to try to compose herself. "Well, we won't be doing *that* again anytime soon," she promised herself and rested there for a few minutes.

*Ding!*

She glanced at the timer on the counter and confirmed it was finally time to take dinner out of the oven. She glanced quickly at herself in the mirror. With the flow gone, her hair had once again returned to its natural blonde, and despite feeling that she'd nearly disintegrated herself, her reflection confirmed that she didn't seem to be any worse for the wear.

Tricia took the casseroles out of the oven and set them on the stovetop to cool for a bit. As they steamed next to her, she put her hands on the edge of the sink and stared at her hazy reflection in the small kitchen window.

"So, one set of flows, flows from the electromagnetic spectrum, flows from light energy, give me strength, speed, light, and heat." she conjectured. "These new flows...these flows repel. These are something very different—not light at all. Shadowy...dark...flows that repel, that push things apart." Realization hit her. "Just like dark energy."

She turned and leaned her back against the edge of the counter. "Both were in the chamber that day. What if...what if the accident didn't just give me a connection to light but also gave me a connection to the dark energy as well, a connection I haven't felt until now?"

Tricia ran her hands up through her hair and clasped them behind her head. "Do I really have the same force inside me that's responsible for the expansion of the universe?!?" She paused for a while, digesting the magnitude of what this could possibly mean for her. It was mind-boggling and overwhelming. Finally, she sighed and let her hands drop.

"Well, whether it is or not, one thing is for sure," she said, getting some silverware out of the drawer and pulling a plate from the cupboard, "my whole plan for this weekend just went out the window."

# Decisions

*These dark energy flows remind me of Rascal when I first found her*, Tricia pondered, taking a long drink of water. She was sitting on the small bench outside the cabin. George glared at her from his spot next to the fence. Despite crashing into the wall last night and all the pushing and shoving she'd given him this morning, he didn't look too shabby. "Yeah, he's probably got a right to be ticked off," she said, taking another swig.

*When I first found Rascal, she didn't want anything to do with me either. Trying to make her come to me was just pointless, but I kept at it, coaxing her, and eventually, she came around. Now, it hardly takes more than clucking my tongue or patting the sofa, and she's there.*

Tricia stood up and stretched. *The light energy is easy; I pull on it or just open myself up to it, and the waves rush in. The dark energy is more stand-off-ish. It wants to be invited, but like Rascal, now it's about just creating space, being available. Both types of energy flows respond to that.*

She closed her eyes, and with her feelings, she created an emptiness within herself. Immediately, she felt the light energy flows rush in, giving her a surge of power that coursed through her body. At the same time, the dark energy flows washed over her. Tricia smiled; being able to access them individually was good, but being able to call on them both at once was nothing short of amazing.

*But learning to do that was just where it started to get interesting*, Tricia reflected. She started poking George with random small pushes, watching the combat dummy wobble back and forth as she poked his right shoulder, then his left, then back to his right, while she considered the events of the day.

She had spent the early part of the morning focused solely on the dark energies and the abilities they gave her, experimenting with the levitation and shields and generally getting a feel for pushing objects around. Tricia was surprised by how quickly she was able to develop a reasonable level of precision with them.

"Turns out, my friend, the hardest part was just tapping the energy flows themselves. Once I got a handle on that, the abilities themselves came rather easily, wouldn't you say, George?" She gave the dummy a harder shove. It rocked back and forth, nodding with its entire torso. She nodded as well. "Glad you agree, George. And to think, it was all because of a spontaneous run...and a glorious face plant."

Tricia had wrapped up her morning exercises and decided to take a quick run before lunch. It was a short trail course, only several miles. She'd run it a dozen times or more, and even at what she now considered a leisurely pace, it would only take a few minutes. She had fun with this course because it offered a few obstacles to keep it interesting, including a dry creek bed. At the speed she usually ran, she had more than enough momentum to clear it, and more to the point, leaping over it was just plain fun.

This time, though, proved otherwise. As she planted her foot to make the jump, she felt an unexpected last-second kick from her levitation ability. Tricia yelped in surprise as she was catapulted forward. Sailing past the creek bed, she wheeled her arms in a desperate attempt to maintain any sense of orientation or control. All sense of coordination or timing gone, she barely managed an awkward tuck as she landed hard, toppled forward, and slid and rolled for several yards.

Tricia had lain there and groaned for several seconds. *I'm sure I just shattered the world record for the long jump*, she recalled thinking as she rolled over onto her stomach, *and likely set one for the most glorious wipeout.* She chuckled and winced, *"Ugh! I wonder what else I shattered."*

She gingerly pushed herself up to sit on the ground and proceeded to check herself over. Fortunately, she hadn't broken or sprained anything, but her shorts were torn, her shirt was shredded, and her back, arms, and legs were covered with multiple cuts and deep scrapes. She brushed the dirt out of her wounds and blotted away some of the blood with the remnants of her shirt. Then, as she sat there, letting her healing knit the torn patches of her skin back together, it had dawned on her: *This is the first time I've used more than one of my abilities at the same time.*

"It was mind-blowing, George, and a game changer," she explained. "I've known for a while that I can't use my light-based powers together. There's no hyper-speed when I'm using my strength, for instance. This morning, I confirmed the same for the dark-based abilities; there's no casting a shield when I'm levitating. When this happened, though, my abilities went to a whole new level."

After Tricia returned from her aborted run and changed out of her ruined clothes, she immediately started a whole new round of experimentation. Using levitation alone, she could just reach the top of the cabin's two-story roof, but by combining her strength with her levitation, she now had a vertical leap that was easily three or four times that height. Repeating the jump she'd done accidentally at the creek, she found she could cover dozens of yards at a time. Her pushing and shielding were no different; combined with her strength or speed, they were greatly amplified as well. Several large rocks now lay in fragments as a testimony to the potential those combinations provided.

Tricia walked over to the combat dummy. "You see, George," she continued, picking it up and turning to walk it back to the cabin, "it has something to do with how the dark energy interacts with kinetic energy. I'm not sure how it works just yet, but I will soon. What I do know is that together, these two sides of my abilities, used together, feel almost limitless."

She sat George down by the cabin door and turned the dummy to face her. *You're a good listener*, she thought, *but at times like this, I wish you could talk back.*

"Don't worry," she chuckled, patting the mannequin's face with her palm, "I'm not going to use you to find out what those limits are. Use of superpowers would probably void your warranty, and I don't want to try to explain it to Larry." She chuckled to herself. "Don't worry though, big guy. Your day is coming, but I do have an idea that might help me to get started with testing them. It's crazy, but it's something. I just need to figure out how to set it up."

Tricia pushed back the flows of energy, and, for the first time, she felt she was somewhat lesser for having released them. For the first time, she truly believed they were a part of who she was now.

"Holy crap on a cracker!" she exclaimed as she felt the bullet whiz past her head, grazing her hair. Tricia released the flows and watched the dark energy shield dissipate. She felt her heart racing and exhaled sharply. "You said you wanted to test your limits, but this...this is borderline stupid!" she muttered to herself.

Strapped to the post in front of her was her father's revolver, pointing straight at her. Tricia half expected that the rounds in the bottom of the gun cabinet in the cabin would be duds, but apparently, the surplus military ammo boxes in which her father had stored them had been very effective at keeping out any moisture all these years.

'Testing her limits' had entailed fastening the revolver to the same post she'd used for her drop test and rigging a cord to pull the trigger. Her speed was normally enough for her to track a bullet in flight, and she could now cast a shield quickly enough to repel the bullet, but the sun was getting low, and this time, a ray of sunlight had caught her in the eye just as she pulled the cord, and she'd lost the bullet in the glare.

"These stupid swirls in my vision don't help either," she grumbled. "Still, I stopped almost all of them. That's impressive."

*But it only takes one, dummy*, she reminded herself.

Tricia looked out toward the horizon through the trees. The sun was getting quite low now, and the woods around her were already starting to get dark. Some of the smaller clouds were already starting to change color for the impending sunset. "Probably a good time to stop for the day anyway," she said and proceeded to take down the revolver, and after unloading the remaining rounds, she secured it back in its case. *Dad would never have put his gun away dirty,* she recalled, and a brief wave of sadness swept over her. *I'll clean it later tonight,* she promised herself.

The sun was now down behind the tree. Tricia could see that the sky was turning a brilliant reddish orange. *I bet that's beautiful,* she thought, *but I'm certainly not going to see it from down here, am I?*

On impulse, she embraced her abilities and levitated herself to the top of the cabin. Adding her strength, she then leaped and pushed simultaneously, propelling her up towards the top of a nearby cedar. *Just like flying,* she mused and smiled.

Tricia landed deftly on a thick branch and put her hand on the trunk to steady herself. She looked west toward the sunset. Small cotton candy clouds were ablaze with reds and oranges as the sun dipped toward the horizon. An old poem tugged at her memory:

> *Red sky at night, sailor's delight*
> *Red sky in mornin', sailor take warnin'*

*Delight or warning? Gift or curse?* Tricia wasn't sure. *It doesn't matter though. I've been given too much for there not to be some purpose, to not put it to some use. Choosing that path, though, means this sun is setting on one chapter of my life, and the sun tomorrow will be rising on a new one.*

The sun started to dip into the horizon. The bright colors faded from the clouds, changing them to deep navy blue silhouettes against an emerging night sky awash with pale blues, sea greens, and soft peach. Tricia thought back on the experience she had in the campus parking lot with the girl and with Jimmy that afternoon.

*I could just try all this behind the scenes*, she thought. *Keep it low profile.*

She sighed. *But that's not really how a difference is made, is it? Sure, one person can make some impact alone, but real change happens when groups of people are inspired...when someone shows them how to be.*

*Beacons don't hide in the background.*

*Beacons shine in the night.*

*Beacons are visible so they can show people the way.*

She made her choice. *No, if I'm going to do this, it can't be under the radar, but,* she then realized, *Tricia Carling can't be the one seen doing it. Using these powers publicly to make any kind of impact would create too many risks, too many problems with trying to live a normal life. No. For that, I need to become something else, someONE else. I just have to figure out who* that *looks like.*

On that thought, the sun disappeared, signaling it was time for Tricia to call it a night. She gave a quick sigh, turned toward the cabin, and jumped. She had done this dozens of times already and had no fear of the multi-story drop. The wind rushed by her as the ground grew closer, and, at just the right time, she pushed with the dark energy to slow her descent. She realized a split second too late that she had slowed herself just a little too much, dropping further to the ground than she'd expected when she released it. Tricia grunted from the surprise hard landing. The gravel skittered beneath her. Her foot slid awkwardly to the side, and she grabbed the fence rail to keep herself from falling. Tricia winced slightly as she rotated her ankle. "Yeah," she cajoled herself, "as a 'someone else' who's had a bit more practice."

A few days later, Marni was working in one of the labs in the Novel Gene Therapy department of the hospital. She was on her fifth pass through the data on the screen. *None of this makes sense*, she thought as she twisted a strand of her curly red hair around her finger and scrolled to the next sample. And the next. And the next. Still nothing.

She was a little over a week into the lab's newest project, working with the reproductive services department. They had recently seen a massive spike in cases related to infertility, and the hospital had formed a task force to investigate what was happening to cause it and find ways to treat it. Marni had been asked to participate. Her remit was to offer whatever she and her lab could do from the perspective of genomics and possible gene therapies, but so far, the project had steadily progressed from exciting and novel to infuriating as the data kept turning up one dead end after another.

She snapped off the monitor just as her commpod chimed. "Incoming call from Doctor Thornton," the device reported to her. Rene's Advanced Genetics Lab at the university often collaborated with Marni's department, so Marni had sent her some of the data she'd been trying to make heads or tails of in hopes she could offer some insights that might give Marni and her team some leads. *She must have something…fingers crossed.*

"Put it through." When she heard the soft beep of the call connecting, she answered, "Hi, Rene! What's new?"

"Hello, Marni," a buttery smooth female voice on the line responded. "I'm getting back to you on that set of samples you sent me. If you have access to them right now, check your messages. There's an attachment we can talk through if you have a few minutes."

"Just a sec, Rene," Marni answered and pulled up the messaging application on her second monitor. "Opening them up now."

"Great. While you're doing that, the short answer is that I think we might be a bit premature in hunting through the gene sequences for the cause of your patients' afflictions."

Marni scowled as she clicked on her incoming messages. "What makes you say that, Rene?"

"Did you find what I sent?" Rene asked patiently.

Marni saw the message from Rene near the top of the list of new messages. "Yep. Have it right here. Reading it now." She clicked the message open, saw the attachment, and opened it. A series of genetic sequences splashed across her screen. Several of them had circles and arrows in different colors. Looking at it quickly, she guessed at where Rene was going to go with this conversation. "I have it open, Rene."

"Great. So, take a look at the sequences I've marked in green," Rene continued, "these certainly look like genomic aberrations as you suggested, and on their own, they could imply something is going on in the chromosomes or base genomes."

"Yes," Marni agreed, "that's why I sent them over to you."

"Sure, but look at the ones in red, orange, and yellow. These imply to me that any aberrations we might be seeing could actually be due to physiological dysfunction, not genomic errors."

Marni looked them over. She squinted as if that would draw out some conclusion she might be missing. *Rene's track record on these kinds of things is pretty good, but I'm not convinced,* she thought. Marni closed her eyes and rubbed her nose. "Hmmmm, ok, Rene. I'll need to look this over a bit more, but what do you suggest we do? The tiger team is looking for an update, and so far, we don't have much to report back."

"I think you should have the pathology lab run the samples through the imaging protocols again and dig into some of the finer structures that might've been passed over in the first run. Their first run was only a coarse screening at best. I think what you're looking for requires a closer inspection."

"But Rene, that'll potentially take weeks. There are over a hundred samples at this point. Don't you think it makes sense to look at the two approaches in parallel?"

"I suppose you could," Rene answered, sounding a smidge condescending and stoking Marni's irritation, "but you could be chasing wild geese. Besides, the more detailed scans could really help you narrow down where you need to look, even if we discover the cause for the cases you are studying is genomic, after all. I'd think after even a few re-scans, you might get enough of a clue to start looking again, but with a more informed lens this time. I included some suggestions in the rest of the attachment on where they might focus some of the imaging series to make it go a bit faster. My recommendations are correlated by the color highlight on the sequences."

*She's got a point*, Marni grudgingly admitted to herself. "Ok, I can recommend that to the tiger team. There's just one problem. As it is, I think they're already pushing the resolution limits of the cellular imaging systems. I don't know how much more they can give us over what we have already."

"Hmmm, well, if it comes down to needing more from the imaging systems," Rene replied, "I think I know someone here at the university who could help."

Marni nodded and smiled to herself. "Now that you mention it, I think I do too."

*I hope you know what you've gotten yourself into*, Tricia thought as she peeked in the window. People were already gathering for Sensei's advanced class. She hadn't wanted to be late for her first one, but clearly, she hadn't really arrived very early either. The oldest in the class so far was easily several years younger than she was, and the lowest rank belt she could see was two or maybe even three levels above her. *This isn't intimidating at all.*

She took a deep breath and pushed the door open. Several people turned to look. A couple whispered, apparently wondering who the new person might be. Sensei saw her immediately and waved her toward him at the front of the room. Tricia focused on him, blocking out the rest of the class to settle her nerves, and briskly walked up to meet him.

"Glad you decided to join us, Carling," he said. "I wasn't sure you'd go through with it, to be honest. I'm impressed. It takes a lot of guts to do what you're doing. You know that, right?"

Tricia smiled nervously, "Yeah, my guts are kinda feeling that right now."

"Don't sweat it," he offered in encouragement. "It's a good bunch, and just remember that at some point, every one of them was where you are now."

"Yeah, and then they reached puberty."

Sensei laughed out loud. "It'll be all right. But look, quickly before we start. First, I'm going to introduce you to the class."

Tricia nodded.

"I want you to take your place right up front," he pointed slightly to his left, "here, and I want you here every class, at least for a while. We are going to do a lot of things you haven't seen before, and being up here makes it easier for you to step out and watch if you need to. It also makes it easier for me to help you through things, if necessary, ok?"

"Yeah, Sensei," Tricia agreed, swallowing a bit. "Makes perfect sense. Being right in front. No pressure at all."

"That's right. No pressure at all. Not yet, anyway," Sensei winked. "When I can, I'll send you some materials to review in advance of class, especially if we are going to review any kata you've not seen yet. That'll help you at least not walk in stone cold. Tonight, you'll be ok. We'll be reviewing a lot of things you should already know, and I'll take the stuff you don't a little slower so you can pick it up."

Tricia gave him a thumbs up. "Appreciate that Sensei. Thanks again for the opportunity."

Sensei nodded to her and pointed to the spot he wanted her to take. Tricia obliged while he addressed the class. "All right, everyone, let's form up."

The rest of the class stopped chattering and quickly shuffled into position on the floor. Some continued to roll their heads, stretching necks and shoulders and shaking out to loosen up.

"Good evening, everyone," Sensei said loudly.

"Good evening, Sensei!" the class responded in unison.

"Before we start, I'd like to introduce a new member of our class," he gestured toward Tricia. She turned and gave the class a small wave. "This is Tricia Carling, or is it 'Trish'?" he asked and looked at her.

"Either is fine," she answered, looking at the class, "Glad to be here."

"Carling normally takes the open class, but I asked her to join us here too. Just to be honest, she is somewhat behind most of you, but I think she's got the stuff it takes, and with us all working with her, I think she'll be a great addition to our group here."

Tricia heard a few claps from the class along with some murmurs of "Welcome, Trish", "You got this", and "We got you, Tricia".

She smiled, and some of her nervousness receded with their warm welcome.

"Ok, let's get going then," Sensei called out. "Tonight, we start with some basic calisthenics to work out that softness you all no doubt picked up while you were slacking off over the break." He grinned, and the group snickered. "Then we'll do some *kata* reviews and some basic technique drills. Got it?"

"Hai, Sensei!" The class shouted in unison.

"Drop down for some knuckle pushups."

*Hah, these I know.* Tricia smiled. The rest of her butterflies evaporated as she assumed the familiar posture on her toes, fists flat on the hard floor, and her elbows at ninety degrees.

"On my count," Sensei said, "*Ichi...ni...san...shi...*"

With her enhanced strength, even a tiny fraction of it, these pushups would be trivial, but Tricia knew she didn't need it. She didn't want it. No matter how much it might hurt, or what she would face in this class, or how much it tested her, she was determined to stick to the decision she'd made before she accepted Sensei's offer. She needed to build the discipline to master her powers without becoming reliant on them, so she would be taking no shortcuts in this class.

*This is for me. Just plain me.*

# Concepts

To Tricia, becoming someone or something else to use her powers in public meant she was most likely adopting a whole new persona, a new identity, one that meant Tricia Carling was completely obscured and out of sight while she was doing it. *My hair comes for free,* she'd thought somewhat whimsically, *but the rest is going to require some kind of disguise...some kind of costume.*

It couldn't be a hack job, either. If she was really going to be a symbol to rally others, she needed to look the part. *No one was going to take some woman in a ski mask and gym clothes beating up bad guys seriously,* she thought repeatedly. A proper costume would be a huge investment in time, effort, and money, but if it helped her make a difference, keep someone's dreams alive, or prevent some kid from becoming an orphan, it would be worth it.

While she cringed every time she thought about it, given how regular fitting clothes impeded her using her powers, she knew it was going to boil down to something resembling tights. She also knew it wasn't going to be easy. Since there weren't any other superheroes on the planet that she knew of, Tricia was going to have to draw on ideas and inspiration from more everyday sources, and she knew this kind of thing was not her wheelhouse. *I'm a scientist...I can figure this out,* she had assured herself. *It is just going to be a matter of form, function, and construction. I got this.*

With her conviction in place, Tricia started doing some research in the evenings and on weekends in between training sessions. Function seemed to her the easiest place to start, and she was soon proven right. A few searches around topics like "high-performance tights" or "body suits" quickly lead her to browsing high-end sportswear for female athletes. It didn't take her long to move past sports like figure skating, wrestling, and weightlifting and narrow the searches down to sports like downhill skiing and track speed skating. These suits were all built for endurance and flexibility and included features that prevented wear and abrasion in high-wear areas of the athlete's body in competition and training. They were lightweight and very form-fitting—again, she cringed at the thought of being out in public wearing one—but they were exactly what she imagined would be important in a working costume for a superhero.

They were also very expensive, but she had already reconciled herself to the fact that this whole endeavor was going to be a substantial investment. Swallowing hard and pitying her credit account, she ordered one of the speed skating options to get her started.

While she waited for it to arrive, Tricia turned to the design side of her costume. This proved a bit trickier; Tricia had to admit that she really had no background to draw on for coming up with a good design for a superhero costume. Most of her reading and media preferences were more in the fantasy genre, so unless she decided an elf or sorceress was the look she needed to go for, neither her time spent at Renaissance fairs nor the books on her bookshelf were going to be of much good to her. Besides, she hadn't been to any of those events in a long time; it was something she did when she was a girl with her father, something they shared and did together for fun, and when he was gone, so went some of her motivation to get back into it. *Dad would probably be sad to hear that,* she thought regretfully. Fortunately, and unfortunately, though, there was a lot of content out on the net boards and websites related to superheroes, so much so she was finding it very difficult to navigate and really get good ideas she could drill down on without spending hours and hours just randomly browsing.

As luck would have it, a couple of days later, when Tricia was walking home after work, she was diverted by construction on the sidewalk, forcing her to take a different side street home. Just a block off campus, right in front of her, there was a comic book store on the corner. *All the times I've walked back and forth to campus, how have I never seen this place before?* she wondered. She stopped for a moment, marveling at the storefront blazing with neon signs and windows covered with posters of various superheroes, villains, and other characters she presumed were from gaming and movies, fists clenched, muscles bulging, threatening to charge out at her from the glass at any moment. "If there's a better place to get some ideas for this, I can't imagine what it might be," she said to herself. Quickly looking up and down the street, she jaywalked across and went inside.

The store was brightly lit inside and featured countless stands of comic books, shelves full of toys and memorabilia, and large glass display cases filled with figurines and other fine collectibles. *Wow*, she thought to herself, *this place is pretty cool.* She pushed the door open. The few customers in the store, mostly younger guys and girls, all dressed in jeans, t-shirts, and hoodies, turned to look at her when they heard the bell at the top of the door ring. Some of them continued to stare at her for several seconds, assessing the new face in the shop before going back to browsing the comics or returning to the games that some of them were intently playing near the back of the store. *Guessing they don't get many random people like me coming in here,* she chuckled to herself. *No doubt, I probably look as out of place as I feel.*

As if on cue, a middle-aged man wearing bifocals and a faded T-shirt that depicted a grinning troll-like creature holding a large bone with the caption "I found this humerus" came out from behind the counter and walked up to her. "Do you need help finding anything?" he asked politely with a broad smile.

"Is it that obvious?" Tricia replied, returning the smile.

"Just a little," he replied, "I've never seen you in here before, and frankly, you look a bit overwhelmed, like a deer in the headlights that might turn and run at any moment if I didn't distract you somehow." He grinned and chuckled.

"Guilty as charged." Tricia laughed back. "I'm interested to see what you might have in the way of female superheroes."

"Sure," he said, clearly in his element now, "Anything more specific in mind?"

Tricia shook her head slightly and shrugged a bit. "Not really. It's been a long time since I've been in a shop like this, so I'm pretty out of touch with what's trendy now."

"Well, ok," he started to gesture to various sections and racks in the store, "We have your mutants, your aliens, your lab accidents..."

Tricia gave a small cough to this. "Lab accidents?" she interrupted.

"Yup, you know, the serum gone wrong, the vat of toxic chemicals, getting bitten by a radioactive something-or-another, that kind of thing."

"Ah, of course," she nodded and smiled to herself. *You missed the 'something exploded' option, but that's probably in here too somewhere,* she mused.

The shop owner went on, continuing to point towards different racks and stands around the shop, "We have the self-made heroines, the vengeful vigilantes, the witches and sorceresses too. We got alternate timelines, parallel dimensions, and multiverses. Then, of course, there's all the legions, leagues, squads, trios, duos, you name it. What sounds interesting to you?"

Tricia thought for a minute, rubbing her chin. "Which ones have the most interesting costumes?"

"Hmm, good question. So, are you into cosplay then? Typically, cosplayers come in here already knowing which characters they are into before they come in."

"Well," Tricia grinned, "I consider myself rather atypical these days."

The shop owner just looked at her, and then a very large grin spread across his face.

Tricia looked back and, after a brief realization, started to blush a bit. "No, um, I mean…that didn't come out the way I'd intended," she stammered, suddenly feeling flustered and a bit embarrassed as a warmth crept up her neck.

The shop owner laughed. "No, it's ok…I get what you meant. And in any event, it doesn't matter. People come in here to have fun with their hobbies and interests, and I'm not one to judge how someone chooses to do that. Heck, I'm a fifty-year-old guy who collects action figures. Who am I to point fingers?"

She chuckled back, relaxing a bit, "I appreciate that. I'm pretty new to all this."

"No worries," he said, "but if that's what you are looking for, some of the villains have some of the best looks."

"Hmm, I'm probably more of the hero type, but why not? Let's have a look. Oh, and if you have them, I'd be especially interested in stories that talk about how the heroes got started, that kind of thing."

"Gotcha. Origin stories, sure. I got plenty of those."

She nodded and let him lead her to a few selections to start looking over. She thanked him, and he wandered back toward the counter at the front.

*Wow, so much,* she thought, a bit shell-shocked, and started browsing.

As she leafed through the issues, feeling a bit overwhelmed by the incredible variety, she noticed a teenage girl looking very intently through some comics a couple of racks over. She had short-cropped jet-black hair, dark red lipstick, and heavy eyeshadow and was very focused on leafing through the assortment in front of her. Tricia looked over at her and asked, "What kinda of things do you like?"

Not looking up, the girl replied, "Mostly the anti-hero kind of stuff."

"Anti-hero?"

"Yeah," the girl answered, now looking up, "the ones that kinda want to do the right thing but have their own moral code: do things by their own rules, where the ends justify the means. It's a bit darker, edgier."

Tricia walked over next to her and leaned in a bit, looking at what the girl was browsing.

"Nah, you don't want this," the girl said, putting down what she was holding. "I overheard part of your convo with Tony. You may be looking more for something like this." She picked up an issue titled *Lady Vengeance.* The cover depicted a very fit woman wearing a dark red halter top, black leather pants, a black ninja mask, and swinging two short billy clubs. The two guys on the cover were having a seriously bad day at her expense.

"Oh, that's good," Tricia exclaimed and took the issue from her, leafing through the pages, picturing herself on the streets of Crystal Bay wearing something like that, trouncing bad guys.

"Maybe this too," the girl offered, handing Tricia a copy of a very thick edition called The Angels. "I really like Death. She's hecka gritty." The girl smiled and winked.

"Great! Thanks a bunch." Tricia smiled back. "This is a big help."

"Sure. Hope you have fun with it. I gotta get going, but just look around this section here, and if you get stuck, Tony's great at recommending things." The girl gave a little wave and headed up to the counter with a few issues to purchase tucked under her arm.

After about an hour of browsing around the comics and even looking over a few figurines and action figures, Tricia finally made her way up to the counter, ready to check out. On the counter before her were a few digests and issues of *Lady Vengeance, The Angels, Solar Flair,* and a thick compendium called *A Heroic History of Superheroines.* She checked out, collected her new treasures, and thanked Tony for all his help.

"Good luck with the costuming! Hope to see you again soon."

"Oh, I'm pretty sure you will," she replied, smiling, and walked out of the shop.

She opted to just pick up some fast food on the way home; one of her favorite burger places was just one block out of the way. After she got home, she sat at the kitchen table, popped a french fry into her mouth, and started browsing through the large tome of superheroines. *The creativity and storytelling in this are pretty amazing,* she admitted to herself. *I can see why people really get into this.* She took a big bite of her burger and looked down at Rascal, who was sitting at her feet eagerly looking for a handout. "You know, Rascal, I wonder what these people would think if they found out they were actually creating instruction manuals for someone like me when they wrote these," she said to the cat, staring at her in earnest and tossed Rascal a fry to gnaw on.

A couple of days later, her speed skating body suit arrived. It was waiting on her doorstep when she got home from the lab. Scooping it up, she tossed her things onto the couch and eagerly tore into it. It was neon pink and green, the worst, but it was on sale and purely for experimentation anyway. She quickly stripped off her work clothes and pulled it on. To her chagrin, she found it took quite a lot of work to get it on correctly— she made a mental note that getting her suit on and off quickly would need serious consideration when she designed her version— but eventually, it fit like a glove. It had some extra padding in the knees, shoulders, and elbows -- again, she made a mental note of how useful that could be for her suit. The suit also had an integrated hood that came up around her neck and down around her forehead, leaving her eyes, nose, and mouth exposed...or at least it would have if her hair wasn't creating such a large bunch wadded up inside it. She tried rearranging her hair and refitting the hood several times, but no matter what she did, her hair was just too long to fit comfortably underneath it. *I could probably do without the hood,* she considered, looking at herself in the mirror, *but I really like how something like this helps conceal my appearance more than just the suit alone. Hmmm, since the top of the hood is the real problem...,* and on a whim, she stripped off the top half quickly, grabbed the pair of scissors off the desk next to her, and snipped off the top few inches of the hood, leaving a circular hole. She pulled the top back on and slipped the modified hood back over her head, letting her blonde hair spill out of the hole she had just fashioned. "Fantastic!" she exclaimed out loud, "that's absolutely perfect!" It was comfortable and simple, with the added benefit that the band across her forehead kept her hair back out of her face.

Again, looking at herself in the mirror, she started thinking about her exposed face and then acted on another spark of inspiration. She took the small piece she'd cut from the top and cut a band a few inches wide from it. Grabbing a black marker, she held the band up across her eyes and over the bridge of her nose, carefully felt where her eyes were, and drew large ovals around them, coming just under her eyebrows to the tops of her cheeks. She cut out those ovals and then, grabbing some tape from the desk, held the strip up so she could look out through the holes. After lining up the openings with her eyes, she taped the edges of the strip to the rest of the hood.

Turning again to the mirror, as wonky as her cutting job was, the result amazed her. *I wouldn't recognize myself in this,* she thought, turning her head side to side. She made a couple more small cuts around her nose, so the newly created mask laid more flush against her face - "I'll definitely need to make a piece, so the final version covers my nose, but yeah, I think we have a winner." Satisfied, she took out her commpad and quickly snapped a few pictures. She took a few minutes to make some marks on the makeshift mask and the hood so she could put it back together again. She then took off the prototype suit and gave herself another mental high-five.

With a basic working concept under her belt, actually building the suit would be the next major challenge. She recalled what the comic book shop owner had said and started her research by looking up 'cosplay' on the Internet. Cosplay, she discovered, was an entire crafting genre devoted exclusively to costuming, to bringing fictional characters from literature, movies, games, you name it, to life. Tricia immediately found it fascinating and awe-inspiring. These people made the most incredible costumes and props from the most basic materials, anything from realistic swords made from dense foam to fully illuminated and robotic prosthetics in their costumes. These amazingly creative people, it seemed to her, are only limited by their imagination – and time and money, of course. Cosplay artists frequently posted photos and videos of their creations, and there were countless websites with how-to videos, patterns, guides, and links for purchasing virtually everything someone could need.

Inspired by what she saw, she made a point of taking some time that weekend to visit some of the craft and fabric stores nearby. Using the videos and tutorials she'd watched on the Internet, she easily located what she needed to make a pattern from the skating suit with which she'd been experimenting. Finally, she gave in to the excitement of crafting her costume and decided to take the plunge.

The shop rented sewing machines and gave some basic classes in how to use them; her grandmother had taught her how to sew when she was younger—it's a skill everyone will need someday, she insisted—but Tricia hadn't sewn anything beyond patching a ripped seam here and there for a long time, and she knew she'd be quite rusty. Plus, these machines were much more sophisticated than the one her grandmother had, so she figured she would definitely need some instruction on it regardless.

Tricia also found that the store conveniently sold patterns for body suits very similar to the one she'd purchased that could be helpful, and they had an entire Halloween section in the patterns department where she found patterns for accessories like gloves and masks, which would come in very handy indeed. Fortunately for her, the store was offering a getting-started class the same afternoon, so she signed up and ducked out to grab a quick lunch before the class started.

It all turned out to be much easier than she'd anticipated. It didn't take Tricia long to remember what her grandmother had taught her, and these newer machines really did a lot of the work for her. In the class, they had her make a white glove that covered her arm up to her elbow. She was quite pleased with how it came out—the first three badly deformed attempts aside— and since this was likely similar to the style she'd want for her costume, it was definitely a bonus.

Feeling a bit more confident now, Tricia signed the rental agreement for the machine. She also purchased some sample patterns, cheap fabric to experiment with, and other materials the cosplay tutorials suggested she use for creating and adapting patterns for her body: clear plastic wrap, adhesive paper, tape, permanent markers, and some very sharp scissors and razor knives. She gladly paid the small fee for delivery and, declaring the day's mission to be a complete success, headed home.

Successful for everything except the actual design. *Yes, I have the style and something to work with,* she thought as she walked, *but what does Beacon LOOK like?*

A few days later, Tricia was relaxing in her tub, taking a long, hot soak. That evening's workout had been especially tough, and a lot of muscles were complaining. A little light jazz was playing in the background, and a glass of Sauvignon Blanc sat on the edge of the tub while she thumbed through one of her comics. Her glasses were pushed down to the end of her nose so she could lay her head on the back of the tub to relax while she skimmed the book.

This was an issue of *The Angels*, a team of four powered women who called themselves Light, Mercy, Justice, and Death—Tricia thought the names were very clever—each with very different powers and very different temperaments, who worked together in very close, and often strained, collaboration to bring down an assortment of baddies.

The center of the comic featured a fold-out mini-poster of the four of them standing together in a set of exceptionally heroic poses. Something about their costumes started to catch her eye. She took a second to wipe the steam off her glasses so she could see them more clearly.

Death's costume struck her first. It looked very much like what she had done with the skating suit and hood; the top was open, unleashing her lavish red hair but leaving her face fully exposed. Her costume was all black, with a black cloak. *That girl was right. She is gritty. Her look is very intimidating, and the dark color really obscures her form and features*, Tricia thought. *I'm not sure an image of 'death' is what I want, but this has a very iconic look and makes a strong impression. People would definitely take notice of something like that…but maybe it's* too *bold?*

Tricia's eye shifted left a bit and stopped on the first heroine, Light. Light's costume was predominantly white with yellow highlights and had a billowing white cape. *Totally conveys the notion of light,* she felt, *but that white just feels too much, too bold, too revealing. The cape is kinda cool, but hmmm, not quite convinced it's practical.* "Let's skip the cape, shall we?" she muttered to herself.

Justice was mostly dark blue – dark blue arms and elbow-length gloves, dark blue legs, and knee-high boots, with a white torso interrupted by a dark blue belt. *Very striking and powerful,* Tricia pondered, *but what if black rather than blue?* —she glanced back at Light—*but then yellow instead of white?* Tricia sat up in the tub and stared at the page, the colors combining in her mind, blending elements of each of the Angels on the page into a single image. "Black not for death, but for the darkness," she explored out loud, slowly at first, but then picking up speed as the pieces clicked in her mind, "but then yellow for the light, coming out of the darkness. Light and darkness, like my powers...light emerging from darkness, like a Beacon.

"Yes! That's it," she exclaimed, everything coming together now, "THAT's Beacon. That!"

She slammed down the rest of her Sauvignon Blanc and did a quick fist pump. *Now,* she had everything.

The next few evenings, she devoted herself to getting a prototype made. She didn't want to ruin the skating suit, so she used the trick she saw in the tutorials of wrapping herself in plastic wrap, then putting adhesive paper and tape over that, and marking where the seams and joints would be with the marker. She'd decided on some small changes to her costume colors; she liked the yellow on the chest but hated the bikini look below. Instead, she decided to leave the central part of her torso in black and let the yellow come down her thighs, stopping at the knee. Her gloves and boots, when she got to that point, would be black but feature a yellow cuff at the tops, just below her elbows and knees, respectively. With that mental image in mind, she used the markers to draw out the differently colored areas on her suit in her new pattern. Since she'd decided on knee-high boots and elbow-length gloves, she could shorten the arms and legs of the body suit a bit for comfort and to make it easier to slip on and off.

It was then a relatively easy task to even out her paper and tape patterns using pieces of the commercial patterns she'd purchased at the craft shop. The mask pattern she'd gotten was easy to blend into the hood of the suit as well. Tricia was also especially proud of the way she figured out how to open and close the suit so she could slip into and out of it quickly. The speed skating suit had a zipper in the back, but she had already decided that a zipper or any apparatus in the back was simply not going to work for something like this.

Alternatively, one of the patterns she'd bought included a simple way for the front to be made of overlapping flaps that didn't require any special hardware or fasteners. Very elegant and very fast, and it would help avoid spending what had felt like hours with the skating outfit tucking and stretching to get everything to fit right. She spent the next evening cutting out pieces of the cheap fabric she bought using the revised patterns, and then the following Saturday sewing it all together.

It took most of the day, but she finally got it assembled. A few seams had to be taken out and redone here and there, and some pieces had to be trimmed to come together right, adjusting the pattern accordingly as she went, but in a few hours, she had a basic first cut of her design. It was missing the colors, of course. She had purchased the cheapest material she could, knowing a lot of it would go to waste, and judging from the floor, she wasn't wrong, but the panels were cut and sewn along the lines where the different colors would be, so her imagination could fill in the blanks. She put it on carefully, not entirely trusting the robustness of her sewing skills, but to her surprise, it went on smoothly, and the fit wasn't terrible.

The hood and mask were especially satisfying. Tricia was impressed that the mask turned out to be such a good fit with the hood on the first try. The gap in the top of the hood worked well for her hair. *It looks just as good as Death's does,* she thought, and she was happy with how well the eye holes and bottom of the mask lined up snugly with her eyebrows, nose, and cheekbones. *Comfortable and functional.*

She turned a few times back and forth in the mirror. Overall, it wasn't bad. She noted several of the seams were rather crooked. Also, she hadn't properly accounted for the stretchiness of the material, so it was saggy and wrinkly in some very unflattering spots. "I'll need to downsize some of the panels in the pattern so it, ugh, fits tighter. But better a bit snugger than looking like, well, this..." she decided as she tugged on one of the baggier sections of material in a very unflattering and conspicuous spot.

Tricia got herself a glass of wine to celebrate, tossed Rascal a few treats—she was happily playing with a few of the material scraps lying on the floor nearby—and decided to do two things right away. First, she went to one of the fabric supply websites recommended by one of the cosplayers she'd found online and ordered some high-grade textured costume material in black and yellow, express delivery. *This is going to look awesome, and there's no good reason not to go for it at this point,* she concluded.

Second, she went back to some of the performance athletics websites where she found the speed skating suit and researched high-performance athletic underwear. She ordered a few sets of premium-grade support tops and shorts in black, also express delivery. *Not wearing proper underwear under this kind of suit is absolutely NOT an option,* she resolved, taking another sip of her wine, and closing the browser.

The new underwear arrived the next day, so Tricia had the chance to give that a try in the gym right away and was very pleased with her choices. The material itself arrived two days later. She had already modified the patterns based on her first attempt and, thrilled with how the new material looked and felt, immediately got to work cutting the panels. She went more slowly this time, making sure each cut was as precise as she could make and that the pieces and edges lined up the way they should before committing them to the sewing machine.

Advanced class with Sensei Tim the following evening offered her a much-needed break from her project. It wasn't unusual for Tricia to get deeply engrossed in projects that excited her, often ignoring small voices that would encourage her from time to time to slow down and take a step back. For once, she decided to heed that voice and take a break, especially for this class. Not only was she really enjoying them, but Sensei had made it crystal clear that unexcused absences were not tolerated; if he was going to commit to being there, he expected his students to commit as well.

Not only was she appreciating the exercise and, frankly, the extra tone she was developing—she was certain that suit was going to need *a lot* of tone underneath it—but she felt she was learning a lot and enjoyed the change of pace this class offered her.

Tonight's class proved to be a good one, even up to the point where she rather spectacularly lost her sparring match, biting on a feint that resulted in a leg sweep, dropping her hard on her hip. She hadn't won a match in this class yet, but given that she usually was fighting at least one or two levels above her, she was, at least, hanging in the matches longer now and had even started to win a point on occasion. She was determined that until she could win without her powers, she could not trust she could win with them.

After class, Sensei came up to her. "Don't sweat that match, Carling. You're really improving. It shows."

"Yeah," Tricia replied, still rubbing her aching hip, "I'm sure it will be showing for sure by tomorrow morning."

Sensei Tim chuckled, "Well, you're really putting in the work. The rest will come, but I get the feeling you're holding something back."

Tricia's stomach twitched. "What do you mean, Sensei?"

"Just that," he said, looking into her eye, trying to read the answer. "Like there's more that you're deliberately keeping back."

"Well," Tricia offered, "I have been really focused on maintaining control, having discipline. Maybe it's that?"

"Perhaps. Those are things we like to work on here, but be careful that you don't confuse the two."

Tricia's eyebrows drew together, creasing her forehead. "I'm not sure I'm following."

"Discipline," he said, "is not about holding back or bottling things up. Look, back when I was in the service, I thought discipline was about holding on firmly, keeping everything in a tight fist. Then, one time, we were on a mission to uncover a terrorist cell. We got ambushed, and it went sideways. A couple of my buddies got hurt badly, and, frankly, my bottle broke. I went off mission and did some things that, to this day, I'm ashamed of. Fortunately, nothing too serious happened, but because I disobeyed orders, I got busted down in rank, and it took a long time to rebuild the trust with my commanding officer and my unit."

He took a deep breath and sighed. "That's when I learned that discipline is not about *constraint*. It's about *restraint*. It's about using the right response in the right amount in a given situation. Control is an element of that, but discipline is so much more. Do you see that, Carling?"

Tricia remembered the confrontation she'd had on campus and how she'd barely pulled herself back from doing something truly terrible. "Yes, Sensei, I see that very clearly."

"Good," he said. "Keep up the good work. Despite the lecture, I'm definitely not disappointed with what I'm seeing from you in this class."

"Thanks, Sensei," Tricia beamed, gave him a bow, and left.

OPEN
anga
THE ANGEL

# Setbacks

Brenda was waiting at her desk when Tricia pushed the door open to the Lab Chairman's office. The outer area was laid out as a small reception and meeting room. Benda's desk was against the far wall, just outside the door to the Chairman's, Doctor Demerov's, private office. Against one wall was a small meeting table surrounded by chairs. Across the room, the other wall held a waist-high set of wooden bookshelves loaded with books. A couple of high-back chairs and a low table were arranged in front of it. The room smelled warm and comfortable, heavy with the scent of leather and books.

As she entered, Benda looked up, smiled, and greeted her warmly, "Oh, hello, Doctor Carling. Thank you so much for coming by a bit early. I'm sure you're eager to get these signed." She held up a light blue folio.

To say Tricia was eager to sign them was an understatement. Roughly two weeks ago, she was delighted to get word that she'd finally been cleared to return full-time. Naturally, the paperwork was taking its sweet time, though.

She wasn't surprised. It was Tricia's experience that Human Resources, like most of the university's bureaucracy, moved glacially even in the most urgent circumstances, compounded in this case by the need for several signatures, including the Lab Chairman's. Even in a world of electronic signatures, the university still insisted on wet ink signatures.

Brenda had called her yesterday to give her the happy news that the papers were finally signed and suggested, since Tricia had this meeting on the books with Doctor Demerov already, that she just come by a little early and get them signed before her appointment. Tricia did not need to be asked twice.

"You bet I'm happy to get them signed," Tricia replied as she approached Brenda's desk. "I was starting to think they'd never get here."

"It feels that way sometimes with these kinds of things," Brenda agreed, taking the papers out of the folio and handing Tricia a pen. The small packet had a few small sticky flags indicating where Tricia needed to sign. Tricia flipped open the packet to the first flag and started scanning the text. Satisfied, she signed and moved on to each one in turn.

"It must feel good to put all this completely behind you," Brenda said.

"Not quite," Tricia muttered absently as she signed the document.

"Pardon?" Brenda asked.

Tricia backpedaled immediately, cursing herself for not being more careful about what she said out loud. "I mean, almost. I still have a six-month check-in, but after that, yeah," she said as she signed the last spot, closed the document, and returned Brenda's pen.

"Well, here's to a new chapter then," Brenda said, toasting with her coffee cup.

"To new chapters," Tricia replied, miming an imaginary cup and returning the toast with a smile.

Brenda tucked the papers back into the folio. "I'll take care of these. You should go in. Doctor Demerov is expecting you." She looked again at Tricia. "Do you have a jacket or blazer by any chance?"

"Um, no. Do I need one?"

Brenda nodded. "It wouldn't hurt. He appreciates a level of formality." She pulled the jacket off the back of her chair and handed it to Tricia. "Here, borrow mine."

Tricia took the blazer and slipped it on. It was slightly too big in the shoulders—Brenda was somewhat wider than Tricia—but it was close enough, and the color matched the light teal silk blouse and dark navy slacks she'd worn perfectly. "Thanks!"

Brenda knocked gently and pushed the door open to the Chairman's private office. "Doctor Demerov, Doctor Carling is here for your meeting," she announced and guided Tricia into the office with her other hand.

Doctor Demerov looked up from behind his formidable wooden desk and, upon seeing them, stood up and beckoned Tricia with his hand. "*Da*, yes, yes, *Privyet*, Doctor Carling. Come in. Please. Sit." Tricia heard the door close behind her as she approached the chair facing him.

Doctor Alexei Demerov was a stout man, roughly her height, with thinning white hair and a perfectly trimmed flowing white beard that overlapped his charcoal suit by several inches. A pair of thin, narrow, wire-rimmed glasses were perched on the end of his nose. Tricia recalled from a holiday function a few years ago, someone who was likely a bit too deep into the open bar had commented that Alexei Demerov looked like Santa Claus. She had not interacted with him much herself, but she knew from his reputation that was where the resemblance ended.

His position as the Lab Chairman for the university was no accident. The various awards and plaques on his walls and shelves testified to his highly accomplished career. He was a stickler for details, and he was deeply passionate about the reputation and contribution of the entire lab complex. It was well known that he fiercely advocated and supported his allies and was equally ruthless with his enemies. There were few people in between, but Tricia always considered herself probably somewhere in the middle. She believed Demerov respected her, or she wouldn't be running her lab, but deep down, she also believed he likely didn't think she'd earned her stripes to be promoted so soon, either.

Tricia reached across the desk and extended her hand. "Good to see you, Doctor Demerov."

Demerov took her hand in both of his and shook it once. "And you, Doctor Carling," he said, gesturing to the chair. They both sat. Tricia perched forward nervously on her chair; no one in her position got called to a meeting in Demerov's office just for tea.

"I am very glad to see you are fully reinstated now, Doctor Carling," he said. "The accident was a tragedy. We were all very concerned about you. You are well now? No lingering effects?"

Tricia smiled. "I'm doing well, thank you. I'm very ready to return full-time. The team has done an excellent job, and we are all eager to move forward."

Demerov smiled and nodded. "*Khorosho*, good...very good." He picked up a stapled stack of papers from his desk and adjusted his glasses. "As to why you are here today, I have been reviewing the report from the audit after the incident. You were aware, yes?"

Tricia nodded. "Yes, Doctor Demerov. I've been aware of the inspectors and auditors who have been visiting the lab. I've met with most of them personally to answer questions and provide any information we could."

"Yes," Demerov replied, nodding in agreement. "The report mentions you and the team were most cooperative. However, there are a few items that concern me."

He flipped past a few pages. "First, for the experiment itself, you introduced a new component, the resonant feedback controller, based on the work of one of your interns." He looked at her over the top of his glasses.

"Yes, we did. We were having problems dampening the resonant harmonics, and simulations using the controller showed excellent results."

"But you changed the operating parameters the morning of the trial, yes?"

"Yes, we did. It was a small change to address some outlier conditions."

"But you didn't re-run the simulation?" he probed.

Tricia tamped down her irritation. Being questioned was not a strong suit with her. "No. As I said, it was a small change, and we didn't feel it warranted running a whole new simulation to confirm them."

"I see," Demerov said, "but then, I have to assume then that no one verified the new parameters were entered correctly, do I not? Clearly, they were not correct, yes?"

Tricia's mouth started to dry up. "I can only assume…"

"Assume?" he asked, his voice growing firmer. "An assumption that almost ended your life, wouldn't you say, Doctor Carling?"

He was right. There was no point in arguing. "Yes, Doctor Demerov."

He sniffed and looked down at the papers again. He flipped to another page. "A few weeks later, it seems you were in the lab on the weekend alone. Is this true?"

The day she used the lab to test herself. Her stomach knotted up. "Yes, I believe that's true."

He looked up over his glasses again. "You are aware of the safety guidelines that prohibit people from doing work in the labs alone outside of normal hours, are you not?"

"I was just checking the equipment, running a few diag..."

"Tsk Tsk Tsk," Demerov said, interrupting her and holding up his hand. "I did not ask you what you were doing, Doctor Carling. I asked if you knew the guidelines."

"I do, sir," she replied.

"Good. I would hope you of all people would be keenly aware of the importance for safety in the laboratories." Tricia's back stiffened, the barb stinging just as he'd likely intended.

He looked at her directly for a second, just for emphasis, and then returned to the papers. "As you say, you were running diagnostics and such, which, to be honest, is not the end of the world, guidelines or not. However, according to the report, there is a discrepancy with the system logs from the morning you were there. The diagnostics are recorded, but it appears that a few hours of log entries are missing. How do you explain that?"

The knot in Tricia's stomach turned into a bowling ball. They'd clearly discovered her tampering after all, but it wasn't clear if they knew it was her or not. She casually wiped her sweating palms on her knees.

"I don't know how to explain it, Doctor," she said calmly and deliberately, looking him in the eye. "I had to do a forced reset on some of the equipment—more than once, actually.

Perhaps that corrupted the logs. Without looking into it with the team, I don't have an explanation at this moment."

Demerov looked at her for a few seconds and finally said, "The auditors had no explanation for it either. They offered it might have been an anomaly in the network, but no definitive cause was listed by them."

Tricia took a deep breath as Demerov set the report aside. He took off his glasses and carefully folded them. Finally, he folded his hands on top of the desk and looked at her. "You can see how these discrepancies during and following your accident might cause me and others some serious concern, can you not, Doctor Carling?"

"I can, Doctor Demerov," Tricia said, "but I hope too that the auditors noted many of the safety improvements and actions the team has taken since…"

Demerov held up his hand again to stop her. "Yes, they have, but still, the concerns persist. I'm sure you can understand how important it is that the university, the trustees, donors, and others have complete confidence in what we are doing here, that our reputation be beyond reproach."

The bowling ball in her stomach turned into a wrecking ball. *Oh my God, he's going to fire me!*

"With that in mind, I, along with the lab council, have agreed to place you and the lab on probation."

*Probation?* Her mind was racing. She'd never heard of a lab being put on probation. *That's a thing here? What does that even mean?*

As if he read her mind, Demerov explained. "For the foreseeable future, a team of three other lab directors, or their delegates, will provide some oversight on the protocols and trials you perform in the imaging lab. They will review proposed trials in advance to make sure proper procedures are being followed and offer any insights or observations they feel are necessary to ensure experiments are being conducted safely and in accordance with established guidelines and protocols. Doctor Teague will lead your probation committee. He will contact you very shortly to discuss how he and the committee will work with you and the team going forward."

The wrecking ball in Tricia's stomach transformed into an unruly mass of swarming butterflies. Tricia could feel her face blanching. Her mind was a whirlwind of shock, fear, regret, and other emotions battling for dominance. A million questions came and went as she struggled to process what was happening, to rationalize and cope with the situation. Of those mission questions, only one seemed to truly matter at the moment. "What does this mean for the next round of our experiment?" she asked tentatively, her voice wavering slightly. "The team has been working very hard to prepare, and we are very close. Do we need to stop?"

Demerov again held up his hand. "No," he answered. "We feel preparations for the next trial are on sound footing, so we do not see any reason to impede your work. Please continue. Doctor Teague will talk with you about how they can support you without interfering unnecessarily."

She nodded. Being able to continue with the next phase of the experiment was good news, but overall, it would take time to process this, what it meant for her, for the team, and for her plans to further develop her abilities.

Sensing her conflict, Demerov softened his voice. "Doctor Carling," he said. She looked at him, and he smiled knowingly. "I understand this is probably very upsetting for you right now, but I want to assure you that we consider you a tremendous asset to the laboratory complex. You have built a good team and are delivering excellent results. We have confidence we all can move past this incident. I ask that you please look at this not as punishment but as an opportunity to benefit from the experiences of colleagues who are more seasoned."

*Older, you mean.* Tricia pushed that reaction away. *Not helpful right now.*

Despite the turmoil she was feeling, she knew she needed to end this conversation strongly—to hide her vulnerability—to not give away anything that might erode Demerov's confidence in her any further. Mustering a measure of composure, she stood up and extended her hand to him across the desk. "Yes, Doctor Demerov. That is excellent advice. I will do my best to take this as an opportunity, and yes, I assure you we will move past this."

Demerov stood up and shook her outstretched hand. "I am pleased to hear it, Doctor Carling. If there is anything I can do to help, or if you have additional questions, please do not hesitate to come see me."

"I will, and thank you," Tricia said and left the room, closing the door behind her.

Brenda had apparently stepped away from her desk when Tricia left Demerov's office. Tricia felt that was likely for the best; she was not in any kind of mental or emotional state to have a civil conversation. She hung Brenda's jacket on the back of her chair, wrote her a short note thanking her for loaning her the jacket, and quickly left the office before anyone could return.

As she left the office, Tricia felt she was losing the battle to retain her composure. Anger, shame, fear, embarrassment, defeat all swirled within her. The ladies room just ahead offered a much-needed refuge in which she could collect herself. She quickly ducked in and pushed the door behind her.

Her heartbeat pounded in the silence of the restroom. Feeling suddenly light-headed, she grabbed the frame of the nearest stall, closed her eyes, and put her head down. She fought for control, to push the torrent of emotions down, bring them to rein. The rage she felt, the anger with herself, with the situation, though, escaped her grasp, and she lashed out with her hand, striking the stall door. The metal immediately buckled, and the door tore free from its hinges, clattering to a stop at an awkward angle against the toilet.

Her eyes grew wide, shocked at what she'd done—*Thank God no one was in there*— but her loss of control only added to her fury. She clenched her fists, pressed her eyes closed, and gritted her teeth, fighting back the scream that wanted to follow. As suddenly as she lashed out, though, the wave of anger passed. Tricia laid both fists gently on the counter, exhaled, and hung her head.

*I'm blowing it,* she thought as she splashed some cold water on her face. *I want to do this. I want to use these powers to help people, but I don't want it at the expense of my personal life or my work. I need to have my real life, too, to keep all this separate, but here I am with my career circling the toilet bowl.*

She couldn't be angry with Demerov or what had happened. Everything he said was absolutely right. It was on her. She let her arrogance make her think she could get away with what she had been doing, but she'd been caught red-handed. If she was going to do this, she was going to have to be much more cautious going forward.

Her next step, though, was figuring out how to break this news to the team.

"Honestly, I'm surprised it took this long," Alex said after Tricia had finished filling them in. "What happened here was pretty serious, and I was expecting some kind of backlash long before now."

Jamal nodded. "And it could have been a lot worse. Probation isn't the end of the world. We know what we are doing, and if we have to handhold the probation committee along the way, we can do that."

"Besides," Nikki chimed in, "you're probably right, Doctor C. Maybe some fresh eyes will give us some good ideas."

Tricia bristled slightly at that but made sure not to show it. Before meeting with the team, she'd called Marni to vent about what happened. As always, she'd been supportive, but without even being prompted, she'd offered the same bit of advice: to look at it as an opportunity.

It infuriated Tricia to hear her taking Demerov's side, but in the end, she knew that was the silver lining she needed to paint on this for the team. They needed to feel there was a constructive path forward, leaving her to shoulder the embarrassment and doubt herself.

Tricia managed a weak smile. It was good they were taking it well. "I'm glad you all feel that way. I do want to say I'm sorry to you all, too. I did some things that contributed to this situation, so I apologize for not being smarter. It won't happen again."

"All good, Doctor C," Jamal said. "Not sure you did anything any of us haven't done at one time or another. Truthfully, it's probably more about multiple small things all at a bad time than any one thing by itself."

"Maybe," Tricia agreed, "but we'll need to be on our best behavior and really run things by the book going forward. So, until we get more information from Doctor Teague, we stay on plan, okay?"

The team murmured its agreement.

Normally, after a day like this, Tricia would have gone to the gym or the pool to work off the frustration and negativity, but she didn't feel like being alone with her own thoughts. Instead, she decided a distraction was more what she needed, and getting her suit together might just be the win she needed.

After a quick dinner, Tricia spent the entire evening carefully pinning panels together, periodically nursing her sore hip, and getting them ready to sew. She double-checked that all the corners and edges were going to join properly if...*if* she did a good job sewing them. *Knock on wood*, she thought, tapping the table three times.

She got an early start on Saturday morning; she was far too excited about seeing it finished to sleep in, and after committing the entire day, save a short break for lunch and a walk to loosen up her sore muscles, here was Beacon, in black and yellow, staring back at her from the mirror.

"Not bad...not bad at all," Tricia said, surveying her handiwork in the mirror. She turned slowly, left to right and back again, looking at the first real version of her suit. "Beacon is born, Rascal!" she exclaimed proudly. Rascal continued to lick her paws lazily on the back of the couch behind her. She would still need to come up with some kind of functional gloves and footwear, and the mask didn't yet cover her eyes, so she looked rather like an inverted raccoon, her blue eyes shining in stark contrast to the darkness of the mask, but here she was, Beacon head to toe.

She turned to the side, took an up-and-down look at her profile, and indulged herself with a brief moment of vanity. *All things considered, you don't look half bad in this*, she mused with a small grin. "What do you think, Rascal? Not too shabby, huh?" Rascal mewed back to her enthusiastically. "Why, thank you! I kinda think so, too." Tricia chuckled to herself.

*Still,* she thought, pushing her hip out slightly toward the mirror, *I might need to reconsider adding the cape. I know I'm really putting myself out there by doing this, but maybe I don't need to put myself out there quite THIS much.*

"Ok, time to give this a test drive," she said, psyching herself up. Tricia reached down and picked up one of the pieces of iron rebar she'd brought back from The Ridge. She gripped it firmly in both hands, facing herself in front of the mirror, and opened herself to the energies around her as she tried to bend the piece of metal.

Nothing.

Absolutely nothing.

She was taken a bit back, surprised. She did a double take at herself and then at the unyielding rod in her hands.

Calmly, she closed her eyes and took a few deep breaths, and, just as she had been training herself to do, she slowly reached out toward the roils and currents of energy she sensed around her, trying to embrace them, to invite them in. To her puzzlement, however, what she felt instead was something in between cutting her off from them.

She could sense them, but it was like watching the waves splash against a glass pane in front of her. Shifting her perception slightly, she focused on the dark energy, the current that was always running beneath the surface. Testing, she coaxed those toward her. The dark torrents came eagerly, and she had no trouble pushing out with them, driving the couch across the room into the far wall. Rascal yelped and sprinted to the bedroom.

With frustration and exasperation, she quickly yanked back the mask and stripped off the top of her new outfit. The arms dangled down her back, hitting the backs of her legs. Standing there in just her support top, she picked up the bar again, and her power came. Not all of it, not full strength, but enough to bend the bar with some strain. She angrily finished disrobing—kicking off her shoes, pushing the rest of the outfit down, and yanking her feet clumsily out of the legs, almost falling over in the process—and tried again. The bar bent effortlessly.

Tricia cursed, loudly. *Just like in the lab, with the lab coat.* She felt the familiar ebbs of energy lapping against her, easily flowing into and around her. She straightened the bar and dismissed those currents, releasing her power.

With a huff, she picked up the crumpled suit by the shoulders and held it up in front of her. "It must be the material...or the fit...or *something*," she said out loud to herself, "Something about it just won't let me tap the energy around me." She cursed again, throwing the disappointing failure into the corner in a heap. Desperate for an answer, she grabbed the first prototype she'd made from the cheap, flimsier material and pulled it on. After confirming her powers failed in that suit as well, she peeled it off and angrily tossed it into the same corner after her other failure.

Frustrated, she half-threw the couch back into its normal place and then flopped onto it, throwing her arms out to her sides and letting her head drop onto the back cushion. She closed her eyes, reached up, and rubbed the bridge of her nose. *All that work, and it's completely dead on arrival. Some scientist I am. Smart scientists test their theories as they go. Ugh. Stupid, Trish! Just stupid.*

And with that, without warning, the emotions of the previous day flooded back, amplified by her failure with the suit. Powerless to prevent them, sobs started to wrack her body. Tears streamed down her cheeks. She sat forward, put her face in her hands, rocking slightly as she wept uncontrollably.

*I'm screwing up my career.*

*I'm letting the team down…the university down.*

*The suit's a disaster, and I don't have a clue why.*

*Who am I kidding? What makes me think I can help people? I don't know what I'm doing. What makes me think I can successfully live two lives when I'm already fricking both of them up so badly?*

She cried, venting the pent-up emotion she had kept bottled up for so long now. When the tears finally subsided, she collected herself, wiping the tear trails from her cheeks, and went into the bedroom where she traded the support top and shorts for a more comfortable t-shirt and pair of sweatpants.

Rascal met her immediately when she laid down on the bed, pressing up against her stomach, purring loudly. Tricia scratched the cat's head as she slowly and painfully came to terms with the realization that she had hit a dead end and was now completely lost about what to do next.

# Options

*T*ricia was standing in the middle of a bright light. It seemed to come from directly over her head and cast an intense white circle of light around her. Just a few feet away, though, it was pitch black. She could hear movement and whispering voices. "Who's there?" she shouted, but there were only the sounds of shifting, scraping, and indistinguishable whispers. She squinted but couldn't see past the edge of the blinding white light around her. There was more rustling moving toward her, and the whispering intensified.

Terror swept over her. She frantically opened herself to her power and felt it flow into her, clenching her fists, preparing herself for what was moving out in the shadows.

She pivoted left, then right, shifting her feet, but she couldn't tell from which direction it was coming. It seemed to be coming from all around her, getting louder now, getting closer.

She drew in more of her power, immersing herself in it. She glanced over her shoulder, and suddenly a pale hand came out of the darkness and grabbed her arm.

*She shrieked and tried to pull away, but her power was gone. It had left her. She was weak, helpless.*

*More hands now seized her arms, yanked her hair, encircled her waist, pulling, dragging her into the darkness.*

*She screamed...*

...and jerked awake, sitting bolt upright in bed. She was sweating, her breathing rapid and shallow, still feeling the cold and clammy phantom hands on her skin. Her covers were askew, half on the floor. The Sunday morning light streaming in the bedroom window clearly told Tricia that it was much later than she usually got up. Even without the nightmare, she hadn't slept well the night before, her mind still churning over the failure with the suit the day before. She had a light breakfast and tried to do a few things around her place, but her mind just wouldn't let it go. If only she'd been smarter about it. If only she'd tested her ideas out sooner. If only she hadn't gotten so caught up with making it in the first place. If only...if only...if only...

Finally, after a few hours of kicking herself around her townhouse, she gave up on doing anything at home, changed into her workout clothes, and headed over to the training facility on the far end of campus. *At least the swanky new underwear I bought will get some use,* she thought. The field house facility was deserted on Sunday afternoon, as she had hoped, so she immersed herself in an intense workout, freely embracing the swirling ebb and flow of her powers. She put herself through a regimen of high-speed agility: stepping, sprinting, and leaping into the ceiling support structure, dropping down to perfectly sticking the landings on the balance beams, or catching herself on the parallel bars.

She knew she was running a huge risk of accidentally being discovered, but, at this particular moment, part of her simply didn't care. *So what if someone catches me? Figures out what*

*I am? Maybe this whole secret identity thing is just a pipe dream anyway*, she thought more than once as she attacked each maneuver.

As she burned off steam, though, she ultimately realized that now, frustrated and discouraged, wasn't the time to make that decision or to keep taking the chance that someone else would make it for her. Collecting herself, she decided to move on to something less risky and began to run through a series of advanced *kata*, at first, slowly, not using her powers at all, checking her form after each stance and technique.

Satisfied she had them solidly, Tricia ran through the same series again, this time combining her abilities with the techniques and forms just as she'd previously done in class. She accelerated the stances and kicks, channeled strength with each strike, created shields, and pushed with them for each block and counterstrike. She then did it all again, but switching up the combinations, this time powering her kicks, making each punch a lightning strike, creating distracting flares of blinding light, and projecting pulses of energy on the counters. She focused on making these combinations feel natural so that when the time came, she could draw on them with confidence and without hesitation.

After the kata practice, she cooled down with a few powered punches and kicks with the punching bags and practice dummies, deftly casting shields and maneuvering them to shove around the weighted tackling sleds on the track. Tricia allowed herself a measure of satisfaction with the power and accuracy she was achieving.

Finally, after a few hours of venting her frustrations, she finally dismissed the currents coursing through her. Her brief regret to feel the power recede was immediately replaced by the hunger and weariness that always followed a powered practice session. She sat down, took several large gulps of water, and dipped into the pile of protein and energy bars she kept in her bag. *THESE clothes work just fine...a little resistance, but overall fine,* she pondered, chewing. *The sweatpants and hoodie I wore when I fought the gang in the parking lot had worked, again, not well, but I could at least USE my powers, and they were much thicker and bulkier than her new suits. Even my gi in class seems to be relatively ok.* She sat with her knees up, put her head down, and ran her fingers through her hair. Interlocking her fingers behind her head. she exhaled deeply. "What am I missing here?" she demanded, but no one answered. Like George up at The Ridge, the dummies here just glared at her silently.

After a brief rest, she started walking home. As she walked in the shade of the trees, she suddenly remembered her nightmare and realized that the setback in making the suit wasn't the only thing frustrating and worrying her. She sighed. "The really frustrating part, the really terrifying part," she said softly to herself, scratching the back of her head, "is that this is yet another reminder of how little I really understand about what's happened to me, how it works. Just when I think I'm getting my arms around it, there's a new twist, a new turn, and while I can learn to cope and maybe eventually even use what I've got, I really don't fully know what's going on. *That's* the scary part."

She fished her water bottle out of her bag and took a long drink. Confronting this revelation made her feel a small bit of relief— her demons now had a name—and she was finally able to unwind a bit more on the way home. By the time she arrived at her front door, the frustration and anxiety had mostly abated, and with it, her outlook had improved considerably.

Tricia tossed her bag down by the door and removed her sweaty workout clothes, tossing them into a sink full of cold water to soak while she let a hot shower help wash away any remaining doubts and worries. She brushed her hair and put on some pajamas, but as she was just about to leave the bedroom, her eyes were drawn to her prototype suit still lying in the corner where she'd left it the night before. Tricia paused a minute to pick it up by the shoulders, letting it hang down in front of her. "You do look pretty good. We'll figure out how to make this work. We will. It's what we do, right?" she said to it, making a pact, more with herself than with the suit. She carefully folded it and laid it down with the other costuming materials by the dresser. "And, in the meanwhile, I still have a couple of comics to go through. Who knows? I might find a clue in one of them," she mused and settled down on the couch to read a bit before making it an early evening.

Monday morning found Tricia in a much more upbeat and optimistic mood. Her workout had helped her clear her mind so she could get a good night's sleep, and while the puzzle of the failed suit still lingered in her mind, it was now just that, a puzzle to be solved, and she was sure she'd crack it eventually. Besides, she needed to get her game face on for the team in the lab this morning. It was going to be a big week. After several weeks of recovering the lab, not to mention her own personal recovery, they were going to make a new attempt at the experiment that led to her accident. Thinking about it put butterflies in Tricia's stomach, but it would be an important event for the lab, for the team, and for her personally.

She went through her normal morning routine, a short session of yoga to get the blood flowing. She concentrated not only on stretching muscles that weren't quite awake yet but also on being in tune with the tides of energy seething and churning around her. Her body craved the strength and power they brought, but she resisted, keeping the flows just out of reach. This was her time to feel at peace with just herself. After a hot shower, she decided to skip breakfast in favor of picking up some bagels and breakfast treats for the lab crew. After all, it was going to be a big week.

As she walked toward the bakery, her mind started wandering back to the suit. What options did she have? What could she try next? Maybe cutting slits or holes in it to expose more of her skin? Her mind jumped back to that comic cover with Lady Vengeance and the halter top. *Oh, yeah, there we go,* she mused. *Let's go with that, but hey, why not shorts and fishnet stockings instead of pants?* She chuckled out loud to herself - it was quite the mental image. *Why stop there?* she continued, *let's go all in and just wear a bikini. That will REALLY make a big impression while fighting the bad guys,* laughing a little, and shaking her head. *Who knows? Maybe the 'Beacon Bikini,' the 'Beac-ini'*—she snickered again—*will become a real thing? Crime fighter AND fashion mogul.*

Adding to her amusement, an old song about an itsy-bitsy polka-dot bikini suddenly popped into her head. She started humming it happily as she walked. She knew this ditty would not only haunt her the entire day but that she didn't regret it even the slightest bit.

She arrived at the lab a few minutes late—the line at the bakery was insane—and saw the entire team was already there. They were huddled around Jamal's monitor, intently watching the morning news stream. Tricia set her bag and the bagels down on her desk and walked over.

"G'mornin," she said, "What are you all so glued to over here?"

"Oh Hi, Doctor C," Jamal replied, throwing her a quick glance in her direction before turning back to the screen, "Did you hear about this?"

Tricia leaned in to get a look. The screen showed a live reporter broadcasting from downtown with a bold headline at the bottom: "Eco-terrorists strike again." As she leaned in to get a better look, the view switched to the local police on the scene, where an officer was speaking with another reporter.

"Turn it up a bit, will you please, Jamal?" Tricia asked. Jamal tapped up the volume a couple of bars.

"...a small explosive device was detonated near the Genomitech main office center downtown earlier in the morning. Fortunately, no one was injured, and there was no significant damage, but an appreciable quantity of some blue and green chemical substances was dispersed into the air. Preliminary analysis indicates the substance is harmless smoke and was likely more for dramatic effect than to cause any harm. We ask that people avoid the area until we've completed our investigation at the site."

Behind him and the reporter Tricia could clearly see the Liberators of Gaia logo painted on the wall. There was still some green and blue mist lingering in the air, but it was rapidly fading as the morning breezes started to pick up.

The broadcast switched back to main news desk where the morning anchor was introducing the police commissioner who appeared next to her in a small picture-in-picture cut out.

"Welcome to our broadcast, Commissioner Weathers. What more can you tell us about the incident this morning?" the anchor asked.

"Thanks, Maria. Glad to be here. We have confirmed that the Liberators of Gaia are claiming responsibility. We can also reassure the public that the blue and green substances dispersed by the explosion are not harmful in any way. These substances are very similar to the colorant used in smoke devices they have set off in two previous events and represent no concern to public health and safety."

The commissioner's tone became more serious as he continued, "Previously, Liberators of Gaia have not generally demonstrated any dangerous tendencies, and while this device doesn't appear to have had any intent to harm, the fact that they have escalated to using larger, potentially more dangerous devices, in highly populated areas of the city now requires us to officially classify Liberators of Gaia as a terrorist organization. The mayor and I are in agreement that all the resources of the regular police and anti-terrorism units will now be brought to bear on preventing any future acts such as the one we witnessed today."

Jamal turned the volume back down and closed the window on the news stream. They all stood back up and shared a collective sigh.

"Wow," Jamal said, "They better get these Gaia nutjobs before something bad happens."

"I admit after they first appeared on the news, I read the manifesto they posted online," Alex said. "They make a lot of really good points about how we can live in better harmony with the planet and how the companies they called out are doing some really harmful things."

"True," Jamal said, "and I get what they are saying. Don't get me wrong. I'm all for saving the planet, but I think this is going about it the wrong way."

They all mumbled and nodded in agreement. "Well, on a lighter note," Tricia said and pointed toward her desk, "Help yourself guys."

They didn't need to be told twice. After swarming the box of goodies, Tricia huddled them all up to review the preparations for the experiment this week. Jamal and Nikki would handle setting up and configuring the sensors and data collectors in the chamber. Steve and Alex would take care of the emitter array and double-check the software. Tricia would run some final simulations to confirm the experimental parameters, and she would also personally handle setting up the newest piece of equipment: the automatic emergency fail-safe interrupt. There would be no repeats of the last time they attempted this test if she had anything to do about it. After asking if there were any final questions, she sent them to go about their tasks.

After the others left, Nikki approached her tentatively, "Um, I just wanted to say I'll be sure everything is absolutely right this time, Doctor Carling."

Putting a hand on her shoulder, Tricia gave it a reassuring squeeze, "I know you will, Nikki."

Nikki smiled, nodded, and went over to join Steve, where he had started to set up the emitter rack.

After running a few simulations to confirm a few of the more critical experiment parameters, Tricia stood up, stretched, and went to check on the progress of the rest of the team. Nikki and Alex had already gone to lunch. They had won the game of Rock-Paper-Scissors-Lizard-Spock, so Jamal and Steve kept working until Nikki and Alex relieved them. Tricia wandered into the chamber where Jamal was setting up a bank of energy flow detectors. Much of the rest of the instrumentation was already in place. At this pace, they could probably run the experiment a day early, depending on how the emitter setup was progressing.

She came in just as Jamal had finished plugging in some cables and had started to drape an oddly textured piece of fabric over the detector units. Tricia's gaze fixated on the covering. Something sparked in the back of her mind. *That fabric,* she searched her memory, *I'd forgotten about that. There was something about it...something special...*

"Hey Jamal," she called out, "Just popped in to see how things were going."

"Hey, Doctor C!" he looked up, grinning, "Yeah, things are going great. Feels like it's all coming together really smoothly. Might actually be a bit ahead of schedule, I think. Gives us a chance to run a few extra tests before the big moment."

"That's really awesome," she praised, and then changing direction a bit, Tricia pointed at the fabric draped over the detectors. "That cloth you're using there...is that the stuff you got from the Advanced Materials Sciences lab earlier this year?"

Jamal nodded. "Sure is. Glad we got it, too."

"Why is that?"

"Well, it's fabulous stuff. It not only seems to dampen some of the electronic noise, but the detectors almost seem to work better with it. I need to make sure it fits flush against them, but it really helps give us great readings for the kinds of precision measurements we'll be taking."

He tossed the piece to Tricia. She caught it and started turning it over in her hands. It was a light gray color and felt very thin and lightweight, almost silky. She tugged on it slightly; it had a bit of elasticity to it. An idea started to form in Tricia's mind, "Could we use more of it? For some of the other equipment?"

"Probably," Jamal said pensively, "I'm not sure how much they have, but I'm pretty sure some of the other equipment could benefit from the same kind of thing if they have more and are willing to part with it."

"Hmmm, ok," Tricia said, her mind now running at full speed, "I'll give them a call and see. Not sure we want to introduce anything new this week, mind you, but after we nail this experiment, maybe we can go on over there and see."

Jamal gave her a thumbs up and went back to setting up the array. Tricia swung over by Steve to see how the emitter configuration was going. Like Jamal, he and Nikki were making great progress putting it together. *Looks like we might be able to do the experiment early at this rate.* Good news.

She had a hard time containing her excitement and concentrating the rest of the afternoon. After the lunch breaks were over, the team really knuckled down and wrapped up most of the setup by mid-afternoon, easily a full day ahead of schedule. They had a quick huddle to review what had been done, take a quick pass through the checklists, and agree on their plan for the next day. She congratulated them on their exemplary work for the day and let them take off early. Not only had they earned it, but she now had something else she was eager to follow up on.

Rather than head home afterward, she decided to walk across the research quad to the MatSci lab and see what she could find out about this material. The main door to the lab was open, so Tricia let herself in. She wandered the halls for a bit until she came across someone who appeared to be a grad student and asked where she might find the director. He routed her toward the back of the building to one of the main labs. The room was somewhat dimly lit, and seemed deserted, so she tried knocking on the frame of the open door and called out, "Hello?"

A head, covered by a full-face shield, popped up at a nearby table. He stood up quickly and stared at her with a startled look on his face. He was tall and lanky, wearing a lab smock and elbow-length rubber gloves. "Yeah, Hi, uh, can I help you?" he called back, fumbling to remove the face shield. The heavy gloves were being anything but cooperative.

"I hope so," she said, making her way over to the table, "I'm Doctor Tricia Carling from the Optics and Imaging lab. I'm looking for the director."

"Yup, that's me," he replied, pulling off the rubber gloves, "Doctor Harold Baskins. Pleased to meet you, Doctor Carling." He extended his hand toward her.

Tricia shook his hand. "Is this a good time? Are you in the middle of something? I can come back if it isn't."

"No, no, it's a perfectly fine time. Just don't get many visitors over here...uh, do you mind if I see your badge? Just to be sure...you know."

"Yeah, of course, no problem." She dug out her badge and showed it to him. He squinted as he looked at it, glanced at her, and nodded. She stowed the badge back in her bag.

"How can I help you, Doctor Carling?"

"Trish, please, Doctor Baskins..."

"...Harold..."

"...Harold, yes, thanks. I'd like to talk to you a bit about some material my lab tech says he got here earlier this year. He uses it to cover some of the detector arrays and thinks it's amazing. Do you know anything about that?"

"I sure do," Harold beamed, "it's kind of my baby. I invented it."

"Great!" she replied, "What can you tell me about it?"

"How much time do you have?" he smirked, "It's pretty much my greatest achievement and most likely also my greatest disappointment at the same time. I could probably spend far more time than you want to take talking about it."

"Ok," she paused, "Why don't we start with the basics then? Why does Jamal feel it could be making the detectors work better?"

"Ah, of course. Well, this material was essentially engineered almost at the quantum level, specifically for the ways it interacts with the electromagnetic spectrum. You see, on its own, it's virtually opaque to a broad range of the EM spectrum, including the parts we can sense and feel. However, when in close physical proximity to emitters and receptors of EM radiation, it becomes just the opposite - it passes EM radiation almost perfectly transparently for emitters. Almost zero degradation or impedance. For receptors, it acts almost like a passive collector, measurably improving the incident energy response. Again, provided it's physically touching the emitter or receptor."

"The snugger, the better?" Tricia said, simultaneously cringing and relishing the inside joke.

"Very. Even the slightest gap and the material becomes fully opaque, blocking any energy transmission."

*Guess there's just no way to get away from that 'snug' part, is there?* she thought, doing a virtual eye roll. "Well, I don't think 'snug' will be too much of a problem, Harold.

"Guessing that's also why he's noticed it tends to shield electromagnetic noise from the electronics?"

"Absolutely, that's why, and interestingly, it works the same way if it's stacked in layers. If the layers are all pressed tightly together, it behaves as if there's a single layer."

Tricia nodded, showing a little excitement. "Sooooo, if we wanted to make some, say, covers and such for some of the other equipment, could we? Do you have more of it? Could we use it?" Tricia asked, a bit hesitantly. *Please, please, let this work out.*

"Come with me," Harold said and led her to the back of the lab. He tapped a code on a storage room door and led her inside. The lights came on automatically, and he led her to the back corner. Harold pulled down a green plastic tub that was perhaps four feet long, two feet wide, and about eighteen inches deep. He carried it over to a table against the wall, pushing aside some of the things littering the top of the desk, and set it down.

"There are probably two hundred yards, give or take, of the stuff in this box." he said casually, lifting off the top, and gestured towards the folded fabric in the box.

"Two *hundred*?" Tricia exclaimed. "In that little tub? Seriously?!?"

"Seriously," he confirmed, taking out a small piece that was lying by itself on top, "it's incredibly lightweight and highly compact. However, it's also incredibly wear-resistant and durable. In fact, it's so durable it can't be cut with conventional tools. That's part of the problem with it." He picked up a pair of large scissors that happened to be on the table and demonstrated. He tried several times to cut the sample in his hand, but the material resisted every attempt.

"Here," he said, handing Tricia the piece and the scissors, "try it."

Tricia tried to cut it to no avail. She then tried to poke the scissors through the material. She carefully drew a little power and tried harder to push the scissors through. The cloth resisted the points of the scissors and remained undamaged. When she stopped pushing, the cloth returned perfectly to its original shape; there was no indication of any attempt to cut or tear through it.

"This is amazing, Harold," Tricia said, astounded, turning the piece of material over in her hand, watching it shimmer softly in the light. "And the texture, it's beautiful. So, I have to ask, why is it such a disappointment?"

"Well, sadly, it's too good," he said, pulling out a chair for himself and one for Tricia. He gestured for her to have a seat as he sat down. "We tried to interest people in it, industry, even the military, but it's insanely expensive to make, first of all, and the manufacturing process is very precise, very finicky, and difficult to automate.

"Working with it is very challenging, too. As you've undoubtedly guessed by now, it requires special tooling to cut it, and it can't be sewn. It has to be chemically welded to itself using a special solution. Also, the applications weren't entirely obvious either. I suppose if you wanted the world's most expensive swimsuit, you'd probably tan better under it than your exposed skin would on its own—" Tricia laughed "—but beyond that, we couldn't sell it to anyone."

"But what about the mil..." Tricia started to ask.

Harold nodded vigorously. "The military was the closest we came. They had this idea for suits for their special ops teams. Beyond what we've discussed, it has one other rather exotic property; when it's infused with a certain low-band EM radiation, it will actively scramble EM waves around itself, creating an odd camouflage effect that makes the wearer difficult to see and detect."

*Ooooh, now THAT's interesting*, Tricia remarked to herself excitedly.

"You mean it makes them invisible?" she asked.

"No," he said, "it's not *that* good, but it's enough to create a fairly effective stealth effect for the wearer. But, again, it requires a very even and stable EM field to do it, and designing a device to do that practically that also integrates into a suit was a substantial impediment."

"So, when you add it all up..."

"Yeah, it was just too expensive, hard to work with, and too much additional development was going to be needed to make anything practical out of it. Like I said," Harold held up one hand, "greatest achievement, and," holding up the other hand, "greatest disappointment."

"So, do you think..." Tricia started.

"Sure," Harold interrupted, "look, this stuff is just sitting here. There's a lot of it. If your team can get some use out of it, yeah, we can make that happen. I'll just need to spend some time with you all to show you how to work with it, but it's straightforward. We have everything here in the lab, and I'm sure we could set up a small work area for your team to use temporarily."

"Oh, that's awesome," Tricia said, fully beaming now with excitement and gratitude. "Let me talk to the team about it, and sometime soon, after the big experiment we are doing this week is done, maybe we can set some time up to come over?"

"Sounds like a plan," Harold said. He stood up and snapped the cover back on the tub.

"Oh, do you mind if I hang onto this sample?" Tricia asked, clutching it eagerly in both hands. "I'd like to run a few tests on it."

"Of course. Enjoy!" Harold smiled, picked up the tub, and returned it to the shelf. He walked Tricia back out to the lab entrance. She shook his hand, thanking him again, and absentmindedly started humming to herself as she turned to leave.

"Hey, that song," Harold called after her, "it sounds familiar. What is it?"

"Oh, just a silly old ditty that popped into my head this morning," she replied, smirking to herself.

# Breakthrough

That evening, Tricia sat at her table at home. She had her storage tub of crafting supplies sitting next to her on the floor. Her two suits were laid out on the table in front of her. She sat there, holding the new piece of material in her hands, looking it all over. *I have to be smarter about it this time, more scientific, before just going all in like I did with these,* she thought to herself. But how, was the real question.

"Like any experiment, we establish some baselines," she said to herself, and went into the bedroom to fetch the performance underwear she'd purchased to go with her suit, or rather, undersuit, as she'd taken to calling it. She changed into it, grabbed a piece of rebar, and let the energy flow into her. It came easily, flooding through her. She closed her eyes and relished the feeling for a moment, before easily bending and unbending the piece of rebar. *On a scale of 1-10, we'll call that a 10,* she thought to herself.

She then grabbed the first prototype suit she'd made, the one made from the cheap material, and put that on. She opened herself and again, felt nothing. She took a deep breath and felt inward for the currents and flows. *No, not nothing, very little, but something*, she realized. Not enough to bend the rebar, but when she tried to lift the couch, it was noticeably easier than when she tried it without using her powers. *Definitely not zero, but a pretty weak 1*, she decided.

She couldn't cut the material, so she decided to do the next best thing. Grabbing a marker, she held the fabric up to her midriff. It was just long enough to wrap around her and spanned from the bottom of her ribs to just above her hips. She marked that section on her suit, took it off, and cut the marked area out of the suit. *Hey, looks like I've got that halter top after all*, she joked to herself. Tricia put on the two remaining pieces, and then wrapped the portion of material around her exposed midriff. She used a small piece of tape to secure the seam, and then tucked the top of the material under the bottom of the suit top and pulled the waist of the suit bottom up over the lower edge of the material. It didn't have to hold long, just long enough.

Tricia carefully squatted down to pick up the piece of rebar, taking it slow so as not to pop her makeshift patchwork. *Ok, here goes nothing*, she thought, crossed her fingers, and drew on her power. She gasped slightly in relief as the currents surged into her. To her surprise, she had also felt the material around her stomach contract slightly. *Maybe that's how I will know it's working?* she wondered. *Harold hadn't mentioned that bit*. Tricia took another deep breath and focused; she could almost feel the roiling currents in her body centered exactly where that material was circling her waist. It was a unique and amazing feeling. She tried the rebar, and, with some strain that made her muscles shake slightly, the rebar finally bent. She tried to pull a bit more and was able to partially straighten the iron rod; it still had a kink that she still wasn't strong enough to bend out. She carefully bent down to grip the bottom of the couch—the material hugged her close, showing no signs of shifting—and easily lifted the couch.

She did a quick test of her dark energy, effortlessly pushing the couch a few feet across the floor.

*Calling that maybe a 4,* Tricia thought, both relieved and excited. *Probably need to be more scientific about this, quantitatively anyway, but we're going to call this a success!* She pressed the flows away, and, as her powers released, she felt the material relax slightly. Tricia pulled the piece of material off, tossing it onto the table, and then exchanged her sacrificed prototype for a t-shirt and lounge pants from her bedroom. She picked the piece up and held it in front of her by the corners, giving it another careful inspection. "You are my most favorite thing right now," she told it, satisfied she had a way forward. She then turned it over in her hands a few times. "But now how do I turn more of you into a whole suit?" she asked it. It shimmered in the light but stayed silent.

Tricia clicked her tongue in mock disappointment that it didn't answer, but she knew she'd need a plan to get the suit she needed but without raising any suspicion. Making a few equipment covers was one thing, but crafting a multi-color full body suit was quite another. She let the gears in her mind start to turn, but quickly realized that without more information from Harold, the next step would remain a mystery.

*I'll find a way to pick Harold's brain a bit more, and then we will see how this unfolds,* she decided, chuckling at her tortured pun.

The days in the lab found Tricia and the team still completely consumed with getting the final setup in place for the big experiment. Granted it was the second time they'd set up for it, and they were still running a bit ahead of schedule, but the team was being particularly careful setting up and meticulously double-checking each other's work. They were all nervous and determined not to repeat what happened last time they attempted this particular scenario. Tricia knew Nikki still blamed herself to some extent for the accident, but she and the team were very supportive of Nikki, and everyone had really gone above and beyond to make sure this second attempt went flawlessly.

Tricia had shared a bit of her conversation with Doctor Baskins with the team about the potential benefit of making some additional equipment covers similar to the one Jamal was using on the detector banks. Jamal had happily done a little show-and-tell for them, and they were very excited by the prospect. Steve and Alex were especially enthusiastic to see how the material would interact with the emitter array. They were all in agreement that after they nailed the experiment and finished popping the champagne, they would be ready for a little arts and crafts time as Nikki had put it. Happy the team was on board, Tricia had arranged with Harold for the team to come over Friday afternoon to get some instruction on how to work with the fabric for their project, provided everything else went as planned.

After a short huddle and rechecking the preparation checklist, the team broke so everyone could get some relaxation before the big day. There was no martial arts class this week, but Marni had reached out for a dinner and catch-up anyway. Part of her was still occupied with what to do next on her costume and wanted to just huddle up and think more about it, but Marni eventually won out.

Tricia was grateful she'd chosen one of the smaller, quieter places to meet tonight. The last thing she needed was an exhausting evening dealing with a noisy crowd. When she walked into the restaurant, Marni waved to her from a corner table.

"You read my mind," Tricia praised, noticing the glass of Chianti waiting for her on the table as she took a seat.

"We are having Italian tonight after all," replied Marni, holding up her glass.

"*Grazi!*" Tricia clinked her glass against Marni's.

They both picked up their menus, but before Tricia could even get through the appetizers, Marni, never one to be content with silence, prodded the conversation, "So, what's new in the world of optical science?"

Marni couldn't have asked a better question to get the conversation started. Tricia excitedly filled Marni in on the prep for the big experiment going on the next day, breaking only for them to give the waiter their order and to tuck into some of the basket of bread he brought to the table. She shared how proud she was with the team and how they'd really pulled together to get ready early.

Marni frowned slightly with concern. "This is the same experiment you were doing when you had your accident?"

"Yes, it is," Tricia replied, "but the entire team has checked and double-checked everything, and we've put in some additional safety precautions. It should go without any problems."

"Hmmm, all right. Just be careful, ok?" Marni relented. The furrows in her forehead made it clear she wasn't entirely satisfied.

"We are. Don't worry." Tricia reassured her, smiling. "Anything new going on at the hospital?" she asked, deliberately changing the subject. She loved Marni, but she didn't need any mothering at the moment.

"Mostly same old, same old," Marni answered between bites, "We are having some good results with some of the newer therapies we've developed. The FDA has bumped up some of the reporting requirements so they can stay on top of what we are doing. Being one of the few research hospitals in the country that's been authorized to develop and administer on-demand gene therapies is a big honor, but it's a lot of pressure, too. Lots of potential, but a lot of people think we are going to cause the zombie apocalypse. They keep us on a short leash."

"Sounds very exciting, though," Tricia said, washing down a bite with a sip of Chianti. Finally, Marni was learning to order a decent wine.

"It really is, but a few weeks ago, something *really* exciting happened too. I was invited to participate on a tiger team," Marni said with a little glint in her eye.

"Ooooh, a tiger team," Tricia teased, making air quotes with her fingers, "Sounds very important. What's this 'tiger team' all about?"

"Well, it's an interesting problem, actually. There's been a sudden wave of couples having trouble conceiving. The hospital has seen nearly triple the usual rate of cases in the past few months. The puzzling part is that none of the standard therapies are working. Stranger yet, many of the couples have previously had children without any issues."

"Sounds really weird. Any clues?"

"Some. The team is working a lot of angles: anatomy, physiology, genetics. They've pulled together specialists from a number of departments to see if we can come up with anything, maybe find something they haven't seen or haven't thought of yet. Something really outside the box."

"That's an awesome opportunity. So why am I only just hearing about it now?" Tricia needled her.

Marni shrugged. "Honestly, I just wasn't sure it was going to amount to anything, so I didn't want to make a big deal out of it. However, it has developed into something really meaty and challenging that can really help some people in areas where my department doesn't usually get involved."

Tricia pondered for a few moments. Granted, she and Marni weren't in any hurry, but she imagined the heartbreak those couples must be experiencing. They'd finally decided to start a family, only to have that choice ripped away from them. A lump formed in her throat just thinking about it.

"I can only imagine how devastating this is for those poor people, Marns. They are lucky that they have you working on it for them. If there's anything I can do to help, don't hesitate to let me know, ok?"

"I won't, Tricia," Marni replied. "You know I won't."

Tricia raised her glass. "Well, looks like we both have some big, exciting things coming up."

"Yup," Marni agreed, clinking her glass with Tricia's, "They save the biggest problems for the smartest people."

Tricia laughed. They dove back into dinner while their meals were still reasonably warm and occupied the rest of the evening with more random small talk. After a couple more glasses of wine, they paid and walked out. Standing on the sidewalk, Tricia gave Marni a big hug. "Thanks for convincing me to come out tonight, Marni. This was a great way to relax before tomorrow."

"Knock 'em dead, Trish...and remember, be safe." Marni took Tricia's hand. "If things go sideways, promise me you won't try to be some kind of hero this time, ok?" she pleaded, her worry poorly masked by a small smile.

Tricia smiled, squeezed Marni's hand, and nodded. "I promise."

A couple of days later, Riptide, Scorpius, and Harmony were huddled in front of the morning news stream at the Liberators' meeting and lab space. Opus had asked them to meet him there this morning, but he was uncharacteristically running late. While they waited, they were watching the report coming in on their latest protest. Even with Opus away, it had gone without a hitch and there was a flurry of activity at the site.

The reporters were interviewing various witnesses. The reporter had just asked a middle-aged woman what she thought of their activities. "Honestly, I'm not a huge fan of them setting off these smoke bombs downtown," she said. "It seems dangerous, but I have to admit, they have made me think about these companies they are calling out, and, after reading their manifesto online, I am rethinking some of the products I buy."

"That's what we want to hear," the deep voice behind them said. They turned to see Opus standing behind them in a business suit. He had slipped in while they were engrossed in the broadcast.

"Scared the crap out of me, mate!" Riptide said. "How was the flight?"

"As good as any redeye can be, I supposed," Opus answered. "It got in on time, but needless to say, traffic was a bit backed up getting here." They all chuckled at that.

"Yeah, shame about that," Scorpius said and winked. "How was the governors' conference?"

"It went well," Opus replied. "I think we were able to convince a number of the governors to consider implementing stronger regulations and oversight on some of these companies that have been skirting the regs for years."

He pulled up a chair, unbuttoned his jacket, and sat down. "One governor, in particular, said he's very opposed to the tactics the Liberators of Gaia are using, but he had to admit that they've made him much more acutely aware of the liberties some of the companies on our manifest have been taking. So, while they may not approve, what we are doing is definitely opening the doors for 'concerned business leaders' like me to have constructive conversations for change."

"That's awesome!" Harmony exclaimed. "Great to hear all this work is paying off. I wish Purity were here to hear about it, too. Where is she, by the way?"

Opus looked at each of them in turn. Clasping his hands in front of him, he answered, "I didn't ask her to join us today. I wanted only us to talk for a bit. I've been having some concerns about her lately, about how driven and single-minded she seems to have become recently. I wanted to hear what you all might think about it."

Riptide, never short on an opinion, answered first, "Yeah, I've noticed she's gotten a bit more intense, but honestly, I don't mind it. She brings a lot of energy and focus, and I think that's helped us stay on track."

Scorpius nodded. "I agree. She can get a bit over the top sometimes, but she's done a lot for us, and I really think we wouldn't be having anywhere near this level of impact—" he pointed at the news stream on the monitor "—without her."

"I tend to agree," Harmony offered reluctantly, "but I admit there are times when I wonder about her motives. She comes off as having her own agenda sometimes, but so far, I agree with the others. She's a huge part of the team, and I'd hate to be without her."

Opus looked at them and nodded. "Ok," he said. "I'll talk to her then, but it might be best if we kept this chat just between us, all right?"

The others nodded in agreement.

About the time the Liberators were discussing their teammate, Tricia and her team had met at their lab and were headed over to the Materials Sciences building together. Yesterday's experiment had been a huge success, and judging from how Jamal and Nikki looked this morning, Tricia was glad she'd only brought in a single bottle of champagne to celebrate. It seems the team more than made up for it at dinner, however. Alex was far from her normal chatty self as well. Her sole choice for celebratory beverages was tequila, not champagne, and since hard liquor was strictly off-limits in the lab, she declined the champagne but made a point of catching up to the rest of the team in the evening and, from the looks of her, passing them well afterward.

The pressure spiked somewhat when Doctor Teague notified them that the probation team would be attending. Initially, her team was nervous about having them there, but Tricia just kept reminding them to trust their work and that if they stuck to their plan, the probation committee would take care of itself. "Eyes on the prize" became their mantra. Besides, having them witness a success of this magnitude in person could go a long way to 'reducing their sentence,' as she put it. In the end, the probation team was extremely impressed with the result and joined them in a celebratory toast. *Here's mud in your eye, Alexei*, Tricia had thought smugly to herself when she raised her glass.

There would be the normal reports to file, IP and patent applications to submit, and all the usual paperwork to be done in addition to analyzing the data, but the team was riding high after the big win and doing some crafts was a welcome change of pace for today. With the pressure of the experiment off their shoulders, they had become somewhat excited to see how the material Jamal had been using would improve the effectiveness of the other equipment.

Jamal had a small detector unit under his arm that he intended to use for a working model. Tricia had picked up donuts; she always believed a little bribery never hurt when asking for favors, and this was going to be a big one...even bigger than the team or Harold knew if things went her way.

When they arrived, Tricia led them toward the back where she'd found Doctor Baskins earlier in the week. She knocked on the lab door, and in a few moments, Harold appeared. He peeked at them through the glass in the door, smiled, and unlocked the door. He pushed it open and, holding it for them to enter, gestured for them to come in. Tricia followed the team in, and after exchanging nods, Harold released the door behind them and locked it again.

Harold noticed Tricia watching him locking the door and drawing a shade across the window. "Might be best to keep our little craft time to ourselves for now." he whispered to her.

"Of course," Tricia agreed, and flourishing the box of donuts, "Beware of optical lab technicians bearing gifts."

"Ah, well, bribery will get you everywhere." Harold smiled, and with a low bow, he gestured toward the lab with a flourish of his own, "My lab is your lab."

They popped open the box of donuts on a side table near a small cluster of desks. This table clearly served as a small break and refreshment area for people working here, much like the break area in their own lab. There was a full pot of freshly brewed coffee on the table as well, along with a box of assorted teas and some compostable coffee cups. Harold told them to help themselves to whatever they wanted, including water or whatever from the small refrigerator against the wall. He then disappeared for a few minutes, eventually returning with the tub he'd shown Tricia on her previous visit.

While they stood around enjoying the donuts and refreshments, Harold started out by giving the team essentially the same overview he'd given Tricia: what the material was, its unique properties, and why they'd had so much difficulty finding suitable applications for it. The team was really engaged and asked a lot of questions, which only fueled Harold's enthusiasm even more. Tricia smiled. Knowing everyone was going to have a lot of fun would make it all the easier for her personal plan to unfold as well. *It's a win-win*, she thought. *Fingers crossed, everyone is going to get something they are excited about today.*

After finishing their morning treat and wiping their hands with some disposable moist towelettes, Harold gave them all a set of latex gloves. He explained that there were a lot of substances in the lab areas where they'd be working and that it was better to be a little on the cautious side. "The decontamination shower is pretty cold, just warning you," he joked.

Their first stop was the precision laser cutter. Harold explained that the durability of the material made it very difficult to cut with conventional methods, but the laser cutter was the best option they'd found. It made a very clean cut and left the edges such that they wouldn't fray or deteriorate. The team eagerly took notes as he demonstrated using a small scrap from the tub. He also showed them how to create, scan, and create templates to guide the cutter. The cutter could be operating manually using a small joystick, but the programmed templates could cut much faster and knock out identical cuts very quickly. The scanning function, in particular, was very useful in that an existing pattern could be scanned, traced, and smoothed by the cutter's software so that even rough sketches could be used to make clean and accurate reusable templates. Tricia took a special interest in this feature.

"So, if the material is so tough that it takes a laser to cut it, how do you stitch it together to make other things?" Nikki puzzled out loud.

Harold pretended to slip her some money from his pocket, smiling. They all chuckled. "Glad you asked that. Come over this way." He waved them towards a steel-topped table against the far wall. The table had a runoff tray around the edge that connected to a floor socket labeled 'Hazardous Waste Drain'. Above the table on the wall, there were racks of glass bottles containing various colored and clear liquids.

Harold explained that while the material resisted most chemical reactions, making it very inert, stain-repellant, and generally non-absorbent, there was one solution they'd found that catalyzed a welding reaction when placed on the seam between two pieces of the material. He drew a small amount of the solution using a pipette from one of the larger bottles on the wall and demonstrated using two pieces of the fabric he'd cut on the laser cutter earlier. Laying the edges of the pieces together, Harold carefully applied a small amount of the solution using a small brush and gently pressed the seam together. "The bond forms almost immediately, so once the pieces are pressed together, you won't get much opportunity to correct a mistake. It's not unlike using contact cement," Harold said, pausing occasionally between words as he concentrated on making the seam smooth and clean. Tricia was impressed with the skill and precision with which he worked. *He must've had lots of practice doing this*, she surmised.

Finishing with the seam, he went on, "Now that the seam is done, it only needs to set for a few minutes. The seam will be quite strong at that point, but any real stress should wait for about 24 hours for the bonding process to be fully complete." he gave the seam a quick but gentle tug, and already, the two pieces almost looked like they'd never been cut. Jamal let out a low whistle, expressing the collective impression of the whole team. Harold smiled, "Yeah, we think it's pretty cool too."

With that, it was nearly lunchtime, and the team collectively decided it was a good time for a break. Harold gladly took the team up on its offer to treat him to lunch as a thank-you for the time he was spending with them. They walked over to a nearby campus cafeteria. It turned out that Harold and Alex shared a fandom of old movies, so the team spent the balance of the time talking movie trivia. Tricia was happy to see the team enjoying themselves so much. It had been a big week, and a fun change of pace like this was great for the team...*and me, too*, she had to admit.

After lunch, it was the team's chance to try out what they'd learned. Using the detector Jamal had brought, the team took turns making templates for pieces of a cover, cutting the material, and putting it together using the bonding solvent. Each of them, including Tricia, had a chance to try each step. After about an hour, they had assembled their first prototype cover. After it had set for a while, Harold assured them it was solid enough to try it out on the device.

Jamal slid the cover over the device while Steve connected his commpad wirelessly to the unit, allowing them to monitor the performance of the unit. Jamal crossed his fingers and pressed the button, initiating the detection diagnostic sequence. The first pass of the diagnostic tested the electronic noise contamination, and the team was ecstatic to see that the noise was significantly suppressed by their new creation.

The second stage of the test was on the detection sensitivity, but their excitement shattered when the detector failed to report any activity. Jamal's face sank. Tricia's stomach dropped too, but she did her best to not show it.

Harold leaned in. "Haven't you forgotten something?" he cajoled, holding out a rubber band.

"Ugh," Jamal exclaimed, slapping his palm to his forehead, "Of course, it has to fit tightly to the detector."

*Oh, of course, we can't forget the snug fit, can we?"* Tricia joked to herself.

Jamal took the rubber band and tightened the cover materials up against the detector plate. He re-ran the diagnostic sequence, and this time, Tricia could see the material contract over the detector face the same way it contracted on her midriff during her test. She glanced at Harold. He crossed his arms, smiled, and nodded back. *Looks like he was expecting that after all*, she noticed.

The team let out a small cheer as Steve's commpad reported a substantial increase in detector sensitivity. They re-ran the test a couple more times just to make sure, but it seemed their project was quite successful.

With a new detector cover in hand, the team assembled at the break area in the front of the lab for their second celebration in as many days, happily clinking bottles and mugs of various beverages. Now that she had a good grasp of how to work with the material, there was still one major question on Tricia's mind: would she have to settle for a boring, dull, monochromatic costume, or could she have the black and yellow that her heart was set on? Mentally, she crossed her fingers.

"So, Harold, does it only come in gray?"

"Um, why do we care about the color, Doctor C?" Jamal asked.

Tricia paused for a second, hunting for a plausible answer. "Well, Jamal," she finally said matter-of-factly, "if every piece of equipment is just gray, we are going to have a hard time telling it all apart, aren't we? If we could maybe color code the covers, we could easily identify the equipment without, well, lifting up its skirt, right?"

Jamal nodded, and the team laughed. Underneath, Tricia felt relieved by that bit of quick thinking.

"Unfortunately, no. It always comes out gray when it's made." Harold said, obviously aware he was likely disappointing her and the team. Tricia's stomach fluttered a bit.

"But," he continued, "we did find a way to color it." Tricia perked up.

Harold explained that the material's composition resisted dying and other conventional coloring methods. It could be painted, but it didn't take long for the paint to wear off and chip away. However, by using a highly diluted bath of the bonding solution and a colorant— they'd found that ordinary acrylic paint seemed to work quite well—the material would bond with the colorant. In fact, it didn't just adhere to the surface of the material; it blended through the entire thickness of the material, essentially turning the gray material completely into the desired color.

"Can you show us how to do that?" Tricia asked excitedly.

Harold nodded, looking at his watch. "Sure, we have time I suppose. I have some basic acrylics in the back. Anybody have a favorite color?" The team chose a couple of simple colors; Tricia made sure black and yellow were on the list.

Harold suggested someone cut a few yards of material for each color while he went back to get the tubes of acrylic: black, yellow, green, and purple. Nikki had heavily influenced the team on the last two. Steve and Alex cut some sections of material on the cutter while Harold prepared a few small tubs, mixing water, a small dab of the acrylic, and a pipette of the bonding solvent in each. He joked that it looked like they were dying Easter eggs but using ostrich eggs instead. Everyone snickered at that, and he put a swath of material in each tub to soak and set a timer. Tricia took very careful notes on the proportions he used; if she was going to "borrow" some of this material, she'd need to replace it. Granted, Harold was being very generous about all this, but her suit would take more than a few equipment covers and he—or worse, the entire team—might start asking unwanted questions if larger quantities of the colored material went missing.

The fabric only needed to soak for several minutes, and after the timer went off, Harold promptly took the material out of the colored baths with a pair of tongs. He explained that if it soaked too long, it could cause the material to start to bond to itself in the bath, leaving it wrinkled and unworkable. He gave each section a quick rinse in plain water to remove any remaining bonding solution and waved the team over to help carry the newly colored fabric. The colors in the fabric were very rich, and the sheen of the material really made them vivid. *This is going to look great*, Tricia thought to herself.

Harold, carrying the dripping pieces of material, then led the team toward a row of heating units against the far wall. They laid the material out in the heaters and set another timer for an hour. The low heat would both dry the material and help with the curing process, Harold explained.

"This is just amazing," Tricia told Harold on behalf of the team while they waited. "We can't thank you enough." The team murmured and nodded their heads in agreement. "What would be the best way to carry on making what we need without creating a lot of disruption and inconvenience for you and your team here?"

Harold smiled and thought for a second. "Well, you guys seemed comfortable working with the equipment, so I don't see any reason we can't just give you all general access to the lab for a period of time. There's another door that opens with a key code. Campus Security hates that we still have it, but it's there, and you can use it whenever you want." He wrote down the code on a piece of scrap paper and handed it to Tricia. "Best to come in late afternoons or after hours if you want to work on your own. If you need to come in the day, just call first to make sure nothing's going on. I'll go ahead and fill out the departmental transfer for the material so it's all above board and get that submitted to the research lab administrative office for you."

The team thanked him once again for all the help. He smiled, shaking all their hands. Tricia shook his hand last.

"Thanks again, Harold, for all the help. I can't tell you what it means to me...and the team, of course."

"Glad to help, Tricia. Anytime. Don't hesitate to call."

The team was already at the door, holding it open, waiting for her. She turned to follow, humming that old song again.

*This couldn't have gone more perfectly if I'd tried,* she thought, closing the lab door behind. *But don't get ahead of yourself,* she reminded herself; she'd been here before only to fail, and Tricia knew that she must not let her excitement or optimism get ahead of her pragmatism again.

# Persona

Her hand slipped again for the umpteenth time. The stench of the solvent permeated the air. Tricia reached up and wiped her nose with the back of her hand, grateful there was a dry spot still on her gloves. "I don't remember this stuff smelling this badly earlier today," she muttered under her breath. Trying to work quickly, she realigned the seam she was working on and kept working.

*Harold definitely had a LOT of practice doing this,* she thought, huffing the hair back out of her face.

Tricia hadn't intended to do any assembly of her costume tonight when she snuck into the lab, but setting up the patterns on the laser cutter and cutting out the panels had gone far more smoothly than she'd anticipated, so she decided to keep working. The larger workspace in the lab was extremely helpful as well. No matter how compact and lightweight the material was, working on a full-body suit, with all its curves and odd shapes, was just awkward.

Her hand slipped again. *I may regret that decision before the night is over.* Tricia swallowed another slight pang of guilt.

When she arrived and typed in the keycode Harold had given them, she had paused for quite a while. She knew she was taking advantage of Harold's generosity and her position at the lab, but she tried to assure herself that appropriating a few yards of cloth— very rare and expensive cloth— would ultimately serve the greater good.

*Yeah, just keep telling yourself that, Trish,* she mocked herself accusingly and kept working the seam.

Just as she finished joining the rest of the seam, her commpod chimed in her ear and spoke, "It's time to check the drying unit, Tricia."

*Ah, the extra material must be ready,* she thought, hoping it had come out. Knowing she was going to be using most if not all, of the black and yellow they had made that afternoon, the first thing Tricia did when she got to the lab was color a new batch of black and yellow to cover her tracks. *Fingers crossed,* she prayed as she opened the drying unit and inspected the material inside.

*Perfect!* She breathed a sigh of relief. The new batch not only looked great but was a perfect match for the material she was using from the afternoon. She laid it out on top of the counter to let the unit cool while she finished working. *All I have to do is rearrange it back in the unit before I leave and hopefully no one, especially Harold, will be any the wiser come Monday morning.*

As she worked, she also to admit she was enjoying the thrill of the secrecy, of painting outside the lines, much more than she thought she would. Tricia had always thought of herself as creative and inventive, but neither she, nor people close to her, would ever call her a 'rule breaker'. *Yet here I am, having a blast. Marni would fall over if she saw me now.*

Anxiousness started to crowd out the thrill, though, when Tricia heard a banging sound out in the hallway. *Must be time for the nightly cleaning crews*, she surmised. *I need to get out of here ASAP. I don't want to have to explain what I'm doing to anyone, even the custodians.* Fortunately, she'd finished the last seam and was just doing the final bit of cleaning up and covering her tracks, which included downloading the patterns from the cutter to a memory stick she'd brought with her and erasing them from the device. There was no way to completely wipe away all traces of what she'd done, but she was hopeful if she did her job, no one would have any reason to dig any deeper and find any either.

The banging of the carts in the hall was getting closer, so she picked up the pace. Tricia carefully folded her suit, along with other pieces for the mask and gloves she'd cut but not yet assembled, into her bag. She also tucked a small glass jar of the solvent into the side pocket of her bag. With luck, she figured she could finish some of the smaller pieces where she wasn't as likely to get caught.

Tricia took one last look around to make sure she hadn't forgotten anything. The machines were shut down. *Check.* The vats were clean and drying right where Harold had left them earlier today. *Check.* Colored batches rearranged in the heating unit. *Check, check, and double check.* Satisfied, Tricia clicked off the work light and let herself out the side door, away from the cleaning crews. Tomorrow, she'd know just how much her efforts had paid off.

The next morning, she woke up very excited to see the results of the previous evening's labors. Her suit was still waiting for her on the table with one addition; Rascal was lying right in the middle of it. As soon as Tricia walked into the room, she started mewling and making biscuits on the black and yellow nest she had made. Tricia chuckled to herself, *Well, if it can't stand up to the cat's claws, it's probably not going to get the job done anyway.*

"Oh, I'm sorry, Rascal," she crooned, picking the cat up gently. Rascal tried to dig her claws into the fabric, but the suit just fell away as Tricia hoisted her up to her shoulder and started scratching her head and neck. "I've been neglecting you lately, haven't I?" Rascal purred, soaking up the attention. Tricia quickly put some food into Rascal's bowl, and while Rascal proceeded to gobble down her breakfast, Tricia picked up her suit from the table and flicked off the layer of cat hairs.

She tugged on some of the seams, testing their strength. They were solid. In fact, they were so clean and smooth she could barely see them. *This really is beautiful material*, she reflected admiringly.

*I know Harold said to wait twenty-four hours for it to fully cure, but I promise to be careful.* Giving in to her excitement, she quickly put on the undersuit, took a deep breath, and slipped on the suit itself.

The silkiness of the material allowed it to slip on very easily, much more easily than the material she had previously tried. It felt like a perfect fit, gliding over her skin and hugging her just enough to be snug but not constricting. She didn't even have to adjust or tuck it into place like the other suits she'd made. It just fit. *Almost as if it was made for me*, she snickered to herself.

She walked over to the mirror and did a quick top-to-bottom check. "Yep...yep...not too bad...not too bad at all," she murmured as she turned left to right, then turned around and looked over her shoulder at her back and legs, finally pausing at her hips. *Yeah, not so bad,* she thought, but looking again at her exposed figure in the mirror, a blush of modesty washed over her. *But I think I am going to need that cape after all.*

Taking a deep breath, she whispered, "Now for the real test..."

Tricia opened herself to the currents swirling around her, but, to her surprise, they didn't just flow in. They rushed in like the surf breaking before a storm. She inhaled sharply with the sensation. She also felt the material contract slightly, sculpting itself to her body. The feel of it was luxurious and intense.

For her, it was like swimming naked in the ocean, with no barriers, no constraints. Just her and the currents, surging and seething around and through her. Her hair had shifted to the black and blonde streaks and flowed out of the top of her mask down to her shoulders. "Wow," she said under her breath, struggling to absorb what she saw and what she felt. "This is just...incredible. *This...that...*is someone entirely new."

She went into the main room and retrieved one of her pieces of iron rebar. Effortlessly, she tied it into a knot. With a satisfied chuckle, she straightened it again. Tricia pulled forth the dark energy. Gone was any reluctance it had shown before. It obeyed her more smoothly and precisely than ever before, pushing the couch several feet across the floor effortlessly. Smiling, Tricia pulled the darkness back into a shield, which formed fluently into a precise circle in front of her. She quickly ran through a few of her class *kata*; her powers responded as if she wasn't wearing anything at all, no binding, no sluggishness. It was like they had been set free and felt nothing short of wonderful.

Tricia stopped, took a deep breath, and reached within herself. She focused her mind on all the power flowing through her far more effortlessly than she'd ever experienced before. She opened her eyes, took another deep breath, and pressed back the torrent. Her power reluctantly abated. She looked at Rascal sitting in the bedroom doorway, alternating between watching her and licking her paws. She knelt down to scratch the cat's head again. "Well, fuzzball, it took a while, but I think we're finally there."

Thrilled with the costume, she carefully peeled it off and hung it up with a hanger on the shower curtain rod in the bathroom to let the solvent finish curing as Harold had recommended. Tricia then opened the browser on her laptop and opened the shopping website for a particular pair of very high-end running trainers she'd been researching. They were expensive—she swallowed hard at the price—but two pairs of tattered trainers sitting by the door had proven to her that conventional shoes could not take the punishment of her speed and strength. She had come this far, so there was no sense in settling for lousy shoes.

The store site showed them backordered. *It's ok. I can wait a little while,* she decided. *I still have plenty to do to finish this costume.* The suit itself was ready, but she would still need the other accessories—the mask, gloves, and now a cape—to make it complete. Tricia was already working some ideas for the mask and gloves but finishing them would still take some time. She pressed 'Submit Order' and closed the laptop.

Marni executed the takedown and rolled Tricia over, locking in the armbar, just as the exercise they were working on called for. Class with Marni that week gave Tricia a welcome break from the hectic pace she'd been setting as well. She had actually been looking forward to it, secretly glad it wasn't the intense advanced class this week. She had a tendency to obsess over new projects, so slowing things down a bit gave her a chance to catch her breath and focus on some other parts of her life for a change.

Tricia winced as Marni secured the hold. *Wow, she's really got this one down,* Tricia admitted and patted the ground to tap out.

"Not so fast," Marni said, keeping a tight grip on Tricia's arm. She pursed her lips and looked up like she was thinking. "Say 'Marni is a beautiful goddess," she instructed.

"Seriously?" Tricia asked. She tried to turn to stare Marni down, but her back was pinned tightly to the floor.

"Say it," Marni drawled and pulled down on the hold slightly, putting a bit more pressure on Tricia's elbow for emphasis.

Tricia winced again. *I probably had this coming,* she thought. "Ok, ok," she said, and then, in a mocking voice, "Marni is a beautiful goddess."

"...who should be worshipped and adored by all," Marni added on and applied a bit more pressure to Tricia's bent wrist.

"Ow! Ugh!" Tricia exclaimed, rolling her eyes. "Who should be worshipped and adored by all."

"That's more like it," Marni said approvingly. She released the hold and sat up on her knees with her feet tucked under her, facing Tricia. Tricia laid on her back for several more seconds, rubbing her strained elbow, before slowly rolling up to sit cross-legged across from Marni.

Tricia looked up at Marni sitting in front of her, looking very pleased with herself, and couldn't help but smirk back. "I think you are enjoying this just a little too much," she teased, shaking her arm out.

Marni put on a playfully evil grin. "You know how much I like it when they submit," she said mischievously.

They looked at each other and giggled. The giggles turned into muffled snorts, which quickly escalated into uncontrollable belly laughs. Normally, this wouldn't have been that funny, but in this moment, it was absolutely nothing short of hysterical. In no time at all, they were bent over, holding their sides, laughing uncontrollably.

The laughs, though, were quickly cut short by a booming deep voice. "Haskell! Carling!" Sensei called out from across the room. "I don't know what's so funny over there, but let's see if you find twenty knuckle push-ups to be amusing. Class, help the ladies count them out."

Shooting each other one last look, they assumed the starting position on their toes, feet spread apart, with fisted knuckles firmly planted on the hardwood floor, and started their penance with the class counting each pushup in Japanese. With each pushup, their knuckles dug into the unforgiving wooden floor, and it didn't take very many to completely dispel any remaining urge to giggle.

As Marni and Tricia were packing up after class, they heard Sensei Tim call out, "Carling. Haskell. Can I have a word?"

Marni gave Tricia a brief 'oops, we are in trouble now' smirk, and they walked over to face the music.

Sensei Tim looked at them both, a small grin on his face. "You two were the life of the party tonight, weren't you?"

"It's my fault, Sensei," Tricia admitted. "I made a joke, and I guess it just got a bit out of hand." Marni shrugged and nodded.

"Ok. I do like to see students enjoying their time in class, but try to keep it under control in the future. Another disruption like that, and you'll owe me twice as many pushups, understood?"

"Yes, Sensei," Tricia and Marni said in unison, feeling a little sheepish.

"On another note, besides enjoying yourselves more, which I have noticed and do sincerely appreciate, it's also obvious you two are putting in a lot more effort, too. It's showing. You both are starting to show more of what I think is your real potential."

Marni beamed. "Thank you, Sensei!"

"If you two think you are ready, I'd like to schedule you for your next belt test week after next. I believe you've finally found the right attitude, and you've got the techniques in pretty good shape. Practice a bit between now and then, and you should do all right."

Surprised, Marni blurted out, "Of course, Sensei. That would be great."

He looked at Tricia. "What about you, Carling? Think you're ready?"

Tricia suddenly realized Sensei had been right all along when he told her that if she took it more seriously, Marni would come along as well. It wasn't just the extra classes. She was taking it all more seriously now, and it was rubbing off on Marni.

"Of course, Sensei. Thank you," she replied.

"Great. I'll put you down on the schedule. The test content is on the class site, so look it over and practice."

Marni smiled, nodded, and, after giving him a small bow, turned to go.

Tricia also gave him a bow, and as she made eye contact, he smiled and gave her a knowing wink and a nod, returning the bow in kind.

Tricia cursed under her breath and hit the 'Cancel' button just in time to avoid punching a hole in the processor. She took off her glasses and rubbed the bridge of her nose. *Alex is so much better at this than I am. I wish I could ask her to help me with this.*

Even if she wanted to, Tricia couldn't ask Alex for help. Alex, and the rest of the team, were over at the MatSci lab having "Craft Time," as they called it. They were still working on a set of covers using Harold's miracle fabric for the equipment to use in their upcoming experiment.

The team was dividing time between designing and setting up for the next phase of their experiment and working over in the MatSci lab. Tricia usually went along with them, but today, she figured it would be good for team building if they did some of it themselves.

Selfishly, it also gave her some private time in the lab to tinker on her own personal projects without burning the midnight oil all the time. In all honesty, the pace she was keeping was starting to catch up with her, and she knew, superpowers or not, she'd need to find time to relax here and there before she got completely burned out.

Tricia had discovered the solution for her mask problem in a scrapped VR headset she found in Alex's parts recycling bin at the back of the lab. A pair of the headset flex-plate lenses and the supporting micro-electronics were spread out on the mat in front of her.

Getting the components working again had been a fairly simple matter. While the swirling and pulsing she saw in her vision when using her powers helped her visualize the energy flowing around her, after she almost took a bullet practicing up at The Ridge, she knew she needed to find a way to make them less distracting. She still had not yet figured out if those patterns she saw served some purpose or were just a side-effect she'd have to tolerate, but she had remembered how the polarized sunglasses she'd used during her confrontation behind Lehman Hall had helped diminish the effect and wanted something that would work similarly without the darkening qualities.

Not only did a simple tweak to the polarizing filter give her what she needed, but the lenses themselves were packed with a variety of other potentially useful features such as night vision enhancement, a head-up display connection for her commpod, and they could dynamically correct for her far-sightedness. *Superheroes need to read the fine print, too.*

The only task in front of her now was to put in a micro-cable that would allow her to move the electronics pad back behind her ear in the mask. The electronics fit fine in the original headset's hard frame, but in her mask, the discomfort from the electronics pressing on her face or forehead was a non-starter.

*Come on, Trish,* she thought, shaking out her hands and pumping herself up, *it's not rocket science. It's only a cable. You can do this.* Carefully, she realigned the electronics pad and the cable in the computer-controlled electronics connection splicer and reset the program for attaching the micro-cable. The laser was the only instrument they had for joining circuits this small, but as she'd nearly just experienced, when it was mishandled, the splicer was quite capable of ruining them as well.

The precheck gave her a green light, and she pushed the button. A few flashes later, the unit signaled it was done, and she slid out the newly joined cable, lenses, and electronics. *Looks good,* she thought, carefully inspecting her, and the machine's, handiwork. *Only one way to really know, though.*

Taking a pair of safety goggles, Tricia taped the flex-plate lenses to the inside of the goggle's eyepieces and gently put them over her eyes, carefully stringing the electronics pad back behind her head. She pressed the electronics pad up against the skin behind her ear and, holding her breath, carefully drew in a small amount of her power.

*Yahoo!* she thought when the visors snapped into life. The swirls in her vision sharpened into vividly crisp wavelets of energy. *Much less distracting.* The visor's control interface glowed in the upper right of her field of vision. Using specific eye movements, she quickly cycled through some of the other modes just to make sure it was working. Glancing down at the workspace, Tricia was happy to see she could clearly read the print on the papers piled there without her prescription glasses. "Perfect. Just perfect." She said admiringly.

Glancing around to make sure she was alone, she reached down into her bag and pulled out her mask piece. The gloves almost fell out as she extracted the mask—*Nope, you stay in there. I'll finish you another day*—and she stuffed them back in.

Delicately, she stretched the mask down over her head, trapping the safety goggles in the eye holes and tucking the electronics pad and cable over and behind her ear. After settling the mask fully over her head and neck, she pulled her hair free and removed the ponytail, letting her hair spill out of the top and down to her shoulders. She then drew on her power and took a look at herself in the small mirror on the workstation.

"The transformation is remarkable," she whispered to her reflection, turning left and right, "and honestly kinda weird." The natural yellowish tint to the flexi-plate lenses blended perfectly with the colors in her mask and the striking blonde and ebony streaks in her hair. "Weirdness aside, it couldn't be more perfect."

As she slid the mask off, again, careful not to pull apart the electronics, she realized she'd need an inner lining on the mask to trap and secure the lenses and electronics. *This mask needs to go on quickly,* she thought. *It can't be this putzy and slow in real action.* She sighed. *That means another unscheduled trip to the Material Sciences lab to create a lining. At least then,* she conceded with a shrug. *I can attach the mask to the rest of the suit.*

*Meh,* she remembered. *I need to go anyway, mask or not, for this.* Tricia reached down into her bag and pulled out the package that had arrived from the cosplay supply site the other day. The package contained two important pieces to finishing her new persona.

Tricia folded the mask and tucked it and the lens electronics into her bag. She opened the package and took out the pattern she'd purchased for a knee-length cape. She spread it out on the table in front of her. The cape was reversible with an integrated tuck-away hood she could pull up to cover her head, helping her stay out of sight when needed. A cape that could help her either blend in or stand out, whichever a given situation required. With a quick flick of her wrists, it could be black or yellow. Dark or light.

In the palm of her other hand, she held the circular resin magnetic clasp she had also ordered. The clasp, when finished, would attach the cape to her suit magnetically, making it easy to don or remove. The clasp would bear her insignia, her symbol: a gleaming oval of white shining with two semi-oval waves, one on each side, over a field of black. A light in the darkness. The emblem for a Beacon of hope.

# Primed

The floorboards groaned and crackled as Tricia slammed her hand into it, her frustration triggering an unintended burst of strength. *Harold had said the suit's camouflage could be triggered with the right electromagnetic frequency,* she thought, hugging her knees to her chest in exasperation, *but I'll be fracked if I can find it.*

She pushed herself up off the floor and ran her fingers through her hair. *Just one more infuriating disappointment on top of another,* she fumed.

Tricia had come up to The Ridge this weekend full of hope, excited to try out her new suit. It didn't take long, though, for that hope and excitement to collapse. While her new cape came out beautifully, and she was thrilled with how it completed the look of the costume, it only took a few attempts at running through some drills and exercises to show her that adding the cape created a whole new element to master.

*Show me what a pain it is in the very thing it's supposed to be covering up, I mean. Pffft.*

More than once, as she turned, the cape would twist around her, trapping her arm or catching her leg on a kick, and mess up the entire flow of the kata she was practicing. After spending a few hours fighting with it, she decided to take a break, questioning if the aesthetic (and the modesty, to be honest) was worth the aggravation.

Despite the frustration of feeling like she had to learn nearly every technique again from scratch, she had started to make some progress. However, it was clear to her that it was going to take a lot of practice to make the movement of the cape feel natural so she could use it without it interfering with, or worse, compromising her movements, especially in a fight. The cape still lay on the back of the couch where she'd tossed it in a huff.

After lunch, she had decided to set the cape aside for a while longer and, instead, experiment a bit with the mimetic properties of the material. *I should have found a way to ask Harold more about it when he mentioned it,* she thought, stretching her arm across her chest, *but at the time, it just didn't make sense to ask about it.* In truth, it not only didn't make sense, but she was sure asking about a feature that was almost in direct conflict with its use for the equipment would have led to questions she couldn't have answered.

To her right, George, the combat dummy, scowled at her from the middle of the floor. "What are *you* looking at?" she taunted it, turning in its direction. George just glared back.

Distracted momentarily from her irritation, Tricia smirked in amusement. "You got something to say?" she asked it, giving it a poke with dark energy. George wobbled but stayed silent.

Tricia grinned more. "Come on. Out with it." She goaded the silent foam mannequin, casting a small shield and bumping him with it. Again, he rocked back and forth but refused to answer her.

Taunting George yet again, she pooled a larger shield. "What's the mat..."

*Wait...what?*

Where the dark energy was pooling on her arm, she felt...a tingling. *No, not tingling...humming.* Looking down, she could see some of the dark energy permeating her suit, and where it did, there was a definite vibration.

*It's like striking a tuning fork or plucking a guitar string*, she thought. *Not with sound, but with energy...*

*A resonance frequency?*

She shuddered a bit at the sight of those dark eddies passing into her suit. The last time she'd turned the flows inward, she was sure she was going to shatter. The memory made her want to recoil, but she restrained the urge to pull them back. *If it's just the suit, I might be ok?*

Holding her breath, Tricia directed more of the dark energy into the fabric, careful to avoid touching herself with it, and the vibration strengthened, became more stable, more precise. *Yes, just like a tuning fork. Could this be the frequency Harold meant?* she wondered.

Focusing on that precise frequency, she drew on the flows of light around her and began twisting them until they matched the thrum, the tone of what she was feeling. When she had it, she released the dark energy, pushed the light into the suit, and felt the entire suit *shift.*

Opening her eyes slowly, Tricia could see the suit was shimmering, like warm air above the pavement on a hot day. She increased the flow, and to her amazement, the suit began to look like a mirage, shifting and conforming to the colors and patterns of the cabin walls and floors around her. *This must've been what Harold was talking about,* she marveled, slowly rotating her hand and arm back and forth, watching the patterns and colors shift. *It's one of the most incredible things I've ever seen, and that's saying something.*

Tricia released the flow, and the suit instantly became fully opaque, returning to its original color and texture. She quickly tried to repeat the specific frequency again, but the suit did nothing. "Ugh, lost it," she muttered.

Once again, she touched the suit with dark energy to pluck the string, and once again, she matched the energy flow with the suit's reverberation, causing the suit to shimmer, cloaking her.

*This is going to be like a tone-deaf person learning to sing,* she thought, *but it's going to be like my speed and strength. I need to find the "feel" of this ability before I can call on it.*

Whenever she'd gotten to this point with her other powers, Tricia was reminded of her childhood fascination with magic. As a young girl, she was determined to learn to do magic tricks, so she practiced sleight-of-hand routines until her fingers ached. She palmed coins, flipped poker chips, cut cards, all of it, relentlessly, but no matter which technique she was learning, her pattern was the same; she would fail over and over and over until she finally did it right that first time. Once she did a trick and knew what it felt like, she could then repeat it and, eventually, master it. Even to this day, she could still flip a stack of poker chips in her hand, one at a time, without thinking about it. Her powers were like her tricks; the *feel* of them was essential to her mastering them.

The same had been true of her speed, then for the light, heat, and later the levitation, pushing, and shields. *The same will be true for this,* she thought, encouraged. *Once I get it, I'll have it.*

*Not an entirely frustrating day after all,* she decided, but before she could tap the dark energy for another try, her commpod chimed in her ear, startling her. She jumped a bit and put her hand on her chest. Shaking her head, she asked the device, "Who is it?"

In its slightly mechanized female voice, the commpod responded, "It's Marni, Tricia."

Tricia released the flows and tapped the commpod. "Hi, Marni. How are you?"

"Oh, Hi Trish! Did I catch you at a good time?"

"Sure, Marn. I'm just up at The Ridge for the weekend."

"You sound exhausted, Trish. Everything ok? You aren't overdoing it, are you?"

Trish huffed a bit. "No, no, I'm fine. I've just been doing a lot up here today, but yeah, I'm going to sleep good tonight." She stretched her arms up over her head and grunted a bit. "Really good. What's up?"

"No worries, Trish, I'll make this quick. Could we get together for lunch, maybe sometime this coming week? Would you have time?"

Starting to nose through the refrigerator, Tricia replied, dividing her attention between Marni and what she could pull together for dinner, "Of course, anytime. Glad to. Anything special going on I should know about?"

"No, nothing special," Marni reassured her, "but I have a little problem at work, and I think you're just the person who can help out."

Tricia was impatient to keep playing with this new discovery but forced herself to be patient and hear out Marni's unexpected suggestion. "I am? Well, you have definitely piqued my curiosity. I'm looking forward to hearing more about it."

"Awesome! Very exciting, Trish!!" Marni exclaimed. "Hey, sounds like you want to get on with something so I can let you go. I'll shoot you a message later, and we can set something up, maybe Wednesday or Thursday?"

"Yeah, sure. Sounds great, Marni. Looking forward to it. Take care!"

"Toodles, Trish. See you later this week," and Marni hung up the call.

Tricia tapped her commpod to close the call on her end. *Well, that sounds interesting*, Tricia mused and once again touched her suit with dark energy, producing the vibration—the specific tone—that she would need to memorize and master to add the suit's mimetic properties to her arsenal of abilities.

Tricia watched the door close behind Alex and Jamal as they headed out for an early lunch. She checked her watch; her lunch with Marni was on the later side of the day, leaving her with just a couple of hours to finish sorting out the augmentation she was working on for her gloves.

*It really needs to be today,* she thought, putting some pressure on herself, *if I'm going to make today the last visit to the craft shop over at the MatSci Lab.*

She wiggled her toes inside her new trainers. They had come the previous day, so she'd decided to test them out by wearing them a bit before putting in the work of adapting them to her costume. If all went well, she planned to finish the final pieces sometime after lunch with Marni.

Tricia pulled some prototype components she'd been tinkering with on and off from her workstation drawer. The goal she was working toward was simple: more precise focus with her heat projection abilities. She had no problem creating general fields of intense heat, but so far, at least, concentrating that heat into a form that she could more accurately direct, something more *useful*, had eluded her.

As with the enhancements for her mask, she had found her solution, or a potential one anyway, right in her own lab. The high-resolution holographic systems depended on nano-collimators to reshape the lasers and focus them into even more highly organized and compact beams that would then be shaped into the desired holographic forms.

Tricia turned her glove inside out and delicately started fitting a small array of these nano-collimators to the inside surface. *I'm no laser by any stretch of the imagination, but these little beauties should still be able to help me focus my heat*, she thought as she carefully positioned the tiny components with a set of tweezers, *and, since they are self-contained, I don't even need a power source.*

As she worked, she again reflected on the fact that each piece she made was more than just another component of her costume. Each piece was a step towards her new persona, towards becoming a new force for good for the city, and she drew strength and resolve from that knowledge.

Tricia checked her watch again. *Still plenty of time.* She placed a small scrap of the suit fabric over the end of her finger and, positioning the nano-collimators gently on the tip of her finger, she rolled the glove finger right-side out over her own finger. She then wadded the rest of the glove into a ball and held it in her palm with her remaining fingers and thumb.

She held her finger up in front of her and gently curled and flexed it, testing the feel. *Looks good*, she thought, admiring her handiwork, *can't even tell there's anything in there.* Tricia then surveyed the lab. "Hmm, now, what can I test it on?" she mumbled to herself, considering her options.

The soda can on Nikki's desk caught her attention. Tricia grinned, her mischievous side getting the better of her. "Howdy, partner," she said in a heavy Southwestern drawl, pointed her finger at the can, and pushed a trickle of energy through the end of her finger.

At first, nothing happened, so she paused and tried again, carefully channeling a bit more power. Again, nothing happened, but when she pushed a little more for the third time, a narrow beam of liquid white light abruptly leaped from her finger, neatly punching a half-inch hole through the can. "Yeehaw," she remarked as she heard the sizzle and watched some caramelized brown ooze trickle out of the hole onto the desk. Her grin evaporated, though, when she looked past the can and saw a dark spot sizzling and smoking on the far wall next to the equipment storage rack. *Ooops.*

Fixated on the smoldering wall, Tricia carefully peeled off the glove. She then fetched a wet dish rag from the break area, and, on her way to inspect the wall closer, she scooped what was left of the can, along with the gooey caramelized soda syrup, off Nikki's desk and into her own trash can. *I'll definitely need to dispose of that on the way out,* she noted to herself.

Tricia then walked over to the wall and inspected the charred spot she'd made on the wall. "This is definitely going to take a little practice," she told herself, flicking her hair back out of her eyes, "but it works like a charm." Having no desire to try to explain the burn mark to the team, she pulled on a bit of her strength and slid the storage rack down a few inches to cover the spot on the wall and hoped the singed smell in the air would clear before they got back.

"Time to leave for lunch with Marni Haskell," her commpod interrupted. Tricia tapped the commpod to acknowledge the reminder and gently packed her work into her bag, along with a few sketches she'd made for an inner glove lining she could easily cut and assemble later. *That lining will not only hold the nano-collimators in place but will add some much-needed padding for her fingers and palm,* she jotted mentally and headed out to meet Marni.

Tricia arrived at the restaurant a few minutes early. She again flexed her feet in her new shoes. *Gotta admit, these are really nice*, she thought, admiring them. *I may need to get a pair to wear when I'm not fighting bad guys.*

She expected to just wait outside, but glancing in the window, Tricia saw Marni already sitting at a table on the far side of the restaurant. She shrugged to herself and went in. As soon as she cleared the door, Marni saw her and waved. *Something must really be up*, she thought, waving back. *Marni's never early for anything.*

Sitting next to Marni was a striking early middle-aged woman. She was wearing very fashionably wide, black-rimmed glasses and had her deep black hair pulled up in a low, twisted chignon just above her neck. Everything about her, from her hair and makeup down to her shoes, said smart, practical, and classy. Tricia felt positively scruffy by comparison. This woman looked very familiar, but Tricia couldn't quite place her.

Tricia wove herself through the dining area and sat down across from Marni next to the window. Marni gave a small gesture toward the woman sitting next to her. "Trish, this is Doctor Rene Thornton. Rene, Doctor Tricia Carling."

"So pleased to meet you," Tricia replied, finally realizing who this woman was. "Director of the Advanced Genetics Lab on campus, right?"

"Spot on." Rene acknowledged, smiling. "You might've seen me in one of the ESG newsletters, too; I'm on the Environmental, Social, and Governance Advocacy Council."

"Yes, yes, I have. I also saw the talk you gave last year at the Research Group Symposium."

"And I saw yours as well," Rene recalled. "I was impressed. There is a lot of innovative potential in your work."

The waiter came around just then, gave them menus, and asked if anyone wanted anything to drink.

Rene took the lead, "We'll have water around," looking at the others to confirm. They all nodded. "And I believe it is five o'clock somewhere, so I'll have a martini done correctly, very dirty, with two olives, one black and one green...no pimento, please."

Marni held up her hand. "Lemonade for me, please. I'm on call at the hospital this afternoon."

"Hmm, why not? I have some time," Tricia answered next. "The house Chianti, if you please."

"Sigh. You researchy types have the easy life," Marni quipped. Tricia and Rene looked at each other, smiled, and played into Marni's teasing by nodding vigorously.

The waiter thanked them and left. All three women picked up the menus and started browsing. After a minute or two, without looking up, Rene smirked and broke the silence, "So, a brunette, a blonde, and a redhead walk into a bar..."

Tricia lowered her menu and put on a mock puzzled expression. "Hmmm, why do I think I'm about to become a punchline?"

They all looked at each other and laughed.

A few minutes later, the waiter came back with their drinks and took their orders. Taking a sip of water, Marni kicked off the conversation, "So, Trish, this is not entirely a social call. Do you remember when we talked a while back about this tiger team I was asked to join? The one about the infertility cases?"

Tricia nodded.

"I asked Rene to join us because she and her department have been working in collaboration with my genetics treatment center at the hospital for a long time now. It's been a great partnership. She and her team have helped us with a number of difficult cases in the past, and she's also been collaborating with me and my team on this project, too."

"That's great!" Tricia remarked, "Have you turned anything up yet?"

Rene responded next, "Some, but we are at a bit of an impasse. Marni's team has been researching any pathology related to the genomes of the affected patients, but based on the data, I'm fairly convinced that we haven't thoroughly examined the physiology closely enough yet. I'm not ruling out something genetic, but so far, the data, in my opinion, just doesn't support a detailed investigation there quite yet. I've been advocating that we explore the imaging protocols in more depth before jumping to conclusions about the genomes."

Tricia nodded, looked at Marni—she expected some kind of reaction, but there was none—glanced back at Rene, and then at Marni again, still expecting some retort, but it seemed that Marni, uncharacteristically, was not going to push the matter.

Instead, Marni chose to jump straight to the point. "And that's where you come in, Trish. Taking Rene's recommendation, we turned back to the affected patients to take a closer look at their reproductive systems and the gametes themselves. The problem we have is that the imaging systems we have don't have the resolution we need to look at the details of the structures we think might be causing the problems."

Rene took over again, "I suggested the Advanced Optics and Imaging Lab might be able to help. Marni said she knew you, and voilà! Here we are, having a lovely lunch." She picked up her martini, gestured it toward them, and then took a sip.

Tricia thought for a moment, rubbing her chin, and then finally replied tentatively, "Pretty sure we can come up with something. To start with, I'll need the specs on the equipment your imaging teams are using. What resolution are you looking to achieve?"

"Sub-micron," Rene offered.

"Challenging, but not out of the question," Tricia responded, still processing the problem, "I have some time right now. We are between experiments, and the team has the ball on analyzing the last round of data and pulling the draft reports together. Have your imaging techs send me the specs on the equipment you have, and I can spend some time looking into how we might upgrade or augment the imaging system."

"We just need to do it soon," Marni cautioned. "Until we can take a closer look, we are almost at the end of what we can investigate further with what we have."

"Ok, but there's only one complication," Tricia responded hesitantly. "I'm still on probation, so anything new we take on at the lab must go through the proper channels. We need to do it by the book."

"Leave that to me," Rene chimed in. "I'll talk to Alexei and get it cleared. His niece was an intern in my lab a couple of years back, and, well, let's just say he owes me for getting her out of a situation after she mishandled some particularly nasty viruses." Rene winked at them.

Tricia grinned and nodded. Marni beamed, reaching across the table to grip Tricia's arm. "This is exciting! We don't get to work together very often. It'll be fun." She gave Tricia's arm an enthusiastic shake for emphasis.

"Yeah, it really will be," Tricia agreed, "I was thinking the same thing after you called."

"Count me in, too, ladies. I know a good party when I see one," Rene added, giving a wink for good measure.

As they toasted each other with their drinks, the waiter returned with their meals. Napkins went to laps, and they started eating. As she ate, Tricia's mind continued mulling over ideas. She also had to admit she was looking forward to working with someone like Rene. She didn't take to people easily, but she honestly felt there could be a really good connection between them and was optimistic about the potential.

As planned, Tricia had stopped by the MatSci lab after lunch, and when she got home that night, her bag contained an upgraded set of gloves and her new "boots". She thought what she had made more resembled a slipper-sock—a very expensive slipper-sock—than a boot, but she was hopeful it would be very easy to slide on; the laceless shoes adjusted to her feet automatically, and she could just unroll the top up her leg, rather like putting on a set of nylons. Plus, she'd added a couple extra layers of fabric to pad the gloves so they would protect her hands and conveniently avoid leaving fingerprints as well.

Rascal greeted her with a rub against her legs. Tricia bent down and scratched Rascal's back, making her arch and purr. Rascal then started sniffing the bag and pawing lightly at the top, trying to get inside.

"Sorry, girl," Tricia told her, picking up the bag and putting it on the table, "nothing for you in here." Rascal stared at her indignantly for a few seconds, flicked her tail, and went to inspect her food dish.

Tricia looked longingly at the bag. "I know I should wait," she debated with herself, "but if I'm *really* careful..."

"Oh, what the heck!" she decided and vanished into the bedroom to retrieve the rest of her suit.

It took her only a few minutes to strip off her street clothes and slip on her alter-ego, being extra careful with the newly worked gloves and boots. After slipping the mask up over her head, Tricia pulled out her ponytail, shook out her hair, and positioned herself in front of the full-length mirror, wearing her new suit in its entirety for the first time. She first turned left, then right, and then did a full turn, flaring her cape for effect. She smiled approvingly.

She drew in her power, savoring the sensation created by the ebb and flow of the energies around and through her, and mercilessly contorted a piece of rebar from her stash in the corner. Satisfied, she tossed the twisted metal onto the floor, and took one more long look in the mirror.

"There you are Beacon, finally. Now, all we need is a crime."

# Debut

Tricia was starting to think that the hardest part of being a superhero was actually finding a crime. She figured that, in a city of this size, it would be fairly easy, especially with what had happened on campus, but she'd been trying to intervene in one for nearly three weeks now and had no luck at all.

She had started by listening to the police bands. Her commpod had an application for that, but every time she heard something, it was either too far away, or the police were on the scene too soon. Clearly, just sitting around listening for some activity wasn't going to work if she really wanted to get engaged and make an impression doing it. Beacon needed to get ahead of it somehow.

It wasn't a complete waste, though. By listening, she started to get a feel for where crimes were routinely being committed and at what times of the day they were typically happening. Equipped with that, she'd started frequenting those places around those times to see if she could catch something in progress. She'd also decided that at some point, she could task one of the analytics AI bots at the lab to create some models of criminal activities that might help even more, but for now, all she needed was just one.

*Just one. How hard can it be?*

That's where she found herself today, walking around a seedier part of the city, keeping both a low profile and her eyes and ears open. A small gang of thieves had been hitting this area repeatedly over the last several weeks, so she was hoping she might get lucky. *Never thought I'd see the day I was wishing for a crime to happen,* she caught herself thinking, but without one, her superhero career wasn't getting off the ground.

Just in case, she was as prepared as she could be to act and act quickly. Her suit was light and comfortable enough, so she was already wearing it under her street clothing. That saved her from carrying any bags that would only slow her down. Plus, the last thing she needed was finally to stumble across a crime and make an idiot of herself with some clothing malfunction or miss it entirely because she couldn't get her boot on in time.

Her costume was fully covered by a tracksuit she'd picked up. The track pants were the long style that came down past her ankle and had very wide legs made to slide easily off over a pair of trainers. She had a light track jacket on over the top, fully zipped up to conceal the top part of her costume. Underneath, her mask was folded down her back, and the cape was wrapped around her, secured at her waist with the back support belt she used when she lifted. It would easily come off with a single hard yank. The only part she wasn't wearing was her gloves; they were rolled and zipped up inside the deep inner pockets of the jacket.

She had distressed the jacket and pants, so they looked a little worn and well-used. Any kind of brand-new, expensive-looking athletic gear would really stand out in this part of town and potentially make her a target. Nothing would be more ridiculously ironic than if she were the victim of the crime for which she was looking.

It was getting late in the afternoon, but still well ahead of the typical times crimes happened in this part of town, so she was just walking randomly, getting a feel for the neighborhood. She was concerned that her prominent blonde ponytail would also make her stand out, but no one seemed to pay any attention to her. She casually browsed some of the storefront windows; most were closed Sunday afternoon, and almost all of them had some kind of metal screen or fencing across the glass, confirming she was in the right part of town to find trouble.

Tricia was standing in front of what looked like a pawn shop, admiring an antique necklace in the window. She wasn't much of a jewelry buff, but it looked just like one she remembered seeing her grandmother wear when she was little.

The sudden clattering of an alarm bell somewhere down the block rudely interrupted her fond memories of cookies and mashed potatoes. She turned to look. *Seems my luck is about to change,* she thought as she saw others look and start to wander towards what looked like a jewelry shop at the far end of the building. Her stomach clenched a little, but it was now or never, and she was determined it was going to be now.

With the people around her distracted, she ducked to her left into the little side alley. Seeing it was deserted, Tricia drew on her power—more difficult in this track outfit, but it was enough—and deftly leaped up to the roof of the low plaza building. She ran down to the end of the building, careful to stay out of sight of people on the street, and looked over the edge. Sure enough, there was a beaten-up car parked in the side lot of the shopping plaza with a shabby, rough-looking guy sitting in the driver's seat having a smoke. Tricia rapidly peeled off the tracksuit and, with nothing to obstruct it, felt her power flood into her. She pulled on her mask and gloves just in time to see another man leaving the side door of the building carrying a heavy canvas bag and starting to make his way toward the car.

Beacon took a deep breath and jumped down into the lot, facing the car and the two apparent robbers. They didn't notice her at first. She cleared her throat and called out, "Hey! Didn't your mothers teach you not to take things that don't belong to you?" It was the best she could come up with on short notice. *I probably should have practiced something in advance*, she lamented to herself.

The two men froze and looked up at her. They looked at each other, and then...they laughed. Loudly. Beacon was taken aback a bit. She hadn't expected this response. After a few seconds, the driver opened his door and stepped out, still laughing. He shouted out to her, "What the heck are you supposed to be, sweetheart?"

"The start of a bad day for you by the looks of it," she shouted back. *Yup, I definitely need to rehearse some lines to use*, cringing a bit at how corny she sounded.

They laughed again, even harder this time. "Honey," the other one said, "you have been watching waaaaay too many movies." They both guffawed even louder. One slapped his leg, howling with laughter.

Beacon felt her face flush and was thankful she had the mask on to hide the wave of embarrassment that came over her. She had not even remotely anticipated this was how her first crime would play out. Before she could reply, though, she heard the faint wail of a police siren in the far distance.

The thieves turned toward the direction of the siren, scowled, and then looked back at her.

"Gagh, we don't have time for this," the driver said. "Tell ya what, the first one of us that shoots her gets an extra cut." The other nodded, and they started to take guns out from under their jackets.

*Time to move*, she decided. She wasn't feeling confident in her aim yet to get the gun with her beam projection without mutilating the driver, so instead, she pushed with her dark energy, slamming the car door into him. He went sprawling, and the gun clattered across the asphalt.

Beacon turned her attention to the other thief and accelerated in his direction. He already had his gun out and she saw the gun fire, once, then twice. As she raced toward him, the first bullet missed wildly, but she misjudged the second. She felt a searing pain on her shoulder as the bullet grazed her. She grimaced and cursed. *I guess he won the bet*, Beacon thought, but she had no time to check the damage as he fired a third time. A quick shield turned aside the bullet, and she popped a flash burst, blinding him before he could fire again. He flinched, giving her just enough time to finish closing the distance. Before he could react, she slapped the gun out of his hand, and as he grabbed his wrist, a quick leg sweep planted him firmly on his back, knocking the wind out of him.

Seeing a garbage dumpster right next to the car, she grabbed the front of his jacket and hoisted him off the ground. "I know just where to put you," she told him and threw him into the dumpster. She glanced briefly behind her. The gunshots and her flare must've drawn some attention as a throng was forming at the entrance to the lot, watching and taking pictures. She smiled a bit to herself. *Witnesses are good.*

Beacon turned her head and saw that the driver was up and scrambling to make it to his car. She jumped to slide smoothly across the hood of the vehicle and landed in front of him, cutting him off from the car. He reached into his jacket and produced a large hunting knife. He bared his teeth and growled at her, "C'mon sister, let's go."

Without hesitation, he attacked, swiping wildly at her with the blade. He was quick but clumsy, and with the speed she was using, Beacon easily sidestepped the thrust and caught his wrist. With a quick twist, she had him in a very painful chicken wing hold. He gasped and dropped the knife.

"Let's go for a walk," she told him, lifting up on his twisted wrist and forcing him to the tips of his toes. Beacon walked him, whimpering and squawking in pain, over to the dumpster, grabbed his belt at the back of his pants, and tossed him into it. The other guy grunted loudly as the driver fell on him. She then slammed the lid shut and bent the latch, sealing them in.

Satisfied they were contained, she took a moment to check her shoulder. As she thought, the bullet had grazed her, slicing a hole in her suit and lacerating her arm. It wasn't particularly deep, and fortunately, her healing had already started to seal the wound, but it still throbbed like crazy.

Looking up, she noticed the crowd was even thicker now. They were watching her intently, murmuring amongst themselves and taking pictures and videos, but deliberately keeping a cautious distance. Beacon took a few steps toward them but noticed a few drops of blood on the pavement in front of her near where the bullet had caught her.

"Hmm, don't need anyone taking samples," she muttered to herself and knelt next to the spatter of blood. Positioning her hand just above them, she charred the spots on the pavement with a pulse of heat, rendering them useless.

Convinced there were no more drops to clean up, Beacon stood up and again faced the crowd. She could see the stunned looks on their faces. They clearly did not know quite what to make of her, but despite the shock and awe, somewhere in the crowd, someone started to clap. Slowly, more of the crowd joined in, but the growing round of applause was cut short as the police shoved their way through. They surveyed the lot and then, fixating on her, shouted, "Freeze! Don't move. Put your hands behind your head!"

It took barely a split-second for Beacon to decide that she was not letting the police take her in, but in the same light, she wanted to avoid any confrontation with them. Standing tall, she shouted back, "Glad you made it, boys, but no, I'm not taking a ride with you today," and she leaped to the top of the store building. She turned and pointed toward the scene as she called down to them, "But, if you're interested in an actual crime, the loot is by the car, the guns are scattered over there, and the trash is in the dumpster!"

The dumbstruck police said nothing but lowered their guns, still staring at her. Satisfied there wouldn't be any problem now—provided she left immediately, that is—Beacon turned to go, but as she started to turn, someone in the crowd yelled up at her, "Hey! Who ARE you?"

She turned back to the crowd and, raising her voice so she was sure they could hear her clearly, replied, "You can call me Beacon." She paused just a moment for effect and disappeared from the edge of the building.

As soon as she was clear, Beacon wasted no time picking up her things and running as fast as she could to the other end of the building. There was another low building off the back across an alley. After a quick glance around to make sure no one could see, she jumped across it, trying to put as much space between her and the crowd and police as she could.

Believing she finally had some space, Beacon pulled off the mask and gloves, wrapped her cape back around her, and slipped on the tracksuit. She hopped off the back edge and lowered herself softly with a little dark energy levitation into a small parking area. Tricia pushed the tides and currents away, quickly confirmed that her hair had returned to its normal blonde, and took a deep breath as she walked briskly away from the scene.

Tricia pulled the collar of her jacket up over her neck and pushed her hands down into the pockets, feeling her gloves safely tucked away. She wound her way back to the main street and continued to casually walk away from the jewelry store, taking a route that would bring her back to more familiar and more comfortable parts of the city. While she waited for the crosswalk signal to change, she turned toward the storefront on the corner and looked at her reflection in the plate glass window. This one had no metal fencing or screen.

"Well, that's it. For better or for worse, Beacon is out there now," Tricia softly told her reflection, taking a moment to straighten her ponytail and brush a rogue lock of hair back out of her face. She sighed, and when she heard the crosswalk sign change, Tricia turned away to cross the street, continuing to reflect on what had happened. *A bit of a rough start, true, but I did stop a crime in progress, and if the crowd's reaction is any indication... well, I guess maybe it was a pretty successful debut after all,* she concluded, but almost as a reminder to not get too overconfident, her arm twitched, and her shoulder started throbbing again. She winced and shook her head as she gently massaged it, *but clearly, I'm not bulletproof. I obviously need to keep practicing.*

*There's no going back now.*

As she got closer to the city center, Tricia started keeping a lookout for a taxi to take her the rest of the way. She was not only very curious to see how the news streams received Beacon, but more urgently, her growling stomach was eager to get back to her neighborhood and find someplace to grab a bite or, more accurately, several bites.

Tricia came into the lab the next morning bright and early. She winced a little as she removed her jacket. The shoulder was still a bit sore, but a hot bath had helped, and her healing had taken care of whatever was left while she slept. Her suit was patched up as well. She was thankful she had the foresight to bring home a small amount of the bonding solvent just in case. The bullet had made a clean cut, so a small amount of the bonding solvent was enough to fuse the material closed again. By this morning, she could barely see where the bullet had left its mark.

The team rolled in shortly after she'd gotten settled in with a cup of coffee, and as she expected would happen, Jamal made a beeline for his console and flipped on the morning news stream. He shouted out to the group, "Hey, have you guys seen this? Quick come over, it's awesome!"

Tricia had watched the news streams the night before. The media was wild mix of responses; naturally the appearance of a superpowered individual breaking up a jewelry heist was sensational news, and they were milking it for all the clicks and steam impressions they could get, but they were being reserved on comments regarding Beacon herself. None of them were condemning it though. Quite the opposite, the way they were presenting it was making 'Beacon' trend very positively so far.

Witnesses and police had been interviewed live on the scene right after she had left. The police were noncommittal on the subject, simply acknowledging she was instrumental in bringing in a pair of thieves they believed were responsible for a series of robberies recently. There were a few skeptical witnesses, but most showed a lot of enthusiasm for having what appeared to be a superheroine in the city and were all looking forward to her next appearance. All this was great news for her, but she was curious what the team thought; theirs would be impressions and reactions from real people without any editing done by reporters and news producers.

The group huddled around Jamal's console. The news stream showed a reporter broadcasting from what Tricia recognized as the side lot where she'd taken down the robbers the day before. The banner at the bottom of the screen read, "Crystal Bay's New Superhero!" Jamal turned up the volume just as the reporter was introducing footage provided by some witnesses at the scene yesterday. The reporter emphasized that the footage had been verified as authentic.

The scene shifted to a video recording of the latter part of her battle, where she'd just set off the light flash and disarmed the first felon. The clip ended with the police pushing into the lot, her jumping up to the roof, saying they could call her Beacon, and disappearing behind the roof. *Pretty good footage*, Tricia thought. *Suit doesn't look half bad, and I kinda look like I know what I'm doing. Mostly.*

The broadcast cut back to the main desk, where the anchor repeated her line, "You can call me 'Beacon.'" She continued, "In case you're tuning in a bit late, yes, Crystal Bay now has its very own superhero, or rather, superheroine, going by the name 'Beacon.' Joining us now is Police Commissioner Weathers." The screen split, showing the anchor side-by-side with the image of a man in his fifties with slicked-back graying hair and wearing what was probably a permanent scowl, being transmitted from what appeared to be police headquarters. "Commissioner Weathers, do you have a statement for us regarding Beacon?"

The commissioner cleared his throat and spoke clearly and carefully, "We do not have an official position on the powered individual known as 'Beacon' at this time. We do, though, consider her to be a person of interest and ask, if she is watching, to please make herself available to the police for questioning. We want to be clear, only for questioning regarding the robbery yesterday and her involvement. We also ask that anyone having information regarding Beacon or her whereabouts to please come forward."

"Thank you, Commissioner," the reporter said. "Again, for those of you tuning in, a robbery yesterday was broken up by what appeared to be a person, a woman, in costume exhibiting superpowers, bringing down two notorious jewelry store thieves in the process. We have no additional information on this person or her whereabouts, and police are asking the public to share any information they might have. Let's take a look at another video taken by another eyewitness. We know it will be hard to believe, but we have confirmed the authenticity of the video."

A new clip started playing. This video zoomed in a bit closer, showing her sliding across the hood of the car, dodging the knife attack, and putting the driver into the dumpster. Jamal muted the stream and looked around at the team, most of whom were still glued to the video in amazement. "Wow! That's something!" Turning to Tricia, he asked, "What do you think of that, Doctor C?"

Tricia rubbed her chin and brushed her pesky hair back out of her eyes. She genuinely wanted to hear their honest opinions, so she couldn't afford to influence them in the discussion. "Hmmm, it sure is tough to believe, despite what the news reporters say about the authenticity of the videos. What do you all think?"

"I think she's hot!" Steve blurted out. Alex and Nikki simultaneously groaned and rolled their eyes at him. Jamal chuckled, but it only took a glare from Alex to make him hang his head.

"Maybe something a bit more constructive?" Tricia admonished.

"Well, I mean, it's unprecedented and incredible, right?" chimed in Nikki, "Imagine someone with actual superpowers? How does that happen? Where has she been hiding before this? You'd think something like that would be virtually impossible to keep secret, wouldn't you?"

Alex seemed a bit more skeptical, "Yeah, that's the rub, isn't it? Where did she come from? What's she really all about? Is she even human?" They all looked at her. "I'm just saying, we don't know what she is, where she came from, or what her real motivation is. What else can she do?"

"But she broke up a robbery," Jamal offered, but Alex quickly countered, "THIS time, sure, but maybe that's just part of whatever her play is. Just saying, we don't know."

"Spoken like a true scientist," praised Tricia. "I tend to agree. She looks like she's here to help, but Alex is right. We really don't know, so it's probably best we reserve judgment either way until we see more of her in action. Until then, I think we have some work to do, yeah?"

The team mumbled their agreement and dispersed back to their tasks for the day. *This is good,* Tricia thought. *Generally honest, positive reactions. They didn't seem freaked out, so fingers crossed, most people out there aren't either and are willing to give this a chance.* She finished off the rest of her cup and made her way to the freshly brewed pot for a refill; the day doesn't start without coffee after all, some days, more than others.

The mood was less optimistic in another lab. Purity and several members of the Liberators of Gaia were also standing around a monitor watching the morning news stream featuring Beacon. Many of them wore scowls as they watched, arms folded across their chests.

"What does this mean for us, Opus?" Harmony asked, with a worried tone in her voice.

"Hopefully, nothing, Harmony. We need to know more before we react. For now, we stay the course," Opus responded, more to the entire group than just Harmony.

"True," Purity assented, "no reason to panic, but if this 'Beacon' is authentic, she could pose a credible threat."

"What are you suggesting, Purity?" Opus demanded.

"I'm just saying we need to have a plan to neutralize any threat she represents if she interferes."

"We don't kill, Purity," rebuked Opus. "Killing will not win people over to our cause, *especially* if it's a popular superhero."

"Fine," Purity relented, "but if she drops in on us unexpectedly during one of our little events, we just need to be prepared. That's all I'm saying."

Opus looked at her for a few seconds and finally nodded in agreement. The others mumbled in consensus as well. One by one, they peeled away from the group to go about their plans for the day. Purity paused the stream, freezing a close-up of Beacon standing in front of the crowd. Squinting, she whispered to herself, "Hmmm, who are you, and how interesting are you going to make things for me?"

# Progression

"Ow!" Tricia winced as shampoo pooled in her eye. *Slow down...we aren't in that much of a hurry,* she scolded herself as she let the shower rinse out her stinging eye. Truth be told, she actually was in a bit of a hurry this morning. The work on the imaging system upgrades for Marni was going well, but she'd hit a bit of a snag on the electronics. Alex had agreed to meet her a little earlier this morning to help her work through some of it.

She had successfully mocked together a solid prototype of a higher-resolution imaging array, and once this problem was solved, she only needed to refine the software needed to gather and process the sub-cellular images Marni and her team needed. Unfortunately, to get the resolution Rene had suggested, she'd need to break the news to Marni and the team that this wouldn't just be a simple upgrade or augmentation for the systems they already had operating in the hospital. One problem at a time, she decided. When the array was closer to being ready for some real-world testing, she'd run it by Marni, and they'd figure out the best way to make use of it for her investigation.

Finished with her shower, Tricia clicked on the morning news stream so she could watch for some Beacon updates while she got ready to head into the lab. She knew she'd likely see the same thing again, courtesy of Jamal, when she arrived at the lab—he was becoming quite the fanboy—but she wanted to have a little time on her own to see what was being said and process it on her own. *Let's see what they have to say about me today,* she thought as she started to dry her hair and settled in on the couch, still wrapped in her bath towel.

By night, Beacon had been making an impression on the city. Tricia had created the crimes heat map she wanted, and armed with that, Beacon had been routinely patrolling the city. She had started by using the same tracksuit disguise she'd used for the jewelry store robbery. It had worked fine for a few nights, but even that extra step of removing the suit and putting it back on after thwarting some crime started being problematic and, ultimately, unnecessary.

Instead, Beacon found that she could stay in costume and easily use her speed and levitation to move deftly across rooftops and fire escapes while she kept her eyes open for crimes to stop. When she didn't need to be on the move, she could simply find some useful shadows, draw up her hood, and trigger the suit's camouflaging properties to stay out of sight while she watched and waited. On the days she needed her tracksuit at the end of her patrols, she could just leave it on some convenient rooftop or fire escape to pick up when she was finished.

Being in the right places and taking this stealth approach started to pay dividends right away. Over the past couple of weeks, she'd broken up several muggings, car thefts, and nasty situations that would have likely escalated into sexual or some other violent assaults. She hoped…expected…the news to have something to say about last night's fruitful outing.

"Ah, just in time," she said excitedly under her breath as the on-screen headline switched to "Beacon foils mugging attempt." Tricia continued to brush out her hair while she leaned forward, listening intently to the report. The more positively she was received by the public and the media, the more of an impact she could make, and knowing how fickle people can be, the anticipation of hearing how they were perceiving her always gave her a few butterflies in her stomach.

"The Crystal Bay Crusader has struck again!" the reporter announced. "Last night, Beacon appeared on the scene for the third time this week, this time to break up a mugging attempt in the West Hedge district of the city."

Tricia smirked—of all the nicknames the media had been coming up with for her, she liked this one the most—and recalled the previous evening's activities. She'd seen the mugger approach a young woman, pull her into an alley, and threaten her with a knife. As the woman started fumbling with her bag, presumably to pull out her wallet, Beacon dropped off the rooftop, landing right next to the two of them. "Mind if I cut in?" she'd said.

The mugger turned, gaped at her, and then completely fell apart. He threw down his knife, dropped to his knees, put up his hands, and started begging her not to hurt him. She was pretty sure he was crying, too. It was rather pathetic, truth be told.

Beacon told the woman to call the police, then leaned down to the mugger and grabbed him by the collar. "Do us both a favor and just wait here for the police to come, yeah?

I'll be watching, and trust me, you don't want to make me come after you again, do you?"

The mugger whimpered that he didn't, so she released him and asked the woman if she was okay. She said she was, thanked her, and gave Beacon a nervous wave. Beacon smiled, waved back, and vaulted back up to the roof. She hadn't stayed around to watch; she was very sure the mugger was going to keep his word.

The news stream switched over to a live interview, drawing Tricia's attention back to the screen. The reporter was interviewing the woman now. The woman was telling her story of what had happened. "I was walking home from work when this guy grabbed my arm and pulled me into this alley." She pointed to the alley behind her. "He pulled a knife and wanted me to give him my wallet. I told him I didn't have anything, but he just told me, for my sake, I'd better have something, and suddenly there she was out of nowhere. Beacon was just standing there, and he freaked out. He dropped his knife and started blubbering. It was a pretty bad look for him, honestly," the woman added with a measure of disgust. "Beacon told me to call the police and told him to wait for them, and then she was gone. She saved me."

"That's an amazing story," the reporter affirmed but was interrupted by a raspy masculine voice just out of the camera view. "It's a load of crap!"

The camera switched to a man with a scruffy beard and baseball cap standing just behind the reporter. The reporter turned and, holding her microphone towards him, prompted, "You have a different view?"

"Yeah," he said, puffing up his chest, "She's a freakin' menace! We don't need her or anybody else going around terrorizing people with powers and stuff!"

"Terrorizing criminals, you mean." offered the reporter.

"Terrorizing *anyone*," he yelled, punctuating his words by jabbing his finger into the camera, "We don't need freaks like her sticking their noses into other people's business!"

Tricia flashed her middle finger up in front of his image on the screen. "Jerk!" she spat and snapped off the stream.

*He may not actually be entirely wrong, though,* she pondered, making her way into the bedroom to dress. *The jury is still out on that point, but either way, it won't stop me from picturing that guy's face on whoever I'll be sparring in class this week.*

"Point! Winner!" Sensei Tim announced, gesturing toward Tricia and awarding her the match, her first sparring win in the advanced class. She was beyond thrilled with her first victory and pumped her fist in celebration. Sensei cleared his throat, reminding her to recover her decorum. She nodded in apology, and, regaining her composure, she and John, her sparring opponent, bowed to each other and then to Sensei Tim. John gave her a high-five and congratulated her.

It had been a particularly grueling class, so when Sensei announced they would still do a round of sparring before closing anyway, he drew a few groans from the class. Tricia knew deep down he relished knowing he was pushing them to their limits but appreciated how he always seemed to know when not to push too far. That said, Tricia's jaw nearly dropped when he called her and John to the mat as the last match for the night. John was one of the best students in the class, making Tricia more than a little anxious about squaring off against him.

They had gone back and forth the entire match, ending up tied two points each at the end of regulation time. Expecting to end in a draw—which was a win as far as Tricia was concerned—Sensei instead surprised them yet again by continuing to sudden death where the next point would decide the winner. Both Tricia and John were dragging by now, and while she was tempted more than once to just draw on a little of her power to help her finish this, she resisted that temptation, determined to finish it on her own, win or lose.

Just a minute or so into sudden death, her opening finally came. John telegraphed his next move, and when he stepped forward for his strike, Tricia was ready. She blocked it cross-body and stepped through, driving her elbow into his floating rib and then following it with a reverse elbow to the kidney, a combination that was worth two points on its own. She found John's grunt to be very satisfying and spun around into a perfect cat stance, ready for his counter, but the match was over.

Sensei Tim led them through cool down and dismissed the class. As she was packing up, he waved her over.

"Good win today, Carling. You had to work hard for that one. John's going to feel that elbow tomorrow morning, I'm sure."

Tricia nodded and thanked him.

"I'm impressed by what I'm seeing from you recently. You're showing a lot of creativity, putting things in combination beyond just what we've learned in the exercises. It's starting to look very natural for you." He put his hands on his hips and gave her a humorously exaggerated stern look. "You aren't doing any fight clubs or anything on the side, are you, Carling?"

Tricia laughed. "No, Sensei, I've just been, um, practicing a lot lately."

"It's showing," Sensei commended her, "John's one of our best students. He'll be testing for his black belt very soon and will probably start assisting me in the beginning classes after that. When you first came into this class, he would have mopped the floor with you, but to take him to sudden death and win the match is a big accomplishment. I made you two go through sudden death to see what you had left in you, and you showed me. Nicely done!"

"Thanks, Sensei, and thanks again for giving me this chance. It's been great."

"My pleasure, Carling. If you keep going at this pace, who knows, someday you might end up being like Beacon's sidekick or something. She's got some moves."

Tricia grinned, "Yeah, maybe someday."

Late Friday morning, Alex and Nikki walked up to Tricia's desk. Tricia held up a 'just a second' finger as she finished entering some new parameters for the simulation of their next experiment. She looked up at them, removing her glasses and tucking her wayward hair back behind her ear. They were shifting nervously back and forth on their feet.

"Restroom is down the hall," she teased. "You don't need to ask permission."

They both laughed. Alex glanced at Nikki and then back to Tricia. "We, um, were wondering if we could take off now?"

Tricia scrunched her eyebrows. "I suppose. What's going on?"

"Well, the Combined Research Complex group picnic is this afternoon over on the North Quad," Nikki explained. "We are on the organizing committee and wanted to head over to make sure everything was coming together before this afternoon. The caterer is supposed to arrive around noon, and we are supposed to meet them."

"Ah, the picnic. Of course." Tricia had completely forgotten about it. "Absolutely. Take off." She then gestured toward

Jamal and Steve, too. "All of you wrap it up for the day and go enjoy yourselves."

"You're coming too, right Doctor C?" Alex asked.

"Um, well, I'm not really sure," Tricia stammered, "I'd forgotten it was today and have a bunch of things I wanted to wrap up today before heading off to The Ridge later."

Jamal chimed in, "Oh Doc, you really need to come." Besides, you're looking a little pale. Some sunshine could do you some good!"

Tricia touched her face with her fingertips. She knew he was right. She'd noticed her skin tone, or rather lack of it, as well. Sure, she'd been spending a lot of time outside, but much of that time was spent using her powers.

Tricia had recently realized that when she used her powers, rather than allowing her skin to absorb the UV light, she was processing it along with all the other energy. In short, she didn't tan when she used her powers. Not burning was definitely an upside, but her lack of color was starting to make her look peaked and unhealthy. It had also occurred to her that she might need to start taking a vitamin supplement; she likely wasn't making enough vitamin D either.

"Yeah, you're right. It probably would," she agreed, also realizing, grudgingly, that as a lab director, she was somewhat obligated to at least make an appearance. "You guys get going. I'll wrap up here and get over there in time for lunch." Alex looked at her skeptically. "No, really, I will. I promise," she assured them, making a cross over her heart.

"We're coming back to get you if you don't. You know that, right?" Jamal mockingly threatened, emphasizing it with a stern finger wag.

Tricia smiled and nodded, waving them out of the lab.

A few hours later, Tricia was sitting on the grass with her back resting up against a large tree. She'd just finished off a couple of hot dogs and potato salad and was nursing a big chocolate chip cookie with a large cup of lemonade. The chocolate was soft and gooey in the warm afternoon sun, forcing Tricia to periodically lick it off the ends of her fingers.

As she sucked some of the melted chocolate off her thumb, Tricia realized that she actually was starting to burn a bit. Given how pale she was, it was no surprise, but it made her even more grateful that she'd found some relief away from the crowds under the shade of the tree's thick leaf canopy.

She was watching some of the other lab staffers play various games out on the quad. There was a rousing game of volleyball going on in one corner. Another group was playing a game that involved alternatively tossing bean bags into hoops laid several yards apart on the ground. Looked like that game also involved doing shots of some kind of alcohol periodically too.

She smiled as she watched, remembering the fun she had as an undergrad playing and taking breaks on the campus quads. Playing would have been fun, but there was always the slight chance she might momentarily lose control and accidentally trigger a lot of questions and suspicions that she just didn't want to have to deal with. Besides, she was enjoying the breeze and relaxing. It had been a while since she'd just...relaxed. *Maybe instead of practicing this weekend at The Ridge, I should just take some time for myself.*

Tricia had no sooner closed her eyes and rested her head back on the tree trunk, when she heard footsteps approach her on the grass. She looked up and saw Rene Thornton standing there looking down at her. "Hi Trish. Mind if I join you for a bit?"

*Gosh, even in jeans and a t-shirt this woman looks absolutely perfect,* Trish marveled. "Of course, Rene. It's a public tree and you're more than welcome to share it." She smiled and gestured to the grass next to her.

Rene gracefully took a seat next to Tricia and stretched out her legs. "Not out there trying your hand at some volleyball?"

Tricia looked out at the game in progress. "No, not this time. Didn't really dress for it and figured it would be a good day to take it easy."

"Lingering effects from your accident?" Rene asked tentatively.

"Mmm-hmm," Tricia replied with a casual nod. "Yeah, something like that."

Rene nodded back and then switched gears. "How are those upgrades going for Marni's team over at the hospital? She seems rather stuck until she can get some higher-res cellular images of what's going on with those people."

"Actually, they are going great. I've just about finished putting together a new imaging array that should meet the specs we discussed at lunch a while back. I was going to finish it this afternoon and call her, but..." and she extended her hands outward. "I'll get them to her next week. Hopefully, that helps crack this thing. Those couples need an answer."

Tricia huffed. "Besides, it seems to be the only thing I can work on without someone looking over my shoulder," she muttered under her breath.

"Ah," Rene said, "you mean the probation?"

Tricia nodded. "It's frustrating, Rene. I'm always answering questions and filling out requests or reports when I should be getting on with our work."

She turned and looked at Rene. "We successfully repeated our projected solids experiment, you know?"

"Yes, I did hear. That was the one that caused your accident, wasn't it?"

"Uh huh, but we pulled it off, and it was mind-blowing." Tricia sat forward and became very animated, telling as much of the story with her hands as she did with her words. "When the steel bearing hit the surface, we heard it. We actually *heard* it hit. We so successfully simulated a solid surface by blending light and dark energy that it made a sound on impact."

Rene smiled, appreciating her enthusiasm. Tricia threw her hands out in a pleading gesture. "That's what we need to be focusing on. There is so much good we can do with technology like this. We know what we are doing, Rene. They just need to get out of our way and let us do it." Tricia flopped back against the tree trunk.

Rene looked at her and nodded once. "Honestly, Tricia," she offered, "are they *really* in your way? I mean, it's a few questions and a little paperwork, but has that actually stopped you? It doesn't sound like it has." Tricia looked at her blankly.

Rene chuckled. "It wouldn't surprise me if Demerov set all this up on purpose just to put you through a little fire, to strengthen your resolve." She held up her fist for emphasis and added with an exaggerated Russian accent, "Zat vich does not keel you, makes you stronger."

Tricia couldn't help but smile. "I don't think Nietzsche was Russian, Rene."

Rene shrugged. The smile faded from her face, and she looked off into the distance, her voice softening. "Funny how adversity shapes us, isn't it, Trish?"

"How do you mean, Rene?"

"Well, your accident...beyond the probation, I'm sure that's had an impact on you?"

*Just a little bit*, Tricia thought, nodding. "I suppose it has."

"...and you lost your parents too, didn't you?"

"My dad. Yeah." Trish looked down, rubbing her hands in the grass.

"Do you mind if I ask how it happened?" Rene probed, still looking off at the horizon.

"Well, it was summer before my senior year. We were taking off for a long weekend at our cabin in the mountains. We stopped for gas at a little station out in the boonies. He went inside to pay for the gas and walked in on a robbery in progress. They shot him and took off." Tricia's voice hitched a little.

"Must've been horrible for you, especially so young."

"Yeah, it was a tough time. My mom had taken off, so she was pretty much worthless. If it weren't for some great friends and some other really supportive family, I would've likely ended up in a very bad place."

"I'm glad you had that, Trish," Rene said. She looked at Trish and patted her knee. "The same kind of thing happened to me, too, you know." She looked away again.

"Oh? I didn't know. How so?" Trish prompted her.

Rene pulled her knees up to her chest and wrapped her arms around them. "In my case, it was another kind of stupid selfishness – a drunk driver. I was eleven. We were all coming home from seeing a movie, and he plowed into the side of the car while running a red light. I was the only survivor."

"Oh my God, that's terrible, Rene." Trish consoled.

Rene's voice became more agitated, "The despicable thing about it is that it wasn't his first offense, *and* he went out of his way to do it; he deliberately bypassed the blood alcohol kill switch in his car just so he could still drink and drive and my family paid for it."

She exhaled sharply, shrugged a bit, and went on, "My aunt refused to take custody, so I ended up in the foster care system. It wasn't horrible...at first. Even as a kid, you can kinda tell when people are in it for the money, right? Even if home wasn't the warmest place, I was treated well enough. I compensated by diving into my schoolwork. I kind of knew deep down that my way out was with my head, so I became a recluse, focusing as much time on my studies as I could.

"I did some academic clubs, mostly because I knew it would look good on my transcripts and even managed to jump ahead a year. It got worse, though, when I really started to, you know, grow up, and my foster father started taking too much of an interest. Being at home became extremely uncomfortable and scary, and I knew my foster mother knew, but she wouldn't say or do anything for a long time."

Tricia put her hand on Rene's hand. Rene absentmindedly patted it and then pulled her hand back.

"Finally, I couldn't bear it anymore. I went to social services and lodged a complaint. My foster mom admitted what was going on. He was charged, and I was taken out when I was sixteen. Coincidentally—not—my aunt petitioned for custody. At first, I was happy I'd be going back to my real family, but in the end, it turned out she was just after the small trust my parents had set up. At seventeen, I was eligible to start accessing it, so she sued the trust executor for conservatorship. She lost, but by that time, I'd won a couple of tuition scholarships, and before she could officially kick me out, I was able to graduate early and start a new life at university. The scholarships covered tuition, and the trust was just enough to manage living expenses, textbooks, that kind of thing.

"So, believing that school was still my escape route, I did the same thing I did in high school. Every minute I had went into studies, projects, labs, internships, and a part-time job at one of the cafeterias on campus to help keep ends meeting. I was able to finish undergrad six months early and then went immediately into a doctorate program in research genetics."

Rene paused and turned to look at Trish. Her eyes were a bit damp, but she smiled and spread her arms wide. "And here I am today."

Tricia paused a moment, a little choked up at Rene's story and how suddenly and freely this amazing woman had just opened up to her. "But look at the amazing person you are, Rene. All you've accomplished. All you've done for science, for society, for the people at the hospital, all of it."

"True, Trish, true, but frankly, it's hard when you know that for all you offer, no matter how much you offer, people will just keep taking and demanding more. They are selfish, Trish. It's in their nature. It's who they are. That's why I'm on the ESG Advocacy Council. I volunteered thinking that if we can find ways to get people believing they should *give* a bit more, even just a little, this world could be a much better place."

Rene shook her head. "Enough of that. I don't want to completely rain on a beautiful sunny day."

"Oh, don't worry about that, Rene. I'm glad you shared. It meant a lot, and it was nice to get to know you a bit more. In spite of all that's happened, you really are an amazing woman."

Rene smiled, stood up, and brushed the grass off her jeans. "Care for a little advice, Trish?"

"Sure, Rene. Of course."

Rene looked down straight into Tricia's eyes. "Doctor Tricia Carling is the youngest research lab director in the history of this university. That's impressive. Use it to make a difference. But you have to be in it to win it. I hate coming to these things, but I come to stay in touch, in touch with the right people. To be seen. To make the connections. Remember, a lot of careers have been lost sitting under a tree, but someone like you, a woman like you—smart, accomplished, pretty—can really be a powerful inspiration to a lot of people if you try. No matter what happens or who tries to get in your way, just keep being you and making the difference you think you can make."

"Thanks, Rene. I'm definitely going to take that to heart."

Rene smiled and nodded, and after giving a short wave, she walked off.

"Trust me, Rene, I'm definitely taking that to heart," Tricia said softly to herself as she watched Rene walk away.

# Insights

Tricia tipped her head back, letting the sun beam down on her face and chest. Her ponytail bounced gently on her back. The waves washed up over her legs and swirled behind her. She closed her eyes and listened to the sounds of the ocean, the calling of the gulls, and the laughing of other beachgoers playing on the sand.

Today was a free day. She'd worked hard this week and took her own advice for a much-needed day to herself. No bad guys, no superpowers, no patrols. It was a beautiful day, and Tricia had decided that it was the perfect day to come back to the beach. She hadn't been here in years, and there was no better day to change that than today.

As she sat in the surf, feeling the waves lap around her, she reached out a bit with her abilities and felt the waves of energy swirling and pulsing around her. At that moment, she sat in two oceans, both filled with power, both ebbing and flowing around her. So much alike, yet so different. She pushed away from the energy around her and felt it slide away from her, leaving only one ocean behind. Today was her day off, so today, the only ocean she wanted to care about was the warm salty water in which she was currently sitting.

"I need to do this more often," she murmured to herself.

*You know why you haven't, don't you?* The voice inside her head asked.

*Because it's a pain to get here,* she answered.

*Is it really?* The voice challenged her. *Seemed pretty easy to get here today, didn't it?*

*I'm busy and don't really have the time,* Tricia tried again. Deep down, she knew she was losing this argument.

*You were really busy as an undergrad and still managed to have some beach days with Marni and your other friends, didn't you?* The voice countered, punching more holes in her excuses.

*Yeah, we did.*

*So? You do know the truth, don't you?*

There was no way to avoid admitting the real answer, a truth she'd been pushing down, not just today but for a long time. Tricia sighed and confessed out loud, "Because Dad and I had such good times here as a kid, and this place reminds me that we won't be having any more."

*Correct,* the voice answered, *and how do you think he'd feel if he knew you were avoiding coming here because of that?*

"He'd be furious to think I was spoiling those happy times we shared with being sorry for myself, that the best way to cherish the memories we made together is to build on them with new ones," Tricia admitted. "He'd tell me to stop living in the past."

There was no response from the inner voice, but Tricia knew she was right. She needed to keep building on those memories, not avoiding them.

She sighed and looked down at her hands and feet. They were becoming quite wrinkly from the water, so Tricia pushed herself up to a standing position and brushed the wet sand off the backs of her legs and her suit. She turned her back on the rolling waves and walked back up to the spot where her towel was spread out on the sand, anchored down against the breeze by her bag. She plopped down on the towel and started lathering on a fresh layer of sunscreen. She knew she didn't need the protection per se, but since she actually wanted to get some color today, she would need to let it happen the old-fashioned way and keep her powers out of it.

Satisfied that she'd thoroughly covered herself, she tucked the tube back into her bag and took out a small hand cloth. Tricia laid back on her towel, arranged the cloth over her eyes, and relaxed, ready for the sun to work its magic on her pasty skin.

Tricia let her mind wander, but despite this being a self-proclaimed free day, her thoughts returned to the cases with which she was helping Marni. Something about them nagged at her, and, as with any puzzle, she was having a hard time letting it go.

Earlier in the week, Tricia had gone as far as she could on the imaging system without trying it on some real samples. She'd given Marni a quick call, and Marni was more than happy to send over an assortment of patient tissue samples for Tricia to try. In fact, Marni was so excited to hear the news that the samples showed up that same afternoon via a special campus courier.

Tricia imaged all of them over the next couple of days, and the results were fantastic. Sure, she'd had to spend some time calibrating the new imaging array, but that's what the samples were for, and after a few runs, the images were exceptional.

However, there was something else that she'd noticed. The case dates for the samples seemed to have an odd clustering pattern. They weren't randomly distributed as she would have expected. When she called Marni back to give her an update, Tricia had made a point to ask about it.

"Yes, we did notice that too," Marni acknowledged, "but the infertility team said it likely didn't amount to anything."

"Why would they say that?"

"Well, they pointed out that human promiscuity happens anytime, but human procreation does tend to fall on more specific cycles." Marni went on, "People trying to have a baby often pay close attention to things like ovulation cycles, for example. Heck, the team said couples even use biorhythms or even the phases of the moon!"

They both chuckled at that. "So, in the end, we don't see the clustering of the cases to be a point of concern."

Tricia adjusted the cloth over her eyes. While Marni's explanation seemed perfectly reasonable, Tricia felt there was more to it, something eluding her right now, but probably something she'd ultimately figure out that was staring her in the face...

...and she was jolted by a crashing sound near her. She jerked the towel off her face and sat upright just as the sound erupted again. Tricia turned to look and saw a group of high school kids had set up camp right next to her. The racket came from them filling their ice chest with bagged ice they'd probably picked up on the drive to the beach.

A bit annoyed at being startled, she stretched a bit. Judging from how high the sun had gotten in the sky and how warm the sand had become, Tricia guessed she'd dozed off for an hour or so. She bent her knees and noted the slight pink on her thighs, but the small swirling waves at the edges of her vision told her that her body had already been drawing a trickle of power to deal with it. Clearly, at some point in her nap, her body had instinctively dampened the UV, saving her from a very uncomfortable sunburn. She drew a bit more and watched the pink fade away, leaving a light tan behind. *Much better.* Tricia smiled; there was still so much she didn't know, but what had happened to her and what she could do with it fascinated her at times.

"Probably for the best they woke me up when they did," she muttered to herself. Her stomach growled in agreement. "Well, if it's lunchtime, then there's no better way to build on some great memories than lunch at Ernie's."

Tricia had to admit she was more than a little excited to go back to Ernie's—if it was still in business, that is. It had been a while. When she would come with her dad, lunch at Ernie's was tradition.

Ernie's was a small beach cafe that sat at the end of a boardwalk near one of the piers on the beach. Locals would come to fish off the pier, so most of what Ernie's served came from the local catch of the day.

No one went there for the swanky ambiance. Truth be told, it wasn't much more than a small run-down shack covered with peeling blue and white paint, but it had character and charm. More importantly, though, her father was convinced they made the best fried fish sandwich on planet Earth, and so far, Tricia had not had anything that came close to proving him wrong.

Encouraged by the steady grumbling of her stomach, she slipped on a pair of shorts and a tank top over her suit, stuffed her towel into her bag, slipped on her sandals, and started walking up the beach toward where she thought Ernie's would be.

Tricia couldn't help but smile when she finally spotted the place sitting right where she'd remembered it. It looked a little nicer than she'd remembered, though. It had a fresh coat of gleaming white and sea blue paint. It also seemed a little bigger, now sporting a small outside bar with stool seating underneath a couple of bright blue beach umbrellas.

She walked up to the large open window. An old-fashioned bell chime sat on the counter with a small sign 'Ring for Service...Just Once!' She gave it a tap and a graying middle-aged man walked up. He was wearing a white t-shirt covered by a very well-used blue apron and he was wiping his hands with a worn kitchen towel.

"What can I do for you?" He said with a big smile.

Tricia smiled back. "Do you still have the best fried fish sandwich on the planet?"

"You know it!" he responded enthusiastically.

Tricia looked over the revamped cafe again, letting a little nostalgia wash over her. "The place looks amazing. You see, I used to come here when I was a kid. A lot of great memories of having lunch here with my dad. Is Ernie here by any chance?"

"You're lookin' at him," he said proudly, and then, picking up on the puzzled look, he quickly added, "Ernie Junior, that is. Ernie Senior retired a few years ago, and I took over the place from him."

Tricia nodded and stuck out her hand. "I'm Tricia, by the way. Good for him. I'm sure he earned it."

"That he did," Ernie Jr agreed, shaking her hand. "Dad put his heart into this place. Hey, I'm willing to bet he gave you extra fries with your sandwich, didn't he?"

Tricia grinned. "Yeah, I'm pretty sure he did."

"That'd be him all right. He always said caring for people was the key to success, and he always had a soft spot for the cute ones." He winked and chuckled.

"Well looks like you picked right up where he left off," she chuckled back. "The place looks awesome."

"It's the busy season. Lots of tourists. Yeah, can't complain. Business is good. So, do you want fries with that sandwich?"

Tricia gave him a look of mock surprise. "Is there really any other choice?" she cajoled.

Ernie clicked his tongue and pointed a finger at her. "Comin' right up!"

Ernie disappeared to the side, and Tricia slid up onto one of the stools to wait. Toward the back, there was a monitor running the news stream. A few days ago, the Liberators of Gaia had pulled off another one of their stunts, spewing blue and green smoke and some chalky residue all over another office building downtown. The news stream was running a follow-up story about the group and their activities.

As with their other demonstrations, no one was injured, but Tricia was skeptical about how effective these tactics were for their cause. Deep down, she believed in what they were fighting for, but she wondered if these smoke bombs were just drawing more attention to the demonstrations themselves than making people more aware of the need to help save the planet.

She heard the sizzle of the deep fryer, making her mouth water. The news stream switched to a graphic showing a map of the city. The map was marked with the locations and dates of all their smoke and paint tagging. Something about it caught her eye, and she squinted to look closer.

Locations and dates...

The dates...

Her eyes widened as it hit her like a lightning bolt. The dates. The dates appeared to align with the clusters in the patient case studies that had been nagging at her! At least they looked close; she'd need to do a more thorough analysis to be sure. And she'd need more than just the relatively few samples she already had to prove any real statistical correlation that the police would find compelling.

Tricia tapped her commpod. "Call Marni."

"Calling Marni Haskell," the device responded. After a few seconds, it reported back, "Doctor Haskell is not receiving notifications at this time, Tricia."

Tricia huffed. "Try again with high urgency, please." That should be enough to get Marni to at least acknowledge the incoming call.

"Calling Marni Haskell with high urgency," the commpod obeyed.

After several seconds, the call connected, and Marni answered with a little irritation in her voice, "Hi, Trish. I hope you're not *urgently* calling me to gloat about spending time at the beach today?"

Tricia winced a bit; she'd asked Marni to come with her, but Marni had a shift today in the hospital. "No, Marni, not at all. It is rather important, though. I think I've hit on something about your cases, and I need access to all the patient case files to test a hypothesis."

A few seconds passed before Marni answered, her tone now very business-like, "You know I can't do that, Tricia. The privacy regs are very specific about this. I can't give you access to any patient information that isn't directly related to your role on the investigation. Is this something to do with the imaging upgrades you're working on?"

"Um, well, no, not directly," Tricia admitted reluctantly.

"Ok, then. Help me out here. What are you looking for?"

"I think I've hit on something related to the case dates, and I need the patients' full contact tracing logs to test it out." Tricia was doing her best to be honest with Marni while being very careful not to lead into anything that Marni would argue with, making her less willing to perhaps bend the rules just a bit.

She wasn't being entirely successful though. "We talked about the dates, Tricia." Marni said, showing some clear frustration. "The dates are a dead end."

"Look, Marn," Tricia pressed, "I really think I'm onto something. Isn't there anything you can do to get me that tracing information so I can check it out? It's been bugging me for a week now, and I'd really like to either prove it out or put it to bed once and for all."

Marni sighed. "All right, Trish. I know how you get when there's a puzzle in front of you. As it turns out, you're in luck. As part of the pathology study, all the patient tracing was collated into a single model. It has all the relevant dates and location information, but it's fully anonymized. It has no patient identification or other case information, so technically, I can make it available to anyone. Will that work?"

"I'll make it work," Tricia replied excitedly. "Can you send it over right away?"

"I can," Marni answered. "I'll send it to your address at the lab, just so it stays on official channels."

"Thanks, Marn. I'll head over to the lab right away then."

"You know, Trish, this isn't how normal people spend a day at the beach."

"Yeah, but I never claimed to be entirely normal." *Especially these days*, she mused.

"Probably why we get on so well." Marni snickered.

Tricia grinned. "I'll let you know how it comes out."

Marni's voice shifted back to a more serious tone again. "Just promise one thing, Tricia. Promise me you won't just go chasing rabbits. This isn't some academic exercise. These are real people with real problems who need help as soon as they can get it, so we can't afford to waste any more time, ok?"

"Give me a little credit," Tricia replied with not a small amount of irritation. "I get it, but I *do* think there's something here. I won't waste time with it, I promise."

"Ok then. I'm looking forward to hearing what you find. If there's something there, I'm pretty sure you'll find it. But wait until after five to call, ok? My shift is over then."

"Sure thing, Marn. Talk to you later." Tricia tapped the commpod to end the call.

Tricia turned back to the cafe window just in time to see Ernie bring out a plate covered with a massive fish sandwich and a heaping pile of golden-brown fries. Even in the heat of the day, she could see the steam rising off the hot food. The smell hit her nose. It was just as she remembered.

"Looks like there are some extra fries here, Ernie," she teased him, sporting a half smile.

Ernie shrugged. "Guess I inherited some of the old man's soft spots, too."

"Well, it looks and smells amazing, but I think I'm going to need this to go now."

Tricia licked the grease off her fingertips as she stared at the monitor. *Better than I remembered,* she thought as she watched the display update in front of her. She was still in her beach clothes. The remains of the sandwich and fries sat in a cardboard box next to her. Ernie had made sure she had plenty of malt vinegar; they both agreed ketchup and tartar sauce were strictly for noobs.

It had taken some work to get the patient tracing model loaded into the Laboratory Analytical NeuralNet Assistant, or LANA for short. Tricia watched the histograms shift as the system finished importing and structuring the data. Finally, the status bar flashed 'READY' in green.

Tricia activated the voice interface so she wouldn't get fish grease all over her keyboard and mouse. "LANA, internet search: please import location and date information for incidents and events by Liberators of Gaia. Display on a map of the city, please."

"Searching…" the system responded. "Loading…"

A map of Crystal Bay appeared on the screen. Several locations were marked with a red circle and tagged with the dates when their smoke bombs had been set off.

"Overlay the patient tracing logs," Tricia instructed.

LANA responded by creating a massive tangle of lines on top of the map. Each line represented the journey taken by one of the patients over the course of the past several months. They intersected and wound around each other, making the map almost impossible to read. Tricia was struck by how much the display remined her of how frequently people touch each other's lives, often without even knowing.

Shifting back to task, Tricia continued her analysis, "LANA, correlate the patient traces by case dates to the locations and dates of the Liberators' events."

The display shifted. Each Liberator event was given a unique color. Patient traces were then colored to match Liberator events with which they intersected. Traces that didn't correlate became gray. Tricia frowned a bit as there were far fewer colored traces than she had hoped there would be.

"What is the R-squared on the correlations, please?" Tricia asked.

"Correlation strength is 48.34% plus/minus .07, Doctor Carling."

*Ugh. That's really lousy*, Tricia thought. She leaned into the screen, studying the data as she wiped off her hands with the pile of napkins on her workspace. *Wait*, she realized, *they wouldn't be reporting a problem the same day as the event. If they were exposed to something, it would take time.*

"LANA, offset the correlation by one event in the past."

The display shifted again. Most of the lines changed color, and a chunk of the gray ones were assigned a new color, indicating they'd found a match. "Correlation strength has improved to 62.6% plus/minus .13," LANA reported.

Tricia shifted in her seat. It was getting interesting now. "LANA, for traces that show a weak correlation, shift by two events." *It's possible they didn't notice or hadn't even tried to conceive for a few months after exposure*, she theorized.

More traces shifted. The colors became an abstract spectrum on the screen. It reminded Tricia of what she saw when she used her powers, how the energy flows shifted and pulsed, chaotic but still somehow orderly at the same time.

"LANA, remove the traces and show me counts and percentages of traces that intersect with the Liberator events."

The display was replaced with the map, color-coded event location markers, and statistics of correlated events for each location. In the lower corner was a histogram showing counts per location and counts of any patients that hadn't yet correlated. This last one was now quite small. *Much better*, Tricia thought. *Let's just go for it now.*

"LANA, please free correlate any weak or unmatched patients to find a best fit with Liberator events."

"Correlating, Doctor Carling," LANA responded. After a few seconds, the display updated. All but a handful of patients were now matched to having been at Liberator locations at the dates and times of the events within a few months of their reporting to the hospital. The unmatched number was very small, well within the range Marni had told her was a normal case load for the reproductive services department.

"What is the R-squared now, LANA?"

"Correlation strength is 93.42% plus/minus .005, Doctor Carling."

"Remove and tag the uncorrelated patients, please, LANA."

"Updating...correlation strength is 95.23% plus/minus .002."

Tricia thought for a minute. This was pretty compelling, but it wasn't even first sigma yet. It might get the interest of the police, but she needed to see if she could do better. In the end, what she was doing couldn't prove any causality—she couldn't prove the Liberators were the cause of the infertility cases—but if she could give them a convincing smoking gun, something that was hard to dismiss, they might take a closer look. *Those poor couples needed an answer.*

She stood up for a minute and stretched. Some sand fell onto the floor next to her stool. She brushed off the stool and shook her shorts and suit bottom to expel some more sand. *That'll make the custodial staff wonder*, she thought, grinning to herself. She checked the time; she'd want to check back with Marni in a couple of hours.

Something occurred to her as she sat back down. She'd been correlating against the case start date, the date when the patients had reported to the hospital, but it occurred to her she should be correlating against when the patients indicated they first noticed there might be a problem.

"LANA, does the tracing model include onset date information?"

"Yes, Doctor Carling. 86% of the patient traces include onset date."

"Great. Include the previously removed uncorrelated patients and segment the model to temporarily exclude patients without onset date."

"Segmentation complete, Doctor Carling."

"Super. Now, do the same correlation but use onset date instead of case date."

"Correlating," LANA replied. The display paused and then shifted. Interestingly, the more recent, larger events by Liberators increased. The earlier events shifted slightly but remained largely the same. Tricia noted this as potentially significant; if whatever the Liberators were doing was somehow related to these infertility cases, as they went on, the effects became more pronounced.

The display stopped updating. A small number of cases still didn't correlate, but again, these could be cases that would have shown up anyway and had nothing to do with the Liberator's activities.

"The R-squared, please?"

"Correlation strength is 98.06% plus/minus .005, Doctor Carling."

Tricia lightly thumped her fist on the desk. "Yes!" she whispered to herself. One last step. "LANA, what is the average difference between onset date and patient case date in the model?"

"Average difference is 7.8 days with a variance of 2.1 days."

"LANA, compute a distribution of onset date versus case date using the model as a reference. Apply the distribution to the patients that have no registered onset date and include them in the correlation, please."

"Yes, Doctor Carling. Calculating distribution using Monte Carlo algorithm...distribution calculated. Applying to segmented records and correlating."

The display updated. Several of the numbers for the more recent events shifted. "Correlation strength is 99.78% plus/minus < 1 part per thousand."

Tricia sat straight up and slapped both her palms down on the workspace surface. 99.8%. She was right. There was something here. She didn't know for sure what it was, but this was a statistical correlation no one could argue wasn't convincing and compelling.

Tricia spent the next half of an hour preparing a new model that showed the results and a quick report summarizing the results. She sent it to Marni's hospital address with a note that simply said, "Call me when you get this."

Tricia didn't have to wait long. She'd just finished cleaning up her workstation and gathered her things to leave when her commpod chimed. "Call from Marni Haskell, tagged urgent," the commpod reported.

Tricia tapped it to answer the call. "Did you see it, Marni?"

"Yeah, Trish. I did. I didn't go through the full model, but I skimmed the report."

"And?" Tricia prompted eagerly.

"I don't know Trish. We went through this. We expected clustering in the patient records. Furthermore, these downtown locations are very high-traffic areas. Frankly, it isn't a surprise that the patients might have been there."

"That's true, Marni, but the correlation is undeniable. It's too high to be simple coincidence." She pressed her argument, "And, as for the clustering, what if whoever is planning this is using the cycles to help hide what they are doing? Knowing you'd look for that, what if they are planning their activities to use some of these cycles and intervals to help mask what they are doing?"

Marni huffed again. "It sounds kinda paranoid, Tricia. Remember, the police have ruled out any pathogens in the Liberators' smoke and gunk."

"I know, but..."

"...but yeah. I agree with you, Tricia. The correlation is too strong. Let me look over the model at the end of my shift, and I'll take it to the police. I think they have to at least give it some consideration, given the analysis you've done."

Tricia did a quick fist pump. "That's all I'm suggesting we do, Marni. There's a connection, but even though we don't know what it is or what's going on, it's still a plausible lead to check. We need to convince them to take it seriously."

"Leave it with me, Trish. I'll make them listen."

"Thanks, Marn."

"And I have to hand it to you, Tricia. This is some impressive detective work. Hundreds of people have been looking at this for months now, and you're the first one to connect these dots. You're scary sometimes, my friend, you know that, don't you?"

Tricia smiled. Even though Marni couldn't see it, she crossed her heart with her finger. "I promise to only use my powers for good, Marni."

"You'd better. Hey, I've got to get back, and I think you need to take the rest of today to relax. Promise me you'll do that, yeah?"

"Yep. I'm outta here. I really, *really* have to get the rest of the sand out of my suit."

"Don't rub it in." Tricia could hear Marni giggle on the other end of the call before Marni ended it.

*Well done, Tricia, very well done*, she congratulated herself. *Strength and light bursts aren't your only superpower*. Smiling smugly, she collected her things and headed for home.

About the same time that Tricia threw the remains of her lunch into the trash, Purity and Opus were standing in front of the large monitor situated in the conferencing area of their headquarters-slash-laboratory. The monitor showed a map of the city. It was decorated with several yellow dots depicting candidate locations for their next demonstration. The two of them were having a vigorous debate over which location would be best.

Purity had to admit that Opus' choice was likely the best one in terms of making a flashy public display. However, a couple of the other locations, ones that were closer to crowds of people, would be better for her purposes. She leaned in a bit, put a hand on his shoulder, and delivered her counterargument, pointing out another of the yellow dots with her other hand. Opus crossed his arms and, after considering for a few minutes, nodded reluctantly. He tapped the dot Purity had been endorsing, and it turned green.

Purity smiled. She honestly thought Opus was a decent leader and managed the team well, but, like most men, if he wouldn't listen to reason, a soft voice, gentle touch, and a whiff of her perfume usually brought him around to her way of thinking. She wasn't above any tactic— well, almost any— at this stage of her plan, no matter how distasteful, to see her vision unfold, and if she had an advantage she could use to see that happen, she'd use it without hesitation.

They heard the side door open and shut and turned to look in its direction. Their stockier colleague was walking toward them, grinning.

"Did the pickup go all right, Riptide?" Purity asked him. She assumed it had, judging from the grin on his face, but she didn't want to leave anything to chance.

"Easy peasy," Riptide replied with his thick Australian accent.

Opus frowned a bit. He looked at Riptide, then at Purity, then back at Riptide. "What pickup?" he asked, obviously not pleased he was out of the loop.

Riptide looked a little uncomfortable and glanced past Opus at Purity. She nodded, encouraging him to respond.

"Well," he said, looking back at Opus, "Purity put me in touch with someone who could get us some items that might prove useful if Beacon shows up at one of our little parties."

Opus turned and looked at Purity. "Nothing that would kill her, right?" he asked very directly.

Purity shook her head as Riptide replied, "Nah, nothing like that. Just a few things that should slow her down. Plus, I've got a few ideas for enhancements that'll boost 'em up a notch."

Opus seemed to relax. "But still non-lethal?"

"Yeah, yeah," Riptide assured him. "Look, she packs quite a wallop, so we probably need something with a little more kick to slow her down than what comes off the shelf. Don't worry, mate. I've got this. I'll make sure we can keep her off our back if it comes to that, without killing her, but I won't promise she won't be a little worse for the wear."

Opus nodded, assured his wishes on the matter were being respected. Purity smiled to herself, very satisfied that another piece was in place to help make sure her plans went without any disruption. They were too close now for anything to interfere.

# Collision

**B**eacon yawned. Granted, she didn't feel fatigue as much when she tapped her powers, but nearly a week of late-night stakeouts was starting to catch up with her. She was still confident, though, that her hunch would pay off. If the Liberators of Gaia held to their pattern, they were now slightly overdue for one of their demonstrations, and from her research, she was nearly positive that VeriMed would be their next target. The construction site at Meyer's Tower just didn't get the foot traffic that this section of Harbor Street did, and it was obvious that they wanted an audience. VeriMed was one of the few companies left on their manifesto that fit their pattern.

She was currently stationed where she had been for most of the week, crouched on a low rooftop just across Harbor Street from the building that housed VeriMed's corporate headquarters. This position gave Beacon a clear line of sight to the front of the building and the maintenance alley to the side. There really wasn't any meaningful access on the other two sides, so if they were going to do something, she would see it. She had her hood up and her cape wrapped around her, channeling her flows of energy into the suit to activate its camouflage, rendering her nearly invisible sitting there in the shadows. It was tedious and boring, making it even harder to stay awake, powers or not, but Beacon had built a pretty solid picture of the building schedule: when the cleaners arrived, various food and office supply deliveries, and that pizza and Chinese seemed to be the go-to food choices for people working late.

It was just starting to get light in the eastern sky, and Beacon was about to call it for the night when a gray van broke the early morning silence. It looked very ordinary, but she decided she'd go ahead and check it out, and then if it turned out to be nothing, she could pack it in and try again tomorrow night. There was still time to get in a nap before she had to be at the lab.

She studied the van as it pulled into the maintenance alley and stopped. It was a BioMat van, clearly labeled by the name with a brightly colored cartoon virus inside a circle-slash replacing the 'O' on the side. They looked familiar. She puzzled for a second and then placed it; they did the biohazardous materials pickups for the labs at the university. Likely VeriMed was a client as well.

The back of the van slid open, and four people hopped out, three men and a woman, all wearing gray coveralls with the BioMat logo on the back. One of the men was tall and muscular with a trimmed beard. Another was shorter and stockier, also with a beard but bald. The third man and the woman could have been brother and sister; both were of average height and slim with short dark hair. They lifted two hand carts out of the back of the van and wheeled them up to the side door. The taller man pressed the intercom, and after a short exchange with someone on the other end of it, she heard a buzzing sound. They opened the door and wheeled their carts inside.

*Looks fairly ordinary. Probably nothing to see here after all,* she figured, stretching her arms and back, but then the driver caught her eye. While the others went to work, he remained seated in the front of the van, almost as if he were waiting for something. Maybe it was nothing, but it was odd enough to her that she decided she would stay until they left, just to make sure, and crouched back down.

After about fifteen minutes, they returned, their carts loaded with various waste containers she presumed had been emptied from various locations in the building. They wheeled the carts up to the back of the van, and the two larger men started unloading the carts into the back of the van.

While the two men unloaded, though, the other man and woman proceeded to lift an odd-looking canister out of the back and carried it to the side of the building, setting it down between the street and the access door. The canister was brushed metal, about three feet high and half that in diameter.

*Well, well. What do we have here?* Beacon wondered to herself. *This just got a bit more interesting.*

Her curiosity piqued, she sat up straighter and started watching them more intently. The pair of them walked back to the van and went inside. When they came back out, the man had a small device in his hands, like a commpad, only a little bulkier, and the woman was carrying a wire basket holding several smaller cans. The man took his device to the side of the silvery canister and started tapping on it while the woman carried her basket to the building wall. She picked up two of the smaller cans, one in each hand, shook them both for several seconds, and then started to spray paint the wall in blue and green, eventually outlining the familiar symbol of the Liberators of Gaia. *Game time*, Beacon thought.

Beacon quenched her camouflage and leaped off the rooftop, soaring over the street. A short pulse of dark energy slowed her descent, and she landed deftly at the mouth of the alley facing the crew of workers.

"I didn't know you guys made deliveries too," Beacon goaded them, her voice shattering the silence of the alleyway. They all turned abruptly, stared at her, and froze. She could see the fear on their faces and smiled. *Busted!*

The tall man in the van was the first to react. "Time to go, people! Riptide, we need a distraction."

"Copy that, Opus!" the shorter bald man responded, his Aussie accent thick with urgency, and turned to open a narrow case against the inner wall of the van.

"I just need a minute!" the thinner man at the canister shouted. "Harmony, give me a hand!"

The short-haired woman dropped her spray cans and sprinted toward him.

Opus yelled back, "No promises, Scorpius. Get a move on!"

Beacon hesitated for a moment. To one side, she saw the bald man, Riptide, start to level what looked to be a net gun in her direction. On the other, the other two were scrambling, she assumed, to finish arming whatever that canister held inside.

She made her choice in a split-second; stopping the device was most important. The net gun, she decided, wasn't really an immediate threat, something she could deal with when and if the time came.

She moved toward the pair frantically working beside the cylinder when she heard "Incoming!" followed by the air blast that told her Riptide had fired the net gun. Beacon spun toward the sound and saw the net expanding in front of her, propelled by four large weights at the corners. *This'll be an easy catch*, she said to herself but realized too late she'd drastically underestimated it.

The net met her outstretched hand, but the heavy ballast weights flew past her, wrenching her backward off her feet. As she fell, the net wrapped and twisted around her body, fouling her arms and legs. She hit the asphalt hard with a grunt and rolled several feet.

"She's down!" shouted Riptide triumphantly. "Get it in gear, Scorpius! No idea how long that will hold her."

Beacon worked her hands up in front of her chest, grasped the mesh in both hands, and tried to tear the net away. She pulled hard, but the net was clearly made for larger quarry and thoroughly resisted her efforts.

*It must have metal wires woven into it*, she realized. Thinking quickly, she dumped an intense heat pulse into the net in front of her. Within seconds, the net began to smolder, then glow, and finally melt, forming a hole in front of her hands. She jerked as several drops of molten material narrowly missed her waist, sizzling on the asphalt.

Redirecting the energy to her strength, she grasped the net again, pulled hard, and was rewarded by the harsh rending sound of the net tearing way around the hole's edges. The hole opened slowly at first, but as she ripped through more of the threading and material, it parted more easily until it was finally wide enough for her to start to squirm free.

"Hurry up, Scorpius! She's almost out!" Riptide yelled to warn them.

Harmony grabbed Scorpius' arm. "We aren't going to make it. We have to go, NOW!"

Scorpius groaned, but when he saw Beacon pulling the net down over her head, he had no choice but to agree. He turned with Harmony, and they ran toward the van.

It took Beacon only a few more seconds to fully free herself from the smoking net. When she kicked the last of it off, Scorpius was already in the van, and Harmony was just pulling herself up to the open door behind him.

"Get us out of here!" Opus yelled to the driver in front, banging on the inner wall of the van. The van's engine revved in response, belching blue smoke out of the tailpipe.

Beacon raced toward the van and just caught the handrail to the side of the open door. The van lurched, causing Harmony to slip a bit. As she fell to the side, Beacon grabbed a handful of the back of her coverall.

Harmony yelped in surprise. "She's got me!!" Harmony wailed in panic.

The rest of the guys grabbed Harmony and tried to pull her into the van. Beacon pulled back, desperately trying to find some purchase with her feet as the van started to pull forward. A two-way tug of war ensued, on the one hand between Beacon and the van and between her and Harmony on the other. The thick smoke and stench of the tires spinning on the pavement made Beacon's eyes water.

Despite her best efforts, though, the van finally started to pull away slowly. Her feet started to skid and slide on the pavement. *I'm going to lose this*, Beacon's mind yelled at her as she strained to hold back the van and attempt to extract Harmony, along with any other Liberators, that she could.

Abruptly, her toe slid up against the frame of a drain grate in the street. She desperately stomped down hard on the grate, once, then twice, and on the third time, the grate bent and twisted in its frame, giving her a foothold. She planted her feet and leaned back into it, drawing more strength and pushing hard with her legs. The van's tires started to spin again, spewing more smoke.

"I'm slipping!" Harmony screamed again. Beacon could feel the team losing their grip on Harmony. Unfortunately, she could also feel the handrail start to warp in her grip. She knew something was going to give pretty soon. She just didn't know which would give first.

"Hold on," she heard Riptide say, "I got this."

Beacon glanced over just in time to see Riptide unzip the front of Harmony's coveralls. The fabric jerked backward and tore free at the seams, leaving Beacon with a handful of torn gray cloth. The recoil sent Harmony and the team flying into the front of the van. Beacon dropped the torn piece of the coveralls and reached for the bumper to get a better grip, but the handrail finally buckled under the strain and snapped loose, sending Beacon sprawling on her back. Abruptly freed, the van skidded wildly to the side and started to pull away.

Beacon snapped back up to her feet and raised her hand. Pointing toward the rear tire, she projected her power into the emitter in the finger of her glove, sending a blinding beam of light toward the van. Fortune was on the Liberators' side, though, as the van hit a pothole at the last second and bounced, causing her to miss the tire and melt a long ugly gash along the lower section of the van's body panel. Determined to chase it down, she started to sprint toward the van when Riptide appeared in the back door. He grinned and waved his fingers at her as he tossed two fist-sized blinking spheres into the road behind the accelerating van.

"What the..." Beacon muttered to herself and drew back as she watched the small spheres bounce down the alley toward her. Not having any idea what to expect, except perhaps the worst, she instinctively crouched and cast a shield up in front of her just as the devices went off. Waves of intense sound impacted her shield.

The shield took most of it, but the remainder drove Beacon to her knees. Momentarily stunned, her shield dissipated, leaving her kneeling on the asphalt to catch her breath. Her ears were ringing, and she felt a small trickle of blood coming from her nose. *Riot control ultrasonics,* she realized, wiping her nose and looking down the alley. The van had vanished.

Beacon stood up slowly and groaned a bit as her back sharply reminded her of what she'd just put it through. She stretched gingerly, brushed off her knees, and walked back to where she'd dropped the torn coveralls. She held the piece of gray fabric up by the corners and studied the logo staring back at her. *What is BioMat's connection here?* she wondered and tapped her commpod to call the anonymous emergency response line for the police.

She was looking over the inactive device when the police arrived a few minutes later. The patrol car pulled up, lights flashing, highlighting her with its front headlights, and two officers climbed out of the car.

"So. It's you." one of the officers said to Beacon in a somewhat irritated tone. "Are you the one that called us over here?"

"I sure did," Beacon replied.

The officer grunted. "Well, I hope for your sake it's something worthwhile."

She ignored the officer's tone. "I just had a run in with the Liberators of Gaia. Looks like they were in the process of setting up one of their goodies, and I got in the way."

"Where are they?" the officer asked, now clearly much more interested in the situation.

Beacon sighed. "Unfortunately, they got away, but they did leave a few interesting items behind." She tossed the piece of coverall toward them. "You'll want to look into this. Looks like there's some connection between them and BioMat." She then patted the top of the canister. "You'll want to have the lab guys dig into this too. They didn't get a chance to set this one off, so I'm hoping there might be some useful clues hidden in here."

The two officers surveyed the alley, making note of the coveralls and canister, and nodded to her. The one she assumed was the senior officer then looked at her directly. "Of course, we'll need you to come along too. There will be questions we'll need answered."

"Now, officers," Beacon admonished them, "we've had this conversation before. I don't accept rides from strangers, and besides, I think these little party favors will give you plenty to do without me tagging along."

The officers looked at each other and started to draw their guns, but when they turned back to place her under arrest, Beacon was already gone.

Purity sat at one of the tables in their makeshift lab, watching the genome resequencing simulator while she waited for the team to return. Despite the early morning hour, she was feeling particularly happy this morning. She had made the extra effort to be here with the team, to personally double-check that the colorant in their signature blue and green smoke generators was properly tagged with her extra ingredient and fully ready to deploy.

The team had to leave while it was still dark to make sure their latest demonstration was in place and set to trigger first thing in the morning as people started to make their way to work. They wanted to make sure this display would be seen by a large audience. To Purity, that meant making sure as many people were exposed as possible.

She was humming contentedly to herself, stirring her tea as she watched the computer work through the simulation. It was the same song that always brought her comfort as a girl when she could escape from her foster parents—the only time when she could truly feel safe.

*...became my own story's hero,* she sang along silently, as she always did, with her favorite line.

Today, though, the song was inspired not by relief but by the hope and optimism she felt about this final test. After the device did its work this morning, it would only be a few weeks until she had the data confirming what she already knew: that this was the culmination of her years of work, that this final strain was indeed what she would need to bring her plan to fruition. Purity was so confident, in fact, that she used her time waiting for the team to return to start the sequencing she'd need to blend in the final component, her *pièce de resistance* that would ensure her genetic cocktail would spread far and fast when it was released as part of the Liberators' big finale, the big demonstration that marked the end of the campaign they –she – had planned.

Purity was just cross-checking the simulation's progress with the data on her commpad when she heard the van pull up outside the receiving door. She checked her watch. They were back right on time. Shortly, she heard the door open and the team's footfalls on the floor as they came in. Without looking up, she smiled and cheerfully asked, "So, how did it go?"

Opus answered, his voice sounding slightly raspy, "We ran into a bit of a problem."

Purity sat upright, her stomach tightening, and turned toward them. "What do you mean prob..." she started to ask but broke off when she saw them straggling toward her. Harmony's coveralls were torn, and she was rubbing her shoulder. Scorpius had his arm around her, helping her walk. All of them looked stressed and haggard. Her knuckles turned white as her grasp tightened on the commpad.

"What happened to you?!?" Purity demanded.

Riptide answered for them, "We got a surprise visit by Beacon."

"Beacon!?" Purity repeated. "Did she follow you here?"

"We don't believe so," Opus assured her, but his voice was anything but confident.

"And the device? What about the device?"

Scorpius answered this time, "We failed to get it set. It all happened so fast. We were setting up, and suddenly, she was there. The team tried to give Harmony and me time, but she was too strong, too fast. We barely got out. She almost got Harmony."

Harmony nodded, still rubbing her shoulder.

"And you just left it there?!?" Purity raged. The team nodded. Purity cursed loudly and threw her pad at the wall next to her. It shattered, and the pieces scattered across the floor. The team jumped, startled by her outburst.

"Great! Just great!" Purity continued to rebuke them. "Beacon didn't get Harmony, but do you know what she did get? She got our device...*intact.*"

"What's the problem, Purity?" Opus asked. "It's not like our names are written on it. It's clean of fingerprints or anything else that could identify us. So what if she got it?"

"It's not like you can just buy that thing and what goes into it down at the local U-Save, Opus," Purity reminded him, running her hands up through her hair. "When they take it apart and analyze it, there's a pretty good chance they can trace it back here, trace it back to *us*. We are officially out of time now. We've got to step up our timeline. We may only have days to get to our final demonstration at this point, a week at the most."

Opus and the team just stared at her. Purity looked away and composed herself by smoothing down her lab smock, adjusting the bun in her hair, and straightening her glasses. She couldn't afford to alienate them now when she was so close. Choosing a calmer voice, she changed direction, "How did the net gun and sonic compression charges work? Did you get to use them? Did they have any effect on her?"

"Yeah, we used them," Riptide reported. "The net gun bought us some time. Gave Scorpius and Harmony a chance to at least get back to the van. The compression charges definitely slowed her down. If it weren't for them, we probably wouldn't have gotten away."

"Slowed her down?" Purity said, exasperated. She took a deep breath to stay calm and forced herself to maintain a more even and calculating tone. "Well, I am glad you all got away — really, I am — but trust me, if she figures all this out and shows up here, slowing her down will not be remotely close enough."

"So, what do you expect us to do, Purity?" Opus challenged her, now expressing some irritation of his own.

"We have a lot of work to do, so we need to get going on it. *That's* what I expect," Purity snapped, backing him down. "We also need to get some precautions and contingencies in place for when Beacon shows up. And yes, I mean 'when', not 'if'. You can take it to the bank when I tell you. Beacon will figure this out, and she will show up here. When she does," Purity pointed at the team sternly, "rest assured, we will deal with her my way."

DMAT

# Connections

Tricia sat at her workspace, loudly crunching her chicken Caesar salad and reading her screen. She had been spending her spare time the past several days researching BioMat, trying to draw some connection between them, the Liberators of Gaia, and the investigation Marni had drawn her into. The lab was empty except for her, giving her a chance to continue her own side of this investigation with some privacy.

As far as BioMat itself was concerned, she hadn't found anything particularly noteworthy. It had been founded a few years ago and claimed to specialize in more environmentally friendly approaches to gathering, storing, and disposing of biohazardous waste produced by a variety of industries.

Tricia was right in that the university contracted with them to handle the waste removal for the various labs on and around campus. That contract was relatively new, and signing it was touted as a major accomplishment by the ESG Advocacy Council as part of their program to move the university toward more sustainable and eco-friendly services. Since Rene had said she participates in the Council, Tricia had made a mental note to perhaps talk to Rene about what she knew about them but hadn't gotten around to it just yet. She had also called Harold to see if he knew any more about them, but he said he didn't. He said they came during the off hours, and no one in the lab typically had any contact with them.

Besides the university, BioMat had contracts with dozens of other companies in Crystal Bay. Interestingly, many of them were on the Liberators of Gaia's naughty list they had published in their manifesto earlier in the year. If the Liberators were to use a legitimate business as a front, BioMat certainly would be an excellent choice, but so far, there was no obvious direct evidence that could provide a link between the organizations, at least none that anyone would take seriously.

Having tugged on the BioMat thread as far as she could, Tricia had turned her attention to the founders themselves. She had to admit to herself they were a fascinating story, and she was completely absorbed in reading about them while she worked her way through her salad.

Jeremy McKinley came from a rural agricultural background and was a rising college football star when an injury prematurely ended his athletic career. He poured himself into his studies and graduated with degrees in agriculture and physics, an interesting combination.

After completing his graduate degree in business and economics, he went on to form several startups, all in the areas of environmentally conscious alternatives and sustainability: clean energy, cleaning products, agricultural methods, and so on. He really hit paydirt, though, when he got involved in biofuels. His company was credited for making the real breakthrough that allowed fuels created from agricultural animal waste to be an effective alternative to petroleum. He was catapulted into the spotlight when his company made the first coast-to-coast trip with a biofuel/electric hybrid automobile that did not require recharging or refueling during the trip.

It was at this startup where he met his wife, Kym. She was the Chief Scientist for the startup and bore an impressive range of degrees in engineering, chemistry, and bioengineering. They had worked closely together on the hybrid trial and, as many close work collaborations go, it developed into something more. From then on out, they were inseparable at work, in public, and in the media, and were married shortly after.

They caught a real break, though, when the federal government, eager to drive the nation's plans for energy independence and green clean energy, became active in blocking sales of emergent green energy companies to overseas oil production interests. Eventually, the courts ruled that the government was overreaching in blocking these sales, but the years in court, plus generous federal subsidies, had given many of these fledgling companies, including the McKinley's, the time they needed to become sustainable and establish themselves.

Once the hybrid transcontinental run was a success, the company rocketed to the top of the investor hot list and became a darling in the high-tech and clean energy sectors. The McKinleys took the company public and, after a suitable transition period, turned the company over to new leadership, but not before securing a big fat pile of stock, options, and agreements for licensing residuals.

Equipped now with several lifetimes of financial security, the McKinleys went on to become a major power couple in the city and nationally as well. They still founded and funded a number of startups, BioMat being just one example. They commanded a very strong public image in the media and at conferences or other speaking engagements. Jeremy had obviously continued to work out, and with his deep voice, chiseled jawline, and dark hair just starting to gray at the temples, he looked and spoke like the strong business and community leader that he was.

Kym hardly looked any different now than she did in her twenties. She was still thin, tall, and beautiful, and with her auburn hair, piercing blue eyes, and immaculately tailored suits, she was as much a media celebrity as her husband, if not more so. In addition to working with Jeremy on various startups and ventures, she had also become a major advocate and driving force in multiple charities, foundations, and programs related to women's healthcare, child services, and education.

Tricia twirled the lock of hair hanging in front of her face around her finger. She found Jeremy and Kym McKinley to be an interesting and complicated conundrum. They had made their fortune in eco-friendly ventures and were still very active in numerous causes related to the environment. There was clearly a fit there, but Kym's charity work seemed to run in direct opposition to the infertility cases Tricia believed were somehow linked to whatever the Liberators of Gaia were actually up to. Why would someone so active in these kinds of charities be deliberately trying to cause infertility, or was it something else?

Further, despite their altruistic endeavors, they both had been instrumental in bringing to Crystal Bay many of the technology, pharmaceutical, and bioengineering companies that were blacklisted on the Liberators' manifest. Maybe that was to give them more influence in their practices, or maybe it was to drum up business for the other startups like BioMat, or maybe it was just an act.

Either way, Tricia could not help but be impressed with Jeremy and Kym McKinley. Deep down, she sincerely hoped they were not involved with any of this—that BioMat was somehow a red herring—because, in every other way, these people seemed like just the kind of positive visionaries and influencers society genuinely needed.

*As impressive as they are though,* she repeatedly reminded herself, *I have to keep letting the evidence lead where it leads. Again, a lot of threads that fit, but nothing that ties them together.*

One other thing about her encounter with the Liberators continued to gnaw at her; clearly, they had prepared for her to catch up to them at some point, but all their countermeasures were deliberately non-lethal. They could probably have chosen weapons to use against her that were much more devastating, but they'd sacrificed firepower and effectiveness to avoid trying to kill her. While this was consistent with their modus operandi for their other activities—none of their demonstrations had come close to hurting anyone or causing any real damage—it wasn't consistent with any scheme she could think of for causing any of the infertility symptoms Marni was tracking. It was a big puzzle, and clearly, quite a few of the pieces were still missing.

Tricia sat on her couch, still in her workout clothes, eating ice cream from the container while Rascal purred, pressed up against her thigh. Truth be told, she was full from the burgers and fries she'd picked up on the way home from the gym, but her father had told her there was always room for ice cream.

*Ice cream always fits in the cracks*, she told herself, scraping down the sides of the container and licking off the spoon. When she was finished, Tricia held down the spoon, and Rascal happily finished cleaning it off.

Her workout today had been another confusing mix of discovery and worry, but Tricia had become used to feeling that mix routinely when it came to her powers. She had intended to have a normal workout and started her routine as usual with a round of cardio on one of the elliptical cross-trainers. After working up a good sweat and getting thoroughly warmed up, she had planned to do some resistance training with the free weights. However, when she found the gym was relatively empty this evening and that the weight room in particular was deserted, she had changed her plans, opting to do a little precision practice with her powers instead.

It had been a while since she'd done these drills, and the extra privacy offered a chance to make up for it. Normally, she would start with a heavy set and draw just enough power to lift the weight and set it back down. She would then add more weight and repeat until she ran out of plates or someone walked in, whichever came first. If she had time, she'd work back down, finishing with some unpowered lifts just to make sure she got in a real workout.

Today went very differently, though. By now, Tricia had developed a very good feel for how much power she needed to apply for a given weight, but today, it all felt off. At each level, she was consistently applying too much strength for the weight, requiring her to draw back and repeat multiple times until she got it right. In fact, she hadn't felt this lack of control since she'd first started training. Puzzled and frustrated, she had to pause frequently, wiping off the sweat with her towel and taking long drinks to settle herself and stay focused.

After a few more sets, it finally dawned on her. She had always thought the power she drew from the energy around her simply added to her strength, that the effect was generally constant with how much she tapped. Comparing her performance today, though, she had realized that her powers were, in fact, *multiplicative*, not additive. As she had been working out more at the gym, the extra training with Sensei Tim, and weekend work at The Ridge, she was becoming physically stronger, and as she became naturally stronger, she deduced that her powers were amplifying her natural increases in strength. To lift the maximum weight here at the gym today, she needed to draw far less on the energy around her than she had several weeks ago.

This was a major and astounding revelation for her. It meant that her full potential was substantially higher than it had been before. It also meant that her upper limits were not just about how much energy she could draw but also depended on her own physical capability. The harder she worked, the more powerful she could become.

That, by itself, would have given her a lot to think about, but once again, she had discovered yet another thing about her abilities completely by accident, renewing the feelings of anxiety, confusion, and lack of control she had felt early in her journey.

With these feelings came one that had also started to accompany each new discovery: loneliness. More frequently, she was reminded of the burden she carried and how she had to carry it alone. True, it was by choice; she was choosing to protect others by not involving them in her secret, but it didn't prevent how alone she felt doing it.

The walk home gave her time to deal with the now-familiar cocktail of excitement, fear, wonder, and worry. Setting the emotions aside for the time being and thinking through it analytically, her confrontation with the Liberators now made much more sense, given this new discovery. When she faced them, she had used her powers for the first time at a very instinctive level. In the heat of battle, she had simply *reacted*.

Using them so naturally was progress that pleased her, but it also meant she hadn't really been thinking about what she was doing at the time. If she had been thinking about it deliberately and empirically, given what she had known then, she would never have tried to stop a van the way she did with raw brute strength.

She *had* tried, though, instinctively without thinking, and she had succeeded. *Maybe my body knows, even if my brain doesn't*, she thought. *Maybe it's time for me to just trust myself more and stop overthinking it. Like Sensei said, stop constraining. Stop gripping so tightly, and trust it. Trust myself.*

It was a lot to mull over, and Tricia knew she'd need time to fathom it all, but the more she walked, the more her prolonged use of her powers at the gym caught up with her. She was even starting to feel a little light-headed. Giving in to her growling stomach and plummeting blood sugar, she took a small detour to swing by her favorite burger joint and picked up a double order of cheeseburgers and fries. It was a good decision. The burgers and fries helped her mood just as much, or even more than they did her appetite.

Tricia got up off the couch, much to Rascal's objection, rinsed the ice cream container and spoon, and put the spent container into the compost recycling bin under the sink. She walked into the bathroom and started to draw a hot bath. A good soak would do wonders for her muscles and her spirits.

As steam started to fill the bathroom, she started peeling off her sweaty workout clothes, tossing them into the sink; they could take a soak as well and get washed later. She'd just tested the temperature with her hand and was ready to get in when her commpod chimed. She reached up and tapped the device in her ear to trigger the commpod's built-in assistant.

"Who is calling?" she asked it.

"Marni Haskell is calling," the assistant responded.

*Bath first*, she thought. "Tell Marni I'm about to get into the bath, and I'll call her back shortly."

"I'll tell her, Tricia," the assistant acknowledged and ended the exchange with a ping.

Tricia took the commpod out of her ear and slipped into the hot water.

About an hour later, Tricia was dried and comfortably in her pajamas, sitting on her bed. She put the commpod in her ear and started brushing her hair as she called Marni back.

"Hey, Trish!" Marni answered right away.

"Hey yourself," Tricia answered back. "Sorry about earlier. I'd just gotten back from the gym and rather desperately needed a bath. You caught me just as I was getting into the tub."

"No worries at all. It was a tough workout today, I take it?"

"It was," Tricia paused for a moment, trying to pick the right word, "...revealing."

"Revealing, huh?" Marni chuckled, "What happened? Did you tear out your tights doing a lift?"

Tricia snorted. "Har har, Marni. No, smartie, nothing quite like that. Just one of those workouts that, well, tests your limits, let's just say."

"Very mysterious, Trish," Marni chided her. Tricia expected Marni to question her more but realized this might not entirely be a social call when Marni pressed on instead. "Anyway, I appreciate you calling me back right away. I'm here at the hospital and was hoping to talk to you before I left."

"Wait, you're still at the hospital? At this hour?" Tricia inquired, a bit concerned. Unless she was on the late shift, Marni wasn't one for staying late, so something must be up.

"Yeah, I am," Marni said. "It's been, well, revealing here today too."

"Ok, you've got me a bit worried. What's going on there, Marn?"

"Sooooo, you remember, after you found that correlation between the Liberators incidents and the infertility cases, we took that to the police for more follow-up?"

"Yeah, I remember."

"After Beacon broke up their latest attempt, she managed to get the police one of their devices intact."

*Yeah, I remember that too*, Tricia thought.

"The police took it apart and gave it a thorough going over. They decided it was pretty much like the others. It's on somewhat of a bigger scale, but essentially the same kind of low-yield explosive device with that smoke generator and blue and green coloring. Their analysis showed the same thing they'd found before; while the smoke and colorant made a big display and a big mess, it was generally biologically and chemically inert, completely nontoxic."

Tricia scowled a bit. She had been hoping for a bit more. "Ok, Marn. So, what happens next then?"

"That's just the thing, Trish," Marni went on, "since we'd showed that possible connection between the Liberators' activities and our cases, they sent over samples for us to look at, samples from both the device Beacon captured, as well as samples of the residue taken from previous incidents. We ran them through some tests of our own."

Marni paused a bit before letting the other shoe fall. "It's not inert, Trish."

Tricia sat bolt upright. She pushed her hair back and tossed her hairbrush down toward the end of the bed, startling Rascal. "What is it then?" Tricia asked.

"We don't entirely know yet. We do know it's some kind of organic material, but it also seems to have some kind of genetic payload. It's clearly carrying a variety of gene sequences."

Tricia's stomach tightened. "What kind of genetic payload?"

"We're still working on that. However, at this stage, all we know is that it isn't inert. The police lab tests were right in that it isn't directly poisonous or harmful, but their test protocols wouldn't have found this. We don't know if it's harmful or not, but given the correlation you found, we are currently treating it as an unknown pathogen and as a potential cause for the infertility we've been chasing."

"Wow. That's incredible, Marni." Tricia was both excited and anxious, excited that something had come from what she'd done and that they might be onto an answer, but also anxious that this now looked much less like something coincidental or accidental. More and more, it looked to be deliberate and malicious, that someone was planning it, someone incredibly smart and incredibly devious.

"Yeah, well, it's quite a lot to process. I'll tell you, Trish, if you hadn't figured out the correlation between the cases we were working and those events of theirs, and if Beacon hadn't gotten her hands on these samples, we might never have found this, whatever 'this' actually is."

"I'm glad I could help. I'm sure Beacon is, too." Tricia smiled to herself, "I really appreciate you sharing this with me, Marni."

"Well, there's a little more behind me telling you than simply sharing, Tricia. I found something else."

"What else, Marni?" Tricia asked, that anxious feeling intensifying.

Marni's voice became very serious. "Just how much do you know about Rene Thornton and the people in her lab, Trish?"

Tricia's eyes widened. "Honestly, Marni, I guess I don't really know her or them very well at all. I met Rene for the first time when we went to lunch, and I've only bumped into her a handful of times since then. Her reputation is stellar, though, Marni. Why do you ask?"

"Because," Marni explained, "while we don't know what these gene sequences are or what they do, we think the way they were made is very similar to edited genomics we've gotten previously from Rene and her team. We've been collaborating with her lab for quite a while now, more recently including these cases.

"Different gene editing techniques leave, um, fingerprints that can give us clues as to how gene sequences are sliced and diced and recombined. These samples have a lot of the telltale signs that they were made using techniques that are commonly practiced by Rene and her team at the Advanced Genetics Lab there on campus."

Tricia's heart sank. She hunched over and ran her fingers up through her hair. "I... I can't believe it, Marni. Someone on Rene's team responsible for something like this?" she finally stammered out.

"Look, Trish," Marni said quickly, walking things back a bit. "It's just an observation, maybe nothing more than coincidence. As I said, we don't know enough about this to do anything, and honestly, a lot of genetics and bioengineering labs use these same methods, so it may just be nothing. It might be a complete red herring, but, you know, it just looked too familiar to at least not ask about, right?"

"Yeah, sure, Marni. Of course, it makes perfect sense to ask." Tricia agreed, still holding her head in her hands, possibilities already racing through her head. "And no question that we, uh, we have to follow the evidence wherever it leads, don't we?"

Marni's tone softened, "You ok, Trish?"

"Sure, I'm good, Marn." Tricia assured her, "Look, I'm really glad you've finally got a solid lead. I'm thrilled, honestly. As for the rest of it, we'll just have to wait and see until you know more, right?"

Despite what she told Marni, Tricia had already decided that waiting was *not* going to be her next step.

"Exactly. Well, that's all I wanted to share, and it's getting late. I should think about getting out of here. See you at class later this week?"

"Absolutely. And thanks again for the call. I appreciate you letting me know, and I'll keep my eyes and ears open around campus. If I catch wind of anything, I'll let you know, ok?"

"Sounds great, Trish. Have a good night!"

"You too. Be safe getting home." Tricia signed off, tapping the commpod to end the call.

While they'd been talking, Rascal had climbed up next to her on the bed and was rubbing her head against Tricia's hip. Tricia pushed her hair back once again, leaned against the headboard, and scooped Rascal up to her chest. Rascal purred loudly as Tricia scratched her head between her ears. "Just when you think we've had enough surprises for one day, huh fuzzball? Looks like we've got some new angles to look into now, don't we?"

Rascal squinted at her happily and mewed in agreement.

# Ensnared

Just after dusk, Beacon sat poised on the top of the roof of the building next to the Advanced Genetics Lab. She had her hood pulled up, and from where she crouched in the deepening evening shadows, she had a clear view of the back of the lab building.

After the call with Marni, Tricia did a bit more digging into BioMat and confirmed that this particular laboratory on campus, along with a few others, was one of their routine stops. She'd chatted a bit more with Harold, just on the slim chance there was even the slightest tidbit he could add to the emerging picture, but given Marni's concerns, she'd held off on tapping Rene for any information on BioMat or the contract with the university.

Tricia had also used a couple of lunch hours to scout around that part of the campus. The lab itself was relatively new and sat adjacent to the original lab building which now was supposed to be mostly abandoned and relegated to storage.

Tricia had noticed that while there wasn't much noteworthy around the lab itself, there were more signs of recent activity around the back of the old lab than she might have expected, given its supposed level of disuse. Fresh tire marks and footprints by the doors and loading area, as well as new trash in the bins, all indicated there was more going on here than met the eye.

*At least the eco-terrorists aren't litter bugs*, she had mused. Regardless of who was behind it all, the more she snooped around, the more the pieces fell into place, and the more they pointed here. Furthermore, after Beacon's timely disruption of the Liberators' latest attempt, Tricia was sure they suspected they were exposed and would likely be accelerating whatever plans they had.

Judging from the level of activity Beacon was currently observing at the back of the building, she was probably right.

As Beacon watched from the nearby rooftop, people wearing those gray coveralls were actively milling around the loading platform. The casual observer would simply see a familiar BioMat van and workers going about their business, just like they did at the other university labs and dozens of other businesses in the city.

To Beacon, though, it looked much busier than a simple pickup of hazardous waste. The van itself was the final piece of the puzzle. She had no trouble spotting the scar on the back corner of the van just above the rear tire; no doubt this was the same van the Liberators had used during their encounter on Harbor Street.

Even with the night vision setting on her mask visor, she decided that she needed a closer look if she was going to sort out what was happening. Cautiously, Beacon crouched her way to the edge of the building nearest the lab and warily peered over the edge. Any kind of stealth entry from the back was out of the question, and the front that faced the quad was too much in plain sight for the people milling about the campus, even at this time of night. The side, though, was not easily observed, and while there wasn't a side door, there was a very convenient fire escape.

Quickly glancing side to side, she hopped over the edge and gently lowered herself to the fire escape, landing at the second-floor window without a sound. *Nicely done there, Beacon*, she congratulated herself. The window was latched, so she placed her hand on the latch plate and focused heat into it. After a few seconds, the latch began to glow, and with a sharp shake, it obediently fell away. Beacon quietly slid up the window frame and slipped inside.

The fire escape opened into a deserted hallway right next to the stairs. She silently opened the door, listened for a few seconds to make sure it was empty and stepped into the dimly lit stairwell. She made her way briskly down the stairs, keeping her fingers crossed that she wouldn't meet anyone. At the bottom, she cracked the first-floor door and peeked out. The halls were dark, hopefully indicating that any students and staff who might be using any of the classrooms or offices in the old building were gone for the day. Getting her bearings, she slid through the door and made her way down the hallway toward what she believed was the back of the building in the direction of the area where she'd likely find the Liberators of Gaia busy at work.

Beacon passed a few small conference rooms and staff offices, but just when she thought she might have to double back, she came to a recessed door marked 'Storage'. Softly trying the door, she found it unlocked. *Unusual*, she thought, but it was worth a look. As soon as she cracked the door, she heard voices and movement from the far side of the large storage area. She checked the area around the door quickly and seeing no one nearby, she slipped in and carefully pushed the door closed behind her. This side of the storage area was dark, but the far side was well-lit and obviously no longer just storage.

Peeking around from behind some racks of equipment and boxes, Beacon could see what looked like a well-established working area and laboratory. There were some partitions dividing portions of the room into small meeting areas, some lab tables with equipment and glassware, and an area with some large monitors for computers. Most of them were dark, but some showed maps of the city while others had some random data displays she couldn't make out at this distance.

At the very far end, she could see the open loading area. Most of the people she could see—people who were obviously not students or staff in her estimation—were busy in the loading area, by a set of racks against the far wall, or in the glass isolation room in the corner.

Staged in a row near the racks stood a set of identical metallic, and very intimidating, devices of some sort. A small team of workers was securing the device nearest the loading area to a metal hand truck; apparently, this one was going somewhere soon.

Beacon could hear a lot of conversation going on with all the activity, but she still couldn't make out much of what they were saying or see exactly what they were doing. She pulled up her hood and drew her cape around her, hoping the black material would help her blend into the shadows as she slipped her way around the walls. Moving slowly and quietly, she made it to the first set of partitions separating the working part of the room from the cluttered storage where she'd entered. Finding it much easier to hear what was being said and see what was happening, she again drew her cape around her and triggered the camouflage ability in her suit.

She checked for the familiar shimmer, and while the effect wasn't perfect, given that she was already somewhat out of sight, she was sure it would be good enough to keep someone from casually noticing her while she got a closer look.

Intently, she tried to make out parts of the conversation...something about cleaning out the essential equipment...would they need to purge the computers...no, not yet, not until they were back...making sure the device was secure...and purified? Did she hear that correctly? *Ugh, why couldn't this have come with super-hearing?*

Beacon closed her eyes and held her breath, hoping it would help her track the conversation better, but before she had the chance to eavesdrop further, she heard a soft footfall just behind her. She turned sharply and gasped in surprise but was too late to avoid the sudden blow across her stomach. She tried to groan, but all the air had been driven from her body. Her powers flooded away from her as she collapsed to her hands and knees, her hood falling down over her shoulder.

"That's a pretty neat trick, mate," growled a deep, raspy voice in an Aussie accent, "but it didn't fool the sonic motion sensors."

Another blow across her back drove her hard into the floor, and her arms and wrists were roughly pinned down by several strong hands. Someone yanked her head back by a fistful of hair and pressed a noxious-smelling cloth over her nose and mouth.

Starving for air, she had no choice but to inhale the fumes. Instantly, her muscles turned to jelly, and she was overwhelmed by a nauseating wave of vertigo. The room spun wildly, and any attempt to draw on her power was like trying to pick up a wet bar of soap in the shower; no matter how hard Beacon tried, it just squirted away from her, out of reach.

Her vision narrowed, and she felt consciousness slipping away from her. Just before everything went dark, she again heard another voice, "She's done. Go tell Purity that Beacon took the bait just like she thought she would. Let her know we have her."

Tricia's eyes fluttered as she started to regain consciousness. Her head was throbbing, forcing her to squint against the bright light directly above her. She noticed immediately that her mask was pulled down and bunched up behind her neck. She tried to bring a hand up to her aching eyes but found she couldn't move her arms. Her wrists were secured in the small of her back with what felt like some kind of metal cuff, and when she tried to bend her arms, her elbows bumped up against something hard. She tried moving her legs, but they were the same. Her ankles were also cuffed, and when she bent her knees, they hit something above them.

Looking down, Tricia saw that she was encased in some kind of storage canister like the ones she saw against the wall when she came in. It was just wide enough for her shoulders and a few inches longer than she was tall. She could move, but not much. The lid was open from about the center of her chest to the end of the canister just above her head. She tugged again against the cuffs holding her wrists, drawing on her power to break them, but barely a trickle responded to her. The cuffs held her fast.

*The case must be shielding me from my powers,* she deduced. *From the light side of them, at least.*

Probing carefully, Beacon could feel the dark energy, though, and drew on it, driving it against the walls of the canister. However, when she pushed, she felt an increasing pressure on her own body, and as she channeled more to try to break free, the pressure finally grew so intense that she was forced to abandon her attempt. Without her strength to back it up, she would probably crush her own ribcage before the canister gave way. She exhaled sharply and squirmed in frustration.

Her fidgeting, however, seemed to have attracted some attention as Tricia heard footsteps start to come her way across the hard floor. Heels from the sound of them, accompanied by an all too familiar voice, "Well, well, are we awake?"

That voice. Tricia turned her head in its direction just in time to see Rene Thornton appear in front of her. "Welcome back, Tricia," Rene said to her, smiling broadly.

Tricia was dumbstruck. All she could do for several seconds was stare wide-eyed at Rene, who just looked back at her, still smiling, apparently savoring the moment. Finally, Tricia stammered out, "You? You, Rene? You're the leader of the Liberators of Gaia?"

"Well, actually, they call me 'Purity' around here," Rene replied softly, "and I wouldn't say 'leader' as much as I might say 'highly valued and influential contributor.'"

Tricia started to raise her voice, "*You* are the...," but Rene placed her finger across Tricia's lips, cutting her off.

Rene leaned in, still pressing on Tricia's lips, and lowered her voice, "Now, now, Tricia, let's keep our little chat civil, shall we? Everybody here is quite busy getting things ready for their big finale, so they have left you to me. No one else has seen you unmasked yet, and it would be in both of our best interests to keep it that way. Please don't put me into a position where I might be forced to make a very harsh decision that I know I'd really regret. Hmmm?"

Tricia and Rene nodded in unison. Rene took her finger off Tricia's mouth and stood back up, maintaining eye contact with her. Cooperating, Tricia decided, at least for now until she could find a means of escape, was in her best interest.

Keeping her voice low, Tricia continued, "You are the one responsible for poisoning people with this stuff, with whatever this is that you've been putting into the smoke and bombs the Liberators have been planting?" Tricia winced and shifted again, trying—and failing—to find a position where the hard bottom of the canister wouldn't keep digging the cuffs into the bruised area on the small of her back.

Rene put her hands on her hips. "I am responsible for this stuff, as you so eloquently put it, yes, but I'm not poisoning anyone, Tricia. I'm not killing anyone with what we are doing. People will take care of the dying and killing on their own, just as they always have. I'm just making sure there aren't any new people to take their place when they do."

"So, it's true then?" Tricia glared at Rene, "You are responsible for the infertility cases?"

"Yes, I am." Rene tapped her nose with her forefinger. "Although, it might be more accurate to say 'contraception' than 'infertility'. You see, the affected people are still quite fertile in the sense they are producing healthy gametes. It's just that those gametes are no longer compatible, either with each other or with those from unaffected people. They simply can't conceive."

Tricia stared at Rene again for a few seconds and then shook her head. "This is your plan, then? To just keep setting off these devices, making small groups of people in Crystal Bay unable to conceive? Doesn't seem like that will get you very far towards your grand vision." Tricia scoffed for emphasis.

"Of course not, dear." Rene smiled again. "They wouldn't, but these little *experiments* have been invaluable."

"What do you mean, experiments?"

"Exactly that. These types of things don't just happen overnight. Like any good scientist, we try something, take data, and correct as needed until we get the results we want. These little demonstrations by the Liberators have taught me a lot in terms of how to disperse my little cocktail, and the collaboration with the hospital has been priceless in supplying me with a large amount of data on how people respond to it for analysis without raising any suspicion. In fact, your friend Marni has been a perfect lab rat herself. Turns out she loves a good lavender latte just as much as I do, and the samples I get from her cups have given me excellent first-hand data with which to work."

Tricia closed her eyes and groaned softly. *Oh no, Marni...*

"Oh, don't worry, sweetie. Like I said before, she's not in any real imminent danger. In fact, I can tell you she's healthy as a horse overall."

Rene patted Tricia's shoulder and continued, "No, the real deal is coming together even as we speak and will be much more spectacular. Between you and me, the Nuclear Physics lab hasn't yet discovered they are missing some small devices that, when triggered properly, will provide a substantial yield. Loaded with my concoction and detonated at a sufficiently high point in the city, they'll do an excellent job of giving a good dispersion pattern."

"Meyer's Tower!" Tricia blurted out.

"Very good." Rene congratulated her. "Yes indeed. My colleagues here in the Liberators like that as a site for a demonstration, but—still keeping this between us, mind you—they have no idea just how big a demonstration it will be. To get the dispersion I need, that device will level the tower and likely destroy several city blocks around the tower site. It will be quite a show."

"So much for not killing anyone," Tricia chastised.

Rene shrugged. "You know what they say about omelets and eggs, right? But true, when my colleagues see what happened, they will be very unhappy, so I've made alternative arrangements to get the remaining devices loaded onto planes where we can repeat the process in major cities in Europe and Asia. It does need to go global to be effective; Crystal Bay alone isn't enough."

"Even so, it hardly seems that seeding this stuff in a few locations will be sufficient to get the uptake you need in the population to end it."

"Right again, Tricia." Rene leaned on the edge of the cylinder next to Tricia's head and smiled down at her. "You know, I really appreciate the scientific curiosity you're showing here, Tricia.

"As Marni would affirm, the real key to any genomic treatment is the delivery mechanism. It isn't just enough to administer the treatment. We have to guarantee that the body incorporates it and that it can be self-sustaining once that happens. The brew that's going into these devices is a much more advanced version, one that self-replicates like a virus. Once inside the body, the body's own immune system starts creating it. People become carriers, and since it's completely asymptomatic, they have no knowledge at all that they are carriers.

"Furthermore, I've made sure it will be very difficult to detect, so any kind of test will be a long time coming. And, as an added bonus, one I didn't even anticipate but was quite happy to discover, is that the material will invade the biosphere— plants, animals, food sources—spreading it even faster and making it *very* hard to eradicate."

Tricia took a bit to process this. She wasn't sure Rene technically was clinically insane, but she had to admit, as psychopathically off the rails she sounded at this point, her plan was devilishly clever, and there was no question she was a genius.

Vying for time, hoping that some means of escape might miraculously appear, Tricia prodded Rene to keep the conversation going, "Still, it's going to take a long time— generations, I'd think—for all this to play out, Rene. There are a lot of very smart people out there. They will figure it out before, um, the end."

Rene tapped her fingers on the lip of the canister opening, considering Tricia's observations. "Possibly. Marni and her team started getting close much faster than I had anticipated. I did have to do some work to throw them off the scent in our consultations, but, in reality, time runs out much sooner than just waiting for everyone to die off.

"Remember, Tricia, people are fundamentally panicky, brutish animals, and in the end, the final blow will come from humanity itself, and it will come rather quickly."

"What do you mean?" Tricia inquired, genuinely curious now despite the horrific implications of what Rene was unfolding before her.

"I've been running some interesting models, and they are quite fascinating. Events run their course in a matter of only a few decades, give or take, not generations, and the point of no return happens even sooner. "

Rene got that faraway look in her eye again. "Think about it, Tricia. Think about how much of our society and economy is dedicated to servicing our young. Food, furniture, toys, education, government, cleaning, and personal hygiene. It's huge. As my compound disperses, it turns out birth rates drop very dramatically. Very shortly after that, demand for all those products and services drops sharply. Supply chains collapse. Entire segments of workers and staff are without jobs. The global economy spirals downward as the effects of these collapsing chains ripple throughout adjacent sectors. Stock markets collapse, and recessions deepen. Panic starts to set in."

Tricia bit her lip. Rene nodded to her and continued, "Once people learn what's going on, they react in only a few predictable ways. Many will flee the population centers, trying to avoid being affected, but that only makes it harder for unaffected people to find each other and help shore up the plummeting birth rates.

"Rioting and looting will skyrocket; thousands will be killed by people trying to hoard precious resources, trying to preserve themselves at the expense of everyone else. Finally, the majority of the population lacks the most basic survival skills to care for themselves without others supplying food, water, power, and other essentials, and will rapidly die of dehydration, starvation, infections, or just stupid accidents.

"In only a few years, most of the world's population end up in small, isolated groups, which, without the ability to procreate, expire very quickly. At this point, even if scientists do figure out what I've done and find out how to counter it, it will be too late. People will go the way of the Sumatran Rhinoceros, extinct, without a viable diverse gene pool from which to rebuild."

Rene took a deep breath and looked down into Tricia's eyes. "So, you see, humanity at its finest."

Tricia looked back into Rene's eyes. She felt tears start to well up, not only from the dread and sadness of Rene's apocryphal vision but also from the very real possibility it could actually come to pass. She fought back a sob, her voice catching. "But *why*, Rene? Why? Someone like you, someone who's done so much good, someone who is respected, even admired. Someone who only a short time ago told me the value of being an inspiration to others. Why would you resort to *this*?"

"You see, Tricia," Rene began, "when you grow up the way I did, you see the world for what it is. There are your foster parents who really don't care about you except for the money...and whatever else they can force from a teenage girl...and there is your family who is also just in it for the payout, and countless others you meet along the way, and as you get older you realize that they aren't necessarily bad people. You realize this is just what people really are. We try to paint ourselves as advanced and evolved, but really, our perception of how civilized we are is a very thin veneer, and it doesn't take very much for our true selfish nature to show through it."

Rene paused and clasped her hands. "I'm not even talking about ancient history here, Tricia. We see it every day, the way people treat each other, at best with apathy and at worst with disdain and violence. The way they act is what keeps a superhero in business, right?" Rene winked at Tricia.

"It wasn't that long ago that a few dedicated people successfully waged a campaign of misinformation and manufactured fear to create a platform of hatred and bigotry and division that dominated our government and society for almost two decades. At a time when we should have collectively condemned the hatred and outrage, millions lapped it up, willingly manipulated by a group of politicians who only wanted to be in power to satisfy their narcissistic egos. They proudly wore their hate and outrage and elected those liars and hate-mongers into office solely on the promise that they would bully and persecute the people their followers wanted to be bullied and persecuted, which, by the way, was pretty much anyone who didn't think like them or didn't look like them.

"And what do we have to show for all this hatred? Millions dead every year from endless religious wars, terrorism, racial violence in the streets, and almost weekly mass shootings, in *schools* of all places." Rene hung her head a moment and sighed deeply.

"But the damage doesn't stop there, with just the people, does it? Arrogant human selfishness spills over into how we treat everything, including the very world we live in. Our planet is just another thing to take advantage of, to suck dry for whatever we can get." Rene leaned forward again, resting her elbows on the edge of the canister.

"For nearly a century, we were warned. Extinctions at an all-time high. Glaciers vanishing. Water and air polluted to near toxic levels. Global temperatures rising. The planet was virtually screaming at us for help. Some saw, sure, and tried, but corporations spent billions, not to clean things up but to secure lobbyists, pay off politicians, and pump out propaganda to deny it all and block regulations because, for them, it was cheaper to keep doing business as usual, destroying the world around them, than to do things right. They didn't care about what they were doing because they knew they wouldn't be around when the bill came due. As long as they got rich, someone else could deal with the consequences."

"But we did respond, Rene," Tricia chimed in, seeing an opening, "we did pass the Climate Recovery Acts. We did take some big steps, yes, perhaps later than we should have, but we did."

"Yes, Tricia, we did pass the CRA, but what did it take?" Rene countered. "It wasn't until a series of superstorms obliterated several coastal cities – hundreds of thousands of lives and trillions in damage. Yes, that scared people into acting. That fear, in that moment, was enough to overcome the lies and denial, but we don't really learn, do we? We pat ourselves on the back and go back to same-old-same-old, waiting for the next disaster to come along to wake us up again."

Rene slapped the back of her right hand into her left palm. "Even now, the corporations and their billionaire backers are back at it, trying to delay the deadlines, trying to pull the teeth out of the regulations, again, solely to boost their profit margins, to satisfy their own greed. Knowing the truth, they still would put their own avarice first and keep ravaging the planet, bleeding each other dry, and sacrificing the futures of their own children and grandchildren. It's been this way over and over and over and over again throughout human history.

"So you see," Rene concluded, "that...that is the one thing this plan depends on, the one thing that has been a constant since the beginning of time, that when humanity is faced with its own collective demise, we can count on people to enthusiastically contribute to it, and as far as I'm concerned, they've more than earned the chance to do so."

Rene stopped, took a few steps back, and composed herself, smoothing down the front of her lab coat and pressing her hair back. Tricia stared after her for a few seconds, processing the depth of Rene's rage, then twisted her body and arms, desperately testing the cuffs at her wrists once again, hoping against odds that they weren't secure, that they'd magically pop free so she could put a stop to this, but to no avail. Rene walked back to the side of the canister, folded her arms on the edge, and rested her chin on her forearms.

"And it was all going so smoothly, too...until you came onto the scene."

Tricia snorted. "Sorry to spoil the party."

Rene chuckled, "Almost. I had a feeling when I first saw you on the news that you might end up causing us trouble. It took a while, but eventually, you did just that when you interrupted our last demonstration. Fortunately for me, the test itself was expendable, but you really put the pressure on us to pull up the timetable for our grand finale. Do you know the police actually visited the BioMat main headquarters?"

Tricia shook her head.

"Well, they did. Fortunately, nobody they could talk to had any idea what we were doing, so they couldn't give anything away. The truck we are using was officially 'scrapped' months ago—" Rene made air quotes with her fingers "—so there were no leads for them to follow, but I knew it wasn't going to be long before you connected the dots and ended up here. Based on what I'd surmised of your abilities, I thought something like this storage canister might be effective in hindering your powers. So far, it seems I'm right." Rene patted the canister.

"I'm not going to lie, Tricia, you could have knocked me over with a feather when they brought you in here, and I pulled down your mask. Tricia Carling was the last woman I expected to see as 'The Bay Bombshell'. I know you, Tricia. You're a loner. You've seen the same tragedies that result from human greed and selfishness in your life that I've seen. Why would someone like you go through all this effort and trouble for them?"

"You're right, Rene. I have seen those things," Tricia admitted. "But I've also experienced what happens when people do show their good side. I've seen the result of their compassion and seen that people can do better when they are given a second chance. I'm walking proof of that, and I know others have the same qualities that I do if they are given the chance.

"I don't need to like people to believe they deserve the chance to be the best version of themselves or to have the sense of moral outrage to want to stop people that hurt others and take those opportunities away from them."

Rene looked down at Tricia, and her facial expression softened. "I admire that, Tricia. I really do. Even though I think it's overly optimistic and naive, I respect and admire how you feel about this and what you're trying to do, but you also must realize that I cannot allow you to interfere any further with my plans."

Tricia heard a voice calling from what sounded like the loading area. Rene turned to look in that direction. She listened, then nodded and held up her first finger, gesturing for whoever was talking to her to wait a moment.

"Well, sweetie, that's my cue. Time for me to do my part so we can set this little gem and start the big show. The Liberators are eager for a big demonstration in the city, and so am I. I figure this canister is doing its job so far. I'm pretty sure if you could escape, after what I've just told you, you probably would have already, so once I close this lid, I'm confident you will be out of commission and no longer a threat to my plans."

Tricia scowled and snapped out, "Look, Rene, if you're going to kill me, please just do it instead of leaving me to suffocate inside this thing."

"Oh, Tricia, I have no intention of killing you." Rene's voice softened, and she reached down to brush Tricia's hair back out of her eyes. "I really like you. Honestly, I do, and I was sincere when I said I admired what you were trying to do. The world is going to need people like you when things start to crumble, but I can't take any chances you'll interfere before then. No, you won't suffocate. This is an environmentally controlled storage canister. I can create any environment in here that's needed to store anything, organic or inorganic. Even superheroines.

"So, you'll have air, but so we aren't taking any chances, it will be mixed with a small amount of Neurostatin."

Tricia's blank look prompted Rene to explain, "Neurostatin is the compound they give to critically ill or injured patients to induce a state of biological and physiological stasis, slowing down the body's function to the point of an induced coma, giving doctors time to treat the patient's disease or injury. You'll essentially take a nice, prolonged nap, just like a princess in a fairy tale, and in a few weeks, when I'm finished executing my plans, and I'm sure there's nothing you can do to interfere, I'll make sure the police get an anonymous tip where to find you."

Rene reached down and pulled Tricia's mask back on, adjusting it onto her face and smoothing her hair. In a last desperate attempt, Tricia implored Rene, "Rene, please. It isn't too late. Stop this now. Let's find another way. Be the inspiration you encouraged me to be. Think of what we could do *together*. Help me make a difference."

Rene looked down once again and replied, with a slightly sad smile, "Sorry, Tricia. The time for inspiration alone has passed. For every one like you or even me who wants things better, there are ten or a hundred who would gladly sacrifice it all for their own agenda. On top of that, and perhaps the worst part of all, for every one of them, there are thousands or millions who just don't care. No, my dear, inspiration won't cut it now. There have been too many chances already. It's like that old superhero movie where the bad guy snapped his fingers, and half of everyone disappeared. He was on the right track, but he just didn't go far enough. It's time for me to finish the job. Goodbye, Tricia."

The darkness enveloped Tricia as Rene pulled down the lid. She heard the latch click into place, sealing her in. Swallowing hard, Tricia pushed down the wave of panic that started to well inside her. She closed her eyes in the dark, took a deep breath, and forced herself to stay calm, to keep a clear head. She had just started thinking through options and ideas for escape when she heard the canister's environmental control unit whirr into life, signaling she had only minutes to spare before the Neurostatin completely incapacitated her.

# Tower

Beacon yanked at her wrists and kicked with her feet one more time. No use. Her restraints remained tight, refusing to budge even a single iota. If anything, her struggles may have actually made them tighter.

*Well, we're really in a pickle now, aren't we?* she thought to herself. Her mind raced. Too little time. Fear gnawed at the edges of her mind. *Easy...easy...step back*, she calmed herself, taking deep breaths. *There's a way, I just have to find it and I won't if I lose it.* She forced herself to breathe more slowly, and using her training, she looked inward.

She was completely cut off from the light, but she felt the dark energy seething and churning. She'd never felt it this keenly before, probably because the light was always there on top. Exposed, it seemed to be calling to her, tugging at her.

*No*, Beacon realized, *it isn't pulling at me.* Her body was pulling her towards it, craving the dark energy, trying to draw it in. She recoiled from it, remembering the last time she'd tried to let the dark energy inside, how she felt she would fly apart, how it terrified her. She hadn't tried that since, but her body felt like it was pleading with her, pushing back on the fear in her head, to use that dark energy somehow to save her.

*Trust me,* it said. *Trust yourself.*

She realized she had no choice, no analytical options. Control by force of will was not going to save her now. It was time to trust her instincts, the experience she'd gained, the journey she'd taken so far. Time to let go.

She took a deep breath and carefully opened herself to admit a small trickle of the dark energies. Sensei's words rang in her mind: *discipline is about restraint, not constraint.* She felt it draw into her, coursing throughout her body, and she felt herself expand slightly. It wasn't a physical sensation, but she was suddenly acutely aware of the canister she was in, the cuffs at her hands and feet, even the air around her. She sensed them on a different level, a non-physical level.

Beacon suppressed a sudden flash of panic over the feeling and pushed the fear away. *Focus...focus...a little more...* Keeping her eyes closed, she steadied her breath and opened up the flows a bit wider. More of the dark energy wove through her. She felt lighter, and her awareness broadened. The feeling was exhilarating. She inhaled sharply at the sensation. She could now feel the entire lab around her. Without being able to see it with her eyes, she knew the lab was empty except for the equipment and furniture. She could feel it all.

Beacon felt something else, too: slow but perceptible motion. Somehow, she was sliding downward, sinking through the canister wall. She could feel the edge of it start to pass through her body. The panic tried to return, but again, she shoved it away, maintaining focus and sharpening her awareness. She forced herself to relax—to just go with it—and she started to sink a bit faster.

Abruptly, the cuffs caught on the inside of the canister, stopping her. Her concentration wavered. *This is no time to get stuck...focus...keep it together*, she chastised herself and drew in a bit more of the dark energy. The ethereal sensation increased, and with a sharp pop, her wrists and ankles slipped through her restraints, leaving the cuffs inside the canister as her descent continued once more.

Abruptly, she felt the edge of her prison pass through the front of her body, leaving her looking straight up at the bottom wall of the canister above her and the frame supporting the canister on either side of her. Her hands and feet were clear. *Free!* Reluctant to keep tempting fate, Beacon closed the conduit for the dark energy. She felt her body snap back to normal. Her physical senses returned. The extended awareness was gone, and she fell.

Beacon gasped in pain as she hit the floor. She landed hard squarely on the ribs where she'd taken those hard shots during her capture. She lay there on her side motionless, trying to slowly breathe, to get some much-needed air through the pain. Her ribs didn't seem to be broken, but still, every breath felt like someone was twisting a knife in her side. She spread her fingers and pressed her hand flat against the floor, testing it to see if it was real, then pressed her hand against her own chest to make sure *she* was real. That sensation she'd felt was incredible, but now, having released it, part of her felt a bit empty...tinier.

As she lay there, another thought hit her. The cuffs had come off, but her suit hadn't. By all rights, she thought she should be lying here naked right now, but she wasn't. *Was it something about what I'd done? Maybe it was something about the suit itself? Another unexplored property of the material?* She would have to figure that out at some point, too, but at the moment, there were more important concerns facing her.

She rolled over onto her back, groaning a bit in the process. There would be time to explore all these new aspects of her abilities later, but she needed to get moving if she was going to stop Rene and the Liberators. Beacon drew on the light energy now ebbing around her, and the pain in her side diminished almost immediately. "Well," she mumbled, slowly pushing herself into a sitting position, "there may be a lot I don't know about all this, but I am definitely loving the healing part of it right now." She rubbed her ribs. They were still sore, but her healing was doing its job, and she could at least breathe normally again.

Beacon stood up slowly, straightened her mask and costume, and started toward the door, eager to catch up with Rene and her team, but as she looked around the lab, she thought twice about her next steps. *They haven't been gone that long,* she deduced. *If I fail to stop her at Meyer's Tower, I need to make sure she can't carry out the rest of her plan.*

She looked around the lab. Even if she destroyed or disabled the remaining devices, Rene could still make more using the data and notes in the computer, so taking those out of her reach would be her first stop. Beacon walked up to the monitor and keyboard. Rene had it locked, and not only did Beacon not have enough time to try to hack through it, but she knew if she made too many attempts, she'd be locked out. Thinking quickly, she changed users; she may not be able to get into Rene's account directly, but the system administrator's account might be easier.

Late last year, when the team was setting up the computing systems in her lab, Tricia and a good bottle of red wine managed to convince the IT admin for her lab to give her the root password. It was technically a breach of policy, but it had not only saved a lot of time getting the lab set up, but it had greatly reduced the demand on the short-staffed IT department as well. She'd observed then that the root password looked like it was based on a formula. Fingers crossed, they used the same method for the system passwords in this lab.

It took a couple of guesses to find which abbreviation for the lab name they'd chosen for the password, but she got in. As expected, Rene did not keep her data on the network storage but kept it locally under her own user directory. Satisfied that she'd found it all right there, Beacon encrypted the entire account and stashed the decryption key in a file under the root account. The police, and likely Marni as well, would be very interested in the data she'd secured.

The devices themselves posed a more interesting problem. She didn't believe she had enough time to try to dismantle or destroy them, and without a lot of work and a lot of time that she didn't have, she couldn't be sure she wouldn't leave Rene any opportunities to recover them and carry out her plan anyway.

Fortunately, the lab was equipped with an isolation chamber, one that was very similar in structure and looked to be just as secure as the Hot Spot in her own lab. The root account gave her access to the application that controlled the access codes for the chamber as well. She quickly changed the access code on the isolation chamber and recorded the new code in the same file as the decryption key.

Using her strength and speed, she quickly moved the rest of the devices, Rene's samples, and the genome sequencer into the chamber and sealed it. It had felt like it had taken an eternity, but all told, she'd only lost about twenty minutes. Those minutes were well spent, buying her confidence that even if she failed to stop them at the Tower, Rene would find it difficult, if not outright impossible, to finish her scheme. Even if she did find a way, hopefully, the data and devices Beacon had tucked away would give Marni and other scientists the head start they'd need to contain the effect of Rene's virus and stop it before it spread too far.

Beacon stepped out of the lab into the brightening morning. No one was around, but they soon would be. *How do I get to Meyer's Tower?* she pondered. *Superheroes don't exactly call ride shares, do they?* Rather than waste time thinking about it, she decided to do the first thing that came to mind: she started running. She drew heavily on the energy around her and ran faster and faster, faster than she'd run before, so fast that she was glad the speed limit didn't apply to runners.

As Beacon neared the city's edge, though, the morning traffic was starting to pick up, making it increasingly difficult to travel at any speed and still safely avoid vehicles in the streets and people on the sidewalks. Fortunately, the rooftops offered her another path through the city. These had become familiar territory for her, and feeling confident that she was really in her element now, she pulled even harder on the energies around her.

The level of power she was drawing gave her speed and endurance like she'd never experienced before. She leaped like a gazelle from building to building, feeling the thrill of flying from roof to roof and the wind sweeping through her hair. People saw her soaring over them, shouting and cheering as she flew past them, but she didn't have the time to acknowledge them beyond the occasional quick wave. She was already feeling desperately short on time, and, truth be told, if she broke her concentration, she was afraid she'd end up as a smear on the side of a building.

Beacon touched down in the construction lot in front of the partially completed Meyer's Tower building. Even though she knew she was pressed for time, she also knew she couldn't afford to be surprised again and would need to exercise some caution. She took a quick look around the lot. It was still early, and the lot looked to be vacant, or rather, mostly vacant. There were a few construction workers milling around the site office trailer.

She jogged toward the trailer and shouted to get their attention. They looked up, and their jaws dropped when they saw her. One of them shouted out, "Hey, look, guys! It's that Beacon chick. She's here!"

She rolled her eyes behind her mask—*Chick? Seriously?*—but there was no time to deal with that comment. Staying on task, Beacon waved her arm and shouted back, "You need to get out of here! Clear the area!"

"What? Why? What's going on?" one of them shouted back.

"I don't have time to explain, but I believe there is a bomb in that building that will destroy this whole area. You need to get people out of here! Call the police too!" she ordered them.

They waved and started scrambling. Confident they got the message, Beacon jogged toward the building itself.

As she drew closer to the front, she slowed to a walk. There was no sign of the van or any other vehicle at the front of the building, but she did find a ramp to the side going down toward an underground parking area. The barricade in front of the ramp had been torn open. *Bingo,* she thought and jogged down the ramp into the underground lot.

At the bottom of the ramp, she paused and surveyed the lot. Not seeing anything immediately, she slowly walked in, looking side to side for any clues as to Rene's whereabouts.

After walking about halfway, she finally saw the van carefully parked against the far wall behind one of the concrete support pillars. Before she could make her way over to it, though, the quiet was broken by the chime of the elevator echoing loudly through the deserted parking area.

Right in front of her, the elevator door opened and out walked Rene and the rest of the Liberators of Gaia. She recognized them immediately as the same group she'd encountered at VeriMed. They turned toward the van, chatting amongst themselves and pushing an empty hand cart, the same hand cart she'd seen at their lab. *Am I too late?* she wondered.

Realizing they hadn't seen her, Beacon shouted toward them, "Stop!" They turned toward her and came to a halt. She took several more steps in their direction and faced them.

"Well, look who's come to the party?" Rene said. "I have to admit, I'm surprised to see you here. You're far more resourceful than I gave you credit."

"What have you done, Rene?" Beacon demanded. "Where is it?"

Rene pointed upward. "But you're too late, dear. The reaction has already started. You'll never get there in time, and besides," she waved a small pad in the air, "without this, you don't stand a chance of stopping it."

Beacon paused to think. She didn't think she could get to Rene fast enough, and there was no doubt in her mind Rene would destroy the pad if she tried. She would need help getting her hands on that pad, so she decided to play a hunch.

"Hey, Opus!" she yelled to the Liberators' leader. "Do you know what she's really setting off up there? Do you know that device up there will completely destroy this building and several blocks around us? Do you know you're helping her kill thousands today?"

She saw the Liberators stiffen and look at each other. Opus turned toward Rene and asked, "Purity, what is she talking about?"

Rene waved her hand at him dismissively, "Don't listen to her, Opus. Can't you see she's just trying to rattle you? Turn us on each other?" Despite her efforts to project confidence and maintain her poise, she was growing visibly unsettled by the Liberators murmuring amongst themselves.

Encouraged by their questioning looks, Beacon kept pressing their buttons and her growing advantage. "That's not the worst of it, you know. Not only are you helping her kill thousands, but you're helping her end the human race entirely."

The Liberators were dumbstruck. Opus, clearly shaken, again pressed Rene. "What does she mean?"

Rene was now agitated herself. Her cheeks flushing, she gritted her teeth and snapped back, "Shut up, Opus. She's making all this up, playing you. Don't listen to her."

Opus turned to Beacon. "What do you mean she's ending the human race?"

Beacon knew she had them. "All those little demonstrations she's been helping you with have really been so she could test a virus she's developed that makes people sterile. She's been using you to help her perfect it so this device, and the others like it that she plans on setting off in other parts of the world, can spread enough of it to stop humans from reproducing entirely. Humanity dies in decades...and you've been helping her."

Harmony gasped, putting her hand to her mouth. Riptide's face was blank. Opus was livid, his fists clenched. He rounded back on Rene. "Explain yourself. Right. Now," he demanded, his voice cracking.

Rene took a step back away from them. She looked at the Liberators team gaping at her, dumbstruck, then back to Beacon. Looking back to Opus, she suddenly threw her hands down and broke, "Fine. Yes. It's true. What we planted up there is more than just a big light show. We are standing in what will soon be a crater a dozen blocks in diameter, and when it goes off, we will have taken the first step toward freeing this planet from the scourge of people. Isn't that what we all wanted? To free the planet?"

Beacon cautiously took a few steps closer. The entire team just stared at Rene, completely in shock. Fixated on Rene, no one noticed her, and all she needed was just a few more steps to be assured she could snatch the pad from Rene's hand before anyone could react.

Opus shook his head. "I thought we were on the same page with this, with our mission, what we were trying to accomplish."

Exasperated, Rene responded, "We ARE on the same page with this, but you weren't willing to go far enough to get it done. Your spray paint and manifestos weren't going to make any real change. The problem is the people, how they are, their nature. They've had more than enough chances and have failed over and over. They aren't going to change."

Rene jabbed her finger into her chest. "I'm doing what it takes. I'm pushing the reset button, giving the planet a chance to start over without people, and it all starts today, right here, right now!"

"No, Rene," Beacon said softly, walking slowly toward them and reaching out toward Rene, "It's over. It stops now."

Rene snapped her head toward Beacon. Without warning, she dropped the commpad onto the concrete. In unison, the Liberators lurched forward to stop her, but her foot came down on the pad, shattering it.

"No, sweetie, it's not over. Not by a long shot," Rene responded, and when they all looked back up from the remains of the shattered pad, she was suddenly pointing a rather nasty-looking handgun in their direction.

Rene locked eyes with Beacon. "Now, I know this won't be very effective against you—frankly, I see I should have killed you when I had the chance, but c'est la vie, I suppose—but you have a choice. You can keep fooling around down here, or you can use what precious time there might still be left to try to stop it from going off. It's a hundred stories up on the observation deck, so I wouldn't take too much time deciding."

Rene then looked towards the Liberators. "As for me, I don't plan on being around here either way. I've got more work to do, so I'm going to take that van and get well away from here before that thing goes off. If you hustle, you might be able to get some distance and find shelter yourselves."

Beacon had already made her choice and immediately ran to the elevator door. She pressed the button, and, as she hoped, the doors opened immediately. Just as she started to step inside, Opus called out to her, "Beacon, for what it's worth, I'm sorry. We didn't know it was coming to this. We just wanted to make things better."

Beacon turned her head and replied, "I know, but you're getting a second chance now...at least if I have anything to say about it. Find a better way."

Opus nodded. Beacon then turned to Rene and lowered her voice, "You will answer for what you've done, Rene. I will see you again."

"No, dear, I don't think you will," Rene said smoothly and smiled at her, keeping the gun trained on the stunned Liberators of Gaia.

Beacon turned into the elevator, leaving Rene and the Liberators to sort things out behind her. She knew the elevator itself would be far too slow, but it did give her quick access to the elevator shaft. After punching her way through the maintenance hatch on the top of the elevator car, she stood on the roof of the car, looking up into a thousand feet of shaft.

After Beacon disappeared up the elevator shaft, Rene turned back to the Liberators standing before her across the parking area. Their eyes were locked on her, and as she saw them start to separate and slowly move toward her, her hand tightened on the gun.

"It doesn't have to go like this, Rene," Opus said calmly, holding up his hands.

"No, it doesn't," Rene said with a sly smile, forcing herself to remain cool and collected. "You can just stand aside and let me get in that van and leave."

The Liberators continued to fan out and close the distance slowly. "You know we can't do that," Opus said, taking a calculated step toward her. "We can't let all these people die, Rene. That was never our mission."

Her eyes darted from one Liberator to another, watching them advance cautiously, and she cursed silently to herself. *They are trying to surround me,* she realized, biting her lip. Rene raised the gun, pointing it directly at Opus' head. "If you all don't stop and let me by, their deaths won't be the ones that you will need to be concerned about."

"I'm sorry, Rene, but I won't be responsible for a nuclear holocaust," Opus said softly. "*Now!*" he suddenly shouted, and the Liberators rushed her.

Rene swore and took a quick step back. Seeing that Harmony was closest, Rene swiveled right to bring the gun to bear on her and fired. Harmony squealed and fell, clutching her upper arm. Rene turned again, but not in time. Riptide's full weight slammed into her, knocking them both to the ground.

Her hand, and the gun it held, was trapped between them. Rene desperately tried to claw at his face, but Riptide grabbed her wrist and twisted it, making her yelp in pain. She struggled beneath his bulk as he maneuvered to pin her to the ground, squirming and writhing to get free. Just as he almost had her, Rene sensed an opening and pulled her knee up sharply, driving it up between his legs.

Riptide groaned, shifting his weight slightly and freeing her to try to work herself loose. Rene glanced over his shoulder. Opus and Scorpio were closing on them rapidly. "No, you won't!" she grunted and, in an effort to free it, wrenched at the gun trapped between them. Before she could pull it free, however, Riptide drove his elbow into her arm to stop her.

Rene's finger jerked, and she heard the muffled blast from the gun still wedged between them. Something slammed into her chest like a pile driver. She tried to cry out, but her breath only seeped out of her in a silent gasp. There was no pain, just an intense cold spreading through her body. *Doesn't matter*, Rene thought, as the world around her faded into darkness. *I've still won.*

Each leap carried Beacon roughly a dozen floors upward, but it still felt like it was taking too long to make the ascent to the observation deck. She considered stretching the jumps, but she was worried that if she pushed it too much, she ran the risk of missing a landing and falling hundreds of feet was in no way part of her plan right now.

In reality, though, it had only taken her just over a minute to finally land at the door to the observation deck. She slid her fingers into the crack between the sliding doors, and they opened easily, admitting her to the observation deck. The construction wasn't finished, so most of the room was still nothing more than open steel infrastructure and framing. The wind whipped through the openings where windows would eventually be, tugging furiously on her cape and hair. Around her spread a commanding view of the city and surrounding landscape. It was stunning and sharpened her resolve– it deserved saving.

In the center of the deck floor was the device itself. Beacon could feel the low thrumming sound it made reverberate through the floor. Despite the filtering of her mask visor, it was nearly invisible amidst a raging maelstrom of energy. Currents swirled and cascaded around the device, and she could feel them throbbing against her.

Beacon paused for a moment to figure out a game plan. There were no obvious seams on the device itself, nor any apparent way to access it or the control mechanism. If she just started tearing into it, it was very likely she'd set it off, probably vaporizing herself in the process.

*Rene had said she'd taken the core of the device from the nuke lab*, she recalled. They had been working on some micro-nuclear systems that harnessed resonant energy to increase the reaction yield. If this was one of those, it didn't just implode like other nuclear devices did. It used a progressive build-up of the core reaction, creating resonance in the energies. Without a regulator, it would eventually reach a critical threshold and catastrophically release all the energy in one massive burst. She could see the surges and currents whirling around the device were indeed gaining strength, getting brighter and pulsing faster. No question it was building toward a cataclysmic overload.

Thinking that siphoning off the energy might cripple the device, Beacon opened herself fully to the energy around her. She felt her power swell, but, as she'd experienced before, she was drawing equally on all the ambient energy around her, having little or no effect on the device itself.

Breathing deeply through her nose, she closed her eyes and concentrated, reaching out with her feelings. She'd never been able to draw from a specific source before, but Beacon could feel the radiant energy of the device, raging and churning, contorting and twisting the other energy waves in the room. It was unmistakable, and she pushed toward it, reached for it, stretching with her power.

Stretching to what she thought was her limit, Beacon felt something abruptly give way, and she was immediately flooded with overwhelming power from the device. As she started to siphon off its energy, every inch of her body felt like it was on fire. She groaned, fighting back the urge to just pass out. Beacon shook her head, forcing back the pain. The energy on the device had diminished somewhat, but she couldn't contain it. *It's working, but if I keep this up, I'm going to die...and I'll have failed,* she told herself, gritting her teeth.

Seeing no other options, she stubbornly held on, but the raw energy and excruciating pain tearing through her body inevitably became too much. Overwhelmed, she began to fade, but just at the cusp of losing consciousness, Beacon felt her body instinctively take over. She reached out with her right hand, and without thinking, her body pushed...*hard.*

Instantly, the pain was gone. Shaking the fog from her head, she realized that she was no longer absorbing the energy from the device, but rather, she was now redirecting it. A massive beam of blinding light was emanating from her hand out of the side of the observation deck. *Well, what do you know?* she marveled. Her body again had shown her it knew what she hadn't, channeling the energy externally, funneling it away instead of letting it burn her out. "Well, if no one knew there was something going on up here before, the entire city probably does now," she said to herself, watching the sky around her flare into a blaze of light.

Turning back to the device, she confirmed the power levels were lower, but they were still building, albeit much more slowly. While she was no longer in physical danger, she found that redirecting this magnitude of power was exhausting, and she wouldn't be able to keep it up forever. If her strength gave out, the device would quickly reach its threshold. *I've bought myself some time, but if I don't find a way to shut down the reaction, it is still only a matter of time until I've failed…again.*

With the few precious moments her new discovery had bought her, she quickly reassessed. *So, what do I know? Even though they manage the energy differently, these micro-cores still rely on chain reactions of colliding particles,* she reasoned. *Reactors are moderated by inserting materials that dampen the collision rates, which, in turn, slows the rate of the reaction.*

The light came on for her. *Dark energy exerts a repelling effect on normal matter. Dark energy is what accelerates the expansion of the universe. That's why my dark energy abilities give me the ability to levitate and push.*

"Maybe," Beacon quickly mumbled to herself, "I could do the opposite of what I'm doing right now. Like I'm channeling the EM energy away from the core, I could instead channel dark energy *into* the core?" Theoretically, it could work, but it was yet another thing she'd never attempted before, and she couldn't help but wonder when her luck spontaneously trying new things under crisis today would give out. On the other hand, she could hardly keep debating what was her only option. "What's the worst that could happen?" she mused, "I'll just blow myself and half the city to smithereens." She had already reached the inescapable conclusion. "If I don't try, that's going to happen anyway, so what do I have to lose?"

As she'd done multiple times while becoming familiar with her other abilities, Beacon focused for a moment on the feeling of her body channeling the energy out into space. She held that sensation in her mind and then reached for the dark energy currents. They surged toward her instantly.

Mimicking that feeling, she reached her left hand toward the device and gently pushed, inverting the flow into the heart of the device. The dark energy responded, flowing past her into the core. As the dark energy entered the core, she felt the reaction pulsing back through the dark energy in ripples and waves. The pulsing and thrumming slowed. She opened her eyes and watched the energy flows around the device start to dim and dissipate. The skyward beam from her hand also began to shrink and fade.

She could feel a cold sweat break out on her chest under her suit. Droplets ran down her cheeks. *Just...a...little...longer,* she demanded, but her reserves were nearly gone.

Finally, the thrum in the dark energy ceased. The siphon she'd created winked out. The device had gone cold; there were no more waves or pulses of energy coming from it at all.

*It's done.*

Beacon released her powers and sank to the ground, exhausted. She let her head hang for a moment, taking deep breaths and gathering her strength. Finally, she managed to sit up on her knees, flipped her hair back, and wiped the sweat from her face with the back of her glove.

Out of the corner of her eye, she saw some movement by the elevator door. Grouped at the edge of the observation deck, a small team of police and firefighters stood there watching her. Their faces wore a mix of awe, shock, and amazement. She had no idea what was going to happen next, but at least the city was safe, and for the moment, Rene's plans were blocked. For now, she'd won.

*Time to face the music*, she thought to herself. She closed her eyes and sighed deeply, letting her shoulders rise and fall a couple of times. Feeling more herself, she turned to face them, smiled, and raised her hand in a wave. "Glad to see you guys. It's been quite the party up here."

One of the police officers hesitantly waved back at her.

Beacon ran her fingers back through her hair and slowly stood up to face the group of responders. "Hey, any of you guys have anything to eat on you by any chance?"

# Debrief

*There it is,* she thought, *Right where they said it would be.* A yellow and black pennant was fluttering slightly in the breeze by a second-floor corner window on the backside of the Bureau building.

After shutting down the bomb, Beacon had to settle things with the police when they arrived. She told them about the lab Rene and the rest of the Liberators of Gaia had been using, how to access Rene's data, and where to find the remaining devices. She was pretty sure they were going to try to take her in as well—she could only imagine what these guys thought of her, standing there in her costume at the scene of a near-cataclysmic disaster—but in the end, she agreed to meet with the DA and was released on her own recognizance. She smiled to herself; more likely, they were completely freaked out by her and just didn't want to start something where they might be over their head. *Frankly, they were probably right,* she mused.

They gave her a secure messaging link she could use to work out the details of the meeting with the DA's office. Given her spike in popularity since Meyer's Tower, she was reluctant to show up at the front door of the Bureau of Investigations building in her costume in broad daylight. She sighed. It would have been a mob scene, so they arranged a back way into the DA's office directly, out of direct public view, and there it was as promised.

*Still, time to back out,* she thought, watching the pennant flap in the breeze above her. It wasn't the first time she'd considered bailing on the whole meeting with the DA. She didn't know what was waiting for her in there; it could easily be a trap of some kind. In the end, though, she knew she had to follow through. It was her duty, after all. Beacon was the only person who knew the entire story, the only one who had all the pieces the DA would need to get an accurate, truthful picture of how everything transpired.

It was also the right thing to do. While the Liberators of Gaia had things they needed to answer for, they were also deceived by Rene, and it was only fair that they were held accountable for the actions that were solely on them. The court needed the facts for justice to be served. Trap or not, she had to share what she knew. With luck, this would be over quickly, and she'd be on her way.

*Let's get this over with.*

That small second-floor balcony was an easy jump for her, so she looked around the alley quickly just to make sure no one was looking and stepped back into a little alcove to get into costume. Tricia had thought ahead and wore most of her suit underneath her street clothes, so it was a simple and quick change. She tucked her street clothes into the small satchel she carried and took a deep breath. Her heart was already racing—this could go any number of ways—but setting things square was the right thing to do. There was a lot the DA needed to know for the investigation, and since she was sure that she was already in some deep hot water, cooperation probably was the best way to begin with him.

One more deep breath, a quick look around, and Beacon drew in a small amount of the bright sunlight, just enough for a quick sprint down the short distance to the building and a perfect leap up to the balcony by the open window. *I bet that looked good*, she chuckled to herself, securing her bag on the railing of the balcony, and tucking it neatly out of sight.

Beacon cautiously stepped in through the window and surveyed the office. Empty, again, as promised. *Stay sharp, Beacon. This still could easily be a double-cross*, she thought, but again, trust starts somewhere. She just hoped this wouldn't be another blow to the gut and fast track to a cell.

District Attorney Harris appeared from a small side room. "Beacon, I assume?"

"What gave it away?"

"Just a hunch," he jibed. "You really could have used the private elevator. It's quite secure, and no one would have seen you."

"I'm trying to keep a low profile." She noticed her black and yellow reflection in the display case across the room. "Well, as low a profile as I can manage, I suppose." *Besides, small, enclosed spaces make me a bit leery lately thanks to recent events, but he doesn't need to know that...too much information too soon*, she decided.

Harris chuckled, "Well, you don't need to worry much about that here. As we agreed, there is no one here but you and me. There are no surveillance devices of any kind in this room. No one is watching or listening. The interview room is this way." He gestured to the room from which he'd entered. "We use this room for the conversations that require extra privacy and security: high-profile depositions, WitSec cases, that kind of thing. It has no recording or listening devices either."

"Okay," she said, relaxing a bit, "Shall we get started then?"

Harris gestured for her to lead the way into the room. It was austere, a single table with a few basic office chairs. No windows and no other doors. There was a smaller table next to the wall with some water and glasses.

"Would you like something to drink? Anything before we begin?"

"No, I'm good, thank you," Beacon replied, taking the chair across the table from the door. She felt much more comfortable facing the door here. If something was going to go sideways, she wanted to see it coming.

Harris sat down in the chair across from her. He pulled out a small device from his coat pocket and laid it on the table. "This room has no recording devices in it, but if you are okay with it, I would like to record what you have to tell me. None of it will be directly admissible in court, but I am hoping you will give us enough leads that we can pull together evidence and probable cause that we will need when we track these guys down."

"Rene and her terrorist friends got away then?"

"We found Doctor Thornton's body in the parking garage in the bottom of the building where she tried to set off her device, where you stopped her. It seems the Liberators of Gaia felt they needed to be liberated from Doctor Thornton as well. The rest of them did get away, but we have a few leads we will be chasing down. We just need a clearer picture of what they and she were doing before the incident a few days ago."

Beacon breathed a small sigh, partly in sadness and partly in relief. *Rene's last words to me turned out to be rather prophetic after all.* Rene was brilliant and might've been able to change with the right help, but she wouldn't get that chance now. Selfishly, at least, Rene wouldn't be giving away her identity either. That much was safe again.

"I'm not comfortable with you recording me during this chat. I don't need a voice print, for example, giving me away. Despite all this, I would like to have some kind of life when I'm out of this suit."

"Ah, of course. Rest easy. Again, when we gather testimony from high-profile types, we use a recorder that scrambles the voice, making it unidentifiable. No one will be able to identify who you are from this recording, I promise you."

*Harris is very good at this*, Beacon thought. Easy to see how he got elected and why he was respected as one of the best DAs in the state, if not the country. *Maybe this is someone I can trust after all - we'll see.*

She nodded her consent, and Harris started the recording. "District Attorney Robert Harris debriefing the person known as 'Beacon' regarding the events prior to and leading up to the attempted terrorist action at Meyers Tower."

"Now, go ahead and tell me what happened and what you know. Please be as specific as you can. I'll ask questions as I need to elaborate the points I feel need more information."

The interview went on for nearly three hours. Beacon related everything she could remember about her encounters with the Liberators, her investigation of the test explosions, her discovery of the nature of the payload of the bombs, Rene's plot to condemn the human race to slow extinction, her capture, and ultimately how she tracked Thornton and the terrorists to Meyers Tower and used her powers to prevent the nuke from going critical. Harris interrupted frequently to ask questions and probe on certain points. Clearly, they already had some information, and he was looking to connect some dots and build a more accurate timeline of what Rene and the Liberators were actually doing.

Beacon did have to obscure, or even leave out, certain details that would have divulged too much about potentially who she was, what connections she had, and so on. If it was just her, it might've been different, but she was not getting Marni or anyone else dragged into this.

Harris sat forward in his seat, "Is there anything else you can remember, or anything else at all you think will be important to the investigation?"

"No, I think that's pretty much everything," Beacon replied as she looked toward the small table. "But some of that water would be great right about now." Her throat felt two sizes smaller, and her tongue was two sizes larger, it seemed.

"Thank you," Harris said as he turned off the recorder. "Sure, let's have some of that water. We've done a lot of talking. I'm parched, too."

Harris walked over to the table and poured two glasses from the pitcher. He brought them back, setting them on the table. Beacon looked at hers, then looked at him. Harris smiled and took a drink from his. She smiled, raised her glass as a miniature toast, and did the same.

"So, now, completely off the record. Anything you want to share about you and your situation?"

She used the drink she was taking to buy her a few moments to consider. Setting her empty glass back down, she smiled and said, "Hmmm, no, not just yet. Maybe sometime, sometime later, but not yet."

Harris nodded his head to the side, "Fair enough."

They sat there for a few moments regarding each other. Finally, Beacon sat back in her chair and broke the silence.

"So, what happens now?"

Harris sat back in his chair and made a roof shape with his fingers. "That somewhat depends on you, actually. Technically, you haven't broken any laws that warrant charges of any kind, and you did save a lot of lives."

She breathed out again in relief. *But there's more to it,* she thought, *I'm sure.*

"However," Harris continued, "neither I, nor the police department, can formally condone someone in a costume being an active vigilante in the city. You must see the problems that would cause legally and with setting some bad precedent for others less capable than you are to do the same.

"On the other hand, it would be less than honest to say that some help wouldn't be appreciated from time to time, especially with certain unique and problematic situations that arise occasionally. Someone with your abilities can take action and intervene in ways that might not be possible for someone in a more official capacity."

*Ooookaaaay,* she thought, *this is going in a direction I didn't expect.* To her, it was starting to sound less like she was in trouble and more like a recruiting pitch. Oddly, that didn't make her feel any more at ease.

"Do you intend to keep going out there and doing the superhero thing?"

"Well, I do have this really cool suit, and I'd hate to see it go to waste." She smirked a little, hoping to diffuse things a little.

"It is an awesome suit, but if you do, I can promise you it won't be easy. You've got a target on your back now. When you were just getting started, you could stay a little under the radar as a novelty, and while you had a lot of fans, people didn't take you very seriously.

"But with what you did a few days ago, you're out there now. The real deal. You've shown you're someone to take seriously, and a lot of people are going to pay attention. They are going to want to know all about you. Reporters, journalists, photographers, every big leaguer, and two-bit hack is going to be on the hunt to get the scoop on who Beacon really is. They will hunt you mercilessly to be the first to tell the world the big secret.

"Worse, there are bad people out there with a lot of big plans and a lot of resources who will now see you as a threat. The dumb ones won't take you seriously. The smart ones, though, will want to stay ahead of you and use whatever they have to figure you out. Not just who you *are*, but your powers, your weaknesses, your friends, your family, anything they can use to get an advantage over you and, if necessary, take you out of play."

She slumped just a little. *Yeah, this is getting real pretty fast.*

"Yeah, I get it. I'll be honest. I'm not sure what I'm going to do next," she admitted. "I'm committed to helping, to using my abilities and my image to make a positive impact. I just don't know if I'm the type that will keep going out looking for people who need my help or if I'm the type that will wait for something big to come along that actually needs me.

"I guess I've always been the type that feels differences are made in small ways every day. I believe that being out there gives people a regular reminder that someone is going the extra mile for them, and that becomes a symbol for them to do better by each other."

Beacon shrugged. "Up until now, though, I was more caught up in whether I *could* do this than if I *should* do this, but now I'm past that part. With the crisis over, I probably have some things to sort out about all this."

"Yes, you definitely do. It will take a lot of commitment and a lot of guts. People will love you, and people will hate you. It's going to take courage in ways your powers can't help with."

Harris leaned forward again, "But, maybe we can."

*Here it comes*, she thought.

"If you were willing to work with us..."

Beacon snapped forward, pointing at Harris, mouth open, but before she could get any rebuttal out, Harris pressed on quickly. He knew he was only getting one shot at this.

"WITH us, not for us...hear me out."

She tightened her mouth and put her hand down on the table, steeling herself for the rest.

"We can help keep some of these people off your back. We can keep information and details out of the public eye that will help keep nosy people off your scent."

"Such as?"

Harris got very serious, and his tone became very calculated and deliberate. *Ok,* she thought, *here comes the lawyer, the negotiator.*

"Such as if, for example, you were Doctor Tricia Carling..."

Beacon's breath caught. She was glad her mask hid her eyes because they were the size of dinner plates right now. *How could he know?*

Even with her mask, Harris had no trouble reading her reaction. "Look, someone with a sublime mastery of investigation like me," he smiled coyly, "could easily look at recent events, compare timelines, pull together a quick history of when and where your activity started, and possibly make a connection to a certain accident at a certain university, and whether right or wrong, you and whoever they thought you were could be in immediate jeopardy. It took me only a few days of digging. Granted, I'm above average," there was that smirk again, "but with enough resources, someone else could do the same, and quickly."

Fury welled up inside of her. She put both hands flat on the table, pushed her chair back with her legs, and leaned across the table toward Harris. The smirk vanished from his face.

"Was that your agenda all along?" Beacon asked. "I come in here willingly, in good faith, because I believe that giving you the whole story is the right thing to do, and you start dropping veiled threats about exposing me? If you're trying to convince me to join your *team*—she spat the word, making air quotes as she did—threatening me is a pretty lousy way to do it."

Putting her hands back on the table, she leaned in a little further to make her point. "Trust me, DA Harris, if you try to yank my chain or go toe-to-toe with me, it's not going to work out well for anyone."

Harris leaned toward her, perfectly maintaining his composure. "I assure you I intended no threat, veiled or otherwise. If that's how it came across, I sincerely apologize." He gestured toward her seat, clearly hoping to de-escalate the situation. Beacon looked at him for a few seconds longer, then pulled her chair back up to the table and sat down.

"So, what *are* you trying to say then?" she asked.

Harris sat back as well. "All I'm trying to emphasize is that the risk of exposure is very real, but I can promise, even if you were her, that I would make sure personally any speculation about your identity would never appear in any official, or unofficial, file anywhere in this office. We could even seal a few hospital and first responder records, leave a few false breadcrumbs, obscure some reports here and there. Generally, make it hard for someone to make those connections."

"Ok. I would certainly appreciate that, but I still feel like there's an 'if' here somewhere. What exactly are you proposing?" Beacon asked. She struggled to keep her voice steady, and there wasn't enough water on that table to quench the desert her mouth had become.

Harris took a small box from his jacket and slid it across the table. Beacon took it and opened it.

"A commpod?" she asked, puzzled.

"If you decide to work with us...if YOU decide...yes, this is a special secure commpod. It is untraceable and untrackable, even by us. It will give you a direct link to the response unit at the department, bypassing the normal front desk. You'll have backup whenever you need it. You will also have a direct line to me. Both are already programmed in. It's lightweight and hardened military grade. From what we know of your powers, which isn't much, honestly, it should be compatible, but we are also confident you can sort out those details when the time comes."

Knowing he had her attention, Harris pressed on. "The Commissioner and I discussed this option, depending on how this conversation went and what kind of a person I decided you were based on it. He isn't crazy about the idea, just so you know, but he also believes the help in certain situations could be valuable, and he trusts me. I'm also pretty sure he'll make sure I fry if this goes badly, but I'm willing to take the risk. You seem like a good bet based on your actions to date and our talk here today."

Part of her wanted to say something stupid like "I won't let you down," and she'd be lying if she said it didn't feel good to have someone believe in her and what she was trying to but decided maybe it is best to keep that to herself for the time being. Part of her still felt played a bit, and trust was going to come slowly.

She took the case, holding it thoughtfully in her hands. She turned it over a few times.

"Are you sure it works?" she asked, showing a mischievous smile of her own.

"Pretty sure."

Beacon thought for a moment and sighed. "All right. I need to think it over. I owe it to myself to sort out how I'm going to do this, and frankly, you've just thrown something new into the mix that I need some time to digest."

"It carries a lot of responsibility," Harris said softly. "Someone like you, though, can not only be the symbol you mentioned before, one that inspires people to be a better version of themselves, but also a symbol that makes the worst of us think twice. Let us know what you decide."

As if on cue, Beacon heard the chime that indicated Harris had an incoming call. He held up his first finger, gesturing to her to wait, and tapped the commpod in his ear. "Yeah, Harris here…. Uh, ok. That's just great," he said sarcastically. Harris rubbed the bridge of his nose, "Yeah, ok. Hold on. I'll be right down."

He tapped the commpod again, ending the call, and turned back to Beacon.

"Seems quite the crowd has gathered out front. People waving signs. Reporters. Looks like we didn't do as good a job keeping this little meeting a secret as we thought."

"Does that happen often?" Beacon asked him.

"The press is an occupational hazard," Harris shrugged, "I need to go down there and give them a statement and, more importantly, distract them for you. Unless, of course, you want to come down and say something?"

Beacon thought for a second and decided, "No, not yet. I don't think I'm quite ready for that."

"You probably will have to be fairly soon, you know."

Beacon nodded, "Yeah, I know…just not now."

"Ok then," Harris replied. He went over to the desk and tapped a couple of buttons on the pad there. A screen lit up on the side wall of the office, showing the news stream being broadcast live from the front of the building. She could see the people out front chanting. Many of them were holding up signs with 'We 🧡 Beacon', 'Free Beacon', and 'Beacon is our hero!'. She couldn't help but smile at the crowd's enthusiastic show of support.

"You can watch from here if you want. I suggest you let me get their attention, and then you can duck out when you're ready."

Beacon nodded, turning to face him. He reached out to shake her hand. She paused for a second and returned the shake, adding just a little extra firmness to let him know that even though she might have a lot to figure out, she was going to do it on her terms.

"Good grip," he grinned.

She smiled back. "You have no idea."

Harris left Beacon standing in the room watching the news stream. No sooner had the doors shut behind him than his commpod chimed again. "Yeah, yeah, I'm on my way down right now," he said impatiently. He listened for a moment and replied, "Yeah, she's still in my office...no, let her leave when she's ready. We're good here."

A few minutes later, as Beacon watched the stream, she saw Harris come out of the building. He was swarmed immediately by several reporters, each of them pushing a microphone into his face. The crowd cheered, raising their signs higher. A petite brunette reporter shoved her way to the front and shouted out the first question, "DA Harris, is it true that Beacon came into your office today?"

Harris straightened his tie and replied, "Yes, it is true that the individual known as Beacon came into our office to provide testimony regarding the averted terrorist attempt by Liberators of Gaia a few days ago."

"Can we talk with her?" demanded another reporter.

Staying calm and collected, Harris answered, "Beacon is not present to make a statement currently, but she asked me to convey her gratitude at the overwhelming show of support you've all given her today and that she's glad she could be of service to our great city and its citizens."

*Wow, he is good,* Beacon remarked to herself.

Another reporter quickly followed up, "What is the department's official position regarding Beacon and her actions?"

*Oh, this'll be interesting*, Beacon thought, holding her breath.

"While the department cannot openly condone private citizens acting as vigilantes, the department has concluded that Beacon's actions to date do not warrant any filing of criminal charges at this time. Further, under the recently expanded Service to the Community statutes, we have determined that she is also immune from other civil suits and penalties as well."

The crowd cheered, and Beacon breathed a sigh of relief. On that note, she decided it would be a great time to leave and made her way to the balcony window. She fetched her bag and leaped over the railing, fusing a little dark energy to slow her descent to the ground. She changed quickly and started on her way home, more comfortable now that she was back in her street clothes.

Tricia could feel the weight of the new commpod shifting in her bag, adding to the weight she already bore on her shoulders as she hurried toward the end of the alley. She wanted to put as much distance between her and the DA's office as she could. Clearly, her secret was now somewhat exposed, and if they couldn't keep a simple meeting quiet, how could they keep other things under wraps? What expectations would they have of her in this arrangement if she accepted it? More questions. Always more.

She gave a small sigh and shook her head, deciding there was no point in worrying about it now. *It is what it is*, and it was just one more thing to factor in as she thought about the future. Pausing briefly at the end of the alley, she closed her eyes to compose herself before stepping forward onto the street. Instantly, she was immersed in the chaotic energy of the city, the symphony of sounds and motion, the thrum of rhythm and purpose as people were starting to head home after work, running errands, or whatever business they had that day. She took a moment to let it wash over her. *These people, their lives, this is what it's all about.*

As she started to dial up her ride home, Tricia glanced first right and then to her left, and there, in that split second, on the small newsstand by the bus stop, her attention froze on the newspaper headline boldly glaring out at her:

## WHO IS 'BEACON'?

### What is the story behind our new superhero?
### Heroine or Hoax?
### Miracle or Misanthrope?

*Good questions,* she thought to herself. *I definitely have a lot to sort out, but Harris is right; I need to get more in front of what people are saying about me. I need to be more involved in how people see me.*

# Images

Beacon sat in the production trailer, staring at herself in the makeup mirror. Xia, the makeup technician and hair stylist, was just putting the finishing touches on her makeup. Despite the mask covering most of her face, Xia had put a lot of work into getting her ready for the interview. Beacon barely recognized herself in the mirror.

Just thinking about how soon it would start stirred up the butterflies in her stomach all over again. *What have I gotten myself into?* she wondered.

Within a few days after she gave her deposition to the DA, the full story about what happened at Meyer's Tower broke, and things got very frantic. DA Harris called her on her special commpod. He had received two calls on the same day, both asking to get messages to Beacon if he could.

The first message was from the mayor. She wanted to do a big parade and celebration for Crystal Bay's superheroine in honor of what she had done to save the city (and most likely the mayor's job, the DA added privately). The second message was from the program director for CrystalClear, the city's morning talk show and current events video magazine. They wanted to do a special live interview segment with Beacon.

Tricia wanted nothing to do with any kind of parade or party in her honor; that was completely out of the question. However, the interview segment intrigued her. After her meeting with Harris, she had come to realize that her image was perhaps her most powerful weapon for truly reaching people, and that image depended on the public getting to know her, empathizing with her, and understanding she was there for them. That required her to not only tell her story but also to dismiss the various speculations and rumors that had naturally popped up surrounding her. No matter how uncomfortable the prospect was for her, Beacon had to get in front of them.

She made her intentions plain to the CrystalClear production team, and after some negotiation, they all reached a compromise. They would arrange the interview segment with Beacon, and the mayor would announce plans to put up some commemorative plaque or something similar at Meyer's Tower in honor of Beacon's service to the city. CrystalClear would get its interview, and the mayor would get her publicity. Everyone wins. Tricia even thought the format they had proposed for the interview was clever. She felt it would come off as very informal and personal, and more importantly, was something she could probably get through without throwing up.

When Harris heard about the interview, he called Tricia and asked her if she thought she was doing the right thing. When she reminded him what he said about getting ahead of the narrative, he had no choice but to agree it was a smart move. He cautioned her to watch what she said during the interview and gave her some coaching on how to prepare.

Given the expertise he showed handling the crowd during her visit to his office, Tricia gladly took any advice he was willing to offer.

A couple of weeks later, here she was, sitting in a production trailer behind a broadcast stage erected on the Meyer's Tower construction site. Beacon absently reached up and touched the small disk next to her throat buried under the neck of her suit; Harris may not have fully agreed with her decision, but he agreed enough to arrange for her to get the scrambler she was now wearing. It was a larger version of what he had used when she gave her statement and, according to Harris, would prevent anyone from identifying her voiceprint from the broadcast stream.

"So, what do you think?" Xia's chipper voice snapped Beacon back to the present.

"Uh, sorry. My mind was wandering," Beacon apologized. "What were you saying?"

"All good. It's just hard to tell with the mask." Xia winked at her, smiling. "I was asking what you thought about taking out the pony and letting your hair down for the interview."

"Oh, that would be fine. Whatever you think is best."

The technician grabbed the hair tie and slid it off. She let Beacon's black and blond tresses fall naturally and started to brush and arrange it.

"Wow, this one bit really has a mind of its own, doesn't it?" Xia exclaimed, holding a wild lock of her hair out for Beacon to see. *THAT lock, but of course.*

"It always has," Beacon smiled.

"Well, it never met me before," Xia asserted and froze it into place with a blast of hair spray. "Good to go!" she proclaimed and gave Beacon a chef's kiss in the mirror. Beacon smiled.

"Do you approve?" Xia asked her.

Beacon turned her head from side to side. "Yeah, it looks great...really great."

Xia beamed. "Not everyone can say they are the hair stylist to superheroes, can they?"

Beacon smiled and shook her head. Xia leaned in a bit, looking at their reflections together in the mirror. "Gotta say, for the record, I don't know what you look like in real life, but you slay in that costume. You're gonna own it out there."

Beacon looked up at the technician's reflection in the mirror. "Thanks," she said. "I certainly hope so."

Xia's response was interrupted by a knock on the door. Without waiting for an answer, a young woman cracked open the door and stuck in her head. "Hi! I'm Casey, the guest handler. Are we ready?"

"Well, I'm not sure about the 'we' part, but I guess I'm as ready as I'm ever going to be," Beacon answered, conscious of the wavering in her voice.

"Nervous?" Casey asked, coming into the trailer and closing the door.

"Does it show?"

"It's natural," Casey assured her, patting her shoulder, "Look, you're going to do great. We've got a good crowd out there, all pulling for you. Just focus on Tamara. She's fantastic and will guide you through it. Follow her lead, go with the flow, and be yourself. Easy-peasy. Remember, you wanted to tell your story, so relax and tell it. There's a whole crowd out there excited to hear it. They are going to love you. Shall we?"

Beacon took a deep breath and followed Casey out of the trailer. Casey led her to a small backstage waiting area and handed her a paper cup of water. "Here, wet your whistle with this. You'll hear Tamara introduce you in just a few minutes. When you do—" she pointed to a small set of steps at the side of the platform "—just go up those steps, smile, and take a seat next to Tamara."

They waited backstage, Beacon doing her best not to fidget. "You said there's a crowd?" Beacon asked, trying to distract herself. The waiting felt like an eternity.

"Oh yeah, there is," Casey affirmed, grinning ear to ear. "We put out seating for a hundred. There is easily four to five times that out there. You're popular. Standing room only."

Before Beacon could reply, though, Casey suddenly reached up and cupped her hand over the commpod in her ear. She looked at Beacon, held up a single finger, and silently mouthed, "One minute." Beacon closed her eyes and took a few calming breaths. *Show time*, she told herself.

Casey started counting down to Beacon with her fingers, five, four, three, two, and at one they heard the crowd erupt, and the CrystalClear show jingle started playing over the monitor speakers. Beacon looked at the stage, then back at Casey. Casey gave her a thumbs up and a smile.

"Good morning, Crystal Bay!" called the voice of Tamara Rawlins, host of CrystalClear. "We are broadcasting live this morning from outside Meyer's Tower, and we have a very special and amazing show for you all today." The crowd applauded loudly. *Jamal would be SO jealous if he knew*, Beacon thought to herself.

"Let's waste no time, shall we?" Tamara continued, "We'd like to welcome our special guest. Live with us here today, none other than the Crystal Bay Crusader...our Angel of Light...Crystal Bay's very own superheroine, Beacon!"

Casey excitedly started shooing Beacon toward the riser steps to the broadcast platform, mouthing, "Go go go." Beacon trotted up the steps and emerged onto the broadcast platform. The crowd erupted in cheers, whistles, and thunderous clapping. She was taken aback for a second until she saw Tamara standing beside her chair on stage, warmly waving her hand for Beacon to join her. Beacon smiled and met Tamara behind a small round table midstage. A beautiful orchid flower arrangement sat on the low glass table, which was centered between three chairs facing the exuberant audience.

"Pleased to be here, Tamara," Beacon said, shaking Tamara's hand. Tamara gestured to the center chair on her left, and they both sat. Tamara gave the crowd a chance to quiet down a bit before starting the interview.

"So, before we start, I have to say this look," Tamara gestured toward Beacon, "is absolutely stunning. It is awesome, isn't it, folks?" The crowd applauded. "Did you come up with this yourself? Where did you get your inspiration?"

"Yes, I did come up with this myself, Tamara. Honestly, I got a lot of ideas and inspiration from comic books...," she suddenly she thought of Tony, the comic book shop owner, and, just in case he was watching, quickly added, "and movies and old TV shows."

"Really?" Tamara questioned, "Comics?"

"Well, Tamara, there isn't exactly a how-to-be-a-superhero website out there I could research." The crowd tittered in amusement. "But a lot of extremely talented and creative people have been imagining this kind of thing for a long time. There was a lot of material to work with."

"Very cool," Tamara nodded, "and I notice that you're wearing a yellow cape today. Black is your usual, isn't it?"

"Black is my usual, true, but today is a special occasion, Tamara. In my line of work, sometimes it's good to be seen. Other times, it's best to avoid being seen. Today's definitely the former."

"It's fantastic, Beacon, and the hair? I assume that's a wig?"

Beacon reached up and ran her fingers through it, careful not to mess up the makeup artist's hard work. "Nope, this is all me."

"Wow, it is a very distinct coloring, those streaks of black and blonde. You must really stand out in a crowd when you're out of costume."

Beacon smiled, "I said it was all me, but I didn't say I was like this all the time. It happens when I'm being...this."

"Ah, I see," Tamara smiled, "so what is it when you're not being...this?"

"In a ponytail usually," Beacon smirked. The crowd laughed.

Tamara chuckled as well, "I see then. Well, you look great, and we are excited to have you here. When we were arranging this, you said there was something you wanted specifically to get out of this interview. Can you share that with us?"

"Sure. I said I felt it was important that now that I'm getting more in the public eye, for people to get to know me, know the truth about me. My dad used to tell me that when people want to talk about something, they will gladly make things up if they don't have the facts. I'm pretty sure people are talking, so it's time to give them some facts."

"Very true," Tamara agreed, nodding her head. "So, with that in mind, let's walk through some of the interesting headlines we found out on the streams and outlets about Beacon and separate some reality from myth."

Tamara pointed toward the monitor. "Here's our first exciting headline." The monitor shifted to an image of one of the city tabloids proclaiming:

## BEACON IS AN ALIEN

### And I Have Proof!

"So, how about it, Beacon? Can you give us E.T.'s phone number?"

Beacon grinned. "No, sorry, Tamara, I can't. I'm all human, born and bred, Earthling."

"Can you narrow that down for us a bit? Where on planet Earth do you hail from?"

"I can give you North America."

Tamara chuckled, "We all probably guessed that one. But you do call Crystal Bay home?"

"I do. It saves on the commute." The audience chuckled. Tamara smiled, too.

Tamara waited for a few more seconds, but when it was clear Beacon wasn't offering any more on the subject of her origins, she pressed onward.

"All right then, how about this one?" The monitor shifted again to one of the city's open discussion forums, showing a thread titled:

# I AM BEACON'S LOVER

Beacon laughed out loud. The crowd burst into laughter with her. "So? How about it?" Tamara prodded.

Still laughing, Beacon managed to force out a reply. "Sorry to burst that guy's bubble, but emphatically no. Doesn't matter who it is, it's no."

Tamara grinned and leaned forward, "So you're saying there's nobody holding Beacon's flame?"

"Not now. Needless to say, I've got a lot on my plate, and trying to juggle a romance with everything else just isn't in the cards right now." Tamara raised her eyebrows, taunting her to go on.

"Seriously, Tamara, there isn't. Yeah, ok, maybe someday, but I have a lot to figure out first, and let's face it," she gestured toward herself with both hands, "whoever gets involved with this is going to have their hands full."

"No doubt," Tamara replied, "but you just either broke a lot of hearts or gave some people a lot of hope. I guess we'll see how that develops. However, in the meanwhile, let's take a look at our next headline". The monitor shifted once again.

# BEACON IS A HOAX

"So, the conspiracy theorists are having a field day with you, dear," Tamara said. The crowd booed. "What can you say to convince people you're the real thing?"

"I don't have to say anything, Tamara. We are live, aren't we?"

Tamara nodded. Beacon smiled and rose up out of her chair, lifting one knee and raising her hands. The crowd gasped, and Tamara's eyes widened as she stared in amazement at Beacon's ascent.

Her cape fluttering in the breeze, Beacon hovered several feet off the platform, then channeled just enough of her power to make her hands glow a bright, piercing white. The crowd cheered in approval.

Tamara shook her head, recovering her composure. "She sure looks like the real deal to me, wouldn't you say, folks?" The crowd's whistles, cheers, and applause confirmed their agreement. Beacon nodded and lowered herself gently back into the chair.

Tamara fanned herself with one hand. "Wow. To see it on video footage is one thing, but to see that right here in front of us is nothing short of breathtaking."

Beacon smiled. "I'm glad we could put that myth to rest so easily."

"But, while we are on the topic of your abilities," Tamara continued as the monitor started showing pictures of Beacon in action, "let's explore them just a little bit more. You just gave us a firsthand, and very impressive, display of flight and light, but we've seen speed, strength, and some ability to move objects at a distance. What else have you got going on?"

Beacon paused for a moment and offered, "I also heal very quickly."

"No doubt that comes in very handy. Anything else?"

"I have a few other tricks up my sleeve."

"Such as?" Tamara pressed, drawing out the 'as' for emphasis.

"Such as.... honestly, it's a work in progress, Tamara." Beacon deflected a bit. "I'm continually learning new things about what I can do all the time. Anything I might tell you today might be different next month or even next week."

"I see," Tamara replied, clearly not satisfied with her answer. "So, is that the hardest part of your journey as a superheroine?"

"In part, but the most challenging part is about maintaining control. When I use my powers, they really *want* to be used. It's hard to hold them back, especially when I'm feeling very intense emotions, so something I focused on early and still train and practice regularly is how to use just enough of what I can do in any situation so no one gets seriously hurt."

The crowd murmured its approval, with a few claps of applause mixed in. Tamara nodded in agreement. "I can't imagine what that must be like, but I think I can speak for all of us when I say how impressed we are and how much we appreciate your sense of responsibility and commitment to discipline." The crowd applauded again.

"Now, let's move on to our last headline." The monitor shifted to an all-too-familiar image:

# BEACON FOILS TERRORIST PLOT
## Thousands of Lives Saved

"Just a few short weeks ago, right here—" Tamara gestured behind them at Meyer's Tower "—you intercepted an attempt by Liberators of Gaia to blow up The Tower along with a substantial part of the city." Beacon nodded. "Can you tell us, in your own words, how that all unfolded?"

Part of the advice Harris had given her included the official story being distributed by the authorities, along with a strong recommendation that Beacon stick to it if any questions came up during the interview. The official story made no mention of Rene or her real plot to wipe out humanity. Plus, the university was very keen to downplay any possible connection between the incident and the university itself. Even though they had no knowledge or connection to what Rene was doing, the fact that she was using university facilities as part of her plot would reflect very badly on them. Tricia felt a sense of obligation to try to protect the university's reputation and had already decided she would avoid mentioning anything about the university in her public version of events.

Bearing all this in mind, Beacon shared as much of the story as she could, being careful to omit certain details and, most importantly, not to lie; being caught in a lie now, or later, would seriously undermine the positive image she was trying to foster with the media and community. She shared how she'd made the connection after encountering the Liberators outside of VeriMed, tracked them to their base of operations, discovered their intent, and then caught up with them at Meyer's Tower. All are true, if not complete, in every detail.

When she finished, Tamara picked back up on the interview. "That's an incredible story. Can you share a little more? Like, where was their base of operations?"

Beacon paused, knowing her answer wasn't going to be well received. "I'm sorry, Tamara, but I can't disclose that right now. There is still an active investigation going on, and it's considered a crime scene. The police are still going through it and have asked that its location remain undisclosed for now."

"I see," Tamara answered curtly, "Ok, then, can you tell us more about this person?"

The monitor changed to show a professional headshot of Rene. Beacon's stomach flipped a bit. *Ok, this is getting interesting now,* she thought. This wasn't in the format they had agreed to, so clearly, someone felt the show needed spicing up and decided to surprise her.

"Is this someone you believe is associated with what happened here?" Beacon dodged.

"This is Doctor Rene Thornton. Some of our sources have linked her to the incident, implying there may have been more going on than a simple excessive demonstration by an eco-terrorist organization."

"So, I take that as a 'yes,'" Beacon responded, smoothly and calmly. "As I said before, Tamara, it's an active investigation. I can't reveal any information about specific people, locations, or events that the authorities haven't already made available to the public. I'm sorry."

Tamara sat back in her chair, visibly showing an element of frustration. "So, help me out here, Beacon. You said you wanted to clear the air, dispel myths, help the public trust you, but if I may speak bluntly, you have seemed somewhat evasive at times here today."

The crowd went stone silent. Beacon took a deep breath to regroup, thought for a second, and then decided to just go with her gut. Harris said to be honest. Casey said to be herself. Time to put it on the table.

"You're right, Tamara. I have been vague on certain points," Beacon started, keeping her tone even but direct and confident. "I do want to be as open with everyone as I can. I need people to trust me, and that comes hard when you're wearing a mask.

"But I need everyone to understand that what I do requires a level of privacy, too. I protect my identity because what I do makes a lot of enemies and people I love, not to mention me, could come to harm if I gave away too many clues about how I am in real life, and someone uncovered that.

"The same goes for my powers. Yes, I can do some amazing things, and I'm learning more about them all the time, but it's also the element of surprise that gives me an advantage. Over time, the full extent of my powers will all become public knowledge. I know that, but I need to hang onto that edge for as long as I can because I believe it might just be the difference between life and death at some point."

Beacon paused for effect. Tamara was riveted by what she was saying, and she could sense the audience was on the edge of its collective seat.

"As far as the police are concerned, it's about building their trust, too. I'm not trying to take their place. I'm trying to help them—be an asset to the city—and if they see me as untrustworthy, it will compromise what I'm really trying to do here. Let's be clear: I don't work for the police, but we need to be on good terms for this to work."

"So, you say you don't work for the police. What do they think of you?"

"I don't work for them, so I can't speak on their behalf. If you want to know officially what the police think of me and what I do, you need to ask them." Tamara frowned a bit and started to interject, but Beacon spoke over her, "*But,* if you want to know how *I* feel about it, I see us as having an uneasy but cooperative relationship based on mutual goals. To keep building that trust, though, I need to respect what they do, and I believe that as long as I respect certain boundaries, they will let me continue doing the good work and making the difference I believe I can make."

The crowd applauded enthusiastically. Tamara nodded and waited for the crowd to settle down. "Ok, I can see that. I think we can all appreciate and respect the fine line you must walk to keep being our Angel of Light, even if that means we need to be kept in the dark on some points here and there."

"Thanks, Tamara," Beacon said, relieved that she'd gotten through that relatively unscathed.

Tamara shifted into a new gear, sitting forward in her chair. Putting on a big smile, she addressed the audience. "Speaking of making a difference and doing good, I'd like to share something Beacon and the team at CrystalClear discussed and agreed to leading up to the interview today. As amazing as Beacon is, it takes a community to truly make a difference.

"To assist our resident superheroine, our production company, in conjunction with a generous donation from Meyer's Corporation, will be creating a foundation called 'Beacons of Hope'. This foundation will operate as a non-profit and will create partnerships with a set of local charities and community service organizations, curated with Beacon herself, for the express purpose of helping anyone in Crystal Bay get involved, whether it's through donations or volunteering or other means."

The monitor shifted to an image of a scannable code and contact information for the fledgling foundation. "There's still a lot of work to do to get it off the ground, but anyone interested in getting notified as we move forward can use the information on the screen to get on our newsletter subscription and updates list. This contact information is also available on the CrystalClear site."

"I really love this, and I'm excited to be a part of it," Beacon added, following the script they'd coordinated in advance. "I used to be someone who didn't get involved. When I found out what I could do, I didn't know if it was a gift or a curse, but I knew not being involved was no longer an option. I'm really optimistic that this will help us connect with people and help empower them to find a cause that they are passionate about and get involved."

Tamara nodded and softly clapped her hands. The audience added generous amounts of real applause, mixed with whistles and cheers.

"Further," Tamara continued, "the foundation will also support Beacon by assisting her with a direct media outlet she can use to engage with you all more directly. It will include discussion groups about the foundation and Beacon herself. She has graciously agreed to occasionally share her personal insights, answer questions, and generally use it as a means to be more directly connected with our city as part of her mission."

The audience applauded again. Beacon smiled. "Thanks again, Tamara, to you, CrystalClear, and Meyer's Corp for their support. I'm excited about the work we can do together and grateful for all the support from you and our great city."

Tamara returned Beacon's smile and stood up. "So, on the note of gratitude, I'd like to welcome our next guest, Mayor

Katherine Reynolds!" Tamara nodded to Beacon. Taking the cue, Beacon stood as well.

Tamara started the round of welcoming applause as the mayor joined them on the platform. Clearly, the mayor was far more comfortable with this kind of appearance. She smiled broadly and waived vigorously to the audience as she crossed the stage to her chair. Her short, graying hair was perfectly styled, carrying just the right balance between fashion and practicality. Her navy blue suit was impeccably tailored, accented at the neck with a black and yellow-striped scarf.

*Nice touch with the scarf*, Beacon thought admiringly, watching a polished politician work the stage. *She's clearly in her element now. No doubt she's kissed a lot of babies in her career.*

They all shook hands at the center of the platform and took their seats.

"Welcome, Mayor Reynolds. Thanks for joining us here on CrystalClear this morning."

"Glad to be here, Tamara," the mayor replied, settling into her seat.

"So, Mayor, you have an announcement for us?" Tamara prompted her.

"Indeed I do," Mayor Reynolds confirmed. She turned to meet the assistant who had followed her on stage and took a large leather portfolio from him. She laid the portfolio on the table and unzipped it. "Originally, I was going to share with you all our plans for a plaque commemorating Beacon's heroism. However, after further discussions with Meyer's Corporation, they and we have agreed that, instead of just a plaque, we will be constructing a small plaza right here in front of Meyer's Tower in honor of our intrepid heroine."

The crowd cheered as the mayor started taking out some conceptual art posterboards from the portfolio on the table. Beacon swallowed hard, stunned by the news. Mayor Reynolds held up the first posterboard, which depicted a small circular plaza with the anticipated entrance to Meyer's Tower right behind. The plaza would be constructed using a lot of grass, trees, and flowers arranged around a central stone display adorned with her Beacon insignia. Children were playing in the plaza while families sat on small benches arranged on the outer perimeter. It was overwhelming and humbling.

"If you can zoom in on this a bit, you can see that Beacon Plaza will..." and as the mayor walked Tamara and the audience through the plans, Beacon became lost in her own thoughts. *Is this my life now? Charities and media interviews? Commemorative plaques and parks and this and that? Is this what I signed up for?* Her mind spun as the mayor continued the presentation but resigned itself to the reality of her situation. *Yeah, I guess it is. Granted, a lot of this today is politics, for the show, but no question that part of being the symbol is being seen. In fact, probably the biggest part of it is being seen. Whether I signed up for it or not, like it or not, I'm a celebrity now. I need to get used to that.*

Mayor Reynolds jarred Beacon's attention back to the moment, "So, what do you think?"

Beacon collected herself briefly and replied, "I'm speechless, Mayor. Honestly, this is just beautiful. All I can say is that I'm deeply honored, and I will do my best to keep being worthy of it."

Tamara again started the applause, encouraging the audience to join in. Beacon shook the mayor's hand. When the applause died down, Tamara reached over to shake hands with Beacon, "Thanks again for joining us, Beacon. It was fantastic having you here."

"Thank you, Tamara. It was quite the experience for me as well. I'm glad you had me on the show today."

The cameras then zoomed in on Tamara herself, "And now, we'll be taking a short break so Aaron and Maria can bring us up to date with the latest news and happenings around the city. When we return, Mayor Reynolds will continue sharing her administration's plans for additional development and renovations for Crystal Bay."

The monitors shifted to the news anchor desk back at the studio. Tamara, Mayor Reynolds, and Beacon all shook hands once again. There was a brief round of photographs with the three of them, then of Beacon one-on-one with each of Tamara and the Mayor. Immediately after the photographer was done, Tamara was pulled aside by the director and programming chief for a side conversation. The mayor was likewise swarmed by her assistants eager to prep her for the upcoming segment. Done with her part of the show, Beacon turned and started walking toward the side of the platform, where she saw Casey smiling at her from the bottom of the steps.

Casey squeezed her shoulder when she entered the backstage area. "You were amazing! I told you they would love you!"

"Yeah? You really think it went all right?" Beacon asked.

"It could not have gone any better. Tamara can be tough sometimes, but you handled yourself like a pro. The audience ate it up."

Beacon smiled and nodded to her. "Thanks."

"By the way," Casey shared, "I know a few of the people who will be on your social media team as part of the foundation. They are awesome, and they are really excited to be a part of it. The potential to really make an impact is huge. I think it's going to go spectacularly."

"Glad to hear that, Casey. It's definitely a part of the job I didn't quite see coming, so I'm grateful to have some good people to help me through it."

"Sure thing. So, I've got to get back to some other things. Are you good? Do you need me to arrange some transportation?"

Beacon smiled and shook Casey's hand. "No, I think I'm covered. Thanks again, Casey. Really appreciate all your help and encouragement today." Beacon stepped out into the lot and, after turning to give Casey one last small wave, deftly leaped first to the top of the production trailer, then onto a nearby rooftop, and disappeared.

Casey slapped her palm to her forehead. *Nice one, Casey. 'Do you need me to arrange transportation?' Duh.*

A couple of hours later, Tricia was standing in front of her bathroom mirror, scrubbing her face with a makeup removal pad. She'd already taken a hot shower, but it seemed no matter how much she washed her face, the makeup stubbornly refused to come off. *No wonder people on the streams always look so perfect*, she thought. *This stuff is indestructible.*

As she tossed the pad into the trash bin, she heard the chime of her Beacon commpod in the other room. She hustled into the other room, picked it up off the charger, and answered it, "Beacon here."

As she expected, DA Harris' voice responded, "Hey, I just wanted to tell you that the interview was excellent. You really killed it."

"Thanks," she responded, "Your advice really helped."

"I'm going to be honest. You've been quite the topic of conversation around the office here. A lot of people were feeling the jury was still out as far as you were concerned. What you said today really won you a lot of points with some important people."

"I'm glad it helped. I know this will take time."

"Yeah, but if things keep going as they are now, you'll win them all over and be able to do even more good for this city than you already are."

"Well, I guess we'll have to make sure things keep going as they already are then, won't we?"

"Yes, we will," Harris agreed. "By the way, I checked the stream to make sure the voiceprint scrambler was working properly. It was. No one should be able to print you from the stream or any recordings made from it."

"Thanks for checking that," Tricia replied, and then, pausing a bit, she added, "Just wondering, does this commpod have a scrambler in it too?"

"Yes, Beacon, yes it does," Harris confirmed, and then added, teasing her, "What? Don't you trust me?"

"Getting there, Harris, but let's just say the jury's still out," she teased back. "But...it is going in the right direction."

Harris chuckled, "Fair enough. Like we said, we'll just make sure we keep it going that way."

"Thanks Harris. And again, really appreciate all the help today." She then remembered the loaner she still had, "Hey how should I get this scrambler back to you?"

"Keep it," he said, "Pretty sure you're going to need it again."

"Probably. Thanks again, and thanks for letting me know how it went."

"My pleasure. Let me know how I can help. Be safe out there."

"I will." Tricia ended the call.

*He's right. I probably will need it again. Suck it up, Buttercup. This is going to be more of my life going forward now than I'd want it to be,* she admitted to herself and put the commpod back on the charger.

# Disclosures

Several days later, Tricia decided to head into campus a little early and enjoy breakfast at the faculty cafeteria near the research quad close to the lab. She was feeling on top of the world this morning, probably the best she'd felt since Meyer's Tower. Class the night before had been a huge personal victory, and she was still glowing inside about it.

Last night, she'd passed her test for her first advanced belt. Her kata demonstration had been spot on – Sensei Tim had made only a couple of small observations and corrections. She killed her technique drills, and for her sparring session, Sensei Tim himself was her opponent. He didn't make it easy, pushing her a bit, but in the end, she "won" the match 2-1. After Sensei announced to the entire class that she'd passed, he pulled out her new belt, and they faced each other. He bowed. She returned the bow. As he handed her the belt, he said to her, "I'm very proud of you, Carling. I knew you had it in you," and smiled.

She smiled back as she took the belt from him and replied, "Thank you for believing in me, Sensei." They both turned to face the class. Marni gave out a loud whoop and a big fist pump from her spot in the front row, and the rest of the class joined her in cheers and applause.

It was a great feeling, especially since she'd stuck to her commitment and did it entirely on her own. Tricia had fully accepted that her powers were now a fundamental part of her, but it was still important to her to know that she could challenge herself and be successful without depending on them.

After class, Tricia let Marni talk her into a celebratory drink. They went to a little place just a block or so off campus. It was essentially deserted on a weeknight, so they chose a small table in the corner. Tricia ordered a Cabernet Franc. Marni went with a prickly pear margarita: "Sweet and strong, just like us," Marni toasted, and they clinked glasses.

The belt test wasn't Tricia's only good news. "I found out yesterday that my probation was lifted," she told Marni.

"That's fantastic, Trish!" Marni exclaimed. "How did that all unwind?"

Tricia went on to explain that having two major lab incidents—her accident and Rene's use of the genetics lab to help the Liberators of Gaia— in a span of several months had created some seriously bad press for the university. Despite their attempts to downplay it, the trustees were up in arms, and they were getting some serious questions from some major donors and corporate sponsors.

To settle things down, Doctor Demerov lived up to his reputation of doing whatever it took to protect the university; he fell on the sword for the lapses in oversight and resigned his post as the Lab Complex Chair.

Tricia felt it was a real loss for the labs on campus and for her in particular. Despite her probation, she suspected Demerov had pulled quite a few strings to protect her, and, as he had suggested, she did learn quite a bit from the situation. It would definitely take them quite some time to find a replacement who was as qualified and committed as Alexei Demerov.

After his resignation, the board canceled the probation with the guarantee that 'more comprehensive protocols across the entire lab complex would soon be coming' to avoid future incidents.

"So, it looks like we all will likely have some additional paperwork and people looking over our shoulders, but we'll cross that bridge when we come to it," Tricia concluded, taking a sip.

"Speaking of the labs," Marni said, "I have some good news as well. Using the data Beacon had secured on Rene's computer, we were able to decode the gene sequences of Rene's infertility virus and finally understand what it actually did to those infected by it."

Marni went on to break down how Rene had put in some specific gene markers she could use to confirm the outcome of her little experiments every time Marni had sent her data from the investigations. Marni felt a little ashamed that she'd been an unwitting stooge in Rene's plans, but once they knew the markers Rene was using, they easily identified the changes in the genome her virus created and devised a way to reverse it.

Normally, it would take months to get any kind of clearance to test it on actual people, but given the unique circumstances, the hospital investigatory review board helped expedite the testing and agreed to allow a limited test on any of the affected people who volunteered. The board essentially had no choice; they had quickly hit the limit of what they could simulate in the computer and test in the lab on samples, and there was no way to test the final antidote except on an affected human.

Marni had confirmed what Rene had told Beacon about her being infected, so she had volunteered to be in the first test group. So far, the antidote has been a complete success. No side effects had been observed—simulation had shown that the probability of side effects was negligible, well in the range of one in a billion—and her body was already starting to produce healthy eggs. It would take a few months for the mRNA vaccine they developed to repair the affected ones, but so far, it looked like she and the other volunteers would make a full recovery. After a few months of observation, if there still were no adverse effects, they would treat the remainder of Rene's victims.

"The reversal rate is about 95%, plus or minus," Marni said, "so the couples may have to try a couple of times, not that they'll mind, I suspect—" she and Tricia both snickered "—but they will be able to have the family they wanted."

Tricia reached across the table and hugged Marni tight, shedding a tear. Marni hugged her back. "I'm so thrilled for you, Marni. So thrilled," she choked back a few more tears, let Marni go, wiped her eyes, and took a long sip of her wine. Tricia didn't know when or even if Marni—or she— would make the decision to have a family, but at least together, they had taken back the choice that Rene had tried to steal.

"Thank you too, Tricia," Marni said, "the help you gave us upgrading the imaging systems was huge." They clinked glasses again. "And, of course, we need to give a big thanks to Beacon. I'll tell ya, Trish," Marni said, pushing her hair back, "if she hadn't stopped Rene and saved us the data from her system, we might not have broken this, or at least not until it was way too late. Rene was a genius. She really covered her tracks, and when we analyzed the payload from the bomb

Beacon stopped, we found that Rene had removed the markers from the final virus. We might've never found it if she'd succeeded in setting off the remaining devices.

"Here's to Beacon, wherever she is," Marni toasted again, raising her glass.

*I'll drink to that*, Tricia silently seconded, smiled, and held up her glass.

Tricia had just finished her egg sandwich and was absentmindedly stirring her coffee while she browsed through a recently published paper on dark matter quantum entanglement. She was just savoring the first bite of her cherry danish when she heard someone clear his throat to her right. She looked up to see Harold Baskins, from the Materials Sciences Laboratory, standing next to her with a tray.

"May I join you for a few minutes?" he asked a bit hesitantly.

"Sure," she said, gesturing to the empty chair across the table. Other than the two of them, the cafe was otherwise empty at this time of the morning.

"I, uh, saw you sitting here and wanted to ask how those instrument covers your team was working on came out. Did they work out for you?" he asked.

"Yeah," Tricia answered, sneaking in a sip of her coffee, "yeah, they worked out great. The instruments are operating at much higher efficiency, and a lot of the noise contamination we were having to filter out in the data has been eliminated. Saves us a lot of work. The team is very happy with them."

"Good...good," Harold replied. He seemed a bit nervous, focusing very intently on his eggs and toast.

"How are things going over at the MatSci Lab?" she asked, prodding the conversation a bit.

"Oh, fine...fine," he said, looking up at her.

Tricia gave him a friendly look, raising her eyebrows slightly, encouraging him to go on. She patiently took another bite of her pastry. He was clearly building up to something, and part of her was faintly amused watching him work himself up to it.

"Um, I was wondering if perhaps you might've seen the interview the other day? The one with Beacon on that morning talk show, uh, CrystalClear, uh, yeah, that one," he stammered a bit.

"Mmm," she started, holding her hand up to her mouth as she finished chewing the bite and swallowing. "No, I missed it. I was, um, at home that day trying to sleep off a stomach bug." Harold nodded slightly as she quickly followed up, "But I am planning on watching it sometime. I think it's posted on the CrystalClear site." The thought of watching herself made her want to cringe, but she pushed down the impulse, forcing herself to keep a straight face while she waited patiently for Harold to continue.

"Well, I hope you do, Tricia," Harold said, again intently studying his breakfast as he moved it around on his plate with his fork. "I, um, think she's pretty remarkable, and I believe what she does and what she stands for can do a lot of good for the city. I feel she deserves as much support as we can give her."

"Well, sounds like she made quite an impression. I'll be sure to watch it soon, then." Tricia smiled a bit to herself, being careful not to glow too much from the praise or otherwise give anything away. *Kinda nice to have a fan,* she thought, still smiling.

"Yeah, definitely. Um, when you do, you might want to take a close look at her costume," Harold offered, looking up directly into Tricia's eyes.

Tricia met his gaze and answered, a bit flatly, "Oh? Why is that?"

Harold continued to look directly into her eyes, and lowering his voice, he said, "Besides the fantastic job she did making it, I noticed that the fabric she used is quite unique. In fact, the pattern in the material is rather unmistakable."

A knot suddenly tightened in her throat, and she took another sip of coffee in a vain attempt to loosen it. Maintaining both her eye contact and her composure, she swallowed and replied, "Well, it sounds fascinating, Harold. I'll be sure to pay close attention when I watch the interview."

Harold nodded and took a few bites of his eggs and toast. As unappealing as it had just become, Tricia forced herself to take another bite of the danish. They ate in an awkward silence for a couple of minutes.

Breaking the silence, Harold leaned forward slightly toward her, "I, um, also wanted to let you know that I took the rest of that material you and the team were using and moved it out of the general storage room to a private storage locker that's more safe and secure. Just in case anyone should happen to be looking around the storage room for any reason, I thought it best if it was, well, more out of sight." Harold nodded slightly.

Tricia nodded back, "Ok, well, that sounds like a very reasonable precaution, considering how, um, valuable and rare it is."

"Absolutely," Harold replied, "but you should know that if you, or your team, ever need more of it, it's at your disposal anytime...for any reason."

Tricia nodded slightly, trying to remain patient, as he continued, getting a bit more enthusiastic now, "In fact, there are other applications for that material as well you might find useful. For example, it can be modified so it's much denser and less pliable, something that resembles the texture and feel of, say, the sole of a boot or the gripping surface of a work glove without losing any of its special properties. In that state, it's extremely durable and can stand up to high levels of wear and friction without degradation. You know, just as an example...of the possibilities, I mean."

It had taken a much more roundabout path than Tricia would have liked, but it was finally clear to her where he was going with this. "That sounds like it could have some interesting applications, Harold. Perhaps I...or the team...can circle back with you on that a little later, and we can explore some of the options, yeah?" she suggested, adding a small smile.

"Any time, of course. Seems that somehow the interdepartmental transfer slip for the material you used got misplaced, too," Harold said with a wink.

"That's a shame, Harold," Tricia replied, smiling slightly. "I guess we'll have to sort that out sometime, won't we?"

"Sometime," Harold said with a nod and, putting on a small smile of his own, hurriedly started to collect his tray. "Hey, it was nice having breakfast with you, but I have a morning seminar I need to prep. Like I said, I'm always glad to support someone doing fantastic work, someone who's really trying to make a difference, you know? Anyway, you can count on me for anything that'll, um, advance the cause, or whatever."

Tricia reached over and lightly touched his arm. "Thanks, Harold," Tricia said softly, "Thanks...from both of us."

As Harold walked away, Tricia gratefully added Harold to her growing mental list of 'Team Beacon'. Someone like him, she reflected, would be a great ally, but it also prodded her conscience once again that there was one person in particular who was long overdue to be on the list, and it was time she corrected that.

Tricia and Marni hiked upward in the brisk morning air. The sun had just come up, and they could still see their breath as they hiked up the trail into the mountain foothills. No one else was out, just as Tricia had hoped. She'd managed, with a lot of convincing and cajoling, to get Marni to join her this morning. She needed to get Marni out and away from everyone else, somewhere they could be alone.

When they reached a small crest in the trail, near some small rock formations, Tricia suggested they stop and take a water break. Marni didn't complain a bit. Mustering her courage, Tricia said, "Marni, I've got something I need to tell you."

"Let me guess," Marni jibed, "you're pregnant."

"No, of course not."

"You've been nominated for the Nobel Prize?"

"No, not the Nobel Prize either. Nothing like that. Look, Marni, I'm Beacon."

Marni snorted as she took a drink of water. "Yeah, right."

"I'm serious, Marni."

"Sure, you are. You have as much chance of being Beacon as I do of being the Easter Bunny. Although," Marni cocked her head whimsically, "given how cute I looked in that rabbit costume a couple of Halloweens ago, I probably have a better chance."

Marni started rummaging through her pack and continued, "Look, Trish, if you dragged me up here at this time of day for some silly prank, then..."

"Marni!" Tricia interrupted.

Marni looked out, then slowly looked up. Tricia was levitating several feet in the air, her hands glowing with a bright white light, essentially mimicking the same demonstration she'd given during her CrystalClear interview. Marni dropped her water bottle and her pack as her eyes grew wide.

"T-t-trish?" she stammered. "Is that you?"

"Yes, Marni, it's me," Tricia answered softly.

Marni felt behind her for a rock to sit down on, and, as she continued to stare at Tricia floating in front of her, promptly missed it, landing hard on her backside. She didn't really seem to notice, though, still stunned by what she was seeing.

After a few seconds, she blurted out, "Tricia, your hair!"

Tricia smiled. "Yeah, it comes along with the whole package." She floated back down to the ground and released her powers, returning to normal. She walked over and offered Marni a hand. Marni stared at it for a few seconds and then took it, letting Tricia help her up. Marni brushed off the back of her pants and, this time succeeded in sitting down on the rock. She folded her arms across her knees and lay her head down, breathing heavily.

Tricia put a hand on Marni's shoulder. "Are you ok, Marn?" she asked gently.

Marni nodded and looked up. "Yeah, I'm ok. I just need a moment to wrap my head around this. Wow. Tricia Carling...the Crystal Bay Crusader...Beacon. How did this happen?"

Tricia reached down, picked up Marni's water bottle, and handed it to her. She then proceeded to tell the entire story, slowly and calmly, starting with her accident, going through how she discovered her powers, her training, and making her costume. Marni just listened, nodding her head periodically, as Tricia moved on to her confrontations with Liberators of Gaia and Purity/Rene, the incident at Meyer's Tower, and finally, her deposition with the DA. When she'd finished, Marni just sat there quietly, obviously just trying to soak it all in. Tricia waited patiently for some reaction, content to give her friend all the time she needed.

"So, that time you punched me in class?" Marni finally inquired hesitantly. Tricia nodded. "That really hurt, Trish," she said, rubbing her sternum absently.

"I know, Marni, and I'm really sorry. I didn't know what was going on then. It was a complete accident."

"And it really was Rene behind the infertility cases and the Liberators, after all?"

"Yes, it was. Just so you know, the DA didn't want me discussing anything about Rene's plot and how close it all came with anyone. The official story is that a terrorist attempt by the Liberators was foiled before it got out of hand. The real story would freak people out, and the authorities would prefer not to have to deal with that, ok?"

"Like I'm going to be discussing any of this with anyone." Marni huffed. "My God, Tricia. Just thinking about it...you...you busting up all those crimes...and what you did at Meyer's Tower. You could have been killed...more than once! What the frak were you thinking, Trish?!? This kind of thing just isn't like you. What made you do it?"

"Rene asked me the same thing, Marni. Ultimately, when this happened to me, I had a choice about what to do with it, and through different means, Rene and I came to the same conclusion."

"How can you say that, Trish? Rene was a raving psychotic!" Marni exclaimed.

"What she did was psychotic, Marni, but we were alike in a lot of ways. She had a troubled past, too, but chose a different, darker path. Talking with her really made me realize that when we start seeing the world through a certain lens, how difficult it can be to see it through any other.

"Rene was right, though, in that people will not change without some motivation or incentive, without someone to show them the way. One person with superpowers, I don't believe, can make much of a lasting difference on their own, but groups of people inspired by seeing someone else putting it on the line to make a difference might become the tipping point humanity needs.

"Whether she meant to or not, she taught me a lot, Marni. Part of me is sorry she's gone. She was a remarkable woman in so many ways and could've been so much more if circumstances were different."

Marni nodded. They sat in silence for a few moments before Marni shifted gears. "I saw Beacon...you...on that CrystalClear interview. I had no idea that was you. Even now, I am having a hard time seeing you as the person sitting in that chair."

Trisha smirked. "Well, I guess the costume works."

"Yeah, it does, but it's not just the costume. You were a totally different person. You were amazing in that interview," Marni praised, but then her tone shifted.

"But why?!? Why didn't you tell me sooner, Trish? I'm your best friend. We are practically sisters, for cryin' out loud. Why didn't you come to me sooner, and why tell me now?

"Part of me wanted to, believe me, Marni, but I was scared. I didn't know what was happening or how people would react, even you, and once I made the decision to create Beacon and start crimefighting, I knew I'd be making enemies, enemies that would gladly hurt anyone I loved or cared about, so I deliberately worked to hide my identity.

"And to be completely honest, I still wanted to have a life outside of Beacon, too. I may not want to be Beacon forever, but I will still always want to be Tricia. If people knew who I was, it would be very difficult for them to treat me normally, and trust me, there are times when I desperately need 'normal.'"

"I get it," Marni empathized, "but why tell me now, then?"

"Because I realize I just can't do it alone. It's a lot to carry around. I need someone I trust in my corner. Someone who has my back without question. That's you. It's always been you."

Marni reached over and squeezed Tricia's hand.

"Plus, I need your expertise too, Marn. Frankly, this scares me. To this day, I still don't really know what's happened to me. There's always something new, something I didn't know before, and sometimes that's really terrifying. On top of that, I don't know what it's doing to me either. I don't know if this is killing me or if it will make me live forever. The scary part is just not knowing, and you might be one of the few people with the skills and expertise to help me figure it out."

"We will, Trish," Marni assured her. "We will. So, besides me, does anyone else know?"

"The DA knows for sure. I'm pretty sure the director of the MatSci Lab knows, too. I snitched the material for the suit from his lab, and he recognized it on the interview broadcast. He told me as much over breakfast earlier this week."

"Can you trust them?"

"Well, I'm pretty sure I can trust Harold. He seems pretty into what Beacon is trying to do and sounds supportive. As for the DA, let's just say I trust him to do what he thinks is right. I think he sees this all as an advantage right now, so I believe as long as he sees it that way, I can count on his support. If it goes sideways, though, I'm pretty sure he'll throw me under the bus in a heartbeat." Tricia shrugged. "Time will tell, I suppose, for both of them."

"So, one more thing," Marni said, looking up at Tricia again, "Are these new superpowers of yours the reason we can hike all the way up here and you're not winded at all?" Marni smirked at her.

"No, I'm just in better shape than you are," Tricia smirked back, and they laughed together.

They sat for several minutes more and then hiked back down to the trailhead in relative silence. Marni asked a few random questions along the way, and Tricia did her best to answer. Marni was clearly working hard to process all of this. It might take some time, but Tricia had absolute faith in Marni and their relationship. Marni would get through it, and they'd be ok.

When they got back to the trailhead, Marni excused herself to use the restroom before the drive back. Tricia walked over to one of the picnic tables to wait. The park was surprisingly deserted for such a nice day. It was just her, Marni, and the trash pickup guy making the rounds in his little green cart.

She sat down, and as she took a long drink of water, the garbage cart pulled up to the bins next to her picnic table, and the attendant hopped out. She looked up at him as he passed her carrying a clean garbage bag. Something about him looked familiar to her, and then she remembered...the dance studio. He had shorter hair now, but yes, it was him.

"You staying out of trouble, Jimmy?" she asked after him.

Jimmy jumped a little, startled, and turned to look at her. His eyes got a bit wider, obviously recognizing her. "Yeah, doing my best."

"You're working here at the park?

"Yeah, I have a few shifts here at this park and a couple of the county parks," he said, walking over to her.

"Glad to hear it, Jimmy."

"I gotta admit," Jimmy offered, "you made a big impression on me that day. Got me thinking, you know. You were right; there was a better way for me. I was better than that. I got myself a part-time job busing tables at a restaurant. Didn't pay much, but I wasn't looking over my shoulder all the time for the cops, and there was enough left over to take night classes. I got my GED, and now I'm prepping for my college entrance exams. The owner's daughter is helping me study for them."

"Oh, she is, is she?" Tricia smirked and gave him a wink.

Jimmy grinned. "Yeah, she is. Hey, turns out she's a dance instructor at that dance studio where you and I, um, met."

"Just goes to prove what a small world this really is, Jimmy."

"For sure. Anyway, I recently got promoted to a full waiter, tips and everything, so I'm on a good track there. I picked up this gig too—" he gestured towards the park "—cuz it brings in some extra money, and I get outside a lot, which is nice."

Tricia smiled. "That's really great, Jimmy. I'm proud of you. Really, I am."

Jimmy smiled and looked at Tricia for a few seconds. He came a little closer, leaned down, and, lowering his voice, asked her, "You're, um, you're...*her*...aren't you?"

"Who, Jimmy?"

"You know...*HER*." Jimmy nodded his head toward the city.

Tricia smiled and shrugged, "Actually, Jimmy, I'm just someone like you, someone trying to take her own advice. Trying to be better, maybe make a difference that helps make the world a little better along the way. Whatever else I am doesn't really matter, does it?"

Jimmy smiled and stood back up. "No, I guess it doesn't. Anyways, good running into you, and, um, thanks for what you did…and, uh, do." He flipped her a goodbye wave and drove off to the next trash station.

"You know, Beacon, my dear," she said to herself, "that's it, right there, isn't it? This is our real purpose, what you and I are here for…making a difference by inspiring people, any way we can, even if it's just one person at a time. That's how the world gets better, superpowers or not." She sighed. "Even if we have to juggle two lives to do it."

Tricia watched Jimmy drive off, leaving a small cloud of dust in his wake.

*Rene was right—about that much, at least.*

# Epilogue

The late afternoon was finally fading into early evening. Darci waited in her dimming apartment. Night couldn't come fast enough. To pass the time, she watched the interview again for the umpteenth time, the interview with her, the one they called the Angel of Light. Darci studied it, studied her.

It had been several months now since that day she was waiting in her professor's office. Darci was failing his class. She was there to plead for a second chance, for help to pass his class. She wanted to pass, to do well, but it was difficult for her. She hadn't adjusted well to the entire university experience, and many of her classmates just seemed to have an aptitude she lacked. The professor was running late, so she waited patiently. What choice did she have?

Then, that disastrous accident had happened in the imaging lab a couple of floors below her, the one that had sent the lab director to the hospital. The one that had nearly killed her.

*But I survived.*

Darci had seen her around campus since then. She had made a full recovery and had gone back to having a normal life. Of course, she did. The responders had come for her, taken her to get the best care. No one had come for Darci. No one had found her lying in her professor's empty office. She'd woken up alone and in the dark, feeling as though something had torn her apart and then hastily thrown her back together again.

Somehow, Darci had found her way back to her room. She didn't quite remember much of that part, but for the better part of a week, Darci had wondered if she would live or die. She remembered the pain, the disorientation, the dreams, how the very touch of light itself made her feel like she was on fire. She had thought about killing herself more than once just to make it all stop.

She recovered, though, fairly quickly, all things considered, and had worked hard to pull herself and her life back together. Things started coming easier for her after that: work, school, friends. Her grades improved, and by the end of the semester, she had managed to get herself back into a position where staying at the university was still an option for her.

She had the shadows to thank for that. The light, while still uncomfortable for her at times, no longer burned, but the shadows were her friends now. Darci found comfort in them.

The shadows helped her do things.

The shadows gave her power.

The shadows took her places she wanted to go.

Darci looked out the dark window. Night had finally come, and she did have places to go and things to do tonight. She looked again at the frozen image of Beacon. "You're not the only one who's special after all, are you?" she said to the picture on the screen, and with a flick of her wrist, the monitor went dark.

"Time to go," she commanded and reached out. The shadows responded. They flew toward her, growing and swirling from the corners of the room, answering her call. As they wrapped around her, fully enveloping her in darkness, she smiled and vanished.

Beacon will return in

# Labyrinths of
# Radiance and Shadow

www.ingramcontent.com/pod-product-compliance
Lightning Source LLC
Chambersburg PA
CBHW060815120726
47909CB00006B/1932